OLD BLOOD

DI JAMIE JOHANSSON BOOK 3

MORGAN GREENE

ALSO BY MORGAN GREENE

The DS Johansson Prequel Trilogy:
Bare Skin (Book 1)
Fresh Meat (Book 2)
Idle Hands (Book 3)

The DS Johansson Prequel Trilogy Boxset

———

The DI Jamie Johansson Series
Angel Maker (Book 1)
Rising Tide (Book 2)
Old Blood (Book 3)

Death Chorus (Book 4)

OLD BLOOD

1

THE STREET WAS quiet and dark.

From their beaten-up old BMW, the two men could see a pair of moths whirling in circles in the glare of a streetlight.

But otherwise, nothing moved.

The big man in the driver's seat tightened his grip, the leather of the steering wheel groaning under his knuckles. He looked across at the man next to him and nodded briefly.

A second later, the passenger was out of the car and moving fast down the middle of the road, blurring in and out of view as he slid between the pools of light.

The only sound was the crunching of his boots on the loose stones on the road, and the sloshing of the petrol in the jerrycan at his hip.

His eyes roved the front doors to his right, counting the numbers until he found what he was looking for.

A quick glance around told him no one was watching – why would they be? It was nearly four in the morning.

He mounted the kerb, pushed through the front gate, and approached the door, slowing.

The paint was peeling from it in thin, curling strands.

The man knelt on the step, hugging the wall, his black coat making him all but invisible, and placed the container down next to him.

He fished in his pocket and withdrew a slender device. He placed the nose of it against the barrel of the lock, glanced around again, leaned into the door, and pulled the trigger.

A sharp bang cut the silence, and the lock cylinder hit the floor inside the front hallway.

The man remained motionless, ears pricking for any sign of movement or response to the noise.

Nothing, but he still had to move quickly.

He replaced the pneumatic gun in his pocket, grabbed the container, and then went inside, closing the door behind him.

The man behind the wheel of the BMW kept his hands on the wheel, watching.

His heart beat slowly. Steadily.

He checked his watch, making a mental note of the time, counting in his head how long this was taking.

All around, the street remained still, quiet, and dark, everyone soundly asleep in their beds. Even as a dim glow began to grow behind the windows of the house with the paint-peeling door.

Even as the front door opened and the man with the petrol can slipped back out into the night.

Even as the flames grew, and took hold of the curtains, and the furniture, and everything else, growing and growing until the glass burst in the frames.

The BMW circled in the street and sidled off into the night, the sound of sirens echoing faintly in the distance.

2

36 hours earlier…

Detective Inspector Jamie Johansson got the call at three in the afternoon.

As she walked towards the apartment through the sea of flashing lights, her blood ran a little colder. Her partner, Krimminalinspektör Anders Wiik, was still on leave, recovering from the wounds of their last case. His hand was 'gravel in a skin bag' – that was the term the surgeon had used. Seventeen pins, eleven rods, and his hand stuck inside a metal cage with screws and bolts sticking out of his skin for at least two months. Maybe more. And that wasn't even mentioning the nerve damage and the lack of mobility he'd be stuck with for the foreseeable. And the pain. Chronic. Incurable.

Last Jamie heard, he was seeing a psychologist.

She wanted to talk to him, but he'd stopped taking her calls.

Stopped taking anyone's calls.

But that would have to wait, because right now, shit was hitting the fan.

She hadn't even stepped foot inside the scene yet but she already had a feeling she knew what had happened. And Jamie hated getting feelings. Because they were usually dead right.

'Hallberg,' Jamie called to her interim partner, approaching the front steps to the apartment building.

The woman, late twenties, with her dark, sleek hair pulled back into a low ponytail, turned to face Jamie. When she'd first met Julia Hallberg, she'd worn blouses, blazers. *Shoes.* Polished, smart, with a small but sensible heel. Now, she was wearing combat boots, a thermal base layer, and a sheepskin jacket.

Jamie didn't have the energy to comment, but it was hard to not feel like she was looking in a mirror as she closed ground on her.

'Inspector,' Hallberg replied, signing something on a tablet and handing it back to a crime scene technician who was milling around at the porch with a few other white-over-all-clad officers.

A strip of blue-and-white police tape had been strung across the entryway, and no less than five police vehicles were forming a barrier around it, blocking the street off.

Jamie put her hands on her hips and looked up at the building. 'You been up yet?' she asked Hallberg, a *polisassistent.* The Swedish equivalent to a detective constable.

She shook her head. 'No, I got here about ten minutes ago. Thought it best to wait for you.'

Jamie nodded, struggling to find words. This wasn't going to be pleasant. She cracked her neck, her long, ash-blonde plait swaying between her shoulder blades. It was April, and though spring was coming quickly, today there was a chill in the air. 'Let's do it.'

Hallberg proffered the door to Jamie and she went in,

dark peacoat rustling as she did. Her lightweight hiking boots squeaked on the polished marble stairs as she climbed, getting off on the first floor and following the trail of crime scene techs who were dusting for prints.

Jamie stepped between the evidence markers on the tiles, and headed for the open door to Ingrid Falk's apartment.

Hallberg weaved around her and lifted the tape across the frame for Jamie to duck in. They'd been working together for a week or so and Jamie had hoped that the teacher's-pet act would have disappeared by now, but it hadn't. Jamie liked the kid – hell, she *was* her eight years ago – but now, she was growing tired of it. And the discovery of Ingrid Falk's body wasn't about to make it any easier.

Inside, the apartment was clean and spacious. Nothing looked out of place. Ingrid Falk, the *kriminalkommissarie* that oversaw the violent-crime department of Stockholm Polis – Jamie and Hallberg's department – was a fastidious woman. Private, reserved, and by all accounts clean as a whistle.

But Jamie knew better.

And she knew that despite Falk being found in her bath, her wrists opened, the bloodied razor blade still on the edge of the tub, this was anything but what it looked like.

There was a man standing at the window in the living space, his back to them. His slight frame was silhouetted against the grey sunlight, his head tilted slightly forward, hands on hips, coat bunched around his wrists.

He turned at the sound of Jamie and Hallberg's simultaneously squeaking boots. *'Hälla,'* he said. Hello. 'You must be Johansson and Hallberg.' He came forward, hand extended.

Jamie took it, inspecting the man. He was tall, with thick charcoal hair peppered with grey at the temples and cut short. He was probably sixty, but was ageing well. His tanned skin was lined but supple, his eyes kind, his mouth wide and full.

'Kriminalkommissarie Thomas Karlsson,' he said. 'I worked with Falk for years, and currently oversee Cybercrime.'

That was the division that Wiik's ex-partner transferred to. She wondered if Karlsson and Falk had talked about what happened between them. Their rough parting. Karlsson was looking at her more intensely than Hallberg. She guessed her name had come up between them.

'I came as soon as I heard,' he said, a slight wobble in his voice. He'd clearly been friends with Falk, and this had shaken him. Hell, it was shaking her, too. But she'd been through a lot, and now was not the time to buckle. She was just doing her best not to jump the gun and make any firm assumptions just yet.

'I never expected this,' he went on, shaking his head and turning back to the window. 'Ingrid was always so... in control. She lived for her work... She was lonely? Sure, I guess, but' – he turned back to them suddenly, his eyes searching their faces for any hint of an answer – 'she was okay, wasn't she? Work was okay? Nothing was weighing on her? I checked her cases out – it seemed like everything was okay? Was it?'

Jamie set her jaw. He needed an answer. Something to tell him that this wasn't his fault, that he hadn't missed some-thing, that he couldn't have prevented it.

That he couldn't have saved her if he was a better friend. Had been more attentive.

She didn't have the heart to say what Falk was mixed up in. What Jamie's last case may have stirred up. That this was the result of a long chain of decisions and moves that Falk hid from everyone. And that though all the signs pointed to it, that Falk hadn't slit her own wrists.

Instead, she shook her head. 'Everything was fine. She seemed… fine.' Jamie tried to keep her voice straight.

Karlsson bunched his shoulders, then dropped them and sighed. 'Alright – you can go in,' he said, lifting his chin towards the bathroom door. It was pulled to, but ajar.

Jamie could already taste the metallic tang of blood in the air.

Two techs shuffled around behind them, their cameras clicking and tittering as they moved through the room.

Jamie and Hallberg pulled gloves from their pockets at the same time and snapped them into place.

They moved carefully towards the bathroom, Jamie leading, and pushed the door open.

Behind them, Karlsson headed into the corridor. Jamie didn't know if he'd seen the scene or not, but he had no intention of sticking around when that door opened.

The first thing she saw was the pale and bloodless face of her boss, Ingrid Falk.

She corrected herself – *former* boss.

Her eyes were closed, her head resting on her chin.

She was naked, her breasts hidden beneath the dark surface of the bloodied water. Her right hand was somewhere next to her legs, and her left was facing upwards on the edge, fingers curled loosely toward the ceiling, a razor blade next to it. The blood had long since stopped running. Jamie guessed she'd been dead for the better part of a day, but the forensic report would tell her more.

No doubt Hallberg would have some information on what had happened here. The preliminaries would have been uploaded to the system already, and Hallberg was on that stuff like a hound. It was just her way, which made Jamie's job a hell of a lot easier.

She was good like that, useful – Jamie cast an eye at her –

even if she did look like she'd dressed up as Jamie for Halloween.

She shook that off. 'Who found her?'

Hallberg was right at her shoulder. 'Her sister. They were supposed to get lunch.' Hallberg pulled out her phone, opened the case file quickly, and began reading aloud. 'She was supposed to meet her at a restaurant at one. Falk never showed, wasn't answering her phone. The sister called HQ, and they said Falk never came in. So, she came here to see if she was okay.'

Jamie nodded, processing it. 'What restaurant?'

'Uh,' Hallberg said diligently, scrolling through the statement taken from Falk's sister. 'Niño's. A Spanish place.' She looked up at Jamie. 'Why?'

She shrugged, eyes fixed on Falk. 'Just curious.' Despite the gruesome scene in front of her, she didn't feel anything looking at the woman. No sadness. No remorse. No guilt. Nothing to put her off the thought of food. And she was getting hungry.

Jamie didn't think Falk deserved this fate. But she'd got into bed with some shady fucking people. And this was the result. It was what had happened to her father, and now it had happened to Falk.

You cross Imperium Holdings, this is what happens to you.

'Come on,' Jamie said, turning and motioning for Hallberg to follow her. 'We're done here.'

'Done?' Hallberg sounded surprised. 'What do you mean, done?'

Jamie paused at the threshold of the bathroom, took another look at Falk, and then let her eyes drift to Hallberg. 'Suicide,' she said plainly. 'What else do you want?'

3

'YOU REALLY BELIEVE that Falk killed herself?' Hallberg sounded almost incredulous.

Jamie pushed the shredded lettuce of her salad around the bowl, searching for another piece of chicken. Or at least a tomato. Anything that wasn't more lettuce.

She sighed and dropped the fork, pressing the heels of her hands into her eyes until they ached. 'It doesn't matter what I believe, Hallberg,' Jamie said. 'It matters what we can prove.'

'So you *don't* think she killed herself.' Hallberg slapped the table and Jamie's eyes opened, fixing on hers.

Jamie weighed up the options, recounting the events that had led here.

The murder aboard the Bolstad oil rig in the Norwegian Sea had forced Falk's hand. The company that owned Bolstad – Imperium Holdings – had called in the favour she owed. No, that wasn't right. They *blackmailed* her into breaking the law for them, and she'd dispatched Jamie and Wiik to investigate the crime. They hadn't banked on the real problem being within their own ranks, though. And despite their best efforts, Bolstad had gone belly up. Less than a week after Jamie and

Wiik had arrived home, broken, battered, bruised, licking their wounds, Bolstad's stock flooded the market, and within days, the company was torn to shreds, sold off in parts, and wiped from the face of the earth.

The truth of what happened there would never get out.

Those who survived were all paid off, forced to sign NDAs, and were then sent to the four corners of the planet to make sure that they never crossed paths with each other, or a journalist.

The deaths were chalked up to freak accidents on account of the storm that had ripped through the place. But Jamie knew better.

And the only reason she hadn't talked was because she knew that as soon as she did, she'd suffer the same fate as Falk. And she didn't have all the pieces of the puzzle yet. She still needed to find the man Falk had told her about – Sand-bech – the man who killed her father. One of Imperium's fixers. The one who'd fixed Falk, probably.

Imperium had asked her to do something. She'd failed. And she'd paid the price.

Jamie's father had gone poking around where he shouldn't have, too. And he'd also paid the price.

Two deaths, separated by decades, but mirror images of one another.

A bullet, a razor blade, it was all the same.

Suicide at gunpoint.

Hallberg was watching her like a hawk. But she couldn't tell her the truth.

No, Falk could have talked. Could have told Imperium what she told Jamie. Which meant Jamie could be in the crosshairs right now.

She turned her head and stared out at the city in front of her, utterly exposed in the booth in the window of Niños.

She'd fancied Spanish after Hallberg had said. But now, suddenly, she wasn't hungry.

Though she was half expecting to eat a bullet in the next ten seconds.

Have one come flying through the glass and punch a hole through her cheek.

Decorate the place with her brains.

Johansson brains.

Imperium seemed to like to paint with them.

Jamie grimaced. Imperium had asked Falk to deal with the issue on the Bolstad oil rig. And to get Jamie to do it, she'd offered her a trade. One which Jamie had fucked up. Or at least survived when maybe she wasn't supposed to. Either way, Falk didn't do what was asked, and now she was dead. And whether that was Jamie's fault or not, she was past caring.

She only had one thing on her mind, and that was revenge.

Imperium Holdings.

Sandbech.

Those names were all she had, but it was more than she had before. And that was all she needed.

'Jamie,' Hallberg said then, catching her eye. 'Did you hear me? I said, so you *don't* believe that Falk—'

'I heard you,' Jamie said. 'I just don't want to answer the question.'

'Why not?' Hallberg insisted.

Jamie continued to search the roofs of the buildings across the street for a glint off a rifle scope. 'Because if I do, it opens a door. And then we have to walk through it. And once we do, things will begin to happen. And the end result will be the same. A bathtub and a razor blade, a gun between the teeth, a stumble onto the train tracks.' She met Hallberg's eye, her voice like ice. 'I'm already through that door, okay? But you're not, and trust me, you don't want to be. So don't do it. Don't make the same mistakes I have. Don't follow my lead.'

'I don't understand.'

'Good. Keep it that way.'

'But, Jamie—'

'Look, Hallberg, drop it, okay? Let this play out how it's supposed to. Listen to me. I didn't listen to anyone else and look at me.'

'Look at you?' Hallberg shook her head. 'What do you mean? You're strong, you're smart, you're—'

'Alone, Hallberg.' She let that hang for a moment. 'And anyone who tries to change that ends up with a shattered wrist, or…' Jamie's hands balled into fists on the table. 'Or a knife in the back. Or worse.' She swallowed and shook her head. 'There's more going on here than you know, and telling you about it will only put you in danger. And not normal *danger* like you think you know. Like actual danger, where your body will never be found if they don't want it to be.'

'Jamie, if you're in trouble, or—'

Jamie scoffed. 'I appreciate it. I really do,' she said, pushing up from the booth and onto her feet. 'But forget about it, okay? Falk killed herself. And the quicker you come to terms with that, the better off you'll be. Don't fight me on this, alright?'

Hallberg's eyes twitched as she tried to work out her next move.

'This isn't a game. It's not a test. And this isn't one of those times where I'll be glad you pursued it, regardless of your own safety. I'm telling you to drop it. You're good at what you do, so be good at it for the next twenty, thirty years. Work your cases, rise through the ranks, become a *krimi-*

nalkommissarie, run a department, keep your nose clean, and retire happy. I wish I had.'

'You still can? Can't you?' Hallberg was shaking her head now, her mouth open. 'I don't get what you're saying – you're talking like something has already happened? Like Falk was just… and you're… *next?'*

She smiled down at Hallberg. 'I'll see you tomorrow, Hallberg. And don't do anything stupid before then.' She pointed at her. 'That's an order.'

'But—'

'No *buts*, Hallberg,' Jamie said. 'Drop it.'

'You wouldn't if you were me,' she said, trying to muster some power in her voice.

'No, I probably wouldn't,' Jamie said, turning and heading for the door. 'But that's what got me into this mess in the first place.'

4

HWANG SUNG-SOOK WAS JUST five feet three inches tall – two shorter than Jamie – but he never failed to knock her on her ass.

'Up!' he commanded, motioning her from the mat.

This was one of his favourite exercises, that he said tested both the ability to kick with consistent power, and to take blows without getting tired or breathless.

Jamie had the first part dialled, the second, not so much.

She crawled to her feet and twisted her back, shaking out her left arm, a thick pad set along her bicep, and then held it in position, covering her ribs, fist raised and clenched.

Sung-Sook motioned her towards him and raised his right leg.

He ran a traditional taekwondo gym on the outskirts of Stockholm. Jamie had let her training slip since she'd come to Sweden, but with what was coming, she didn't think there was a better time to get back into it.

Jamie faced her trainer and lifted her right leg, too, foot loose, knee hovering in front of her chest.

Sung-Sook met her eye and then nodded. In unison, they

twisted into their left feet, and fired the *dollyo chagi* – the roundhouse kick – into the other's pad. Jamie wobbled, but then Sung-Sook was nodding again. And then kicked her again.

She kept up.

Three. Four. Five. Six. Seven.

And then she hit the floor, panting hard, arm ringing.

A well-placed roundhouse kick could stun the kidneys, break a rib, split an ear open, or even cave in a temple.

It was one of the kicks Jamie thought she had nailed.

Sung-Sook disagreed.

Jamie landed on her side and keeled onto her back, her shoulder as sore as her foot.

The lights of the gym swam above her, hazy, and strands of hair clung to her sweat-slicked face.

And then suddenly, she was looking at the bottom of a foot.

It plunged down and impacted on her chest.

Jamie gasped, pain rippling through her body, and her heels jumped a foot in the air.

And then it was coming again.

She threw her hands up, felt Sung-Sook's heel bounce off her forearms.

Then he kicked her in the leg and she swore, rolling away from him.

He kept coming and Jamie scrambled to her knees, turning just in time to throw up a block to protect her face from another kick.

She grunted, stumbled backwards to an awkward stance, and watched as he swung a low kick into her calf.

It tensed and clenched, then spasmed in front of her eyes and she pulled it backwards heavily, trying to gain some sort of awareness.

He was still coming at her, left leg extended, right leg behind, hands low, strafing sideways.

Jamie glanced down at his lead foot, switched up her stance and took a step forward, trying to sweep it.

She put force into the move, but it wasn't fast enough.

Sung-Sook hopped clean over it, landed, and then slapped her in the face.

The short, sharp blow caught her off guard, the feeling of his open palm striking her cheek a wake-up call.

'Sloppy!' he called, stepping backwards and dropping his hands.

Jamie was seething, her shoulders rising and falling quickly, her fists still balled. 'I wasn't ready,' she growled.

'You think the men you're going to be fighting will wait for you to be ready?' His English was decent, his Swedish not so much.

'What men?'

'The men you're training to beat,' he said plainly. 'You turn up here a week ago, and every night since, you're in here three, four hours. Asking for training, hitting bags. You think I don't know when someone's training for a fight?' He feigned spitting on the mat. 'You ask me for a favour, then call me stupid.'

Jamie clenched her jaw, tried to calm herself. She had only known Sung-Sook for a week, but she already knew him to be one of the sharpest, and toughest, people she'd ever met.

His brother moved to Stockholm five years before and had opened a restaurant. He'd moved last year, and had set up a traditional taekwondo gym. Most of his members were either native Koreans, or kids who came to weekend classes.

He was an excellent martial artist, but his bedside manner was as inviting as a rattlesnake.

Jamie pulled the pad from her arm and threw it on the mat. 'I don't know what you're talking about.'

'Fine, you lie to yourself if you want.' He threw his hands at her and turned away. 'So long as you pay on time, I don't care. Now, it closing time.' He strode quickly towards the door and put his hand on the light switches, looking back at her with pursed lips.

His skin was tanned, his head bald and gleaming in the glow of the halogens.

Usually they trained until later than this – that was what they'd agreed. Six until nine every night. It wasn't half past eight yet. But she'd clearly offended him, and there wasn't a part of her that wasn't hurting.

She got off the mat and headed for her rucksack in the corner. She opened it and pulled out a zipped hooded sweatshirt, throwing it around her shoulders, keeping her eyes fixed on the loaded SIG Sauer P226 semi-automatic pistol on top of the towel stuffed in the bottom of her bag.

She looked over to make sure Sung-Sook wasn't watching, saw that he was, and then turned half-on, pulling her water bottle out with one hand, her pistol with the other, sliding it into the back of her leggings under her hoodie. She swallowed the water in her mouth and dropped the bottle back in, wondering if he'd seen, embarrassed by it almost.

Then she zipped up the bag and picked it up, heading for the door.

Sung-Sook remained silent, pushing it open as she got close.

As she crossed the threshold, he grabbed her arm. His fingers dug into her skin, his eyes focused on hers. 'If you are in trouble—'

'I'm not,' Jamie said firmly.

His jaw flexed, and then he threw her arm back at her. 'Then don't bring a gun into my gym.'

Then he killed the lights and closed the door, shutting her out in the cold night air.

Jamie sighed, stared up into the mottled, cloudy sky for a few seconds, then headed for her car.

5

FALK'S DARKENED office was already standing as a stark reminder of what had changed. The once brightly lit interior stood like a gloomy tombstone, and Jamie kept clocking the whites of people's eyes as they glanced over at it.

The violent-crime department at Stockholm Polis HQ was without its captain, and suddenly, felt rudderless. Everyone here was a seasoned detective – Jamie looked around and counted eight pairs, a few loose polisassistents who floated between cases and teams – and yet, there seemed to be no order or motion on the floor today. Everyone was waiting for something, but they didn't know what.

Jamie's eyes went to the two empty desks on her right. One belonged to Anders Wiik, her missing partner, and the other belonged to Julia Hallberg.

She checked her watch. It was after nine. Hallberg was never late.

Jamie sat back in her chair and drummed the lid of her pen on the report she was reading over – an attempted burglary and assault she was working on. She had a bad feeling about this.

And then she heard Hallberg's voice.

'—but, sir—'

Kriminalkommissarie Karlsson turned, stopping her six inches from him. 'I said *no*. This conversation is over, and I don't want to hear another word about it.' He met her eye, then turned back towards the floor, straightened his grey blazer, and strode forward.

As he approached the edge of the desks, he slowed and cast his eyes around the room. Everyone was already watching him intently.

He looked tired, but still well, his thick salt-and-pepper hair glowing in the pale LEDs that hung from the ceiling on wires.

'Hello, everyone,' he said, announcing his presence. 'If I could have your attention?' He smiled then, politely, mournfully, almost. 'As I'm sure you will have heard by now, Kriminalkommissarie Ingrid Falk sadly passed away yesterday. The family have requested a closed, family-only funeral, but the SPA are organising a memorial service to honour her thirty-two years of service. You'll receive the details of this event later today via email.' He looked around again, his gaze seeming to rest on everyone except Jamie.

Hallberg had already circled around the outside of the desks and had found hers. She was sitting with her arms folded, scowling, not looking at Jamie either.

Karlsson went on. 'Operations will continue as normal, and while we search for a suitable replacement, I will be your acting kommissarie. For those who don't know me, my name is Thomas Karlsson, and I am the head of Cybercrime. You can find my contact details on the system, should you need me. If you could begin preparing summaries of your active cases, in order to ease this transitionary period, that would be much appreciated.' He clasped his hands, nodded to the room, and then turned on his heel and walked away.

Everyone began murmuring, but Jamie only cared about one person, and that was Hallberg.

'What the hell was that?' she asked, already at her desk.

Hallberg turned, still scowling. She'd always been so obliging, so browbeaten, almost. But without Wiik here to police her policing, she seemed to have evolved spontaneously. And unfortunately, it seemed to be into another Jamie. Which oddly, Jamie wasn't taking too.

'What the hell was what?' Hallberg asked, her tone hard.

'You and Karlsson.' Jamie leaned on her desk now, keeping her volume low. 'I thought I told you to drop it. And by the sounds of it, Karlsson did too.'

She tutted and shook her head. 'You know a letter arrived at Falk's sister's house this morning?'

'A letter?' Jamie tried to keep her voice even.

'A suicide note.' She practically spat the words. 'Saying how Falk had been harbouring thoughts of ending it for months, how she got no satisfaction from her job anymore, how she felt like she'd been living a lie, and that she'd finally come to the realisation that she was "profoundly and irrevocably unhappy".'

Jamie cleared her throat. 'Sometimes people—'

'Give me a break,' Hallberg said, glaring at Jamie. 'Not you too? You knew Falk – did she seem on the verge of killing herself to you?'

'They rarely do,' Jamie forced out, not liking the look in Hallberg's eye. And as much as it pained her to, she said, 'No one thought my father was going to either.'

Hallberg's stare twitched a little, but she said nothing.

'I don't buy it,' she went on. 'I worked under Falk for four years. *Four years,* Jamie. And not once' – she threw a finger up – 'not once did Falk show a single sign of being unhappy. And I should know, I'm trained to spot that kind of thing. She loved her job. She took pride in it. Gave up everything for it. A husband, kids – her job was everything to her.'

'Maybe that was just it,' Jamie said, already feeling like Hallberg was going to be all but immovable on this. 'Maybe she realised the job wasn't all it was cracked up to be.'

'So quit. You don't just jump in the bath and…' She turned her hands out to show Jamie her wrists.

She got the message.

'Hallberg…' Jamie said then, tiredly. 'I know it's not what you want to accept, or what you want to hear, but Falk is dead. There were no signs of forced entry, the neighbours heard nothing, saw nothing. The note will match her handwriting, and the crime scene report will come back revealing that the only person in that apartment was Ingrid Falk.'

'You sound pretty sure of all that,' Hallberg said, the tone of accusation unmistakable. 'You know something I don't?'

'No, Hallberg.' Jamie met her eye now. 'There's no conspiracy going on here. All the evidence says that she did it to herself because she did. I'm sure that you want to believe what happened was something else, but it wasn't. Falk killed herself. And that's all there is to it. But you know who didn't? Who we can help?' She needed to steer the conversation away from this now, get Hallberg's focus elsewhere. Jamie reached down and picked the stack of case files on Hallberg's desk up, dropping them one by one in front of her. 'Mattson. Söderberg. Blomquist. Jensen. Ruberg. These are all people we *can* help. And people who you're ignoring if you continue going after this.' Jamie let out a long breath. 'We have work to do, Hallberg. And as much as I'd love there to be someone that we could make *pay* for what happened to Falk. There isn't.' She struggled to keep her voice from cracking. 'Okay?'

Hallberg was a statue for a moment, and then nodded. Just slightly.

'Good,' Jamie said. 'Now let's get back to work.'

She headed back to her desk and sat, checking on Hallberg out of the corner of her eye.

The girl had a thousand-yard stare. One that went right out of the room, through Jamie's bullshit, right through Karlsson's refusal to pursue this, and then who knows where after that.

Jamie hoped to hell that Hallberg was going to follow orders.

But as she looked at her, a Jamie Johansson in the making, she knew that she wouldn't.

Simply, because if it was Jamie, she wouldn't have either.

6

TWENTY MINUTES AFTER THAT, Jamie looked up from her desk, and saw that Hallberg was gone.

By the time lunch rolled around, her desk was still empty. Which Jamie didn't like.

Her unease was growing by the moment, and at one o'clock, when she saw Karlsson storming around the corner, eyes fixed on her, mouth twisted into a furious pucker, she knew that something was wrong.

'Johansson,' he called, not caring that everyone else could hear – or that they'd stopped working and looked up at him, and then at her. 'Office,' he commanded, pointing to Falk's old post. 'Now.'

Jamie felt her grip tighten on her pen, her mind already working. She dropped it onto the open file in front of her and followed Karlsson into the darkened room. The motion-sensor lights clicked on above, bathing them in a harsh light, and Karlsson swung the door closed behind her.

It drifted slowly to the jamb and they stood there in silence for a few seconds as the seals brushed together. Jamie could feel the anger coming off him in waves. But she couldn't anticipate what was going to come out of his mouth.

'You want to tell me what the *fuck* you think you're doing?' he hissed, conscious of the army of eyes peering over the tops of computer monitors at them.

Jamie took a breath, forcing her fists to loosen. 'You're going to have to elaborate.'

'Don't play with me. You *know* what you've done. But I'm wondering if you know just how stupid it is.'

What Hallberg's done, Jamie felt like saying. 'No, I don't, actually,' Jamie said instead. 'Because I've been sitting here all morning. So why don't you lay it out for me, huh?'

Karlsson's eyes flared. 'Watch it, Johansson. Falk said you were good, but I'm still your senior, and I'll ask that you show me a little respect.'

'With all *due* respect, *sir,*' Jamie said, long past the point of caring, and interest – and already decided on Karlsson's position in all this – 'I'm guessing Imperium Holdings have you by the balls, same as they had hold of Falk.'

His jaw flexed, but he kept the anger.

'And I'm assuming you've dragged me in here because you know as well as I do that Falk didn't kill herself. And that you were under strict instructions by Imperium to make sure that the investigation went no further than ruling it a suicide and walking away. And that Falk and you were cosy enough with each other that she told you what was going on – with me, with my father, with Bolstad. And that you knew giving me her case would need no further managing. That about right? You assumed that I'd glean context and know not to stick my nose in?' Jamie scoffed. 'Hell, maybe Imperium thought that Falk's death would be a message to me. As much as it was to you' – she looked around – 'and every other spineless sack of shit in this place that they can jerk the lead around your necks any time they please. And that when they do, it's time to roll over and show your pasty fucking bellies to them. Is that about the sum of it?'

Karlsson's shoulders were rising and falling quickly. He dug his hands into his hips but kept quiet.

'Look, Karlsson – let's dispense with the pleasantries and formality, alright? Falk fucked up. She got in with Imperium, and they gave her a job to do with Bolstad. She shit the bed on it. There's no denying that's why they came for her. Why *he* came for her.'

Karlsson seemed to stiffen at the mention of 'he'. Sandbech. The man they send. Jamie noted his reaction, that he knew who he was at least, but carried on.

'And frankly, I'm surprised that they haven't come for me, too, yet. Maybe two suicides so close together would bring too much attention. But hell, I keep expecting a car to mount a kerb, or to get mugged and stabbed on my way home from work.

'But whatever timeline they're working on, I've got no intention of putting a bigger target on my back than there already is. If there's *anyone* who knows how dangerous these people are, it's me. And while I'm not carrying any guilt for what happened to Falk' – Karlsson swallowed, his lip quivering ever so slightly at her name – 'I understand that my actions played a part in her death. But was it my fault? No. She blackmailed me into going to Bolstad, and it almost got me and my partner killed. So you can leave the high-and-mighty shit at the door, and just be straight with me, okay? Tell me what's happened, and tell me that the person who did it didn't just sign their own death warrant.'

Karlsson filled his lungs and let out a long breath, all his rage going with it. 'Fuck,' he muttered. 'Fuck!' He bobbed his head suddenly and then bared his teeth in frustration.

'These fucking people.' He looked at Jamie then, still weighing her up, still unsure what to say. But at least he wasn't denying it. It was clear as day that Imperium had him in the same way they had Falk. And probably enough people above his station to make sure that Karlsson took charge of Falk's department, and got Jamie assigned the case. 'Okay,' he said then, lifting his hands. 'So you *didn't* order the funeral home not to take possession of Falk's body and for an autopsy to be carried instead?'

Jamie closed her eyes and drew a slow breath, controlling her own anger. 'No,' she said. 'I didn't.'

'Fuck.'

Fuck was right.

'Well, it's your name on the order,' Karlsson said. 'Any ideas who'd be brazen enough to use your credentials to get that through?'

'I can guess,' she muttered. Jamie ran her hand over her head and then stared out into the office, at the empty desk of the woman who was quickly evolving from unflattering imitation to serious fucking thorn in Jamie's side. 'Julia Hallberg.'

'Hallberg?' he repeated the name, a little surprised. 'She going to be a problem?'

'I hope not,' she said, looking at Karlsson again. 'But I think that just might be wishful thinking at this point.'

Jamie found Hallberg hiding in the break room.

She was sitting at a table, reading a book, eating a sandwich at the same time. She looked up and saw Jamie enter, and in the same moment kicked back her chair and made for the door on the far side of the room.

Jamie halted, doubled back, and dipped back into the corridor, squeezing past a big detective in a green shirt and suspenders.

Her boots thudded on the carpet and she ran the length of the hallway, swinging right around the corner to cut Hallberg off.

Except she wasn't there.

The corridor was empty, and when Jamie checked the break room again, the table was still empty, the book lying open.

Jamie kept her teeth fastened together, listening to her heart beat softly against her ribcage, slowing with each step.

She laid her hand on the book and closed it, rotating it to read the cover.

Forensic Pathology: Practices and Case Studies.

She lifted her eyes, pulling the book from the table, and heading back towards the main office. She was just about ready to promote Hallberg from thorn in the side, though she didn't know what ranked above that.

Jamie thought about it all the way back to her desk.

Hallberg didn't return to hers before the end of the day, and though Jamie managed to cancel the autopsy that 'she' had ordered, she feared it would only light more of a fire under Hallberg.

Jamie closed her computer down and ducked out of the office just before five, heading into the cool late-afternoon air.

It was after six when Hallberg came down the street towards her front door.

Jamie crossed quickly, circling up from behind. At first, she wanted to call out, to confront her peacefully. But as she closed ground on her purposeful, determined walk, she felt something black and unpleasant boil inside her. And instead, she snatched her hand out of the air, twisted it behind her back, forcing Hallberg off balance, and then shoved her against the wall of her building.

She hit the bricks with a dull thud, a few strands of her ponytailed black hair coming loose and flopping over her eyes. They widened in her cheeks, filled with fear for an instant, and then her expression changed to one of frustration when she recognised her assailant over her shoulder.

'What the hell do you think you're doing?' she snapped, pushing herself away from the wall, trying to yank her wrist free.

She turned, made to move past Jamie, but she wouldn't let her.

Jamie grabbed her hand out of the air for a second time and bent it back over her wrist this time. She wasn't fucking around.

Hallberg stopped and slumped backwards again, hitting the wall for a second time, her expression intensifying.

'What I'm doing,' Jamie growled, releasing her and leaning in, 'is saving your fucking life.'

'What are you talking about?' Hallberg rubbed her hand indignantly.

'Using my name to order an autopsy for Falk, after I explicitly told you to leave it alone.'

Hallberg stopped rubbing and looked at her, holding her grit. 'They wouldn't do it if I asked – you were the ranking officer on the case. I didn't have the authority.'

'You think *that's* what I give a shit about?'

Hallberg's eyes searched her face.

'You ever stop to think about *why* I might have told you to drop it? Even for one second?'

She opened her mouth, then closed it.

'Go on, you want to accuse me of something, don't you?'

Hallberg swallowed and broke her gaze.

'Spit it out, Hallberg. You're not leaving here until you do.'

She thought on it for a moment. 'Bolstad,' she said then, her voice hushed.

'What was that?'

'Bolstad!' She looked up at Jamie now, no more than twelve inches between them.

'What about them?'

'I don't know,' she said. 'But I know that Falk was…'

'Was what?'

'I don't know – working with them? *For* them? They had something on her, I guessed.'

Jamie didn't confirm or deny.

'That whole case was wrong from the start. The Spanish police should have been informed the victim was Spanish, and they should have dealt with it. They should have pulled everyone off there and shoved into custody the moment it happened.'

'You're telling me,' Jamie muttered.

'The fact that Falk went along with it… The fact that *you* did…'

'Makes me, what? Dirty? Corrupt? On someone's payroll?'

Hallberg's nostrils flared as she once again measured Jamie.

'Look at me, Hallberg – I seem like the kind of person to take money to look the other way?'

'Falk didn't either,' Hallberg said coolly.

Jamie huffed. 'Sure, that's it. Once everyone else clocks off for the night, Falk and Wiik and me all jump in our Ferraris and drive back to our mansions.'

She seemed to twitch at Wiik's name.

'You're accusing Wiik as well, I assume,' Jamie said. 'Because he went to the rig, too.'

She didn't say a word now.

'You're making assumptions based on what you *think* you know, Hallberg, and that's dangerous.'

'So tell me what's going on. The truth, this time. Falk didn't kill herself, did she?'

Jamie drew back and looked around, inspecting the street carefully. 'If she didn't – *if* – who do you think would have gone after her. And why?'

Hallberg followed her eyes, saw the intense focus there, sensed the angst. 'She… I don't know. Bolstad. They've gone under now as a result of the scandal. That's motive.'

'You think Bolstad killed Falk?'

'Did they?'

'You tell me.' Jamie brought her stare back to the girl in front of her.

'Jesus! Why don't you just tell me the fucking truth!'

'Because I'm trying to save your life!'

Hallberg blinked at her.

'You think if someone, if *Bolstad,* did kill Falk and tried to pass it off as a suicide, that they'd be okay with detectives looking into it?'

Hallberg didn't say anything.

'Or that they'd have *any* fucking qualms about doing the same to those detectives?'

The reality seemed to dawn on Hallberg for the first time. 'So it... *was* Bolstad?'

'It doesn't matter who it was, or why they decided to do it – what matters is that they *did.* And that people know—'

'What people?'

Jamie ignored it. '—and they're trying to make sure that it falls through the cracks.'

'You can't be okay with that?'

'It doesn't matter what I'm okay with, Hallberg,' Jamie said, moving closer, pleading with her. 'What matters is keeping your fucking head attached to your shoulders long enough to figure out *how* to nail the people who did it.'

'So you're... *not* dropping the case?' Hallberg lifted an eyebrow cautiously.

Jamie sighed. 'It's not about this case, or any one case, Hallberg. The people responsible for Falk's death, for what happened with Bolstad, and for so many other crimes – they're powerful. And their reach is... I don't know. Long enough to deal with anyone they don't like.'

'And now...' Hallberg said, her voice thin, 'by ordering

that autopsy… with *your* name…' She swallowed. 'Shit… I'm so sorry, I never meant to—'

'It's fine. I can look after myself.'

'If there's anything I can do, just let me know. If you need me to dig up info on anyone or speak to anyone, I can—'

'Please, don't. I just need you to stop. Stop anything you're doing that has anything to do with Bolstad, or Falk, or anything else.' Jamie bit her lip, hoping she hadn't already put herself on their radar. 'Can you do that?' Jamie was struggling to hold her voice together. If Imperium didn't have her in their sights before, they would now. And they'd only have to learn who her father was before they'd want to shut her down. For good. And she didn't trust Karlsson not to offer her up on a platter the second it would save his ass.

'If they come after you, they come after all of us,' Hallberg said defiantly. 'I won't let you do this alone.'

Jamie swallowed, really struggling to hold it together now. She could shrug off Falk's death, but she couldn't get Hallberg killed. She was good at dragging people into the firing line; not so good at stopping them from getting hit.

'That's where you're wrong, Hallberg. This is has been my fight for longer than you know. So do your work, solve your cases, and forget all about Bolstad, and Falk, and pursuing this. If you don't, there's nothing I can do to help you.' She paused, hoping that would sink in. 'There's nothing that *anyone* will be able to do to help you. And believe me when I say this, if it gets to that point, no one will be ordering an autopsy for you. So, if you're ready to die – because that's what we're staring down the barrel of here – then carry on. If not…' She stepped back and pushed her hands into her pockets, feeling the bulge of her holster and the SIG Sauer P226 in it against her ribs. 'I'll see you tomorrow, okay?'

Hallberg stayed against the wall for a few seconds and

then nodded slowly, stepping past Jamie and heading for the door.

Jamie watched her go, meeting the girl's eye one last time as she looked back.

And then she stepped inside.

Jamie couldn't help but wonder if that was the last time she'd ever see Julia Hallberg alive again.

8

WHEN JAMIE'S PHONE RANG, she immediately thought the worst.

She rolled to her feet, one hand closing around her phone, the other on her loaded pistol.

She held the former against her ear, and let the latter hang loose in her grip, her finger tapping the side of the trigger.

'Hello?' Jamie said, listening for any sounds of movement in her apartment.

Everything was dark and quiet.

Through the blinds over her window, she could just see the milky, almost green tinge of the approaching dawn.

'Is this Detective Inspector Jamie Johansson?' a voice asked in a Swedish accent.

'Who is this?' Jamie asked curtly, her fingers flexing on the grip of the pistol.

'This is Polisassistent Linnea Torell.'

Jamie held her breath, hoping that the next words out of her mouth weren't going to be that Julia Hallberg's body had just been discovered.

'There's been a fire,' Torell went on.

Jamie sank her teeth into her bottom lip, pistol shivering in her hand.

'At your house.'

'My house?' Jamie pushed out, throat tight.

'Yes – firefighters are on scene. I was asked to inform you and—'

Jamie cut her off and pulled on a pair of jeans. She grabbed her rib holster from the headboard where it was hanging, slotted her pistol in, and then threw it over her head, aiming for the door of her apartment.

Twenty minutes later, light had permeated the sky and Jamie could see black smoke rising in the distance. The buildings around her grew smaller, and by the time she pulled into her street, the smoke was dark and acrid, drifting up from behind a cluster of fire engines and police cars. Men in yellow suits sprayed water into the ruined innards of her father's house, and all around, families stood on their lawns, wrapped in heavy coats and bathrobes.

Jamie wheeled her car in at the kerb – an old saloon with a big diesel powerhouse and snow chains that sloshed endlessly around the boot – and kicked the door open, jogging across the street towards the police line.

An officer in a rain mac to keep the spray from the hoses off his back held his hands up. *'Sluta!'* he called. Stop.

Jamie flashed her badge at him. 'This is my house.'

He lowered his hands. 'Oh, I'm sorry,' he said, putting on an apologetic face.

'What happened?' Jamie asked, moving from foot to foot, looking for the fire captain among the yellow suits.

'Electrical fire,' he said. 'That's what they think.'

Jamie was already moving past him. 'Thanks,' she said, aiming for a guy standing next to the engine, clipboard in hand.

'Detective Inspector Jamie Johansson,' she said, approaching, badge flashing once more. 'This is my house.'

The captain was a tall guy, with a scruffy beard and a thick neck. He pushed off the engine and lowered the clipboard, looking Jamie up and down quickly. 'You live here?' he asked, his tone sharp.

'What? No,' she replied, shaking her head.

'But you left the electric on,' he said, tucking the pencil he was using behind his ear.

'I don't know,' Jamie said. 'I haven't been here in weeks.'

He nodded, mind made up. 'Well, you did – a fuse shorted and ignited some wire casings. Whole place went up.'

Jamie set her jaw and looked at her home. The side walls were still standing, but the top half of the front of the house had been burned black, eaten away. And the roof had collapsed.

The doors and windows were broken – either by flames, or by the firefighters who kicked their way inside.

'You know that the electrics in this place are nowhere near up to standard. Old. Corroded.' He pulled the pencil out and pointed at the house. 'An accident waiting to happen.'

Jamie could have stood there and argued herself blue. But there was no point. Because she knew that this was no accident. Not even close.

Instead, she turned away and headed for her car. She'd already removed everything of value from the house. She had intended to sell it, but just hadn't got around to it yet. She didn't know if she ever would have.

'Hey!' the captain called after her. 'I need you to sign some things.'

'Just send them to my office,' Jamie tried to call back, her voice catching on the lump in her throat. She couldn't be there. Couldn't look at it anymore.

She was filled half with anger, half with something else. Something raw. Like the skin beneath a scab. Or a cavity in a tooth. Something sensitive and exposed. Something that hurt to touch.

'What was that?' the captain called again as Jamie crossed the police line. 'Hey!'

But she was already gone, back in her car, and peeling away from the kerb at speed.

The old saloon sidled in a circle and then the back wheels spun lazily, fighting for grip as Jamie accelerated away into the rising sun.

9

WHEN JAMIE GOT to her desk, there was a sticky note on her monitor.

Interview Room 5 – TK.

Thomas Karlsson. Kriminalkommissarie Thomas Karlsson.

Jamie lifted her head and looked around. The floor was still empty – it was barely past eight, after all. Not even Hallberg was in yet. Jamie hoped she was taking some time to consider the implications of her actions, and that it wasn't the alternative.

Her eyes lingered on the empty chair for a moment, and then she headed for the interview rooms.

One, two, three, four… She passed the doors quickly, stopped, and then hooked into five, not knowing really what to expect.

Thomas Karlsson was already inside. He looked drawn, his eyes bagged and bloodshot. But his fast back-and-forth pacing and folded arms told Jamie he was anything but lethargic.

'Johansson,' he said, stopping and looking up. 'Good.'

Jamie hovered at the door, one hand on the handle. 'How did you know I was—'

'I saw you used your key card to scan in downstairs,' he said quickly. 'Come in, close the door.'

Jamie stepped slowly forward, letting it close behind her. She could feel her back stiff, a dull buzzing behind her eyes, her heart beating a little harder. She'd have asked what this was about, but it was pretty fucking clear.

Imperium.

'I'm sorry about your house,' Karlsson said then.

'I have a feeling they hoped I'd been inside,' Jamie replied, struggling to keep the sharpness out of her voice. She didn't know whether Karlsson was someone that Imperium trusted to represent their interests at the SPA, or whether he was a fully-fledged lap dog. She'd need to tread carefully until she did.

Karlsson paused and looked at her. He seemed fidgety. Fuck, it wasn't his house that got burned down.

Jamie kept a lid on her anger. Now wasn't the time to do anything except keep control. She had to be smart here. Smarter than she'd ever been.

'You need to stop,' Karlsson said then.

'Stop what?' Jamie replied, keeping her expression blank.

'Don't play games here, Johansson. You need to stop. Now.'

'I spoke to Hallberg,' Jamie said then. 'She understands what's at stake. She doesn't know what's going on. But she got the picture. And I cancelled the autopsy. Falk's death will slip through the cracks. You can report that back to *whoever* you need to.' She struggled to keep her voice even.

'That's not what I mean.'

Jamie clenched her teeth. 'What do you mean?'

'Hallberg used your name for the autopsy request – I

don't think they know about her. Or at least I've heard nothing. But you…'

'What about me?'

'They know who you are.'

'No shit,' Jamie said cuttingly.

Karlsson's nostrils flared, but he let it slide. 'What I mean is that they know that you're Jörgen Johansson's daughter. And they know you're looking into his death.'

'I'm not,' Jamie said, shaking her head.

Karlsson came forward, slamming his hands down onto the metal table in front of him. The bolts attaching it to the floor rattled. 'They'll kill you. You know that!'

'I do.'

'So then leave it alone! They've looked into you – know who you are, what you're like. They've asked questions, made sure that any stones you turn over, they'll know about. You need to drop this. And you need to drop it now. Falk's death, your father's death, everything.'

Jamie kept quiet.

'And then… And then leave. And don't look back.'

Jamie lifted her head. 'Leave? The SPA?'

'Sweden. For good.'

Jamie bit her bottom lip, nodding slowly. 'Just turn my back on the SPA? The murders, the corruption here? Everything I've learned? Just forget about it? Is that it? How you can stand there and ask me to do that?'

'Because I'm trying to save lives. Yours. And everyone else's. Because Imper—' he cut himself off, regained a little composure. 'Because *they*,' he started again, as if using their name would alert them somehow, 'are ready to clean house. And I'm not about to let that happen.'

'Clean house?' Jamie lifted an eyebrow, inspecting Karlsson across the table. 'What does that mean?'

He took his time answering. 'If they remove you, there'll be ripples. And they only have one way of dealing with those. The people you've involved in this… It won't end with you.'

She didn't answer. But she knew who he meant.

'Your partner, Wiik. Hallberg. Your friend at the pathology lab, Claesson.'

'They'd kill them? Just like that?' Jamie spat.

He nodded very slightly. 'And whether they get you or not, they'll get them. One by one, all at once. However they can. You're on their radar, Jamie. And people don't drop off it. They'll be watching you. And whatever you do next will be the difference between life and death. And not just for you.'

Jamie swallowed, then cleared her throat, turning her back on Karlsson. She folded her arms, thinking. 'And burning down my house. What was that? A warning?'

'A *final* warning.' He stood straight and walked around the table.

Jamie could feel him hovering behind her.

'I'm sorry, Johansson, about everything. But there's nothing more to be done. Make arrangements to leave, and I'll even write you a recommendation. Help you get anywhere you want.'

'Anywhere but here.' Her voice quavered.

'Sweden isn't your home anymore. There's nothing here for you now. Your time at the SPA is over. Move on.'

'And if I don't?' Jamie closed her eyes, listening to the quiet drum of her heart in her ears.

'If you don't,' Karlsson said, barely above a whisper. 'Then there's nothing I'll be able to do to protect you. Or anyone else.'

He moved past her, opened the door, and slipped out without another word.

Jamie picked her head up then, swallowing the bile rising in her throat.

Maybe Karlsson was right. Maybe it was time to leave Stockholm behind.

Jamie thought for a moment, then reached out for the door with a shaking hand, pulled it open, and stepped through it.

10

Hallberg still wasn't in by the time Jamie left HQ and she tried to ignore the unease that was creating.

Before long, her mind was elsewhere. She held her hand up next to the steering wheel as she drove, reading the map on it as she navigated down a narrow street of small townhouses in the residential part of the city. Jamie had never been here before, and didn't know what to expect. But from the neat exteriors and cleanliness of the roadway, she figured it was about par for the course. She found a space a hundred yards down and then backtracked to the front door she was searching for.

Jamie felt a little queasy. She just had a cup of coffee sloshing around inside her, and it was doing little to settle her stomach.

She clenched her shaking hand and thumped it against the wood.

Minutes passed without response. Jamie tried again. Nothing.

She could call him, but it was going straight to voicemail

already, and she thought four missed calls was already looking a little desperate.

But damn, did she need him right now.

Jamie leaned her forehead against the cool wood, the spring air fresh around her, the sun warm on the back of her neck. She knocked again, next to her head, eyes closed. 'Wiik?' she called through the jamb. 'You in there?'

She'd noticed his car on the walk up, so she knew he was home.

His son lived with his ex-wife and step-father in Gothenburg, and he had no one else. He was just as alone as she was. So why the fuck wouldn't he answer?

'Wiik!' Jamie raised the volume a little. 'I need you.' She banged again. 'Please, open the door. Come on.'

Something moved inside and Jamie's eyes opened. She lifted her head and pricked her ears. No, she'd definitely heard something.

She didn't usually resort to that kind of thing, but before she could think about it, she was on her knees, pushing her fingers through the letterbox. The metal flap creaked upwards and Jamie peered into the darkened interior of Wiik's hallway. 'Wiik?' she said through the gap.

Something moved in the shadow next to the stairs.

'Wiik, come on,' Jamie said then. 'I can see your legs. Open the door.'

The legs shifted from side to side, as if deciding whether to run away or not, and then they approached, pausing just in front of the door.

'What if I'd had a dog?' came Wiik's voice through the door. 'He could have bitten your fingers off.'

'Then you'd have had to let me in,' Jamie said. 'I imagine you'd feel pretty strongly about me splashing blood all over these lovely clean steps.' She looked around. They were clean. Cleaner than Jamie's own kitchen, she thought.

'I'd prefer it all over my steps to my floor.' He pulled the door open, standing there in a pair of jogging bottoms and a loose, faded T-shirt that had one sleeve cut off at the shoulder, a gaping hole hacked half down to the ribs. He wouldn't have been able to get it on otherwise – he was cradling his left hand, each of the fingers on it held straight out, a mess of screws and pins holding them that way, attached to an elaborate metal cage that stretched from beyond his fingertips halfway up his forearm.

Jamie tried not to stare.

Wiik was a mess. He looked exhausted. Dishevelled. His usually impeccably swept-back hair was lying in a greasy, lifeless centre parting. He hadn't shaved in a week, and she could smell the sweat coming off him from five feet away. She thought showering was probably disgustingly painful and awkward. She didn't blame him.

'We need to talk,' Jamie said, forcing a little smile.

Wiik didn't seem intent on letting her in. 'About what?'

She glanced around. The street was empty. But that didn't mean they were alone.

Fuck, he really wasn't going to let her in. 'I'm leaving,' she said then.

'Leaving?' He narrowed his eyes slightly. 'Leaving where?'

'The SPA. Stockholm.' She swallowed. 'Sweden.'

Wiik was silent. He just stared at her.

'Not because of you,' she added then, feeling the weight of his eyes.

'I didn't think you were.'

Jamie cleared her throat. 'Look, can I come in? Can we

talk about this? About what happened?' She glanced past him, saw the pile of mail lying next to the welcome mat.

'What is there to talk about? You're leaving.'

'Don't you want to know why?'

'Does it matter?'

All the warmth that had developed between them had now gone. Like everyone else that got hurt around her, they seemed to blame Jamie. Sure, the bruises on her throat were still just about visible, and she'd been concussed for a few days following their last case, but comparative to him, she was unscathed. Wiik, on the other hand, would have to live in pain for the rest of his life, most likely. 'Yes,' Jamie insisted, knowing how easy it would be to walk away. 'It does,' she said, and then shouldered past him. 'Now move, I'm not going to stand on your step and talk to you like we're strangers.'

She stormed into his hallway, glancing up the stairs and then into the kitchen at the back, and made a beeline for the latter.

'Got any coffee?' Jamie called over her shoulder, standing in the middle of what looked like a bomb site. Every cupboard door and drawer was open, every counter filled with rubbish and empty food containers. There were dirty dishes, plates, cutlery, pots, pans… There wasn't a single uncluttered inch of space in there.

'Help yourself,' Wiik said, hovering by the kitchen door, still cradling his cage.

Jamie didn't know where to start. She turned instead and started talking. 'You hear about Bolstad?'

'Saw that they were taken over on the news last week,' Wiik said, looking down at his hand.

'And you heard about Falk?'

Wiik looked up at her now. 'Falk? What happened to

Falk?' Whether he'd read the tone in her voice or just gleaned from context, Jamie didn't know, but the sudden focus in his eyes told her he hadn't completely lost his shine.

'She's dead, Wiik. I tried to call, but your phone was—'

'Dead?' He straightened a little, stepped forward. 'What? How? When?'

'Yesterday,' Jamie answered, watching him. 'Suicide.'

'Suicide?'

'Supposedly.'

He stared at her intensely. 'What do you mean?'

She could see he was thrown, but that it was anger in him, not sadness. Anger that he hadn't been there? That if he was, he might have done something to stop it?

'Same way my father committed suicide.'

He was still then, the wheels turning in his head. 'Talk.'

'There's nothing to say. The company behind Bolstad told Falk to have that mess sorted out quietly. We didn't accomplish that task. Now, Falk's dead.'

'You're saying it's our fault?'

'No, I'm not,' Jamie said, her voice cold. 'Far from it. Falk was in deep with them, and I don't care if it sounds heartless, but she was corrupt, and she made her bed.'

Wiik's jaw flexed, but he said nothing.

'And because she failed, they dealt with her. Same way they dealt with my father.'

'That's why you're leaving?'

'No,' Jamie said, sighing and rubbing the back of her neck. 'I'm leaving because Hallberg disobeyed a direct order, ordered an autopsy for Falk under my name, and now they've burned down my house and ordered me to leave Sweden or they'll kill me.'

Wiik looked at her, unsure if she was joking or not.

'Hallberg disobeyed a direct order?' he asked then.

'That's what you took away from that?' Jamie almost laughed.

'I spent the better part of a year whipping her into shape, making her diligent, obedient, careful. Two weeks with you and she's disobeying orders, using the credentials of superior officers?' He shook his head. 'I'm just a little shocked.'

'I think you're missing the point here, Wiik.' Jamie really needed that coffee. 'They've ordered me to drop the case, drop my investigation into my father, and *leave the country.* The country, Wiik. Not just the SPA and Stockholm. The country.'

'You spoke to them?'

'No, the message was passed along.'

'By who?' Wiik's hand rubbed the cage. She couldn't imagine how uncomfortable that thing must be.

Jamie drew a slow breath. 'Falk's replacement. Thomas Karlsson, head of cyber.'

Wiik seemed to tense up at his mention. Whether he knew the man or it was just because it was the department that his old partner was transferred to, she didn't know. It was a subject she'd been unable to broach with him. Though from what Falk had said, Wiik saw it as nothing short of a knife in the back.

'So, uh,' he said, playing it off and letting his hands hang loose, 'what are you going to do?'

'I don't think I have much of a choice. It's not just my head on the chopping block.'

'What do you mean?'

'Karlsson wasn't bashful about naming those who'd be taken down with me.'

'And as you're standing here talking to me about it, I supposed I'm on that list?'

Jamie offered a brief smile. 'You could take it as a compliment.'

'How?'

'I don't know,' Jamie said. At first she thought it made Wiik one of the closest people to her, but if that list also included Hallberg and Claesson, the pathologist who'd worked the Angel Maker case and helped her father two decades ago, then her life was probably a lot sadder than she thought.

Wiik inhaled deeply. 'So, that's it? You're dropping the investigation into your father and leaving?'

She didn't want to answer that. 'I don't really see that I have a choice. If they want to come for you, you won't be hard to find.'

Wiik was the one who didn't answer now.

They stood in silence for a few minutes, each sort of looking everywhere but at each other.

A clock ticked quietly in another room.

'I never thanked you,' Jamie said then. 'Or apologised.'

'For what?'

'For what happened with Bolstad. On the rig.'

'Forget it.'

'I won't. I can't,' Jamie said. 'I went there to serve my own agenda, and you only went with me because you thought it was a stupid idea for me to go alone. And you were right.'

'And now Falk is dead, I'm lame, and you managed to piss off the people pulling the strings inside the SPA by shutting down the company that gave them a choke-hold on the Swedish energy industry.' He shook his head. 'You know, when I first started – and your father was still around – there was this thing. People used to laugh about it. They called it the *Johansson Effekten.*' The Johansson Effect. 'Your father had an uncanny ability to take a simple case and somehow blow it up. Usually spectacularly.'

Jamie felt her shoulders tense.

'Every one of his cases seemed to snowball into this big… *thing.* And he could never leave it alone.'

'Maybe he was just perceptive. Saw what others didn't,' Jamie said through gritted teeth.

'Maybe he just didn't know when to leave things alone.' Wiik stepped forward now. 'Isn't it enough that you know what happened to him? That you know he was killed, and you know who did it?'

'No, it's not. How could it be, Wiik?'

'I don't see how you're going to fight these people, Jamie. The SPA don't only know about it, they *are* these people. You'll be fighting the police as much as them. You can't hope to win.'

'It's not about winning.' Her voice was growing more barbed.

'Then what is it about?'

'It's about doing something. Anything. It's about not rolling over. It's about—'

'Martyring yourself? Getting those around you killed? I'm sorry, Jamie – you're on your own on this one. I can't help you.' Wiik turned away and headed for the front door.

'I didn't come here for your help,' Jamie called after him.

He reached it and stopped, pulling it open.

Jamie stared out at the bright square of daylight, knowing that it was an invitation to leave.

'Then why did you come?' Wiik asked as Jamie approached.

She slowed at the threshold and reached out for his arm. 'I came… to say goodbye.'

Her fingers touched, just for a moment, and then she pulled them away.

'I came to tell you the truth, in case I don't see you again.'

Jamie walked out onto the neatly looked after steps – the only part of Wiik's property still clean – and started down towards her car.

'Jamie,' Wiik called after her, stepping through his front door for what she suspected was the first time in weeks.

She paused and looked back.

'If you call,' he said, seeming to labour over the words, 'next time, I'll pick up. Stay in touch. Let me know you're safe, at least.'

Jamie nodded, unable to find any suitable words.

And then Wiik closed the door and Jamie was as alone as she'd ever been.

11

JAMIE WAS at the airport when Hallberg called.

She answered, sitting with her trusty duffle between her heels. 'Johansson,' she said, feeling like any official prefix or title was pretty much a moot point right now.

'You handed in your notice?' Hallberg's voice was almost incredulous.

'Hello to you too,' Jamie said tiredly, the momentary relief of hearing her voice gone already. It was just after midday, but she felt like it was the end of a very long week. Or maybe a long few months.

'Karlsson just told me you're leaving.'

There was no point sugar-coating it. 'I already left.'

'Is this because of me?'

It's for you, Jamie felt like saying. 'No,' she said instead. 'There's just nothing for me here anymore.'

'Nothing... for you? What are you talking about? And what happened to your house? I saw the report this morning – someone burned it down? Did *they*—'

'Stop, Hallberg,' Jamie said coldly. 'You may not understand why I'm doing what I am. But trust me when I say that it's better for everyone if you never see me again.'

'Does Wiik know you're leaving?'

'He does.'

'What did he say?'

Jamie didn't need to lie this time. 'Honestly? He didn't seem to really care. This was only ever supposed to be a temporary thing, Hallberg. And this is the right time to make this decision.'

She scoffed a little.

Jamie's fist tightened around the phone.

'I can't believe you're just running away.'

Jamie held her tongue.

'After everything. *Everything* you went through. Everything that's happened. With Wiik, Falk... They burned down your house! And you *know* who's responsible. And you're just turning your back on it. On them. On us?'

Jamie stared up at the board in front of her, watching the status of her flight change from *Boarding* to *Last Call.*

'Call it what you want,' Jamie said flatly, getting up and slinging her duffle over her shoulder. 'Look after yourself, Hallberg. And don't do anything stupid.' She hung up before Hallberg could reply and pocketed her phone, approaching the desk in front of her, the line now empty, everyone else on board.

Jamie handed her ticket and passport to the gate rep and watched them run it through the machine.

A second later, she handed it back and gave Jamie a warm grin. 'Enjoy your trip to Helsinki.'

A little over an hour later, they touched down at Helsinki Airport, the air cool and grey, and Jamie disembarked.

She flew through security, keen to do this as cleanly and quietly as possible, and headed for the car rental booth with the shortest line. Jamie rented a small hatchback and then walked quickly towards the lot it was parked in, checking over her shoulder every few steps.

She was conscious that Imperium would be watching her – their track record didn't suggest that they were in the habit of making empty threats – so she needed to be surgical about this. Give them no time to catch up, or catch her off guard.

If they were watching, then they'd be trying to figure out what she was doing, and why she'd booked a flight to Finland of all places.

She just hoped that by the time they came to the right conclusion, she'd already have accomplished what she needed to.

After she'd left Wiik's, she'd headed back to the office to draft up her resignation letter and offload her cases. She'd also accessed the file from the Bolstad oil rig case and copied out some contact information.

Jamie reached lot C and looked down at the rental paper-work in front of her. Third floor, space 327.

She took the stairs and wound quickly upwards, throwing her duffle over her shoulders and wearing it like a backpack, breaking into a run as she reached the first land-ing, suddenly aware that an empty stairwell was probably a great place to get murdered. Her skin was beaded with sweat by the time she reached the right floor and blipped the keys.

She'd been forced to leave her service weapon in Sweden. As much as it begrudged her to do it, she didn't think holding on to it would convince Imperium that she was dropping the whole thing. So she'd handed it back to Karlsson, along with her badge and her resignation letter.

Which ultimately meant she was now unarmed, and totally defenceless.

Jamie steadied her breathing, looked out for the flash of lights in the darkness, and closed ground on the little Volkswagen. She slid into the driver's seat, scanned the empty floor around her, and then pulled out, tyres squealing on the slick concrete.

As she circled towards the exit, she pulled out her phone and opened the map, the destination already in place. She'd done it at the rental desk while they took her payment.

She was wasting no time.

Jamie pulled out of the car park, joined the traffic oozing onto the road that led to the city, and then snuck into the fast lane, aiming to get that forty-six minute travel time down to an even forty.

Jamie passed Heikkinen Investments thirty-eight minutes later, and looked up at the shining glass exterior. The clouds moved in its reflection, high above the city, silent and bruised.

She continued a few hundred metres down and parked in an underground lot, leaving her duffle in the back seat and heading back towards her destination.

Inside, the air was crisp, air-conditioned despite the freshness outside.

People moved in expensive suits, their heels clipping on the wide marble tiles.

Jamie, as always, was in her boots, skinny jeans, and a hoodie-and-leather-jacket combo that made her look exactly what she was just then – unemployed.

There were two people sitting at the curved front desk.

Above them on a black granite slab were the words *Heikkinen Investments* in embossed silver with an abstract shape that was a mix of the letters *H*, *I*, and what Jamie thought was the alchemical symbol for gold or silver – she couldn't remember which.

'Voinko auttaa sinua?' the young man behind the desk asked.

Jamie dragged her eyes down from the sign and looked at him. Mid-twenties, impeccably groomed, quaffed hair that Wiik would have been proud of.

Her brain stuttered as she realised she wasn't in Sweden anymore and tried to work out what she'd just been asked.

'Sorry?' Jamie said in English, blinking.

'I asked,' the young man said, switching fluidly to English too, 'if I could help you.'

'Uh, yeah,' Jamie said, ignoring the condescension in his voice. 'I'm here to see Simon Heikkinen.'

His eyebrows slowly pushed his forehead into well-moisturised rolls. 'Simon Heikkinen? Do you have an appointment?' he asked, doing his best not to look her up and down. Even as just a receptionist, he was wearing a suit that probably cost more than Jamie's monthly rent.

'He'll agree to see me,' Jamie said, pulling a card from her pocket. She put it down on the desk in front of her and slid it across to him.

'Detective Inspector Jamie Johansson,' the clerk read, picking it up. 'With the *Stockholm Police*?' He seemed dubious about the dissonance between the English title and the Swedish posting. And about the woman in front of him being anything except a dishevelled crazy person who'd just wandered in off the street asking for a meeting with one of the most influential multimillionaire business magnates in Finland.

Jamie nodded, keeping her voice firm. 'Yeah. That's right. And I need to speak to Simon Heikkinen.'

'You'll forgive me if I ask to see some identification,' the clerk said, smiling politely now. The girl next to him – who looked early thirties, smart, well-groomed and dressed, too – was staring at Jamie now.

'Of course,' Jamie said, pulling her wallet from her jeans. She withdrew her driver's licence and put it down on the desk too.

The clerk stared at it. 'And your police credentials?'

Jamie looked down at him, wishing she could just wipe the condescension off his face with the heel of her boot. 'You know what,' she said, pulling her licence back towards her. 'Forget it.' She stowed it in her wallet. 'Just call upstairs, and tell Heikkinen that I came to see him, and that he can reach me on that number. And tell him it's a matter of urgency.'

The clerk put the card down next to his keyboard and clasped his hands on the desk, nodding. 'I'll do that right away for you. Thank you for choosing Heikkinen Investments.'

Jamie's heel twitched, dancing under her. She had to think twice before she decided slinging a spinning kick over the desk was a bad idea.

She sighed and turned away, dragging her disappointed boot with her.

Jamie slumped down behind the wheel, watching as her grip tightened on it, her knuckles rising unevenly on the smooth curve.

She sucked in a deep breath, and then bucked in the seat, screaming at the backs of her hands, trying her fucking hardest to rip the wheel right out of the dashboard.

Her skull banged against the headrest, making the bolts on the chair groan, and only when her hair had fully flung itself around her head, blinding her and filling her mouth, did she stop, spit it out and then hunch forward.

She drew in slow breaths, a sickening feeling growing in the pit of her stomach.

Was this it? Was this the end? Did she really have to turn tail and run away?

Jamie sat up and looked in the rear-view mirror, seeing a tired woman with red eyes staring back. Jesus, she looked like she was about to burst into tears. She grimaced and turned the mirror away, shoved her car into drive and squealed out of the car park.

She'd drive first and think later.

If she needed to get on a plane, then she would. But right now, she just wanted to drive. She'd head out of the city, find somewhere to hole up for a night or two. She'd just pick a town that looked quiet.

With little more than the next hour of her life mapped out, Jamie followed the signs for the E75, the highway that led north, towards Lahti, and resigned herself to silence, thinking about what was to come next.

And not knowing the half of it.

12

JAMIE HAD BEEN DRIVING for a little over two hours when night fell. She hadn't realised the time, but her heavy eyes told her it was growing late.

The roads were quiet now. She'd left Lahti in her wake an hour before, the country growing wilder around her. She passed by lakes on the left, then the right, the road meandering hypnotically between them.

Jamie sighed, rolling down the window and welcoming the refreshing cold air on her face.

Behind her, headlights flared and she glanced down at the speedometer. She was doing a little under the speed limit, but nothing, really. They filled the rear windscreen and reflected harshly in the wing mirror. Jamie squinted, glancing up at the rear-view. Fuck, just go around – the roads are empty.

The SUV behind her weaved a little, revving hard, the lights lifting higher and then sagging back down as it pulled up closer to her bumper.

Jamie stuck her arm out, waving the 4x4 around.

And then it hit her.

The truck accelerated hard and connected with the bumper of her little hatchback, sending it snaking forward.

Her brain switched on suddenly, fear rearing up inside her, the realisation striking like lightning. This wasn't just some asshole in a truck.

One word seared itself in her mind.

Imperium.

Jamie floored it, the automatic box on her little Volkswagen struggling as the car downshifted and hauled itself forward, the engine revving weakly.

The SUV dropped back behind her, then caught up again.

Jamie braced, moving into the middle of the road.

It hit again and she heard the tyres squeal, the steering going light for a second as she wrestled the car straight, easing off the accelerator, and then planting her foot again the instant it gained traction.

Her heart pounded behind her eyes, sweat pouring through her palms, making the rippled faux leather slick in her grip.

Jamie's eyes were fixed on the rear-view as she danced back and forth across the central divider line, the cat's eyes rumbling and thumping under her.

The big SUV lumbered around behind, the lights rolling up and down as it tried to close the gap and stay on the road.

Headlights then. In front.

Jamie's eyes flitted to the road, saw them racing towards her.

A horn blared.

Jamie ripped the wheel right and the wheels slid on the asphalt, the car understeering, careening across the path of the oncoming car, out of the opposite lane.

She screwed her eyes closed, brakes screeching as the car swerved the other way.

The horn screamed in Jamie's ear, and the inside of her eyelids burned yellow for an instant, and then the sound was behind her.

She gasped, her eyes opening, the front wheel of the car juddering over the white line that separated the tarmac from the gravel verge and sinking into the soft ground. The car snaked, threatened to spin out, the engine struggling, revs dying.

Jamie turned the wheel back, the rear of the car sailing around, jumping down onto the verge itself, sending a spray of tiny stones into the fir trees and onto the lakeshore beyond.

Her ears were ringing, her face beaded with sweat. She was breathing hard, the car trying its best to get back up onto the road.

Dust trailed in her wake, clouding the windscreen.

Jamie squinted through it, watching the headlights flicker over boughs of trees, and then catching the reflectors that separated the two lanes.

And then she stopped bouncing in the seat, the car levelling off, the revs climbing again as all four wheels found the roadway and she began to accelerate.

Jamie swallowed, breathing hard, her mouth dry, and checked the rear-view mirror.

Clear.

Nothing.

The truck. Had it gone off the road too? Had she lost them? Where the hell was—

Jamie looked left a half-second too late, the enormous bulk of the black four-by-four crossing the lanes right towards her. Its broadside connected with hers, no more than six inches from her left shoulder.

The sound of rent metal filled the cabin. Jamie's neck

jerked violently, the seatbelt cutting into her shoulder and chest, choking the air from her.

Her hands flung the wheel left and right, but it was no good, the wheels didn't seem attached to the ground anymore.

They hit dirt and the car swung around, throwing Jamie into the door, her head connecting with the glass painfully.

She called out, feeling her weight shift forward, opening her eyes to see the ground rushing up at her as she plunged down the bank next to the road, fir limbs cracking and snapping against the windows.

And then she landed, the front bumper digging into the ground, blasting stones in all directions.

The airbags deployed, the bang deafening her, sending pain ripping through her brain, setting off a high-pitched whine in her ears.

The pain came then, in her face, like she'd been hit with a fucking bible.

Her eyes lolled, watching as a crack lanced through the windscreen, the dashboard lighting up furiously with warning lights as the car speared forward, leaving the ground once more as it barrelled over the edge of what had to be a cliff.

She didn't have time to think about it.

Jamie was weightless for an instant, helpless, dazed, watching the surface of the lake rush up at her. And then water exploded around the bonnet, throwing her against the seatbelt once more. It gushed up over the bonnet, the headlights failing.

The engine stalled, a noisy beeping sounding somewhere around her.

Jamie gasped, coughing blood over the backs of her hands held up in front of her face, and stared forward, not understanding what she was seeing as water climbed the windscreen, spraying in through the cracks.

She looked down, saw that it was pooling around her feet.

Panic set in then and her hands starting waving around, looking for the exit.

She was wheezing.

There was so much pain.

She tried the door, only to be dragged back into the seat by the belt, which seemed to have tightened like a noose around her.

She fumbled for the clasp, the car tilting forward again as the weight of the engine dragged it down into the water.

Shit, it was cold.

It climbed her legs, making her shudder as she fought with the belt.

The lights died around her then, the dashboard going dark, the cabin light that she hadn't realise had turned on stuttering and then blinking off above her shoulder.

The water kept rising, the car sinking faster now.

It was at her stomach, chilling her, pushing on her chest.

What the fuck was wrong with this belt!

Jamie jerked in the seat, kicking at the underside of the dashboard.

And then water was rushing in from her left, over her shoulder, through the open window as the car sank lower, the water level totally over the windscreen, her body submerged up to the neck.

Jamie lifted her chin, shivering with the cold already, sucked in as big a breath as she could, and then went under.

Her eyes stung, but she forced them open, her lungs already burning.

No, focus! You're not going to die like this.

Not here.

Not in a fucking Volkswagen!

Not after everything.

Jamie couldn't get the button down, there was too much pressure on the belt. She needed to pull herself into the seat.

Right.

Yes.

Her mind began working again, the adrenaline in her system taking hold, focusing her. Willing her to survive.

Jamie kicked at the dashboard again, dragging her feet up until she managed to get one against the radio.

She straightened her leg, her heart hammering in her throat, her ears aching and throbbing as the pressure began to build.

How long had she been under? A few seconds? How fast was she sinking? How deep was this fucking lake?

The pressure built as Jamie wedged herself back against the seat, alternating pushing with her leg and pushing the button.

It depressed a little, pain shooting through her ears, threatening to burst her eardrums.

And then it clicked under her thumb and the belt was loose.

Jamie floated upwards, her head bumping against the ceiling, and a stream of bubbles escaped her lips, her body threatening to flatten against the roof liner.

She kicked, her heels hitting the passenger seat, and reached out for where she thought the window was.

It was dark. She was disoriented.

The only noise around her was the rushing of air, from her own mouth and from the various pockets trapped in the cabin.

Her fingers felt the curve of the door then and she scissored her feet, hauling herself over the sill, her hips hitting it, then her knees.

The top of the window hooked around her boot and stopped her, her fingers clawing madly at the water.

She could feel herself being dragged down again.

Her mouth opened, a gargled scream piercing the water.

And then it let go, and she was turning

Jamie blinked, eyes stinging, seeing nothing, her lungs on fire now, empty, spent.

She looked around. Everything was dark.

She needed to go up! Up! But which way was – she saw it then, just a murky shape, a receding black blob over her right shoulder. The car. Sinking.

Jamie wasted no time, turned her back on it, and kicked.

Harder than she'd ever kicked before.

13

JAMIE'S HEAD broke the surface and she raked in a watery breath, filling her mouth with liquid, choking and thrashing as she kept her head above the surface.

She heard a voice in the distance, then another, and kicked herself in a circle, trying to get her bearings.

Her eyes began to focus, burning from the water, and homed in on the glowing white lights in the distance.

Everything took form then – she could see the shore about ten metres away, a steep bank rising to a bluff fifteen feet up, and above it the roadway.

The SUV was parked on the little verge behind the trees, the lights silhouetting the firs. Her car must have gone down the bank, hit the little cliff edge and tumbled over. She didn't even remember that – it was all just a blur of exploding airbags and screeching tyres.

Her ears started picking out sounds then as the water drained from them – shouts, the scrabbling of stones as two shapes slid and ran down onto the ledge, no more than dark figures.

And then there was light – a blinding rosette, cutting the darkness.

Water erupted next to Jamie's head, a geyser, dousing her in it.

The shot echoed around, registering an instant later.

There was another muzzle flash. And another.

Fuck!

Jamie sucked in a deep breath, sank below the surface again, the only thing she could do, and turned, kicking her legs again, swimming away from the shore.

She didn't even think about her breathing, just kept her legs pumping, arms moving in wide strokes, pulling herself forward. How big was this lake? She didn't know. But it was damn cold. Her face was aching, her forehead stinging, her nose throbbing.

Jamie broke the surface again, the sounds of shouts now further in the distance.

She stole a glance back, totally drowned in darkness now, and could see the headlights on the roadway maybe thirty metres away.

The two men strode back and forth on the bank. She didn't know if they could see her, but she wasn't waiting around to find out. The moment she got her breath back, she dived under again, willing her muscles to keep moving, her body to stay warm.

On the third surface, she slowed her pace, took stock of her surroundings. She needed a better plan than to keep swimming straight. The headlights had disappeared from the road now – no doubt that they weren't sticking around in case anyone drove past and stopped. But no one seemed to be.

Jamie waited, treading water for a solid minute or two before another car trundled up the road.

It didn't drive quickly, and Jamie wondered if it was the

SUV doing a cruise-by to see if she'd been stupid enough to head back to shore.

She wouldn't be. But she didn't think they'd quit anytime soon.

They were a long way from any sizeable towns, and if anyone had heard the shots, it would take a long time to scramble police. And even then, would they even know where to stop or what to look for?

Jamie couldn't stick around to find out. She was already getting tired and as the evening wore on the temperature would drop further. A thin mist had already settled on the surface of the lake and her breath was frosting in front of her.

Jamie swallowed, tasting blood. She licked her top lip and felt it warm on her tongue. She kicked her legs, touched her nose with her hand, felt a bolt of pain shoot through her face, the telltale edges of torn skin running across the bridge of her nose. She swore, sinking below the surface, choking on water for a moment before she righted herself again.

Was her nose broken?

'Fuck!' she screamed this time, rising onto her back and trying to float, trying to catch her breath.

But she couldn't, her clothes too heavy, her body not buoyant enough. And she was getting tired. She needed to get to shore, and she needed to get warm. This wasn't sustainable.

Jamie braced herself, looked left and right, squinting into the near-perfect darkness, and then took off at a steady pace, trying to conserve energy as best she could.

Nearly twenty minutes later, she felt stones under her toes and managed to stand. The water had grown shallow, but the shore here was still a little way off.

She dragged herself through the waist-deep water, pushing it out of her path with her knees, arms wrapped around her body, teeth chattering, blood still running down her face.

She spat it into the water, clearing her mouth constantly.

When she got to knee-depth she paused and looked around, seeing nothing but wilderness and trees. She racked her brain, trying to think of any signs she'd seen, any hints of towns. She'd passed one before the lake, she thought, maybe saying there was a town a few kilometres ahead. But she didn't know. She couldn't be sure.

Right now, it didn't really matter. She was alone, unarmed, and she had no way to contact anyone. Her phone had been in the centre console, and now it was at the bottom of a fucking lake.

She didn't even have a jacket.

Jamie looked down at herself – a long-sleeve T-shirt, which was sopping wet, a sports bra, a pair of jeans, and her boots. That was all she had. Just the clothes on her back.

For an instant, she wanted to collapse, cry, scream, punch the water.

And then what? Curl up and die out here?

No. No fucking way.

That wasn't her. It hadn't ever been her. And it wasn't about to be her today.

Just pick a direction and run. You like to run. You were made to run. You eat 20-Ks for breakfast.

Jamie filled her lungs and pulled off her shirt, screwing it up and wringing it out as hard as she could. And then she pulled it back on, wading out onto dry land, and squeezed as much water out of her plait as possible.

And then she started running.

14

BY THE WAY her legs were burning, she guessed she'd run at least ten kilometres, maybe more.

But at least she'd managed to stay warm.

She'd had to stop twice to attend to her nose, and her forehead, which also seemed to be cut.

The airbag exploding in her face was the culprit. Either that or she'd managed to smack her head on the steering wheel when she hit the water. Or punch herself. She didn't know, but her nose was all but broken, split across the bridge, and there was a vertical gash on her forehead, starting between her eyebrows and running an inch upwards.

Both had stopped themselves around kilometre five, she thought.

Though what kind of mess she looked, she couldn't have even imagined.

Jamie climbed an incline, scrambling up through some loose rocks and pine needles, and saw the first glimmer of lights through the trees.

She had to hold back tears of joy. The pain in her face, her chest from where the seatbelt felt like it had cracked a rib, and the burning in her lungs were all enough to make her want to collapse. But she couldn't. She wasn't safe yet.

Jamie sidestepped down the slope and into town – which was no more than a few loops and blocks of low-set houses, a narrow main street with a coffee shop, a post office, and a small convenience store. The former two were locked up and dark, but the shop was open, and Jamie made a beeline for it, panting hard.

As she neared, the lights spilling out of the floor-length windows stung her eyes. She'd been in darkness for so long, scrambling through bushes and over undulating, tree-lined hills, she could barely see.

Jamie held her hand up to shield her eyes and slowed to a jog, heading for the door.

It opened automatically, dinging as she stepped in.

She stopped, looking around, catching the eye of the woman behind the counter. She must have been near sixty, short, with curled grey hair and square glasses on a beaded string. She was staring at Jamie in shock.

Jamie hadn't really thought about what she'd do once she got inside. 'Sorry,' she croaked reflexively, finally looking down at herself. Her jeans and legs were filthy up to her knees and her laces were covered in torn-off fern leaves. Her shirt was crumpled and creased, plastered in blood, and her hands were covered in it too.

She turned and looked at herself in the reflection of the glass, saw her hair a tangled mess, her forehead cut, nose swollen and split, and the bottom half of her face completely crusted over with blood.

Jamie looked back at the woman, still breathing hard. 'Do you have a phone?' she croaked again, realising how dry her throat was.

She wasted no time in crossing to the fridge opposite, pulling out a bottle of water, and draining it.

The woman behind the counter was still staring at her in shock.

Jamie neared now. 'Do you have a phone?' She racked her brain for what little Finnish she knew. Despite being next to Sweden, the languages were nothing alike. '*Onko… sinnulla… puha… pehelin?*'

The woman started to shake her head, backing up until she hit the shelves of chocolates and cigarettes behind her. '*Sinun täytyy lähteä…*' she said. '*Sinun täytyy lähteä nyt!*'

Jamie was the one shaking her head now. 'What? I don't understand.' Jamie put her hands on the counter and the woman recoiled like Jamie was about to launch herself at her.

'You,' the woman said, pointing, 'leave! Please.'

'No, I just need to use your—'

'Leave!' the woman yelled.

Jamie backed up – she needed help, not to terrorise this poor woman. 'Look, look,' Jamie said, feeling the warm trickle of fresh blood on her nose again. 'Please, I was… I was in an accident, okay? You know "accident"?'

'Leave!'

The sound of an engine broke the quiet of the shop then and Jamie turned to see a black SUV rolling down the street. She froze, standing right in the middle of the store, drowned in light. There was nowhere to run.

The car slowed suddenly, rocking on its springs, and pulled to a stop directly opposite. It idled there, tinted windows raised.

Jamie's blood ran cold.

'You leave!' the woman behind the counter said, stretching the limits of her English. Most people spoke it perfectly in Finland, but in more rural communities, with her

generation especially, times hadn't yet caught up. These
sleepy little villages, nestled in the wilderness... This was
probably the most frightening thing the woman had ever seen.

'Please,' Jamie tried again. 'I need help. You see that car?'
She didn't dare point, but risked nodding her head sideways.
'Those men – they are trying to hurt me, okay? *Kill* me, uh,'
she said. '*Tapa...* uh... *minut. Tapa minut?*' Jamie didn't
know if she had that right, but by the way the woman was
pressing herself back against the shelf, her face screwed up
like Jamie was about to spit acid on her. She didn't think she
was getting her point across.

Fuck! Jamie couldn't go out there. And she couldn't stay
here.

No phone, no gun – and who the hell was she going to
call, anyway? She was on her own here. She was stuck,
cornered, and she didn't think she had it in her to go out the
back and run another ten kilometres through the woods
again.

'Leave!' the woman mustered again then. 'Leave, or... or
I... call... *poliisi*!'

It dawned on her then.

The police.

Jamie backed up from the counter. 'Yes, good,' Jamie said
then. 'Call them. Please.'

The woman looked confused.

Oh for fuck's sake! Did she have to spell it out for her?
Jamie turned, took a step, grabbed a display stand with
sunglasses and hair bands on it, and pulled it towards her. It
bowled over, hit the ground, and smashed, sending imitation
Ray-Bans and bobby pins flying.

The woman behind the counter jerked, shrieked, and then
tried to climb the shelves.

What was wrong with her?

Jamie went to the next shelf then, ran her hands along it, dragging tins and packets of rice onto the floor.

She got the picture now, grabbing a phone from under the counter, brandishing it to show Jamie she wasn't joking.

'Do it!' Jamie commanded.

Nothing.

Jamie circled the shelf. Wine. Perfect.

She grabbed a bottle, tossed it over the shelf, heard it smash, watched as red liquid spilled across the tiles.

She couldn't hear dialling, couldn't hear talking.

Jamie grabbed an armful and went back around. The woman was trying to tap the keypad.

Jamie threw down another bottle.

Then another.

The woman was calling now, holding the phone to her ear, back against the shelves, cowering.

Jamie felt sick to her stomach, but she had no other option.

'Hei, poliisi?' she squawked, and then started letting out a stream of Finnish Jamie had no hope of understanding. But it was panicked, desperate, the kind of phone call, when backed by the sound of smashing glass and whimpering – Jamie threw another down just to reinforce the point – that was responded to quickly.

A flood of relief washed through her, her grip tightening around the neck of the bottle. She couldn't risk just being escorted out of here. She needed to make a statement. She needed to make this count. She needed to ensure that they were going to put her in the back of a police car and take her away – and that maybe that would give her some sort of chance to get out of this smudge of a town alive.

Jamie turned towards the floor-length windows, her shoulders rising and falling, eyes fixed on the four-by-four parked across the street, knowing they were looking back at her, and raised the bottle.

She wound up.

The woman behind the counter shrieked and ducked for cover.

And then Jamie hurled it, straight at the window.

The glass turned opaque for a moment, the bottle shattering the pane, and then it fell, straight out of the frame, wine raining down all around.

Jamie stood there, mouth twisted into an ugly grimace, covered in her own blood, more angry than she'd ever been in her life, feeling the cool wind on her skin.

In the distance, sirens began to rise, echoing through the sleeping town.

After a second, the headlights came to life on the SUV and it eased forward slowly, waiting as long as it dared, and then the engine flared and it roared forward out of town, just in time to avoid the first strobe of blue lights playing off the buildings opposite.

Jamie's jaw quivered, her knees wobbled, and she sank to the tiles, staring down at her shaking hands, surrounded by broken glass.

She hung her head, listening as the cars neared, skidded to a stop. As the doors opened and the footsteps clattered.

Hands were on her, dragging her to her feet, pulling her wrists up behind her back.

And then she was frogmarched out of the shop, heels crunching on what felt like the fragments of her sanity, holding herself together with everything she had left.

15

WITHIN THE HOUR, Jamie was sitting in an interview room of a tiny police station on the outskirts of a neighbouring town. It sat on a lonely road that joined the two, with just six officers covering the entire area.

Two uniformed officers, two desk clerks, a single *komisario*, a senior inspector, and the *ylikomisario,* the superintendent, that ran the place.

Jamie had the latter two sitting across the table from her right now.

She'd never felt handcuffs on her wrists before.

They were sharp, and uncomfortable.

'Why don't you go over it again?' the inspector said in accented English, his superior sitting back in the chair next to him.

The inspector was in his late forties, with a bald head and thin glasses. His boss was ten years his senior, a big man with a round stomach, bristly hair, and an old-fashioned sweeping brush moustache that rustled when he moved his mouth side to side. Which he did a lot.

Jamie sighed, lifting her hands and placing them on the

table. 'I don't know what you want me to say,' Jamie said. 'The story isn't going to change.' She just wished it was the truth. But she knew from experience – from sitting the other side of the table – that sitting here spewing conspiracy theories about corrupt government officials and shadowy organisations would do nothing except get her slapped with a psychiatric evaluation and probably thrown in a secure ward for a two-day hold. Maybe three, judging by the state of her. 'I was driving along the main road, and was run off into the lake.'

'Which lake?'

'I don't know,' Jamie said. 'There's a million of them.'

The inspector drew a slow breath, not bothering to even force a smile. They'd both been dragged away from their families and back here long after their shifts had ended. And neither were pleased about it.

'Okay,' he said. 'Let's say you were. Then what happened?'

Jamie ground her teeth a little. 'Two guys fired pistols at me—'

'When you were in the water.'

'Yes.'

He stared at her. 'Go on.'

'I swam to shore.'

'While they were shooting at you.'

'A different shore.'

'You swam off into the darkness? Fully clothed? While under gunfire?' He raised his eyebrows above his glasses.

'Well, I wasn't going to swim towards them,' Jamie growled.

He drew another slow breath. A condescending fucking breath.

Jamie felt her hands tighten into fists, and then immediately released them, noticing the superintendent looking at them.

She cleared her throat. 'I was trying to get away.'

'And you did. You reached the far shore, didn't you?'

'Yes.'

'And then what happened?'

'Then I ran.'

'Ten kilometres. Through the woods. In the dark?'

'Yes. Maybe. I think so.'

'How would you know? You said your phone was still in the car, and you didn't know which lake it was.'

Jamie felt like screaming. 'I run a lot. I know what ten kilometres feels like.'

'Convenient,' the inspector said, laughing and shaking his head.

'Not really,' Jamie sighed. 'Look at me. Anything about this situation strike you as convenient?'

'No, I find it convenient that you claim to be escaping two armed men, of which there is no trace, on a road we can't identify, next to a nondescript lake that could be ten kilometres away. You have no phone, no ID, you've clearly been fighting—'

'With an airbag,' Jamie cut in. 'This is from the airbag deploying when—'

'I've seen enough action to know what it looks like when someone bites off more than they can chew.'

Jamie really felt like screaming now. 'Call the SPA. Check out my credentials. I'm not lying.'

He nodded slowly. 'We will, in due time. Once we've established the facts. Which still remain unknown. You won't tell us why you are in Finland, or what really happened to you. If you expect us to believe that you were indeed run off the road and fired upon – which we can find no evidence for

– then you must tell us the reason *why.* If you don't, we simply cannot help you. All we can do is arraign you for the damage you caused to the grocery shop.'

'And for terrorising a helpless old woman,' the superintendent chimed in, voice gruff under his bristling moustache.

Jamie leaned forward now, bowed her head, tasted copper on her lips and tongue. They hadn't let her wash before stuffing her in this room. She was still a stinking, bloody mess. 'Just call the SPA, please,' Jamie said. 'Ask to speak to Kriminalkommissarie Thomas Karlsson. He'll confirm my credentials at least.'

'And then what? You think that being confirmed as a police officer in another country excuses you from the crimes you have committed here?' He stared right at her.

Jamie wondered if she'd made the right choice. She was 'safe', sure. But for how long? How long could she stay here before Imperium found her again? And then how would she possibly hope to escape when they did? Had she just delayed the inevitable? Could she trust these men? If she did tell them everything, would they believe her? She didn't think she would if she was in their shoes.

She missed Wiik then. Intensely. Painfully. She was so alone. So filled with rage. Out here on a crusade? To do what? Who did she hope to take down, and how? She'd left the peace of her old life behind, taken up the sword against Imperium. But with a loose grip. Ill-conceived. Even more poorly executed. Sloppy. Short-sighted. Jamie grit her teeth, clenched her fists. 'Just call Karlsson. And then… then I'll tell you everything. The truth.' If she could get them to believe she was a police officer, a respected detective who'd worked with the Stockholm Police, then maybe, just maybe it would lend some credence to the batshit-crazy story she was about to lay out for them.

The two guys in front of her took stock of that, and then looked at each other, pushing back from the table. 'Okay, we'll make some phone calls. Don't go anywhere.'

Jamie lifted her handcuffs. 'I'll be here when you need me.'

They left the room then, and Jamie was alone, racking her brain, trying to figure out what the fuck was going to come next. Knowing that, if nothing else, she'd need a miracle to get out of it alive.

16

_____

JAMIE THOUGHT that they'd be back in minutes. Fifteen. Twenty at the most.

But three hours later, by the clock above the door, she was still sitting there, thirsty, hungry, and dirty. She was expecting at any moment for the door to open and for the same suit-clad guys from the lake to enter, lift a gun, and put two in her chest. And for that to be the end of it.

But no.

At 10.57 p.m., the door finally opened, and the inspector walked in and crossed the space, looking stern. He grabbed Jamie's hands and unlocked the cuffs roughly.

Jamie said nothing, instantly massaging her wrists as she stared up at him.

He stood to the side and pointed to the door.

'Did you get hold of Karlsson?' Jamie asked, not sure she wanted to get up.

'I did,' the inspector said, taking the back of Jamie's chair and pulling on it, signalling for her to get up. 'And he said that you were discharged from the SPA pending an investigation for gross misconduct. He said that you were supposed to be booked in for an evaluation with a psychiatrist this morning, but that you disappeared.'

Jamie rose slowly, staring at the inspector in disbelief. She didn't think arguing would be any use. The SPA were no doubt just covering their asses so that when her body turned up in a ditch somewhere, they could claim it was the result of a string of bad choices on her part. No doubt they already had a nice way to frame it.

'Please,' the inspector said, gesturing to the door again.

'Where are we going?'

He said nothing in reply.

Marching me to my death? No, thank you. She glanced down at the inspector's midriff, searching for a holster, for a weapon. But he was unarmed.

'Ms Johansson?' A new voice rang out now and Jamie looked up at the doorway.

A tall man in his late thirties with a clean-shaven pointed jaw and a tailored grey suit was standing there. He tried to keep his expression neutral and friendly, but the shock at seeing the state of her was apparent.

Jamie narrowed her eyes at him, trying to work out whether he was one of Imperium's lackeys or not.

'You need to come with me now,' he said, smiling at her.

Jamie stayed where she was.

'Please, Ms Johansson, we don't have much time.'

Jamie widened her feet slightly, preparing.

The man entered the room, glancing at the inspector, and reached into his jacket.

Jamie braced.

And then his hand was out, a white business card in it.

He reached over the table, holding it out for her.

Jamie stared at it, then grabbed it quickly, reading what

was written there. It said, *Detective Inspector Jamie Johansson, Stockholm Polis.* It was her business card.

Her mind stuttered for a moment, and then she realised.

It was the same card she'd given to the kid at the front desk of Heikkinen Investments.

But this wasn't Simon Heikkinen, was it?

She stared at the guy. The expensive suit, the keen eyes. No, he had the stink of a solicitor on him. In a big way.

Jamie couldn't stand there all night, and she knew that the guy wasn't about to announce on whose behalf he was there, otherwise he would have already.

She just had to trust this. It was that, or refuse to leave, and let what might be her only chance at leaving this backwater town alive walk out of here.

She nodded then, crumpling the card in her grip, and skirted the table.

The solicitor moved quickly, with purpose, leading her down a corridor, into the small reception area and out the front door.

Jamie glanced back at the inspector and the superintendent, both of whom were now standing in front of the reception desk, looking as pissed off as each other. The inspector had his hands on his hips, the superintendent's arms folded, moustache dancing on his face, both their eyes burning into her.

'Ms Johansson?' the solicitor said from behind her.

She turned back, the night air cold around them, and saw that he was standing at the open door to a blacked-out Mercedes, a pale leather interior waiting for her.

'Please,' he said, giving a brief smile. His eyes betrayed his cool exterior as a shell. He was shitting himself inside.

Jamie looked around. The road they were on was empty.

No streetlights, nothing. Just the glow coming through the doors of the station.

Her first thought was to kick this guy in the face, pull the driver out, steal the car, and run. But did she really need anyone else chasing her? Simon Heikkinen had managed to get his daughter onto that oil rig to help her education. To help her succeed in life. He'd used his ties with Bolstad and Imperium to do that. And they'd tried to kill her. So would he still be in league with them? No doubt he'd lost a ton of money when Bolstad had gone under.

Simon Heikkinen was maybe the only other person in the world who had as big an axe to grind as she did. But was she about to bet her life on that?

'Ms Johansson,' the solicitor said again, walking back towards her. He dropped his voice now. 'You need to get in the car right now. Mr Heikkinen is waiting for you. But he won't wait forever. If you want the help he's prepared to offer, then you need to come with me.' He drew a breath. 'Mr Heikkinen can't be seen to be helping you, which means we have to act quickly.'

'So then, why is he?'

The man swallowed, rolling on the balls of his feet, visibly nervous. 'Because you saved his daughter's life. If you hadn't acted as you did on the platform, Noemi would be dead. As would her friends. And Bolstad would still be afloat. Not only did you keep Noemi alive, but you also gave Mr Heikkinen the freedom he required to excise himself from Imperium Holdings.'

She measured him, her brain telling her to run.

But she knew she wouldn't make it a mile. She was exhausted, penniless, with no phone, no means of transport. She'd be hunted down like a dog.

And if nothing else, she knew the power of the love that a

parent had for their child, and vice versa. And what that meant.

Imperium had tried to kill Noemi, and Simon Heikkinen didn't just want to thank Jamie for stopping that, he wanted to see them bleed for attempting it.

Or at least that's what Jamie told herself as she stepped down onto the pavement and climbed into the back of the Mercedes.

The solicitor climbed in after her and then the car accelerated away without wasting a second.

The driver was a bald guy who didn't look back. He just kept his foot planted, pinning Jamie into the leather.

The solicitor wrung his hands between his knees, the pulse in his neck doing a steady 120 by Jamie's count. She was feeling the angst, too, but she didn't think the driver nor the guy next to her were armed, and that was something.

Trees flashed past, the unpainted narrow road winding through the forests endlessly.

No one said anything.

A full twenty minutes passed, the car not dropping below what Jamie guessed was a hundred by the way it was clinging on for dear life in the bends.

And then, suddenly, they were slowing down.

The driver decelerated quickly, pulling left off the road onto a small, single-lane track.

It dived through the trees, tight and twisting, but the driver didn't let up, and threw the car into every corner as though they were being chased.

Jamie suspected there was a good chance they were, though she'd seen no headlights behind them. Still, that didn't mean no one was watching.

Jamie's heart beat fast and quiet as the trees began to break and the track burst into an open field.

She stared through the windshield, seeing that up ahead, there was a junction, a stone lay-by, and another car, head-lights illuminated.

Was this it? Door open, bullet to the head, straight into the boot, and off to some shallow grave?

The car skidded to a halt on the opposite side of the road to the other, identical Mercedes, and the driver let the engine settle to a hot idle.

Nothing moved outside. No other headlights in any direction – which had visibility for probably the best part of half a mile.

They were totally alone.

Jamie jumped as the solicitor opened his door and got out, circling around and opening Jamie's.

The road was bathed in a pale glow, the headlights from both cars lighting it indirectly.

Jamie made no moves, waiting, ready to react.

The back door to the other Mercedes opened, and a pair of legs swung out.

A man exited.

He was maybe fifty, on the short side of average height, with a shock of light blonde hair. He had a tanned face, strong features, and was wearing a pair of suit trousers and a white shirt rolled up to the elbows. But what caught Jamie's attention was his eyes. Electric blue. The same distinct shade as Noemi Heikkinen's. Alight in the darkness. Glowing almost.

She knew that she was looking at Simon Heikkinen.

She exited swiftly then.

He met her halfway, his expression kind, but his manner uneasy.

'Ms Johansson,' he said, keeping his voice low. There was no need to shout. 'Are you alright?' He couldn't help but look her up and down.

Jamie laughed abjectly. 'I've been better.'

'I'm sorry for all this,' Heikkinen said.

'Did you tell Imperium to kill me?'

He met her eye unflinchingly. 'No.'

'Then you've got nothing to be sorry about.'

'You know coming to my office was stupid.'

'I was all out of smart options.'

'They're hunting you.'

'I figured,' Jamie said, trying to stay polite but finding her patience had been totally spent.

'They won't stop.'

'I figured that too.' She sighed now. 'Are you going to kill me?'

'What? No.' Heikkinen looked surprised, shook his head to reinforce his incredulity. 'Why would you ask that?'

'I've had a long day, and if you were, I would just prefer to get it over with.'

He blinked in disbelief. 'You don't strike me as the sort of woman who would give up quite so easily.'

'Easily?' Jamie looked down at herself, blood-splattered and beaten. 'There's nothing about this that's been easy. This just seems like the sort of place you might bring someone before you kill them, you know?' She gestured to the empty fields, the utter darkness, the silence.

'Perhaps. But I am a businessman, not a killer.'

'That's good to know,' Jamie said, though relief didn't seem to come with his statement.

'But what about you?'

'What about me?'

'Are you a killer? A police officer? A coward? A daughter without a father?'

Jamie narrowed her eyes, feeling the asphalt rough under her heels. 'What the hell are you talking about?'

'Imperium,' he said flatly. 'They took everything from you, yes?'

She looked him dead in the eyes. 'Yes.'

'And they tried to take everything from me, too.'

Jamie said nothing.

'And they would have, if not for you. If not for what you'd done on that *fucking* oil rig.'

'I did what I had to.'

'You made them pay. And you saved Noemi.'

'Fat lot of good it did me,' Jamie muttered.

'And then,' Heikkinen went on, the ire and frustration in his voice apparent, 'they killed your boss, they burned down your house, and now – they try to kill you. And what are you going to do about it?'

Jamie drew a slow breath. 'I don't know. What can I do?'

'Anything you want. I know all about you, Jamie. I know what you've been through, what you're capable of. And I think if anyone has the ability to do what is necessary, and the desire to make it happen, it's you.'

She let that hang between them, his electric-blue eyes somewhere between suggesting and pleading.

'And how exactly,' Jamie started, tentatively, 'would I do that?'

He bit his lip. 'You'd take the car behind me, along with everything in the boot, and you'd disappear. And then, you do what you could never do while hiding behind a badge.'

'And what's that?'

'You make them pay. For everything.'

Jamie set her jaw. 'Just take the car? Just like that?'

He nodded. 'A small price to pay.' There was silence between them for a few seconds. 'They won't stop. Ever. If you had any chance of living a normal life before, that's gone now. Coming to Finland, to my office – that was a step too far. And they won't give second chances.'

'How did you know where to find me?' Jamie asked. 'At the police station?'

'I have a lot of friends in high places. Once I found out you had come looking for me, I knew that something was wrong. I had my people keep an ear out. And when I heard that a woman matching your description had been taken into custody, and what for… I knew that it had to be you. And that Imperium wouldn't be far behind. If I hadn't have got to you… Another hour, and the story would have been very different.' He took a breath, rubbed his neck. 'I will always be indebted to you for what you did on that oil rig. For Noemi, for me, too, whether you realise it or not. But despite my wealth, my status… I am not untouchable. Imperium don't like to be crossed, and once they realise you've escaped, they'll come for me, too.'

'So then why do it?'

'Because they'd come for me sooner or later, anyway. At least this way, I can get away on my terms. I can put my affairs in order and disappear. Me, Noemi. New identities, everything. They'll never find us. But I don't think running away is an option for you, is it?'

Jamie kept quiet.

'So if you're going to hit back, then you need to hit hard.' As he said that, the driver in the car behind him opened the door and stepped out, leaving it open. Wordlessly, he crossed the road and got into the car that had brought Jamie here.

Heikkinen dug in his pocket then, and pulled out a black bank card, offering it to Jamie. 'This is linked to a Swiss bank account with twenty-five thousand euros in it. Here, take it.'

Jamie did, staring down at it.

'Untraceable,' he said. 'Use it wisely. In the car,' he went on, turning to gesture to it, 'there's a full tank of petrol, clean clothes, food, water, if you want to stay off the beaten track. Everything you need to survive, until you have a plan.'

Jamie could only nod. Her head was spinning.

'In the glove box, you'll find a handgun, and a prepaid mobile phone. They won't be able to trace that, either. But they'll be searching for you. So if you call anyone you know, make sure that you lose the phone afterwards, and you get as far from that place as quickly as you can.'

He put out his hand then and Jamie looked down at it. Her mouth had gone dry, her heart pounding in her ears. After a moment, she took it, and felt Heikkinen shake and squeeze.

'Good luck. You'll need it.'

And then he pulled his hand from hers and went to join everyone else in the other car.

Jamie turned, still clutching the card. 'Wait,' she said, her mind struggling to catch up. 'That's it? Here's a car, some cash, a gun, off you go?'

Heikkinen stopped and looked back at her. 'I wish I could do more. I really do.'

'Can't you give me a name? Somewhere to start, at least?' She hated how desperate her own voice sounded.

He cracked the smallest of smiles. 'I think you already know as much as I do at this point – Imperium work through the people they control. Police officers, judges, civil servants. Any name I give you would just lead from one to another to another, and never to the people you really need to find.'

'Who do I really need to find?' Jamie shook her head now, stepping forward.

'You're a detective,' Heikkinen said, nodding to her reassuringly. 'You'll figure it out. Goodbye, Ms Johansson, and thank you.'

And then the door closed.

The wheels spun and slingshotted it back into the road in a plume of dust and loose stones.

The engine sang in the darkness and then dwindled.

Jamie covered her eyes, and by the time the dust cloud passed, the car was no more than two orange smudges in the distance. And then it was gone altogether.

She watched, waiting to see if it would come back. But she knew it wouldn't. And that she'd never see Simon Heikkinen again.

He'd said it himself – he was leaving. Not just Helsinki. But the country. This was his final 'fuck you' to Imperium. And he was gone. New identities. The works. No doubt he had enough money to go anywhere in the world, and the resources to ensure that Imperium would never find him.

Jamie, on the other hand…

She looked down at the card she was holding. Twenty-five thousand Euros.

Enough to get away herself, start fresh.

But how could she? She had no passport, no ID, nothing… Whatever came next wasn't going to be easy.

Jamie's knees wobbled under her and she thought they might give way altogether.

She turned and staggered towards the car, the only source of illumination out here, and fell against it, breathing hard.

Her fingers were tingling, her heart hammering, chest tight.

She stared up into the clear night sky, an endless curtain of black pin-holed with light.

It was peaceful out here, somehow. As if none of this shit was happening. As if life was somehow simple and easy, and she was just a person living her life. Her boring, boring life. Wouldn't that be something?

She leaned her head back, concentrated on her breathing, and tried to believe that, if only for a moment.

And then, in the distance, somewhere beyond the line of trees over her shoulder, she heard a low rumbling. The indistinct hum of an engine? An approaching vehicle?

Her heart kicked into overdrive again, eyes focusing.

It was a nice reprieve, for a second. But now it was over. And everything Heikkinen had said came rushing back.

Jamie climbed into the driver's seat and slammed the door, throwing the car into drive, and planting the accelerator.

The rev counter hit the limiter, the wheels fighting for grip, and then she was moving.

Where, she didn't know. But it would be very fucking far from here.

And when she got there, she'd go over what she knew, and she'd make a plan.

And then she'd hunt these fuckers down. One by one, if she had to.

Heikkinen wasn't giving her a name because he couldn't or he was afraid to.

But it didn't matter, because she had one already.

The only one that mattered.

Sandbech.

And she'd find him, if it was the last thing she did.

And it probably should have frightened her more that it was probably going to be the last thing she did. But it didn't, because if she thought she had nothing and no one before, now she really didn't.

Jamie Johansson, just like her father, was now a ghost.

A ghost with twenty-five thousand euros, a full tank, a loaded pistol in the glove box, and the taste of blood in her mouth.

As the speedometer climbed, the night-drenched landscape blurring past the windows outside, Jamie Johansson settled into a cold rage. One that she didn't think would ever abate.

It felt good, sitting in the pit of her stomach, festering, clearing her mind.

No more cases, or suspects, or procedures. None of that bullshit.

Just her and Sandbech.

And the open road ahead.

17

Three months later…

SUMMER WAS LYING HEAVILY over Stockholm.

People thronged in the streets and the multicoloured townhouses glowed in the bright sunlight.

Everyone was smiling.

Everyone except Anders Wiik.

She watched him approach down the busy street and enter the shop of a local grocer. With supermarkets and chains dominating the market, this little shop was clinging on to existence. The owner was a sweet old man who had a deeply ingrained hatred for big business. And for bureaucracy. And the government. And it turned out he also hated the police. He thought them all corrupt, bribe-taking mouthpieces. So using his shop for cover while Jamie waged war on the people behind it all wasn't a hard sell.

Not to the owner, at least.

Wiik entered, scowling, and glared at the owner, who diligently glared back.

He walked down the length of the shop, glancing back as

the owner muttered something offensive under his breath, and ducked through a beaded curtain at the back, climbing the narrow stairs beyond to a storage area above.

'You're late,' Jamie said, coming away from the window, arms folded.

Wiik sighed. 'It took me longer than usual to lose my tail,' he said. 'They're getting smarter.' He was rubbing at his hand. His quirk used to be flattening his hair to his head fifty times a day. Now he constantly massaged the knuckles on his right hand. It was a mess of scars and discoloured tissue, and while he had reasonable mobility in it, it was clearly stiff and painful all the time.

'Smarter than you?' Jamie asked, raising an eyebrow.

He narrowed his eyes. 'Just smarter.' He glanced around the room at the makeshift operations centre Jamie had set up. She'd pinned various photographs and documents to the walls – one side was names and faces, police officers and business people she suspected to be on Imperium's payroll. On the other were newspaper clippings, police reports, obituary entries. Events tied to the faces opposite – unlikely business deals that had come off, untimely demises, and a manner of other strange things that reeked of intervention.

She'd been building it for months, hiding from Imperium. She had the luxury of moving freely, not being an 'official' fugitive, and Heikkinen's bankroll had stretched a long way. She was keeping off Imperium's radar, biding her time. But that didn't mean she could let her guard down. Even for a second.

Jamie waited for him to go on. This was their weekly debrief. 'Well?'

Wiik drew a slow breath. 'Rasmus Allinder.'

Jamie stepped forward. 'Rasmus Allinder? I know that name.'

Wiik nodded. 'He was a kriminalkommissarie in the internal investigations department at the same time your father was working his last case.'

They'd resorted to referring to it as that, rather than saying, 'when your father was murdered'.

Jamie nodded again. 'I reached out to him after the Angel Maker case during my initial enquiries, before I even knew about Imperium. I never got a response.'

Wiik cracked the knuckles on his bad hand. They popped loudly. 'I'm not surprised. He's living a quiet life, outside the city. It took me a little while to track him down. Especially without raising any flags.' Wiik made a point of saying the last part.

He dug in his pocket and then held out a piece of paper for her.

'I really am grateful,' Jamie said, taking it. 'You're risking a lot. Don't think I don't appreciate it.'

He hovered, on the verge of saying something. And then just said, 'Don't mention it.'

Jamie offered him a smile, then crossed towards the window, glanced up and down the street for any sign of Imperium's mercenaries – because that's what they were. Private contracted security staff. Like the guys that had gone to Bolstad with Wallace, the fixer that had been dispatched to clean up that mess before Jamie and Wiik could do their jobs.

They were good at what they did – military trained, efficient, but they didn't exactly blend into a crowd. Which made them easy to spot, and easy enough to avoid. At least when your life depended on it. Still, Jamie carried a loaded gun everywhere she went.

Jamie studied the paper in her hand, reading what Wiik had written. What looked like a rough routine that Rasmus Allinder was following.

Wiik had gone back to work two days a week, but wasn't actively investigating any cases just then. And though he and Jamie hadn't left things on very good terms before she'd left, he seemed to have come around to the seriousness of this. And wanting to help her not get killed looked to be outweighing his not wanting to get involved.

He'd even started looking after himself again. His hair was slicked back as normal, and while his chin was rough with stubble, he appeared to be showering daily. Which was a big step. She guessed it was just hard for him to shave with his bad hand.

For all his faults and his abrasive shell, Anders Wiik had the capacity to care deeply for people, and had no qualms about laying down his life for them.

Right now, Jamie thought that list included his son, her, and Julia Hallberg. In that order. Though he never would have told her that.

'You know,' he said from across the room, 'Karlsson's up my ass about you. Constantly.'

'Saying what?' Jamie asked, wondering how many hours Wiik had spent tailing Allinder, and how much work he was putting into this thing. By what he was saying, Imperium were having him watched pretty continually. And by the sounds of it, Karlsson was under pressure to find her, too.

'Casually asking, mostly,' Wiik said. 'If I've heard from you, seen you, had any contact, that kind of thing.'

'They suspect you're helping me?' Jamie came away from the window, back towards him.

'They can suspect whatever they want. I've had their mercenaries arrested three times for stalking already. They're starting to get the picture that I don't like being followed.' Wiik seemed almost proud of that.

'That's probably why they think I'm back in the city,' Jamie said.

Wiik shrugged.

'But they haven't made any serious moves?' Jamie tried to keep her voice calm.

'No, they keep their distance. It's one thing to go after someone trying to expose them. It's another killing a detective in cold blood. At some point, it's just too much to cover up. I'm safe enough, I think, and I won't give them a reason to get rid of me.' He paused for a moment, nodding to Jamie. 'We're being careful, don't worry.'

'We are, you're right.' She breathed a little sigh of relief. They had been treading lightly, gathering information, approaching people cautiously. But it was obvious they suspected Jamie was in the city.

It's why they were watching Wiik so closely. Hallberg too. But Wiik was seasoned, and he knew the whole story. He knew what he was getting himself into, and that throbbing, aching hand of his reminded him continually who these people were. He wanted to see Imperium burn as much as Jamie, and she knew taking orders from Karlsson was enough to make Wiik sick.

Hallberg had her whole life ahead of her, though. She didn't need to get mixed up in this. She was still clean. Could still make a career for herself.

'Are you going to move on Allinder?' Wiik asked, biting his lip.

'You don't think I should?' Jamie asked, reading the concern in his expression.

'I think he's a solid lead,' Wiik said. 'If anyone knew what was going on with your father's last case, I think it's him. The others so far – they were long shots. Maybe involved with Imperium, maybe not. Hard to say. But none had anything worth telling you, right?'

Jamie watched him. 'No.' It was pretty much gut instinct, but all the people she'd spoken to who were mixed up with Imperium changed the second they heard that name. She'd cornered four people so far. Ex-detectives mostly, those who ran in the department the same time as her father. Three of them looked blankly at her when she mentioned Imperium, and then all of them expressed their condolences, said that they were sorry he was gone, but they were glad to see her alive and well.

All genuine, friendly guys. No alarm bells ringing.

The fourth had reacted differently. He'd been reasonably receptive, said that it was good to see Jamie, that he liked her father. Then, at the mention of Imperium, his face changed. He couldn't wait to get out of there.

Jamie had put him up against a wall. Pulled her gun.

He'd sworn blind he didn't know what her father was mixed up in, or anything about Imperium. Just that he'd taken orders from his kommissarie to lose some evidence on a case once, and then found an envelope full of cash in his desk the next week.

He'd asked his kommissarie about it later, after a few too many drinks.

He'd been talkative.

The next week, he was dead.

It seemed to be a common pattern.

You talked about Imperium. Then it was lights out.

She could see by the fear in his eyes that he didn't know anything. And that he didn't *want* to know anything.

But up until then, they'd been dealing with retired officers and detectives who wouldn't have had the power to be of any use to Imperium. But Rasmus Allinder? Now a Kriminalkommissarie dealing with internal affairs? The man responsible for looking the other way when it came to corrupt officers. There was a man who was of use to Imperium. Someone on Karlsson's and Falk's level.

Hell, Karlsson was the prime target, and Jamie and Wiik had gone over it again and again, looking for a way to get at him. But Imperium knew that he was a liability, a target, and they were watching him even more closely than they were Wiik.

And they were as good as hanging him out for bait.

Except Jamie wasn't a bass and she wasn't about to chomp down on a hook.

They'd had their shot, and they'd missed.

Now it was her turn.

'So you're going after him?' Wiik asked.

Jamie nodded. 'Yeah.'

'He shops at a farmers' market on Sunday mornings. It's busy there, will be easy to blend in. That's when I'd take him.'

Jamie nodded. 'Okay, thanks.'

'You want me as backup? I can run interference? Watch from a distance and tell you—'

'No,' Jamie said, smiling and coming over. 'You've done enough. More than enough.'

'I can help.'

'You've already helped. And I'm sure there'll be more to do. But if they're not watching Allinder already, we can't risk you leading them right to him. Especially not when I'm there.'

Wiik resigned himself to silence. He couldn't argue with that. And he knew as well as Jamie the moment they spotted her, they'd go in for the kill.

If she was back in Stockholm, it meant she hadn't scuttled off to hide somewhere very far away.

And they weren't going to take any chances again.

Jamie approached and put her hand on his shoulder. 'I'll signal again when it's time to meet.'

Wiik nodded, lifted his gnarled hand and put it on hers. 'Just be safe out there.'

She let his touch linger on hers. They were both glad for the contact.

'I will. And you too. I can't lose you, Wiik,' Jamie muttered.

'You won't,' he said back. 'But you have to promise not to be reckless.'

'Me, reckless?' Jamie said, pulling her hand free and meeting his eye. 'Wouldn't dream of it.'

18

Rasmus Allinder wasn't difficult to spot.

He was a tall man, with narrow shoulders, and a thick head of white hair that stuck up from his scalp like he'd been playing with an electrical socket.

The farmers' market was set up on the east side of the city in the Östermalm district, in the Tessinparken. Jamie caught an early-morning bus, wearing a hooded sweatshirt and a baseball cap. She watched the park sail by out of the window, scouting the area for any signs of burly guys in dark jackets, and got off at the next stop. She wanted to be sure that she wasn't getting out into some sort of ambush. It was impossible to know how many people Imperium had on their payroll, and how many people they could be watching at any time.

She was yet to cross paths with them again in Stockholm, but considering Karlsson's actions, and Wiik's entourage – as well as the fact that he was trying his hardest to lose them – it was just a matter of time before they crossed her path.

But Heikkinen was smart, and his help was making it easy enough to stay under the radar. She had the benefit of years of experience trying to track down people who didn't want to be found. You watched their phone, their bank accounts, their homes, and you waited for them to slip up. And then you moved in.

Jamie's phone was still at the bottom of a lake in Finland, she guessed. She had no way to know whether they'd recovered the car or not, and there was no way she was going to go back to her apartment to pick up her mail.

Jamie exited the bus just before eight in the morning, knowing that Allinder had come the last three weeks between eight-thirty and nine. And she also knew that he parked in the car park on the far side. That he drove a three-year-old Volvo estate. And that he'd be carrying a canvas bag and wearing a pair of Ray-Ban sunglasses.

Wiik's research had been thorough, his note-making meticulous. She had to hand it to him, that anal-retentive streak really came in handy when it came to surveillance and good old-fashioned police work.

As Jamie walked a wide circle around the park, checking for any lookouts, scoping ingress and egress points, escape routes, she missed him. Professionally more than anything else. But it was hard to go from being with someone every single day to being on your own. Sure, she could bring him into this, she could ask him to leave his home behind, walk out on his career, and join her in the little cash-in-hand bedsit she was renting in a questionable part of the city. And he would, she had no doubt. But she'd already got him maimed, and partners that followed her on her crusades often ended up with a knife in the back, a flank full of buckshot, or worse.

She already had too much blood on her conscience, and she wasn't going to add Wiik's to it.

Jamie checked her watch a while later, standing under a tree with a clear sightline to the entrance to the car park. It was the only way in, and she watched from under the peak of her hat, putting fresh blueberries in her mouth one at a time. She'd picked up a punnet from a stall on her way past.

She let the juice wash over her tongue as she chewed slowly, confident that there was no sign of Imperium. Yet, at least.

It was now eight thirty-five, and Allinder was due any minute.

Another ten minutes passed before the Volvo estate pulled in, dusty with the city, sidling over the pockmarked gravel surface of the lot. It queued down the central alley and Jamie got a good look at Allinder as he went by. Tanned, wearing a blue open-collared shirt. Sticky-up white hair. Ray-Bans. Just as expected.

She cracked a little smile, keeping an eye on his car, and then it faded.

Her gaze moved down the line, and four cars back, she saw a black Mercedes SUV. It was sleek, big-engined by the low hum piercing the din. But it was debadged, windows tinted. Two men sitting in the front, one bald, one with just a thin layer of hair on his head.

Jamie watched, a blueberry between her teeth, as it went by, the guys' eyes fixed on Allinder's car.

The Volvo pulled into a space, and as the SUV passed, both their heads turned to look at it.

They pulled in at the next available one – one that was too small for the car – and then quickly squeezed out.

Allinder was at his boot already, pulling out his canvas tote and a leather bumbag, which he attached to his waist.

The two guys from the Mercedes were on their feet as well, lingering 'casually' at their tailgate, pretending to talk.

It would be twenty degrees today, maybe a little over. Jamie was already warm in her jeans and grey zip-up, but she was wearing it because it did a good job of disguising the Glock 19 Compact Frame tucked under her ribs. The two guys at the back of the Mercedes were similarly layered – versus Allinder's beige chino shorts, leather sandals, and linen shirt combo.

The bald guy was maybe six-one, and was wearing jeans, lightweight walking boots, a T-shirt, and a green bomber jacket with elasticated cuffs. It was slightly oversized, perfect for hiding a holster. The other was wearing a denim jacket, black jeans, and polished black boots.

Jamie had no doubt that they were both armed.

And that they were both Imperium goons sent to tail Allinder.

And that told Jamie two things. One, they knew she was in the city. And two, Allinder was worth watching.

By the time Allinder set off, ready to take his one-up, one-down lap of the market – where he moved along the left-hand stalls on the first pass, and then back down the right-hand stalls on the return journey – the two guys had exhausted their feigned dialogue, scouted the surrounding area, and fallen into step behind him. They stayed back a decent distance, but Jamie had them clocked from the second they'd rolled in.

As Allinder moved with the crowd, lining up his approach, the two guys broke off from each other, both screwing little buds into their ear as they did. One stayed in the crowd about ten metres back from Allinder, and the other went on ahead, moving down the centre of the market. There were about ten metres between the stalls, and the central two or three metres were occupied with benches, barrels for people to put things on, and general congregations of families and friends.

The bald guy with the bomber jacket wound between them, head on a swivel.

Jamie watched from her position between an artisanal cheese stall and a wine stall that had big stills at the back. She stood behind a billowing Swedish flag hanging from the cheese place, watching as he searched the faces of the crowd. He wasn't watching Allinder. His mandate was to find her.

While the guy in the denim coat stayed on Allinder.

Jamie bit her lip, thinking.

She'd never be able to reach him with these guys on her.

But what they'd do with her if they caught her was the other question she couldn't help but ask.

She didn't think they'd risk putting a bullet in her in the middle of this many people – and hopefully they wouldn't just open fire into a crowded space.

Her mind worked furiously as she sized up the mercenary in the bomber jacket, the endless call of, '*Ost, färk out!*' from the cheese vendor filling her head.

He grunted loudly, hefting a massive gorgonzola up onto the bench in front of his customers, and then pulled out a long length of cheese wire.

The pudgy man in a meshed hat held it over the wheel and began sawing.

Jamie's eyes settled there, watching him work through the rock-hard, stinking lump, and then moved behind him, to the rack filled with cheese-lovers gift sets.

Her mind seemed to put the pieces together for her then, and on reflex, she was reaching for her wallet.

19

WATCH CHECK AGAIN.

It was after nine-thirty now, and Jamie knew that Allinder would be out of there inside an hour of arriving. The market wasn't that big, and he knew his way around. So if he arrived by quarter to nine, he'd be out of there by quarter to ten. And sure enough, he was on the home straight.

Jamie didn't have a lot of time, but she'd need to cut it close for this to have any chance of working.

Allinder, still completely oblivious despite his years as a police officer, was inspecting a butternut squash. The guy in the denim jacket lingered about five metres behind him.

There were two uniformed police officers doing the rounds, and trying to avoid them while pulling this off was going to be tricky.

She needed to separate the two Imperium heavies first, draw the scout away. Deal with him, and then go back for the second.

Jamie was breathing hard when she came up behind him, weaving quickly through the melee.

He was leaning against a lamp post, scanning the crowd

in front of him, when she nudged him with her elbow and then quickly moved off.

He glanced down, and then his eyes chased her.

Jamie was already looking back over her shoulder, still moving.

The second their eyes locked, she pulled them away and sped up.

No doubt he had her face ingrained in his mind.

She could already hear people protesting as he shouldered past them after her.

Jamie aimed for an alley between two stalls – one selling fresh fruit, the other honey, chutneys, and jams.

But she'd not chosen these stalls because of what they sold, but because they had their backs to a dense little copse of trees, and once they got in there, no one was likely to see what was going to happen.

The guy was probably one and a half times her bodyweight and trained. To fight. To kill. He'd be coming for her hard, and with more confidence than he should have been. But that didn't mean this would be easy. Though Jamie knew that this would be a test of her nerve more than her skills.

She ducked into the gap, not needing to look back, her hand in the pocket of her hoodie, clenched around her recent purchase.

The guy followed her in, slowing as he entered the shade, taking his time to let his eyes adjust, not rushing to move into the blind corners.

The white flaps of the stall on either side slapped gently, the sounds of the crowd behind obscuring Jamie's movements.

He unzipped his bomber jacket and reached under his ribs, pulling out a pistol. He held it low, tracing forward, leaning in, listening for any sound of attack coming from ahead.

But Jamie wasn't ahead of him.

The fresh fruit stall had a bunch of boxes stacked behind it, and the rear sheet had a central split the workers used for access. One that Jamie had also just used.

She came up on his shoulder, ducked behind to his right, and then raked a length of cheese wire over his knuckles before looping it over his hand completely.

Before he could even react, Jamie snapped it tight, untwisting her hands to tie the wire over the back of his wrist, dragging it down and past his hip and up behind his back.

The guy immediately started to twist, trying to move his free hand, trying to turn, but the metal was already biting into his skin and a quick jerk let the guy know that if she wanted, she could strip the skin right off his hand.

'Try anything and I'll rip a hole through your radial artery,' Jamie growled at his shoulder, straining against his bulk.

He stilled, breathing hard, the crowd still flowing behind them.

She could tell his mind was working on a solution, his bleeding knuckles laid across his lower back, pistol tight to his skin, facing outwards.

'This is cheese wire,' Jamie said, trying to keep her voice straight. 'One pull, and you'll be bleeding out. So don't move, don't speak, and don't even think about touching that trigger.'

Her voice sounded cold even in her ears.

The guy swallowed, his jaw flexing.

Carefully, Jamie transferred the handle in her right hand into her left, the noose tight around the mercenary's tanned skin. It was already drawing blood, the slashes across his fingers enough to convince him of the sharpness of the weapon around his arm.

'Lift your left arm and' – Jamie tweaked the wire as he moved – '*slowly* take the earpiece out of your ear.' She reached up with her now free right hand. 'And I'm going to take this,' she said, pulling the gun free from his grasp. She glanced down at it – Heckler & Koch USP – and then let it hang at her side, her finger resting on the barrel.

She watched as the guy lifted the earpiece out and held it between his fingers, still breathing hard.

'Now drop it,' Jamie said. 'And crush it under your heel.'

He seemed to deliberate on that.

She tweaked the wire again, heard him grunt a little. And then he obliged and did it, hanging his head. 'You're so fucking dead,' he muttered. He wasn't Swedish. Polish, maybe. Czech. Belarusian, perhaps. She didn't know. And nor did she really care. The clock was still ticking.

'Yeah? We'll see,' Jamie said, pushing his pistol into her waistband and using her right hand to pat him down. 'Keep your left hand where I can see it,' she whispered, moving her hand up his leg, feeling the flat of a phone. She pulled it out of his jeans. 'I'll take this.' She pushed it into her back pocket, then moved onto his, felt the raised ridges of a few hefty cable ties coiled there.

She liberated them and inspected the plastic lengths. Her blood ran a little cold. They were meant for her.

'Left hand against the bar,' she said, checking over her shoulder. No police. No onlookers. She was good, for now. But she couldn't hang around.

The guy moved his hand down and nearer to the vertical support strut at the corner of the jam stall. He seemed reluctant.

'They'll kill you,' he said then.

Jamie gritted her teeth, tried to steady her breathing. 'Hand. Bar. Now.' Another tweak of the wire.

Blood was flowing over his tied-up hand now, dripping from his fingers, running down his leg, staining his jeans.

He held his left hand out, and Jamie stared at it. Fuck, she didn't know if she could cable tie him and hold on to the cheese wire.

She had to think quickly.

'You'll never get away,' the guy said again, letting out a low, dry laugh.

Could she just yank down? Let the wire slice his radial? Let him bleed out? She couldn't let him go, and if she fumbled the cable tie... She couldn't let this get away from her.

She could feel sweat beading on her brow now.

Think, Jamie. Think.

She pushed the ends of the cable ties into her pocket and drew a breath. Right. New tactic. 'Hey, hand up, keep it where I can see it,' she said.

'Hand down, hand up, you're not very good at this, are y —nggghh—'

Jamie couldn't deny that she kind of enjoyed pulling on the wire that time.

'Shut the fuck up,' Jamie muttered, going back over the other pockets now.

She patted down his backside, and then reached around the front, awkwardly going for his left front pocket.

She came up a little short.

'Like what you feel?' the guy asked, turning his head and smirking at her.

She could shoot him, couldn't she?

Not without everyone in the park scattering like fucking geese. Allinder included.

She left his other pocket alone and went to his jacket now. Near side empty, far side empty.

Inside pocket?

Her hand touched something long and solid, and it took her brain a second to work it out.

She peeled back the hem and reached inside, keeping a firm grip on the wire.

The guy had fallen quiet now, his breathing rapid and shallow.

Jamie slipped a suppressor out and looked down at it.

The guy swallowed.

Watch check.

Fuck. She was running out of time.

She needed to move, and fast.

Trust your instincts. They'd kill you if they had the chance. Fuck, he had zip ties, a suppressor! If he'd have spotted you first, you'd be in the back of that Mercedes, bound, gagged, and on the way to the nearest ditch. You wouldn't even be given the care of making it look like a suicide.

Jamie pinned the suppressor under her arm then, working quickly, with focus. She pulled the USP she'd lifted from him from her waistband and held it between her legs, barrel facing forward, then dropped the suppressor into her hand and started screwing it into the barrel.

She could see the guy's free hand flexing next to his shoulder.

But remarkably, he'd taken her advice and shut up.

When she felt the thread tighten, the suppressor in place, she lifted the pistol and turned it over, fingering the trigger, her hand slick with sweat.

Now her heart was pounding.

And she could see that the mercenary's was too.

Jamie took a breath, steeling herself. 'If I let you go, what are you going to do?'

'What?' The guy turned his head, glanced back at Jamie, trying to read her expression.

'Will you run? If I let you go.'

The guy sneered. 'You let me go, and I'll fucking kill you, you dumb whore—'

Jamie pointed the suppressed USP at the back of his right knee and pulled the trigger.

The spit of the muzzle was swallowed by the din of the crowd, the shouting of the vendors, and Jamie watched with grim satisfaction as the front of his patella blew out, spraying blood all over the exposed earth behind the stalls.

Jamie released the cheese wire and quickly stowed the pistol, letting the guy collapse forward, yelling and swearing.

'Thanks for making that such an easy decision,' she said, disappearing through the flap at the back of the fruit stand as people started clamouring and converging on the opening between the two stalls.

20

Jamie was moving now and moving fast.

Her watch said it was less than ten minutes before Allinder would be back at his car, but she didn't want to cut it that close.

As more and more people began to converge on the mercenary with the blown-out knee, people now beginning to shout and scream as Jamie waded against the tide of the crowd, a more solid plan began to form in her head.

She could see the second Imperium guy up ahead, broadcasting his location. He was standing on a bench, craning his neck back towards the spot where Jamie had kneecapped his partner, finger against his ear, talking into thin air.

Jamie locked on, knowing Allinder wouldn't be far away, and knowing, ultimately, that even if he ran, he'd only be going for his car. And she knew where that was, too.

She straightened her blue baseball cap and swept left, skirting the stalls on that side. She had a five-hundred-krona note in her hand and slapped it down on a table as she passed, pulling a bottle of red wine off the surface without even stopping. All the eyes were on the screams in the distance now, but that didn't make Jamie a thief.

She cut right, back through the crowd, straight towards the mercenary in the denim jacket.

Jamie would have to get close for this to work. And now that he was on high alert, she doubted that she'd be able to get him somewhere quiet.

By the time he looked at her, she was right next to him.

They locked eyes for a second and his widened.

Jamie stepped into the crowd and broke into a run.

He leapt after her.

Jamie sidestepped into a group of women and then ducked.

The guy went after her, homing in on her blue cap, and reached out.

His fist closed around her shoulder and he ripped backwards, spinning a blonde woman around just as she was reaching up to take off the hat that had been pulled over her head without her permission.

She stared back at the guy in shock, in fear, in confusion.

And then glass exploded around the back of his skull and the crowd was doused in red wine.

The guy sagged forward, eyes lolling in his head, and Jamie kicked him onto his side, throwing back the hem of his jacket with her toe. 'He's got a gun!' Jamie yelled, pointing at the exposed holster on his ribs.

The woman in Jamie's blue hat seemed to forget she was wearing it and threw her hands to her face, shrieking violently.

The crowd in her immediate vicinity erupted into total panic and chaos, and in seconds, the unconscious mercenary was swallowed in the stampede, disappearing beneath the feet of the people.

Jamie let herself be taken with them, trying not to think about the fate of the guy lying on the ground, and began swimming towards the parking lot.

She couldn't let Rasmus Allinder get away. She knew that much.

But she also needed to get the fuck out of there.

Sirens were already beginning to echo in the distance.

Jamie fought her way between two stalls and up onto the grass verge separating the market from the parking lot, orienting herself.

Cars were spinning their wheels, filling the air with dust, all jostling to escape what, for all they knew, was a terrorist attack.

White Volvo estate. Come on. There. Yes.

And Allinder, making for it, canvas bag clutched to his chest, the leaves of carrots swaying next to his head.

Jamie started sprinting, darting through the running shoppers. She kept her hand under the back of her hoodie, loose around the grip of her Glock, the silenced USP tucked firmly under her left arm. She hadn't spotted any more Imperium goons, but she wasn't going to risk getting caught off guard.

She measured her approach, waiting for Allinder to get close, and then she was on him.

He opened the driver's door and threw the carrots into the back seat, grabbing the handle, ready to pull it closed.

But it wouldn't move.

Jamie had the USP in her hand again, muzzle pressed against his ribs, one of his feet in the footwell.

She held it open, spoke quickly, firmly. 'Rasmus Allinder. We're going to have a conversation, and we're not going to do it here. So get in and slide across into the passenger seat, *slowly,* and I won't have to use this.' She twisted the muzzle into his ribs, the metal biting at his skin through his shirt.

He winced, licked his lips, and glanced around at all the people. Wondering how the hell no one was seeing this. Wondering if he could call for help.

'You're not the only one on my list,' Jamie said, grabbing his attention. 'So either we leave together, or you end up like the two Imperium guys I just left in the market.'

Realisation seemed to dawn then. Whether he knew he was being followed, or just the name *Imperium* and the situation at hand was enough to convince him, she couldn't say. But he nodded then. 'Okay, okay. Just, just don't shoot me.'

Jamie breathed a sigh of relief as inconspicuously as she could and watched as Allinder shimmied awkwardly over the centre console and into the passenger seat.

He eyed the door handle instinctively, but froze as Jamie pressed the muzzle into his shoulder, climbing into the driver's seat.

'Keys,' she demanded, closing the door and holding her other hand out.

He hesitated.

Jamie pulled the pistol from his shoulder and planted it on his knee. 'I've already blown out one kneecap today. Want to make it two?'

He swallowed.

'Give me the keys and you walk out of this, or I pull this trigger and then take them.'

He fished in his pocket and tossed them into her lap.

'That's what I thought,' Jamie said, jabbing the central-locking button on the centre console with the nose of the gun and slotting the key into the ignition.

She shoved the car into gear, keeping the pistol in hand, and wheeled backwards out of the space, driving straight across the line of traffic, mounting the kerb, and pulling onto the road via the grass divider.

Other cars quickly followed suit, not wanting to wait for the proper exit, and then Jamie was away, speeding into the heart of the city as blue lights flashed past in the opposite direction.

Jamie drove quickly towards the underground car park with no security cameras where she'd left a beaten-up old Volkswagen Golf. It had a reliable engine, and she'd purchased it for cash two days before. She parked up next to it and ushered Allinder out of the Volvo at gunpoint, and then into the Golf. The Volvo had a built-in sat-nav, and would be too easy to track.

She caught Allinder trying to send a text as she got into the driver's seat, and quickly relieved him of his phone, tossing it under his car.

Then she pulled out the phone she'd lifted from the Imperium mercenary, slipped the back off, and took out the SIM card and battery. It was a prepaid phone, just like the one Jamie was using, but with some luck she might be able to pull something of use off it.

Then, she peeled out of the car park and drove for thirty minutes straight, as fast as she could, north-east, heading for Täby. Beyond it, the land was crisscrossed by narrow roads and dense with trees.

Jamie didn't want to be interrupted, and the moment that Imperium got wind of Jamie's presence and what had happened at the farmers' market, she had no doubt that Karlsson would have a task force together, painting Jamie as public enemy number one. Allinder would be reported as kidnapped, and they'd be scouring the city and CCTV looking for her, and would no doubt close in on his car and phone within the hour.

So she needed to get somewhere that she couldn't be found.

Wiik had enlightened her to a farm just near Brottby. Some friends of his parents owned it, and had recently gone into assisted living near their daughter in Stockholm. The place was shuttered up now, and empty.

Jamie pulled onto the access road and trundled up towards the house.

It was a lonely old place with a knot of trees behind it, and a small, half-dilapidated red barn off to the left.

Jamie followed the track that ran around behind it in silence and parked up.

Allinder hadn't said a word the entire way, and was now staring out at the fields with glassy eyes.

'I'm not going to kill you,' Jamie said, trying to calm her heart.

'No?' Allinder said, not looking around.

'No.'

He huffed a little under his breath and then shook his head. 'I'm dead anyway. Whether you pull the trigger or not.' He faced her now. 'You know about Imperium, that much is clear. And you want to know more. Or I'd already be dead. So really, this only goes one of two ways. Either I tell you what you want to know, and then they kill me for talking to you. Or I refuse to tell you what I know, maybe you kill me, maybe you don't, but then Imperium kill me anyway. Because even if I tell them I didn't tell you anything, they won't believe me.' He laughed through closed lips, looking down at his hands. 'I didn't have a choice, you know? Back then.'

Jamie gritted her teeth, the fleeting sense of guilt she was feeling replaced by a quiet rage. 'It's funny how often I hear that. But you know what, you did. Everyone does.'

'Your father thought so,' he said.

Jamie met his eye.

'And look what happened.'

Jamie set her jaw.

'What, you thought I wouldn't know who you were?'

'Imperium tell you?' Jamie's fingers flexed around the grip of the USP.

'I used to be a detective, you know,' Allinder said. 'And Bolstad made the news, remember? They showed your face, and your partner's. Wiik, was it?'

Jamie said nothing.

'When I saw your photo, your name, Jamie Johansson, I knew that you were Jörgen's daughter. Right then, I knew there was a connection. Bolstad, your father, you… It was all a little too convenient for you not to be on Imperium's trail. I just hoped that you had more sense than he did.'

Jamie didn't interject. If he was intent on talking – whether this was some sort of absolution for him or he was just stalling – then she'd let him.

'Months passed, and I heard nothing. But then, when I spotted the two idiots following me a few weeks back, I had a feeling it was just a matter of time.'

'Before you were abducted?'

'Before a lifetime of bad decisions caught up with me,' he said, almost wistfully. 'My fate was sealed the moment that I took that offer. So tell me, what do you want to know?'

'Just like that?' Jamie asked, almost hesitant.

'Did you expect resistance?'

'I was prepared for it.'

He looked down at the gun in her hand, then at the barn. 'Take me in there, tie me to a chair, use… *farm* tools on me until I talked?'

'Something like that,' Jamie said through gritted teeth.

He chuckled through closed lips again. 'No, I'd rather skip that, if we could.' He leaned towards the window and looked at the sky. It was bright. 'Looks like it's going to be a beautiful day. What would you say to a walk across the fields instead?'

Jamie narrowed her eyes slightly. Allinder seemed to have accepted his fate extremely quickly.

'Don't worry,' he said, laying a hand on the door handle, 'I won't try to run. And if it makes you feel better, you can keep the gun.'

21

JAMIE AND ALLINDER set off across the fields under a cloudless sky.

She kept a few feet of space between them and held the pistol in her hand the entire time.

'Do you want me to start at the beginning?' he asked, brushing his hands across the tops of the blades of thigh-high grass.

'My father.'

'Hmm,' Allinder said. 'I suspected as much.' He let out a long breath, seemingly reaching for a long-repressed memory. He seemed old, standing next to her then. He must have been at least in his early seventies. Perhaps a little more. For a moment, Jamie realised her father would be nearly the same age if he'd been still alive.

That surreal thought captured her for a second, and then it was gone, and Allinder was talking.

'It started in… 2000, I believe.' He nodded to confirm it to himself. 'Your father led a case the year before, and arrested a man for the murder of a woman by the name of Sonya… Andersson, I think. She was on the city council, and was mugged and stabbed a few hundred metres from her home. In a quiet suburb.'

Jamie kept pace with him as he meandered, face to the sun.

'Your father was relentless and tracked down the man over a course of months. When he finally got him in a courtroom, the evidence was rock solid. The jury convicted and sent the man to prison.'

Jamie listened intently.

'A month later, the killer managed to acquire some rather elite defence council, who filed a motion to have the verdict overturned.'

'On what grounds?' Jamie asked.

'Mishandling evidence, coercing testimonies, and negligence on the part of the investigating officer.' He slowed for a moment, leaned down and plucked a buttercup from the grass, and then inspected it closely. 'They had your father followed, photographed him...' He seemed to labour over the words. 'With certain women. Drinking, too. And driving. Coming into work hungover. Drinking while working. They rounded up complaints from witnesses, warnings filed against him in work, everything they'd need to discredit an investigation.'

Jamie's jaw flexed as she stared into the grass.

'They asked him to resubmit the evidence for the case to a new jury, and when he went to do so...'

'It was missing?' Jamie asked.

'Partially. Enough to make the original conviction shaky. And with his track record and the evidence they had against him, a claim that he'd misfiled it or manufactured it completely in order to convict the killer was enough to throw the whole thing into jeopardy. In the end, the guy walked.'

'Who removed the evidence needed to convict?' Jamie asked, pausing and looking straight at Allinder.

He didn't want to answer that. At least not directly. 'They aren't people you say no to, Jamie.'

Her nostrils flared, fist ratcheting tight on the pistol.

'After that,' Allinder went on, 'your father became obsessed. Paranoid, even.'

They began walking again.

'He was convinced that someone within the department had gone behind his back, had tampered with the evidence. Was responsible for letting a murderer walk. But whether that was the case or not, the evidence against him was impossible to ignore. He was given a final warning and chained to his desk. Or as good as.' He laughed a little. 'God, he hated that. I remember no one would go within ten metres of him.' He turned to Jamie. 'He'd hit the keys on his computer so hard that the whole keyboard would jump after every letter.'

Jamie restrained a smile, imagining that. As much as she despised this situation, she'd been dying to hear someone talk about her father, tell her about him in some real way. Wiik had only known him peripherally – Wiik was barely even in uniform at the time. To him he was just a bogeyman. A story that the detectives told the new recruits. Do your job or Jörgen Johansson will come and rip your head off.

Allinder trundled onwards across the field, the farmhouse growing smaller in the distance.

'A few months later, he requested a meeting with the heads of the departments – violent crime, internal affairs, organised crime, the works. He asked us all to meet after work to discuss something serious, something that involved corruption within the SPA.'

'And you were already on Imperium's payroll by this point?' Jamie asked.

Again, he didn't answer the question. 'We all sat in a conference room and waited. He was sitting at the head of the table, and after a few full minutes of silence, him staring intensely at the six, seven of us that were there, he said, "If it was one of you, I'll find out. If it happened on your watch, I'll find out. And when I learn who let a killer walk free, I'll make you fucking pay for it. I swear, if it's the last thing I do. And if anyone tries to stop me, well, then you're telling me everything I need to know."' Allinder waggled his finger in air, mimicking her father. Then he made a loose fist out of his hand and let it drop. 'And then he got up and walked out.'

Jamie shook her head. 'Jesus. He really did that?'

'Probably the only person in the entire SPA who would have done.'

She wished she'd seen it. She wished a lot of things.

'And it worked, too. He got on with his work, stayed at his desk during work hours, kept his head down. Hell, he even stopped drinking. It was strange, to see his eyes clear, his mind focused. But he *was* focused. More than I'd ever seen anyone.'

Jamie swallowed, trying to hold it together. Claesson, the pathologist that came to her after the Angel Maker case and told her that her father had been murdered, said as much. He was going straight. He was getting his life back on track.

That case had given him purpose, and the murderer had walked free because he was a fuck-up. And he wasn't taking any more chances. He was cleaning up the SPA, and he was cleaning up himself.

'But after hours,' Allinder continued, 'he was building a case. He was working an investigation. He was speaking to people. *Polisassistents, kriminalinspektörs, kriminalkommis-saries*, everyone. One by one.'

'You were the head of internal affairs then, right?'

He nodded. 'But what could I do? I told him that it was our job to do what he was doing, that we'd take over his investigation, if he just gave us access to what he had already…'

'And what did he think of that?'

'He stared at me so hard I thought my skin was going to catch on fire.'

Jamie'd seen that stare. The stare that turned drug dealers and career criminals into puddles of piss. She wished she'd had a chance to get him to teach it to her. 'He refused your help then?'

'He said that we should open our own investigation, and give him access to it. That way, he'd be able to compare his own findings.'

Jamie smirked a little. 'He had you boxed in.'

'In all senses of the word,' Allinder sighed. 'Imperium were worried, to say the least. Worried about being exposed. And your father wasn't stopping. We fabricated an investigation, one which showed that it was a simple clerk's error that got the evidence lost, but he wasn't interested. He wouldn't even speak to me.'

'You think he knew?'

'I don't know. But he began digging deeper, looking beyond the department, the SPA. Looking not just at old cases, but at other deaths, ones ruled as accidents. He was booking meetings with council members, ambushing politicians and business people at their homes, at dinners with their families, rubbing shoulders with unsavoury characters, criminals – the sorts of people he'd been putting away for years, searching for the truth. Hunting it. And that straight, focused man that he'd turned into was gone again. For a moment, just a moment, I thought that he'd slipped. That the investigation would go by the wayside as he fell into worse and worse company. Hell, I even made a play to try and have him removed from the SPA for gross misconduct.'

'What happened?' Jamie was hanging on his every word.

'I submitted the request, and it disappeared.'

'Disappeared?'

He shrugged. 'It seemed someone higher up was more than happy to look the other way.'

'My father was working with someone within the SPA? Someone was supporting him in the investigation?'

'Someone, or someones. Maybe not even in the SPA. Chancellor of Justice, the Ministry Of Justice, or the National Operations Department. It's difficult to say. But trying to find out would have only put the spotlight on me even more.' He shook his head.

'Why was my father meeting with criminals?' Jamie thought back to Claesson's story. To how he'd said that her father had come in to his lab, face a mess with cocaine, stinking drunk, to discuss a body that he'd asked to be autopsied – off the books. And how that meeting had gone. He'd thrown Claesson through thousands of krona worth of lab equipment and left him in a bleeding, unconscious heap on the floor. What had pushed him to do that? What the hell was he doing in those final weeks?

Allinder drew a slow breath. 'I don't know why he was meeting with them. I can only assume he was looking for information on Imperium from all angles. They had a hold over half the city, so maybe ingratiating himself with some bad people would give him an in? Maybe he was looking for information? Maybe something else was going on. I don't know. But I don't think he was doing it alone.' He sighed. 'Imperium wanted to know everything about his investigation – they were pressuring me to find out. But if I pressed too hard… Well, let's just say I'd seen what your father did to people he was convinced were guilty.'

Jamie was the one who didn't offer an answer this time. She knew all too well the *bad* stories about her father. Her mother had made sure she was well educated in that regard.

'So when he put that doctor, the coroner, in the hospital, it was a godsend.' He looked at Jamie. 'For Imperium, I mean.' He cleared his throat. 'The SPA couldn't ignore that. They had to suspend him. Regardless of what he was working on or who with. They were keeping the investigation under wraps, but attacking someone like that? There were limits, it seemed. And it gave Imperium the chance they wanted. In the lull that followed – in those few days it took whoever your father was working for to deal with the suspension – Imperium moved in. They'd been looking for a chance, and they took it.' He stared into the pale blue sky, squinting in the bright sun. 'Imperium killed your father, Jamie. I'm sure of it.'

Jamie's hands were in fists at her sides. 'And I suppose you were the one who told them about his suspension? Who told them where he'd be? Where we lived?'

'They already knew all that. They'd been watching him for months. Waiting for their chance. All I did was pass along information.'

'Information that got him killed.' Jamie's voice was venom.

His eyes drifted down to hers. 'I'm not proud of what I did. But your father's death was on him as much as anyone else. You don't mess with these people. You don't cross Imperium. No matter who you are. Jörgen Johansson or not.'

Jamie struggled to get her words out. 'Imperium – that name comes up so much. But never any *actual* names. No faces. No one. Just a faceless holdings company. Who are these guys? Where are they from? How has no one found out about them, exposed them? How many people have they killed?'

He stared back at her, offering an apologetic smile. 'Honestly, I don't know. They approached me the year I made *kriminalkommissarie*. There were parties... to celebrate it. It was the eighties, a different time...'

'What the hell does that mean?' Jamie stepped in front of him now and met his eye, stopping him where he stood.

'It means... like *your father,* despite being married, despite being police officers, we... indulged. Too much.'

'And they, what, came to you with photos of your *indulgences,'* Jamie said, verging on spitting the words, 'and threatened to tell your wife, your boss?'

'I believe the conversation was slightly more nuanced, but that's about the sum of it. They had me do something for them, right away – misfile a meaningless piece of evidence, and hand it over to them.'

'And then what happened?'

'Then they bought me a new car.'

Jamie scoffed.

'That was it. Blackmail became bribery, and I was locked in. For good. And time and time again, we were reminded of that.' He shook his head, his white hair waving in the gentle breeze.

They stayed in silence for a full minute, each staring out at the horizon.

Then Jamie spoke. 'Sandbech.'

Allinder looked at her, raising an eyebrow. 'How do you know that name?'

'So you know him, too?'

Silence.

'I know he killed my father. Probably delivered the pictures of you. And your new car, too, right?'

He chuckled to himself. 'Once upon a time, saying that name was enough to get you killed.'

'And it's not now?' she looked at him.

'You'd probably have a fighting chance these days,' Allinder said. 'He must have been in his forties in the eighties. Older than me. By ten years, at least. He'd be, I don't know, eighty-five, now? Maybe more.'

Jamie's brow furrowed. 'Well, he's spry for his age, then, because three months ago he murdered Kriminalkommissarie Ingrid Falk in her apartment. Made her cut her own wrists in the bath.'

Allinder shuddered a little. 'That sounds like him.'

'Was he the one you had contact with at Imperium?'

Allinder nodded. 'The only one. He delivered messages back and forth. And they always contacted me. Never the other way around.'

Jamie cursed under her breath. 'And you don't have a way to reach him?'

Allinder coughed into his hand, closed one eye at the sun. Jamie could see beads of sweat beginning to form on his forehead. 'Sorry, no. Once I retired, I became little use to them, I'm afraid.'

'Is there *anything* you can tell me about him? I need to find him. Is Sandbech even his real name?'

'I don't know. I didn't ever ask. But he's not a man you'd ever want to meet. So if I can convince you—'

'You can't,' Jamie said. 'Now tell me something I can use.' She held the gun up a little, to emphasise its continued presence in the conversation. 'Or do you want to go back to the barn?'

Allinder pursed his lips. 'He was in the army.'

'All of Imperium's goons are in the army,' Jamie said. 'What else?'

'The Swedish Army. Special forces.'

'How do you know?'

'He had a knife – showed it to me once.' Allinder looked a little tense now. 'He told me what he was going to do with it if I didn't…' He swallowed. 'He said that they'd given it to him in the special forces, taught him how to use it. Taught him how to a cut a man so he can never walk again, so he can never…' He glanced down at his genitals and then back at Jamie.

'What else? Describe him. What did he look like?'

'He was tall, strong – maybe one hundred and eighty centimetres. Blondish sort of hair, green eyes. A big chin.'

'Don't fuck with me. If you're feeding me a line—'

'I'm not.'

'You've got to give me something else, Allinder. Something I can actually use to find this guy, or…'

His eyes fell on the gun now. 'Or…? You're going to shoot me? Here?' He gestured to the field. 'In the middle of fucking nowhere? Just leave me here for the crows?' His voice was growing louder, his eyes filling.

Jamie took a few steps back. 'Cool it, Allinder,' she commanded.

'Why? Or what? What if I scream, if I yell? Do I not have the right?' He was growing hysterical now.

Jamie narrowed her eyes.

'I supposed it's only fitting, isn't it? You. Jörgen Johansson's daughter. Revenge, they say, is a dish best served cold. Well, Jamie Johansson? What do you say? Do you feel cold? Cold enough to shoot an old man?'

'An old man who let murderers walk free? Who got people killed?' Her fingers uncurled and then curled around the grip of the pistol. 'I've felt worse.'

He stopped then and laughed. 'So this is it. I always

thought it would be *them*. This is what *they* do, you know that?'

'You won't find sympathy from me. They killed my father. They burned down my house. And they tried to kill me. More than once.' Her voice was flat, her heart calm.

'And I can't even call my wife!' He screamed at her now. 'Here, dead, in the middle of fucking nowhere! And you know, because of you, they'll probably kill her, too! So try and sleep with that on your conscience.'

'The wife you cheated on?' Jamie spoke slowly. 'The wife *you* got killed by getting into bed with Imperium? Don't try and get out of this. You said it yourself, whether it's me or not, Imperium will kill you anyway.'

'You're just going to kill me, then? So do it already. Fucking do it!' His voice sustained in the air and then blew away on the breeze.

She let him settle, her eyes never leaving his, and then she looked out towards the horizon again. 'Walk away, Allinder.'

'So you can shoot me in the back?'

'If that's what you want to believe.'

His lips quivered with rage, and then it faded, and he was on the verge of sobbing, his eyes shining with tears. 'What about my wife? What about my children? What will they say? What will they know?'

'Were you a good father to them? A good husband to your wife?' Jamie asked bitterly.

He nodded pleadingly.

'Do they know that you love them?'

He nodded again, flicking tears onto the hot earth.

Jamie lifted the pistol and pulled back the slide, putting a round in the chamber with a cold metallic click. 'Then they'll have more than I ever got.' She levelled it at him. 'Now start fucking walking.'

22

OVER A WEEK PASSED before Wiik arrived.

Jamie had asked the shopkeeper to put out the sign to signal she wanted to meet. *Fresh Peaches,* it read. Pretty innocuous for a greengrocer. But that was the idea.

It had taken Jamie weeks to make contact when she'd first arrived back at the city. She had to be sure she could do it without *anyone* noticing, and eventually, had managed to intercept the guy who walked down Wiik's street posting flyers for local takeaways under people's windshields, and asked him to pop a note under Wiik's. She'd had to pay him five hundred krona to do it, but it was a small price to pay.

The next day, he'd come. No questions.

And yet, it had taken him a week this time.

He slipped in wearing a flat cap, something Jamie had never seen him wear before. And he was also wearing trainers. And a coat she'd never seen either. He didn't look at all like him. But she guessed that was the point.

As he climbed the stairs, Jamie waited impatiently, checking the window three times in the space of ten seconds to make sure there were no signs of Imperium.

Wiik opened the door and Jamie crossed the room, hugging him.

He stood awkwardly, and then held her back, squeezing lightly at first, and then relaxing and hugging tighter.

'Jesus, I thought you were dead,' she said, letting him go. 'What happened? And what the hell are you wearing?'

Wiik rolled his lips into a line. 'Sorry I couldn't come earlier. They've been on me constantly. Parked up outside my house twenty-four seven, following me to work. They even put a tracker on my car. And I think they bugged my house, too.'

'Bugged your house? You sure?' Jamie asked, surprised.

'Pretty sure,' Wiik said, lifting a black device trailing a wire out of his pocket and tossing it onto the drafting table. It bounced and settled. It was definitely a microphone.

'Fuck.'

That was a bit much, even for them. Imperium didn't like to leave trails. And this was definitely a trail. Which meant they were getting desperate. And that meant they'd take more risks, and leave less up to chance.

Wiik cleared his throat. 'I heard about the market. I assume you're the one who blew that guy's knee to bits?'

Jamie nodded quickly and looked away.

'Well, he survived. Spent two hours in Saint Göran's, and was then picked up by a private ambulance and taken away. The other guy… wasn't so lucky.'

'Trampled?' Jamie asked, ignoring the knot in the pit of her stomach.

'Yeah, after he was brained with a glass bottle,' Wiik said dryly. 'Witnesses say he tried to attack a woman, and was then struck. There was a gun found on the body. No ID, though. It's been a bit of a media nightmare. Karlsson's losing his shit.'

'I bet,' Jamie said, balancing between smug and sick.

Wick smiled briefly. 'His head's on the block. He's frantic over this. Your face is *everywhere* at HQ. There's a task force, a city-wide manhunt, the works. They want you on the hook for kidnapping, assault. Murder.'

Jamie swallowed.

'The public is leaning the other way, though.'

Jamie lifted an eyebrow. 'What do you mean?'

'Karlsson's got all of Cyber quashing forums, videos, and petitions, but they keep springing up. People saying an unknown blonde woman saved someone's life. That a guy with a gun tried to attack a lady at the market, and that you saved her. Karlsson – and I guess Imperium – have managed to keep it out of the mainstream press, your name and face, too, but the public are riling against it. They don't like the police trying to sweep a public event like this under the rug. They want answers, and Karlsson's not giving them.'

Jamie bit her lip. 'He'll need to be careful, or Imperium will be after him next.'

'My guess, by the extra grey in his hair, is that he's reached the same conclusion. He's stopped speaking to me completely. Hallberg, too. He's got his team around him like a cocoon. He's scared, Jamie.'

'As he fucking should be,' she spat.

Wiik nodded. 'Allinder is dead,' he said then.

Jamie met his eye.

'Was that you?'

She drew a slow breath. 'No. Almost.' She shook her head. 'I couldn't do it. Couldn't just execute him.'

'Leaving him to the wolves was as good as.'

'He made his choices,' Jamie said coldly. 'We've all made choices. And it's on us to live with them.'

Wiik held his hands up. 'Want to know how they did it?'

She sighed and turned away. 'No, not really. Did they at least leave his wife out of it?'

Wiik said nothing, then stared up at the faces on Jamie's wall. Ex and current police officers, judges, politicians, business magnates, journalists. All possibles.

Jamie walked to the table and spread her hands on it, leaning heavily, staring down at the microphone in front of her.

'So what do you have?' Wiik asked after what seemed like an age of heavy silence. 'Allinder give you anything useful?'

Jamie rattled in a long breath, stood straight, and turned, hardening and leaning back against the table. 'I hope so. You got any contacts in the special forces?'

'The army?' Wiik raised an eyebrow.

Jamie nodded. 'Yeah, Allinder had a *personal* relationship with Sandbech, it seemed.'

'Define personal.'

'He threatened to cut his cock off with a knife.'

Wiik squirmed. He had a strong stomach for blood and justice, but one mention of genitalia in polite conversation and he was shrinking into his shell like a snail after an eye-poke. 'I hope you have something more useful than that.'

'Allinder thinks he must be in his eighties – eighty-five or so – Swedish, was in the special forces. Would have left the army before Allinder made kriminalkommissarie in the early eighties. Can't be many people who fit that description.'

Wiik looked at her, folding his arms. 'You think an octogenarian broke into Falk's apartment and got her to kill herself?'

Jamie had been wrestling with that herself. 'I don't know. We don't even know if that *was* Sandbech. But we have somewhere to start looking, now. We have an approximate age, we know that he was in the special forces, retired in the seventies. Allinder said he was tallish, six-foot-plus, blonde-brown hair, green eyes. Strong jawline. Well-built.'

'You're describing about half the men in Sweden, Jamie.' He sighed. 'And probably about eighty per cent of the guys in the special forces.'

'It's *something,* though, Wiik. Right?'

'It's something that'll get us killed. If I go asking the wrong people—'

'So ask the *right* people then. Come on, you must know *someone.'*

Wiik was a statue then, staring at her.

'I know what I'm asking, Wiik.'

'Do you? Do you, Jamie? Because I've got people in my house, following me to work, putting trackers on my car, taking photographs of me while I'm fucking sleeping!' His voice began to rise. 'I do this, and I have a strange feeling that they're going to step up their tactics. They're not going to believe that I'm innocent in this anymore.'

'They don't anyway,' Jamie said, her voice even. 'The only reason you're still alive is because they think if they watch you closely enough, you'll lead them to me.'

His eyes twitched. 'Is that supposed to make me feel better?'

Jamie didn't actually know. But it was almost certainly the truth. 'Look, if you know someone. Just give me their name. Tell me how to reach them. And then… and then maybe it's time that you took a trip. See your son, maybe? Head down to Gothenburg for a while, get out of the crossfire.'

'And just abandon you here?' He seemed more offended by that than being asked to stick his neck out.

'You've done enough already. Too much. The next step is

you in the boot of a car, bound and gagged, on the way to a set of train tracks.'

'I won't let that happen.'

'Don't be a fool, Wiik!' Jamie could feel her heart rising, her anger growing. 'I'm not going to let you get yourself killed for me.'

'Then just stop!'

Silence fell between them.

Wiik let out a breath. 'Just stop. All of it. Write a letter saying you're done, it's not worth it, and then send it to Karlsson. Whatever money you've got left then, use it to go away. Far away. where they can't find you.'

'You know I can't do that,' Jamie muttered, looking at the ground.

'Why? Because this is who you are? Because this is *all* you are?'

She looked up then, his voice cutting. 'Yes, Wiik. Because this is all I am. Because this is all I have. And if I just leave and let this go. I couldn't live with myself.'

'But you could *live*. You could just find some beach somewhere, and never worry about the polis, or killers, or cases, or Imperium ever again.'

'I don't like the beach.'

'Then the mountains! Or the woods. Or the fucking moon for all I care!'

Jamie blinked, reading the emotions on his face. 'I'm not going to have an argument over this, Wiik. And I'm not going to ask you for anymore help. This is too dangerous now. Thank you, for everything. But I'll find out the information I need for myself.' She stepped forward, put a hand on his shoulder. 'I'll send you a postcard from wherever I end up.'

She breezed past him towards the stairs, doing her best to

hold what she was feeling inside, knowing if she stayed another minute it would spill out everywhere.

'Wait,' Wiik called, her feet already on the stairs. 'Just wait.'

Jamie did, but didn't turn back.

'I'm sorry,' he said. 'I know how much this means to you – and… I shouldn't have asked you to drop it. I just don't want to see you killed.'

Jamie's fists curled but she kept her head down. 'Funnily enough, me neither,' she squeezed out.

'Give me some time. A week. And we'll meet back here. I might know someone who can help. Let me make a few calls.' He sighed heavily. 'Just don't be surprised if next time I show up here, I've got a bag full of clothes and a sleeping bag with me.'

Jamie cracked a smile, not daring to look back. 'Thanks, Wiik,' she said, putting her hand on the old, paint-splattered wooden handrail. 'And if it comes to that…' She forced her cheeks to accept a smile and then glanced back. 'The place I'm staying isn't all that bad. Once you get past the rats. And the cockroaches.'

23

WIIK WAS true to his word. A week to the day later, he sent word.

Jamie had hoped she would see him, but the information came in the form of a letter. Wiik had obviously determined it too risky to contact Jamie directly or show up himself.

The letter was waiting for her at the grocer's, and had been put upstairs on the table. It had been posted as normal, addressed to the shopkeeper, but with the prefix *1st Floor* written before the actual address. Enough to tell the grocer who it was for.

Jamie approached the table quickly and picked it up. The grocer hadn't been upstairs the whole time she'd been there. At least not to her knowledge. She was paying him for the use of it, cash under the table, and he seemed trustworthy enough. Though she'd barely told him anything except she was an ex-detective who'd been kicked off the force and was now looking to expose the corruption ingrained there.

The letter was light and Jamie wasted no time in opening it. She pulled out a single slip of paper and turned it over. There was just one thing written on it.

gammaltblod.se

Jamie stared down at the words, and then seconds later she was fumbling her laptop from the satchel at her hip.

She put it down on the table and pulled her phone out, flicking on the hotspot.

A few seconds after that, she had the browser window open and was typing in the address.

The screen went white, then black. Nothing happened.

Jamie stared down at the cryptic void, wondering what the hell she was looking at. What was this?

She tapped the keyboard and a little green asterisk popped up in the middle. She touched again. Another one appeared.

Password?

Password.

But what password?

This was from Wiik. She guessed, anyway. It had to be. Unless it was a trap. From Imperium? Her fingers retracted from the keyboard.

No. Why would it be? If they knew to send it here, then they'd know where she was. She'd be dead already.

This had to be from Wiik.

Jamie went back to the letter, reluctant to do anything before she thought about it.

If this was some sort of data drop or directions for how to find Sandbech, then she couldn't jeopardise it. It was obviously designed for her, and her alone.

Wiik wasn't technically advanced – he could use a tablet, and was reasonable on a computer – but designing a site like this? Jamie ignored that for now and scoured the letter. Totally blank save for the hand-printed URL.

She went over the envelope then. Nothing.

She even went downstairs and asked the grocer who'd dropped it off. He said it came with the normal mail.

Jamie was back at the screen now, staring at the two green asterisks.

She backspaced and they disappeared.

She clicked around the site. Nothing.

None of the other buttons on the keyboard did anything either.

Jamie even right-clicked and inspected the page source. But it didn't tell her anything other than the fact that she knew nothing about computer code.

What about the URL itself? *Gammaltblod.* Old blood. Jamie bit her lip. What did that mean?

Old blood.

Was it a reference to Jamie's crusade here? Was it supposed to be like bad blood? She tried that then in the address bar. It came up with a page for a punk-rock band based out of Gothenburg.

She navigated back. No point going down that rabbit hole.

The site was obviously for her. Blood. Blood. Her blood? Her family? Johansson? She typed that in, and hit enter. The asterisks disappeared but nothing happened.

Old blood.

Her father?

She tried 'Jorgen'. Then 'Jörgen', complete with the umlaut. Neither worked.

Shit. This was going to be impossible.

Jamie sat back on the little stool, staring at the screen. Nothing had changed. And she couldn't just sit here banging random words out and hoping. What if she locked it for good, or… and then she noticed. Something had changed.

The URL was no longer just *gammaltblod.se,* it now had */tåhattar* after it. Jamie read the words. Toe caps?

She looked down under the table at her boots. Remembered all the shit that Wiik had given her over them. *You can't wear hiking boots to work. They're needless. They aren't smart. Detectives don't wear hiking boots.* But she'd outpaced him on every run, and maintained that they were the best thing she'd ever spent her money on. Sure, they were needlessly expensive, but they were also extremely light and comfortable, great for being on your feet all day, and when she needed to sling a kick into someone's ribs – or head – there was nothing that beat the Kevlar toe caps…

Jamie looked up at the screen then, typed K-E-V-L-A-R, and hit enter.

It flashed white, and then went black again, a little green cursor popping up in the top left-hand corner. It flashed gently.

Jamie smirked to herself.

Clever. No one would ever have known. No one except her and Wiik. Imperium might be able to dig into her life, into her past. But they'd never be able to know something that was only ever spoken about.

Wiik, you cunning bastard.

But what did she type now.

After a minute or two, she settled for 'hello'.

And then quickly added an '?' after it.

'And now we wait,' Jamie muttered, staring at the screen.

Whatever nuances were behind this encrypted website, it was, for all intents and purposes, an instant messaging app.

But as the minutes ticked by, Jamie realised it was anything but instant.

Nearly half an hour later, a response appeared.

> *Jamie?*

> *Are you there?*

> *I have the information you wanted.*

Jamie's fingers twitched, heart racing. 'Okay,' she typed. 'Send it over. Thank you.'

> *Lars Sandbech. Born 1938, Östersund. Served Swedish military 1956–1973. Retired from special forces at the rank of major.*

> *Currently residing near the Sarek national park. Do you want the full address?*

Jamie's heart was pounding in her ears. 'Yes,' she typed, grabbing a notepad.

The address came through and Jamie scribbled it down.

> *Got it? These messages won't be saved.*

'Got it,' Jamie replied, sighing with relief. 'Thank you, Wiik.'

> *Don't mention it.*

> *Good luck.*

> *Also… This is Hallberg.*

Jamie did a double-take and started typing, but before she could even get a word down, the screen went blank and she couldn't type anything.

A minute later, it reloaded itself and showed her a 404 error page. *Site not found.*

Jamie stared down at it in shock, wondering what the hell that was. What had happened to Wiik? What was he doing getting Hallberg involved? Was he alright?

She didn't think sitting there was going to solve any of those questions though.

And there really was no time to lose, and nothing to wait for.

Jamie closed her laptop and stowed it in the satchel next to the table. Then she got up and looked around. Whatever happened next, she didn't think she'd be coming back here again. It wasn't safe. Wiik was under scrutiny, if not in serious trouble – enough to get Hallberg involved in this after Jamie *explicitly,* and emphatically, told him not to.

She shook her head, unbelievably pissed off at him, and

worried sick at the same time. 'For God's sake, Wiik,' she mumbled to herself, brushing the hair out of her eyes. 'What the hell have you done?'

Five minutes later, the walls were stripped bare and everything was stacked in a folder and secure next to her laptop.

She did one final sweep of the room for any last evidence, memorised the address on the paper in front of her, pocketed it, and then headed for the door.

She took one quick glance back from the top of the stairs, and then headed down.

The grocer looked up briefly and Jamie went over wordlessly, putting down a thin stack of banknotes.

He looked at them, then at her.

She nodded, and then left, pausing only briefly at the window to take the sign for fresh peaches down. 'You won't be needing this anymore,' she said, looking at it.

And then she laid it against a box of potatoes and pulled the door closed behind her.

The quiet of the shop immediately faded and Jamie was swallowed up by the thick heat of the city.

24

JAMIE HEADED NORTH in the shaky VW, the dashboard rattling the entire way as the tired engine chugged on.

She'd been driving for well over an hour before she realised she was in complete silence. Jamie sighed and rolled down the window, allowing the wind in.

It caused the loose strands of hair around her forehead to whip at her eyes, but nothing was going to break her focus.

A quick glance at the passenger seat confirmed that her pistol was loaded and ready. It was sitting on top of an old topographical map she'd acquired, which was marked out with the location of the cabin she was approaching – Sandbech's cabin – as well as notes on the surrounding landscape – vantage points, potential attack corridors, and escape routes. She was leaving nothing to chance.

There was a rucksack in the footwell that contained a high-powered pair of binoculars, and a spare magazine for the pistol that Heikkinen had given her.

Other than that, she had the clothes on her back, the boots on her feet, and the knowledge that she was going to try to kill someone in the next few hours.

.   .   .

It was mid-afternoon and hot by the time Jamie arrived.

The approach to the address led her through Östersund, around the Storsjön Lake, and north towards Krokom. After she'd passed through the quaint residential village, everything got very quiet. The road continued to head north; the villages getting smaller with each passing hamlet.

And then her phone was telling her to pull off onto an unmarked gravel track that wound into the dense forest on her left. She could see the tops of mountains beyond, the tittering of birds loud and omnipresent around her.

The GPS was showing that the cabin was just over a mile up the track, but she had no intention of just rolling up to the front door.

Jamie continued on and then swung right and drove towards a tiny spit of a town a little way down the road.

She parked on a little residential street, the old VW blending in seamlessly with the aged cars sitting on the grassy verges, relics all but forgotten by the modern age.

Two houses faced her, but both were silent, as though uninhabited.

The temperature in the car began to climb as Jamie surveyed the area, the seemingly deserted little village totally asleep.

Jamie was in an old, faded T-shirt and a pair of jeans. Nowhere to hide her pistol.

She stowed it in her backpack and pulled it around her shoulders, stepping out into the sunshine.

She expected at least to see twitching curtains or hear the sounds of voices, another engine, anything. But there was just the buzz of unseen cicadas and the tweeting of the local birds.

Jamie locked the car and walked away quickly, making steady progress back towards the main road.

She'd cross it and then head up into the trees on foot. The map showed that the cabin was nestled in a natural valley and backed onto a rise with a pretty reasonable prominence. It was full with trees, and had a river running through it, one of the hundreds that crisscrossed the area, joining the lakes that dotted the landscape.

The only road in was forced to cross the water before dead-ending at the cabin. It was a natural choke point and would be easy to defend, the natural mountain behind forming a difficult angle to attack from. The impenetrability of the landscape around would make any sort of large-scale assault nigh on impossible. All of which made the cabin a place anyone would think twice about moving on without meticulous planning and several backup plans in place.

That old line of a plan being so stupid it just might work crossed Jamie's mind.

The pistol in her pack was all she had with her, and she had no idea if it would be enough. She just hoped that Sandbech wouldn't know she was coming. And that he'd be there. If he wasn't, would she wait? Sit in his house, pistol in hand, waiting for him to arrive? Ask him the questions she wanted, make sure that he was the man who killed her father, make him *admit* to it, and then… shoot him?

Was she really so far gone that she'd execute an old man? Was there any other choice? And then what? What came after? Imperium wouldn't let her go, but she had no clear picture of what was next. Of how she'd tackle things. Of how she'd make it so Imperium couldn't hurt anyone else.

Jamie bit her lip, jogging across the hot, black strip of asphalt and down the verge into the trees. The air was thick with pollen and the smell of sap, the gentle creaking of the pines and her boots sinking into the soft layer of browned needles the only sounds as she wrestled with her mind.

Sandbech would know something, enough to make the difference. To give her the next name. And then she'd find that person. And get another name. And another. And if she had to, she'd go through them one by one until she had enough evidence to build something solid. And then it would be... Interpol? Europol? The Hague? MI5? The FBI? How many federal or cross-border law enforcement agencies did she know of? How far did Imperium's reach stretch?

As Jamie climbed higher, towards the ridgeline over-looking Sandbech's cabin, her mind began to cloud and clear at the same time. Thoughts of Imperium's insipid rot took root in her brain, the anger she felt for what they'd done to her and to everything she'd stood for blocking out everything else.

The ground under her began to level, and she approached the rise with a quiet detachment. She'd need to head down to where the trees thinned and find a good vantage point.

Jamie pulled her rucksack from her shoulder, drew her rib holster from the pack, and put it on. The Glock 19 slid snuggly into it and then she pulled out her binoculars, shoul-dering the bag before she continued down.

The sun was bleeding through the canopy in bright shafts, the ground underfoot a mixture of loose dirt and rocks as it fell away towards the river.

Water burbled gently over round stones, the river shallow and clear. Jamie paused for breath, kneeling at its side. She placed her hands under the surface and lifted them out, running her fingers around her neck and through her hair. The day was hot.

Jamie stayed there for a few minutes, collecting herself. Despite her resolve being unshaken, this was no small step for her. Going into it with Allinder, she'd prepared herself to shoot him and then not been able to. And when it came to the two mercenaries, one had been trampled – which she could reckon with, though it still made her sick to think about it. The other she'd kneecapped, threatened to kill. But doing so was different. In that moment, things were so microcosmic, and he was coming for her. Self-defence was one thing, but to shoot an unarmed man, right in front of you? To look them in the eyes and pull the trigger?

Jamie shook her head, threw water on her face, and stood up. Thoughts like this would only get her killed.

This guy might be old, but that didn't mean he wasn't still dangerous. A career killer – and castrater if Allinder was to be believed. Going into this with any doubt in her mind would be suicidal.

Jamie picked her way across the river and then climbed the bank on the other side, tracing her way around the bowl, and then down to the tree line.

As they began to thin, she aimed for a rocky outcropping and slowed, dropping her bag behind a stout pine and kneeling.

In front, the tops of the last few sporadic trees swayed, obscuring her from the valley below. But she had a clear view. Down to the pastured valley floor, the road coming in, the single-lane bridge that crossed the river, and the cabin that it led to.

Except it wasn't really a cabin.

The alpine-style chalet was nestled in the embrace of a sloped meadow, surrounded by trees. A gravel driveway opened in front of it with two garages built into the basement of the house, overlooked by a wide balcony, a glass frontage, and a white-and-stain paint job that could have put the place in the heart of St Moritz.

Jamie lowered the binoculars. 'Shit,' she muttered. Imperium obviously paid well.

But where was Sandbech?

And realistically, how long could she stay there?

Jamie bit her lip, feeling sweat beading around her collar.

And then she made up her mind.

25

THE IDEA of picking the lock, letting herself into his house, and waiting for him in an armchair, loaded pistol in her lap, crossed Jamie's mind.

But melodrama wasn't exactly what she was going for here.

And anyway, that wasn't her style.

This needed to be clean and quick.

So, as Sandbech pulled up in a nondescript, thirty-year-old Jaguar two-door, brown from the dust on the road in, and levered himself out, Jamie made her move.

The old man took a while to get upright, and then approached the steps to his front door with what looked like a glass bottle of milk in one hand, and a loaf of bread in the other.

His back had a slight hunch, and he moved deliberately. But he wasn't exactly agile.

He climbed the stairs and got to the front door, pinning the loaf under his arm while he fumbled with his keys.

Jamie had made the approach a hundred times in her

head, and now doing it for real, she ran down the hill, hopped the gap from the retaining wall at the side of the house onto the balcony, vaulted the railing, and then came around the corner, pistol raised.

Before Sandbech had even turned the key in the lock, she had the muzzle pressed into the soft patch of flesh under his ear.

He stood in silence, utterly still.

Jamie could feel the nose of her Glock pulsing slowly with his heart. Most people's would double the second they realised they had a gun to their head. But Sandbech just stood like a statue, his heart beating slowly.

'Are you going to pull the trigger?' he asked, hand on the key, not a hint of shake.

Jamie looked around the empty valley, and then pressed a little harder. 'I could,' she said, 'and no one would hear a thing.'

Sandbech chuckled softly. 'Ooh, chilling.'

'Don't fuck with me,' Jamie said. 'We're going to have a little chat.'

'Great,' Sandbech said, twisting the key and pushing the door inward. 'I love chats. And doing them at gunpoint always makes them so much more interesting.'

He stepped into his front room, tossing his keys onto the side table inside the door, and crossed the open-plan living room towards the gigantic island in the middle of his kitchen.

A little thrown, Jamie went in after him, keeping her pistol raised.

The old man seemed totally unphased by its presence. Maybe he didn't think Jamie had the spine to pull the trigger. Or maybe he'd accepted death a long time ago.

Sandbech put the milk on the counter and went around to

the other side. 'Can I get you something to drink? Tea, coffee? Something stronger?'

'I don't drink,' Jamie said sourly, keeping him between the sights.

He smiled at that. 'Not like your father, then,' he said.

Jamie twitched, but kept her pistol straight.

Sandbech was behind the island now, opening a drawer. And then his hands were on the counter, a pistol in one of them, lying on its side under his hand.

'Don't fucking move,' Jamie ordered, stepping closer.

'Come now,' Sandbech said, his green-blue eyes flashing with the sharpness of a much younger man. 'If I wanted to kill you, you'd already be dead.'

Jamie's jaw tensed. 'Push the gun away.'

'I don't think I will.'

'Do it. Now.'

'Or what? You'll shoot me?'

'It's what I came here to do,' Jamie said, voice hard.

'I suspected as much. But had you wanted to kill me, you would have done so the moment I got out of the car. No, you want to… *talk.* They always want to talk.' He shook his head. 'I find talking so *dull.* Don't you?'

He was clearly Swedish, but he spoke perfect English, almost unaccented. Jamie hadn't realised they weren't speaking her native tongue until then. She'd lived in England since she was fourteen, spoke it like her first language. But she didn't know a thing about Sandbech, not really.

'I'm not a huge fan,' Jamie said.

Sandbech grinned. 'It's a little early for a proper drink, but I think the circumstances call for it, don't you?'

He leaned over then, disappearing behind the counter, and Jamie went closer again, keeping the gun fixed on his head.

'I'm reaching for a glass,' Sandbech said, not looking up.

'It's why I brought the gun out first, so you wouldn't get jumpy.' The words sounded squeezed as he stood straight with a little effort, and put a glass on the counter, a bottle of Scotch in his other hand. He poured out a dram, corked the bottle, and set it down. 'Now then, would you like to have a conversation here, or would you prefer to sit? Or have you decided you'd prefer to skip it altogether?'

Jamie thought. Fast. And hard. 'Here is fine.'

How was she suddenly on the back foot? Sandbech had an unnerving coolness about him. And despite being in his eighties, he looked ten years younger, and gave no hint that he wasn't still a capable killer. And that he wasn't still utterly dangerous. He knew who she was the second that muzzle touched the back of his neck.

'How did you know it was me?' Jamie asked.

'I live in the mountains,' he said, taking a sip of whisky. 'Not on the moon. I spent a good deal of time with your father and knew his work quite well. When the Angel Maker case made the news again, and I saw your face and name, I knew it would simply be a matter of time before we crossed paths. If you survived that long.' He chuckled to himself, amused by it. Then he took another small sip through lined lips.

'You killed my father,' Jamie said, a statement rather than a question.

'Yes, I did.' A confirmation rather than a denial.

Jamie swallowed.

'This is the part where you shoot me.' He took another sip. 'No? Then I will sit, if you don't mind.'

He crossed from behind the island and sat at a glass table in the window of his dining area. The windows were slightly tinted on the inside, making the room bright but not unbearable. It was cool in there, and beyond the glass, the mountains looked like a painting.

'I think,' Sandbech went on, 'that you have realised that while revenge is satisfying, it's not wholly practical, a lot of the time, at least. Your problems extend beyond this grudge with me. As you've come to the conclusion that I was merely a cog in a greater machine. Did I force your father to put the muzzle of his snub-nosed-thirty-eight in his mouth and pull the trigger? Did I tell him that if he didn't pull the trigger, I would go to England and hurt you and your mother in horrifying ways? Yes, and yes.'

Jamie's hand was shaking now, her throat a pinhole.

'Do I feel guilt for those actions?'

That hung between them for a moment.

'No. Not a shred of it. I suppose that's what made me so good at my job. Your father was not special in any way – not to Imperium, and not to me.'

'Are you trying to get me to kill you?' Jamie forced out.

'I'm not trying to do anything,' Sandbech said. 'I was curious to meet you.'

'You said you knew my father. You spent time with him… Tell me. Tell me what happened.'

'You look shaken,' Sandbech said. 'Sit, please.'

'I'll stand.'

He stared at her. 'So be it. But yes, I did. I spent time with your father. I met him for the first time in the weeks leading up to his death.'

'How? How did you meet?'

'If you began asking the wrong questions, I was the one they sent. Though I saw something in him I thought we might have used. So I elected not to kill him. Not right away, at least.'

Jamie's grip fastened on the Glock.

'He was looking to bring down the organisation, and I thought that having a man like him at the SPA could have been more beneficial than the other spineless imps at our disposal.'

'Allinder,' Jamie spat.

'Rasmus Allinder?' He raised an eyebrow. 'Among others.'

Jamie narrowed her eyes. 'He's dead.'

'I'm not surprised.'

'You didn't…?'

'Kill him?' He looked at her now. 'No. I didn't. I haven't killed anyone in… several years now, at least.'

He said it with such cold indifference.

'Someone is killing people.'

'Lots of people are killing people,' Sandbech said, taking another drink. 'It's rather an epidemic if you know where to look.'

'No,' Jamie said, shaking her head. 'Ingrid Falk, a kriminalkommissarie. She gave me your name.'

'I don't know anyone by that name,' Sandbech said flatly.

'She said you are who they send.'

'Sent, yes. But I'm retired.' He looked around. 'Don't I look it?'

Jamie furrowed her brow. 'She's dead. Made to look like a suicide, like the others.'

'Yes, an efficient way to do it, of course. And I may have coined the style, but I assure you, my days of doing that are over.'

'So you're saying there's *another* Sandbech?'

'I believe that's what *you're* saying.'

'Don't fuck with me!' Jamie yelled now, walking over so that she was close enough for him to smell the gun grease.

He restrained a smile. 'I was good at what I did, but I was not the only one. Though I admit, it's rather a smart move.'

'What is?'

'Using my name.' He shook his head. 'I don't know if I should be flattered or not.'

'Why is it smart?'

He looked at her as though she was missing a beat. 'Because someone looking for revenge against a man named Sandbech would no doubt land here, at my feet.'

Jamie did feel like she was missing a beat.

'Which makes someone who might have been difficult to find previously, very easy to find indeed.'

It dawned on her then and Jamie stiffened.

'Ah,' Sandbech said. 'The penny drops.'

Jamie's eyes turned to the quiet landscape outside, the natural ridge around the bowl, the vantage points, the panoramic glass. The kill-box she'd willingly walked into.

Was she being sighted through a scope as they spoke?

'I wouldn't worry,' Sandbech said. 'If they were out there, you'd be dead already.' He got up and took his empty glass back to the island. 'But I wouldn't drag my heels,' he said. 'I have no doubt they know you're here, and it'll just be a matter of time.' He poured himself another drink. 'They would have clocked you the moment you got near this place.'

'How?'

'The security cameras.'

'I didn't see any cameras. I checked.'

He raised the glass to his lips. 'They wouldn't be very good security cameras if you did.'

Jamie lowered the gun then, her heart hammering in her ears.

'Right then,' Sandbech said. 'We'd better get to it. What did you really want to ask?'

'You're going to answer my questions? Why?' Was he going to lie to her? Stall for time? What was this?

He shrugged. 'I don't know. Boredom?'

'Boredom?'

He shrugged again. 'I don't have any allegiances to them. Nor to you. I live my life as bait. And this isn't the sort of situation one walks away from. I suppose if I help you, give you something you can use, it makes things... more *sporting*.'

'Sporting?' Jamie was in shock.

'Sporting. Fair. Gives you a fighting chance, you know?'

'What the hell is wrong with you?'

He took another drink. 'What, you'd deny an old man a little fun before he dies?' He laughed again now. 'What do I care what happens to them after I'm gone? I led a good life. One I enjoyed. One that was rewarding in its own way. And who knows, once those cars come over the ridge and thunder down that road, maybe it'll be enough to get my heart racing again. So what do you say, eh? Ready to have a little fun? I could never convince your father of it, but what about you?'

Jamie stared down at the pistol in her hands.

He was mad.

Utterly mad.

A grade-A psychotic old motherfucker who got off on murder and mayhem.

But if he was telling the truth about the cameras, and she had no doubt he was, then he'd be telling the truth about Imperium, too. And in who knew how long, they'd be here. In force. With guns. Looking to kill her.

She glanced up at Sandbech, the man who'd taken everything from her, who'd shattered her life. And her blood ran cold.

But honestly, what other choice did she have? Put a bullet in him and run?

She could, but then she'd have nothing. No leads, no information, and nowhere to go.

No, the only option seemed to be to stay. And to fight.

She was just relieved, in a strange, twisted, disgusting way, that this crazy old man was at least on her side.

26

As Lars Sandbech talked, he seemed perfectly pleasant. If you could ignore the subject about which he was talking. And his history of complete, psychotic violence.

Jamie found it difficult to believe that he would be so forthcoming with information – especially against Imperium. He'd been discharged from the Swedish military for what he said was 'a trivial reason'. Jamie gleaned it was something to do with his conduct, and no doubt to do with his psychotic tendencies. The special forces often attracted men like Sandbech, but they didn't always like the results they got.

Following that, in the late seventies, Imperium snapped him up and put him to work. Mostly killing people.

They'd paid relatively well, and when he'd reached his mid-seventies and he'd become slower than the job required, they'd allowed him to retire. After forty years of diligent murdering. But he said that during his tenure, he'd dispatched almost as many people who had 'retired' from Imperium as had stood against them. And had always expected one of his successors to come knocking on his door with a bullet just for him one day. The circle of life, he called it.

'So quite frankly,' he said, 'fuck them.' Then he took another drink. 'I lived my life, enjoyed it. Got to kill a lot of people. Most for Imperium. Some just for me. There were lots of good times. But now, sitting here, waiting for someone to come and kill me? Well, it's not a fitting death, come to think of it. Go over there, to the cupboard in the kitchen.'

Jamie stood from the table, leaving the notepad full of names and other information about Imperium's inner workings, and headed to the kitchen, pistol in hand.

Sandbech seemed amenable, but she was under no illusions who she was sitting across the table from. And every five seconds, her brain kept telling her that the second he stopped being useful, she'd put a bullet in him. But the more he spoke, the more human-esque he became. He was the lens through which she'd focused all her anger. But it was difficult to hold anger for someone who felt such indifference. Who spoke of the past like a television show he'd watched.

She didn't know whether she'd expected remorse from him, or whether she could get him to beg and plead for his life. Whether that would have made it easier, or harder.

Honestly, she'd hoped that he would have fought back, that they would have tussled, and that she could have distilled it down to the him-or-me scenario that would have allowed her to pull the trigger.

And yet here they were, talking politely across a very expensive dining table.

Jamie headed for the cupboard that Sandbech pointed out. It was next to his fridge. The kind that most people would use to store a mop.

She opened it and stood back, swearing under her breath. What stared back at her was a veritable arsenal.

A marksman rifle with scope, two shotguns – one pump

action, the other a single-barrelled sport shooter – and what looked like an automatic assault rifle.

Then she saw what was hanging on the door. Four pistols. Two matching Glocks, a Browning Hi-Power pistol, and a Heckler & Koch Mark 23. Jamie doubted she'd be able to even hold it up with one hand – it was huge.

'Quite the collection,' Jamie said, turning to face Sandbech.

'Just a few favourites. Call me sentimental.' He smiled, tickled by his own joke.

'I'm not looking to really get into a war here,' Jamie said.

'You're already in one.'

'Don't remind me.' Jamie sighed, sick to her stomach. 'You'd really turn on the people you worked for all those years?'

'As quick as they'd turn on me. It's all just business.' He shrugged, moving his tumbler around the table with his fingers, totally at ease. 'Your presence here has simply precipitated the next shifting of the board.'

'But why help me?' She looked away from the guns. 'That's what I don't understand. Are you just stalling, waiting for them to get here? So you can hand me over?'

'Just satisfying my own curiosity.' He surveyed her. Not as a human does another, but as a lion does a zebra, lounging in the shade. 'I'm waiting to see if you're going to kill me.'

Jamie narrowed her eyes at him.

'I've always found the inability to kill someone fascinating. Such a disadvantage that seems odd to me.' He stared out into the trees around his home. The valley was quiet and unmoving behind the glass. 'Animals do it. Wolves kill deer without remorse. Cats kill mice. Birds kill insects. It is only the human that holds itself to a *moral* standard. A fictionalised vision of right and wrong that renders the majority of them helpless.'

'Don't you mean *us?*' Jamie arched an eyebrow.

He smiled again. 'Yes, I suppose I do. But I've always found it fascinating in those who *won't* kill, what drives them to kill. Others, or themselves. You tell a man to sit down and put a gun in his mouth, and he refuses.'

Jamie stiffened.

'But you tell him that if he doesn't, you'll hunt down his wife and daughter and hurt them in ways that he could never imagine, and suddenly, killing comes easily to him.'

Jamie's fingers flexed on the grip of her pistol, the weapon shaking at her side.

Sandbech's eyes flashed. 'See, there was a glimmer of it then.' He pointed at her playfully. 'I saw it, just for the briefest second – the ability to kill. To lift your gun and shoot me, because you wanted to.'

'I think this is the part where I tell you you're sick,' Jamie growled, unable to part her teeth.

'A diagnosis that has been floated around, certainly.' He sighed, crossing his legs and lacing his wrinkled hands over his knee. 'Though I consider myself quite sane. Simply a bystander. An observer of the human condition. As a researcher might the rats who scuttle around his maze.' Sandbech lifted his hands and twiddled his fingers like a puppeteer.

Jamie restrained a gag. 'I think I'm ready to leave now,' she said, shaking her head.

'Oh, so soon? But our party guests haven't even arrived yet. And we were just getting to know each other.'

Jamie didn't even bother trying to smile. She just crossed to the table, picked up the notepad and tore out the filled pages, and stuffed them in her pocket. 'You're just going to let me walk out of here, right?' she said then, glancing at Sandbech, who was still watching her.

'Why wouldn't I?'

'I could think of a few reasons.'

'No,' he laughed. 'I quite enjoy watching people try to take on Imperium. It's always fun to see how far they get.' He cocked his head slightly then, his eyes unfocusing. And then he looked at Jamie again, sending a shiver down her spine, and turned to the window. 'They're here,' he said.

Jamie followed his gaze to the track beyond the river, and the cloud of dust rising just behind the ridge.

'So what will it be, Jamie Johansson?' Sandbech asked, getting to his feet and walking into the kitchen, towards the still-open gun cupboard. 'Do you wish to be the mouse, or the man?'

27

'I WISH to end this fucking nightmare,' Jamie grunted, watching the dust cloud grow.

'Well, don't mind me, or the floors. The maid comes every Tuesday,' Sandbech said, gesturing to the pistol in her hand.

'Not what I meant,' Jamie said, eyes fixed on the horizon. 'I don't suppose you have a way out of this—' Jamie cut off, turning to look at Sandbech and finding herself staring down the barrel of the marksman's rifle.

Her heart skipped a beat, her skin erupting in gooseflesh.

Sandbech pulled the trigger.

Jamie jolted.

But all that rang out was a metallic click. The firing mechanism falling on an empty chamber.

Sandbech lowered the rifle and laughed to himself again. 'Sorry, I couldn't resist.'

Jamie just made an indignant sound.

'What do you want, the assault rifle or the shotgun?'

'Neither,' Jamie said. 'I'm leaving.' She'd already

mapped the route back to her car. 'Good luck with… whatever it is you're doing.'

'Dying.' Sandbech slotted a round into the chamber of the bolt-action rifle – a polished antique Remington – and then slid the bolt into place. 'Probably,' he added. 'I suspect they'll come in force.'

Jamie watched him lay the rifle on the kitchen island and then return to the cupboard for the rest of his weapons. Jesus fucking Christ, he was really intending to get into a firefight with these people for… *fun.*

She was almost begrudged to be leaving without any closure, but what more was there to be said? Sandbech had killed her father, and despite the hatred that she'd had for him from the moment she'd learned the truth about her father's demise, she was finding it difficult to detangle the man in front of her from the spectre in her mind.

She couldn't be any more angry at him for what he'd done than you could be a spider for eating a fly. It was just in his nature. The cruel irony of it was that had she been more like him, she might have been able to kill him. But if she was, then it wouldn't bring her closure. She'd feel nothing. And she knew if she lifted the pistol in her hand and shot him, that would do nothing except eat her up. She had killed before. Three lives lived on her conscience. And every time she thought about them, it made her want to turn inward. To curl up into a ball, eat her feet, and then disappear. It made her feel angry and sad, full and empty at the same time. It felt like a crushing weight, an outstanding bill she needed to pay back.

And adding one more life to it was not something she wanted to do lightly.

Jamie Johansson was not a killer.

As much as she wished she was at times.

'You should take the truck,' Sandbech said then, pulling

Jamie out of her haze. Keys were flying through the air suddenly and Jamie snatched them before they hit her in the head. 'If you are intent on running away.'

He banged a magazine into the body of the assault rifle, and then carried it out to the front door, along with the Remington.

He opened it and took a deep breath of crisp mountain air.

A breeze blew in and moved Jamie's hair, and she watched, squinting at the harsh sunlight pouring through the open door, as Sandbech knelt with some discomfort, and laid the barrel of the rifle on the balcony rail that Jamie thought would be far better served on quiet mornings, leaned on with a cup of coffee in hand.

She thought about that then, whether she should have taken Heikkinen's advice. Karlsson's advice. Wiik's advice. Everyone's advice. And just left. Found somewhere like this. Lived out her days in quietude. In solace. In peace—

A gunshot rang out. A thundering boom followed by a high-pitched whine as the bullet tore from the mouth of the rifle barrel and arced through the air.

Sandbech absorbed the recoil, then smoothly popped the casing out of the rifle and put another one in the chamber with the bolt.

In the distance, Jamie could see a line of black SUVs hammering through the valley. And then, without warning, the lead car swerved and impaled itself on the left-hand support strut of the bridge.

Smoke billowed into the sky above it and the two four-by-fours behind both skidded to a halt at an angle.

Sandbech took a second, then let another bullet fly.

He looked back casually, grinning, as little figures began to swarm in the distance, the chatter and pop of rifles and pistols distant and seemingly innocuous.

'If you're leaving, now would be a good time. Head past the kitchen, a door on your right leads down to the garage. There's an SUV there. You already have the keys.'

He returned to the scope, ejected the second casing, and loaded another.

Jamie stood and watched. As much as she wanted to get out of there, she wanted to see how this played out, too. Who was coming, and whether Sandbech could fend them off.

Then the first bullet hit the window in front of her and created a little spiders web of cracks. The glass was bullet-proof, but it was still enough to bring her back to reality.

'Where am I supposed to go?' She watched the merce-naries organise themselves in the distance, blocking the only road out of the valley.

As she began to back up, more bullets struck.

One, two, three.

She couldn't stay here. But how the hell was she supposed to escape?

Sandbech fired for a third time, and then was on his feet.

The men in the distance were wading across the river now.

He came back into the house unhurriedly and crossed to the kitchen island. 'Pull out of the garage and head up the valley,' he said, picking up the box of bullets for the rifle. 'I knew I should have gone for the six-round magazine,' he said, almost as a throwaway remark.

He fed three into the body of the Remington with prac-tised ease. 'When you reach the lightning-struck tree, go right up the slope. You'll see a little opening and an old logging path. It sweeps around, up the side of the valley, and meets up with the road a kilometre north.' He pulled back the bolt and then chambered another round. 'Now then,' he said, grinning. 'Where was I?'

Jamie didn't need any more information, and with a dozen armed guys edging closer by the second, and nothing but a gun-crazy octogenarian between her and them, it was time to go.

She patted her pocket to make sure she still had the notebook pages, and then made for the garage.

Sandbech was still picking off soldiers as she ran. And she had no doubt that every bullet was hitting its mark. He was not a man who made mistakes.

The garage was dark, but expansive and clean. Jamie's feet hit concrete and she stumbled, bumping into a gleaming red convertible. Jamie couldn't make out what it was, but the sleek, classic lines told her it was something vintage. Luckily, the SUV was a little newer.

A Mercedes G-Class with knobbled tyres and gleaming black paint shimmered in the darkness, the thin shards of light coming in around the garage door offering just enough brilliance to make it out.

Jamie blipped the keys and climbed up into the cream-leather cab.

As she closed the door, the sound of gunfire disappeared, replaced with a strange sense of calm.

She glanced down at her hands. They were shaking a little, shiny with sweat in the courtesy lighting coming from the headliner.

Hanging from the sun visor, she could see a little black device – the remote for the garage door.

Once she pressed it, she'd be driving straight into gunfire.

Not a very appetising thought.

She took a deep breath, reaching up.

Jamie wondered then whether the glass in the car would be bulletproof too.

And then realised that in about five seconds, she'd be finding out.

Her hand hovered at the button and she cranked the ignition with her other, feeling the car shudder to life beneath her.

Jamie depressed the clutch, breathing hard, and slid the gear-stick into first. The sound of gunfire began to grow beyond the glass.

'Screw it,' Jamie muttered, jabbing the door button.

She stamped on the accelerator and the engine flared.

The garage door rose ahead.

She let down the handbrake, the sunlight blinding her, and then released the clutch.

The back wheels spun, the car twisting before it found traction on the slick concrete floor, and then slingshotted her forward.

The still-rising garage door scraped across the roof of the four-by-four and then she was outside.

Guys in black scattered ahead of her, advancing on Sandbech's bulletproof chalet in a wide line.

The one right in front regained himself and lifted an assault rifle.

And then collapsed spontaneously.

It took a second for Jamie's mind to realise that Sandbech had just put a bullet in him, and then she hung a right, the tyres slashing at the loose gravel, sending a flood of dust into the air.

Bullets pinged and peppered the side of the car as she picked up speed, heading up the valley, and then the back window shattered and rained down into the boot. Guess that answered the bulletproof glass question.

Jamie ducked instinctively, wrestling the Merc left and right as she continued to pick up speed, and then straightened out.

She changed up, the knobbled wheels fighting for traction as she bounced over the meadow, mowing down tall grass in the process.

Behind her, the gunfire wore on. In the rear-view, Jamie could make out several bodies heading for the house, several turning to give chase.

But with the lead car blocking the bridge and the others stranded across the river, they had no hope.

Shit!

Jamie almost missed it.

Her eyes faced forward again, her heel finding the brake instinctively.

The wheels locked up and she skidded, juddering in the loose earth, a tall, blackened husk of a tree standing in front of her. It had been struck by lightning.

What did Sandbech say? Right at the tree, up the slope.

Jamie changed down, and then again. The wheels spun, but then she was moving.

The forest loomed, and she searched for the logging track.

There. Just a small opening. Two deep wheel ruts.

Shit, she hoped she wouldn't bottom out.

She headed for them without caution – there was no time for it.

The wheels sank in, the front bumper gouging the loamy soil as she hit the track.

Her rev counter climbed, the tyres searching for grip, and then she was lumbering up the slope.

The sunlight died behind her and she suddenly shrouded in darkness and the smell of pine.

Up and up the track went, climbing higher as Jamie switched from first to second, second to first, looking for a route that didn't beach her or send her tumbling down the steep drop-off.

She was catching glimpses of the meadow through the trees, but the chatter of gunfire had now stopped.

The ground levelled out ahead, and Jamie eased off the throttle, now at the top of the slope.

Below, to her right, through the branches, she could just make out Sandbech's chalet. And in front of it, a loose circle of guys in black.

Jamie let the engine idle and kicked the door open, stepping onto the mount of dirt that separated the track from the bank.

Two more figures appeared now, walking from the house into the open, into the circle of men.

The man in the front was Sandbech, Jamie could tell from his shirt and the slow, laboured gait.

He wasn't walking hurriedly, but he was walking at gunpoint.

The man behind him was in black, too. From here, Jamie couldn't make anything out except his bald head and the gleam of the silver pistol in his hand, stark in the sunlight.

Sandbech turned slowly, and the man paused, the gun levelled at his head.

Everything was still, and then, without warning, he cracked Sandbech in the temple and he went to a knee.

Jamie guessed that the polite request to get on his knees went unanswered.

She watched, breathing hard, hand still on the door of the Mercedes, engine still idling.

The man stepped closer, held the pistol against Sandbech's head.

The circle of men stilled.

And then a single report from the pistol echoed around the valley.

Sandbech collapsed sideways, executed in cold blood.

Before Jamie could even react, there was a distant glint of silver, then a tiny plume of muzzle flash.

A tree two feet to the right of Jamie's head exploded in a shower of splinters and bark and she ducked, scrambling back into the cab.

She planted her foot once again, stealing only a quick glance at the bald executioner in the distance, pistol still raised towards her.

Though he didn't fire again.

He just seemed to stand there and watch as Jamie drove away.

And then he was gone, hidden behind the wall of trees, and Jamie was over the ridge and descending towards the road, wondering what the hell had just happened.

Who the man with the silver gun was, and whether now that she knew the man who'd killed her father was dead, she felt better about it or worse.

As she drove, she couldn't decide.

All she felt instead was dread.

What she'd hoped would have been an end for her had proved just the opposite.

Sandbech was dead.

But Jamie Johansson knew that this was just the beginning.

28

Two months later...

JAMIE WAS THROWING kicks into a heavy bag in her top-floor apartment in Bergen, Norway, when her phone started beeping.

She lowered her leg, sweat dripping down her forehead and beading on her collarbones, and looked at it.

Her breathing slowed as she walked across the bare boards and picked it up off the ratty table in her weekly rented one-bed. The place was a dump, but there weren't a whole lot of buildings which didn't ask questions and accepted cash.

Jamie picked up her phone and double-tapped the notification. The screen opened to show a feed from a camera she'd put on the third-floor landing, a guy walking carefully across it towards the stairs. The apartment below her was vacant – she made sure of that because she was paying for it, too – which meant this visitor was for her.

She could see a full head of dark hair, a polo shirt, a pair of jeans, boots, an upright posture, well-defined musculature. She figured him for six-foot and strong.

Jamie put her phone down, picked up the loaded Glock 19 lying next to it, and chambered a round.

A minute later, she heard the click and tap of picks in her lock, and then the door swinging open.

The guy stood, waited, listening for any hint of movement, and then entered slowly.

He looked around, moving deeper inside, eyes going over the walls decorated with photographs and newspaper clippings, yarn stretching from pin to pin, making an impenetrable web of information that it would take months to decipher – or assemble.

He stiffened visibly as the muzzle of a gun touched his ribs.

Then he moved, twisting hard, throwing his left elbow back, knocking the pistol cleanly from Jamie's grip. His right hand was rising steadily, going for her neck, his right foot tracing a path forward, ready to hook behind her heel and trip her, putting her on the ground.

But before he even managed to get his foot level with hers, the laces of Jamie's left shoe connected with his flank, hard.

His eyes widened, body stunned.

Jamie parried his rising right with her left, and fired a closed-knuckle jab right into his solar plexus.

He gasped, then took a kick to the outer thigh, and buckled.

The guy went to the ground, fighting for breath, and Jamie stared down at him.

'How did you find me?' she asked flatly.

'Don't… you…' He winced. 'Want to… know… who I

am?' he asked, American accent apparent, even in the choked-out words.

Jamie cocked her head to the side. 'FBI, CIA, I'm guessing.' She shrugged, picking up her pistol, pointing it at him. 'So I ask again, how did you find me?'

'How did you... know?'

She sighed, lowering the pistol. 'No gun drawn coming in here – I guessed you weren't coming to kill me. And only an American would be brazen enough just to pick the lock and come in unarmed. Plus, the polo shirt kind of gives it away. I thought you guys were trained to blend in.'

The guy on the ground grinned with straight white teeth. He had a thick head of dark hair, a thin layer of stubble on his angular chin, and eyes that steely colour of grey-green. 'Beau Simpson,' he said, the Southern accent coming through now. He offered his hand from his position flat on his back.

Jamie stared at it. 'Seriously? Beau Simpson? That can't be your real name.'

He sat up with some difficulty, massaging his ribs. 'My parents weren't exactly the creative type.' He fished in his pocket then and offered Jamie a black leather billfold.

She took it and opened it, seeing his FBI credentials and his name. Beau Simpson. 'You weren't kidding,' she said, tossing it back on his lap.

He held his hand out for a lift up, but Jamie was already walking away, pushing her pistol into the waistband of her workout leggings. 'You going to make me ask a third time?'

'How we found you?' He got to his feet.

Jamie turned back, nodding.

'It wasn't hard.'

'Bullshit,' Jamie said.

'Okay, it was a little hard,' he said, flashing her a smile she expected melted the hearts of all his Quantico classmates.

'Just good old-fashioned detective work. You're slick, but not a ghost.'

Jamie drew in a breath. She didn't feel like asking him to elaborate.

'But don't you want to know what I'm here for?' he asked, his voice normalising.

'I'm guessing it's something to do with Imperium Holdings.'

'Bingo. They said you were good.'

She resisted the urge to roll her eyes. 'Talk or get out. I'm busy,' Jamie said flatly.

Simpson looked around at her project wall again. 'I can see that.' He put his hands on his hips now. 'Emma Hagen.' He looked at her.

Jamie was steel.

'Good poker face.'

Jamie rolled her lips into a line. 'We done here?'

'Why are you so keen to get rid of me?'

'Oh, I don't know,' Jamie said lightly. 'How long have you got?'

'As long as you need.'

He met her eye, and they stared at each other for a few seconds.

Jamie had already made her extrapolations, but she needed to be careful. She was technically a fugitive, wanted in Sweden for the incident at the farmers' market. And every law enforcement agent across Scandinavia was scouring the continent for her. But if Simpson was here to arrest her, then *he* wouldn't be here. It would be a group of tactical officers. And they wouldn't have picked the lock. They would have caved the door in with a battering ram, thrown flashbangs, and then stormed the place.

And he wasn't here to kill her. If he was, he'd know who

she was and what she was capable of, and he'd at least be armed.

There was no way she should be conducting an investigation like this. It was tantamount to vigilantism. Which no law enforcement agency liked.

Which eliminated pretty much every other option except that they were here to ask for her help.

'I have no interest in working with the FBI,' Jamie said. 'Especially not someone who breaks into my apartment. So why don't you let yourself out, yeah? You know the way.' She needed to play her cards close to her chest.

Simpson laughed a little. 'I don't think you understand the position you're in.'

'People tell me that a lot. And yet here I am,' Jamie said tiredly. 'I'm proving hard to kill. And trust me, they've tried.'

'I don't mean with Imperium,' Simpson said then, serious all of a sudden.

'Let me guess, I've managed to piss off the FBI, too?'

'Intruding in a federal investigation is no small matter.'

Jamie was the one who laughed now. 'Tried the carrot, now the stick. I get it. So, what, either I help you out somehow, or you put me in chains and ship me off to Guantanamo?'

'That's the CIA, but about the sum of it.' Another radiant smile. Another failed attempt.

'Let's just cut to the chase then, huh? What is it that the FBI thinks I can do that they aren't able do for themselves?' Jamie folded her arms, not breaking Simpson's intense stare.

'Emma Hagen. You know the name?'

'I do. She's one of the leading lights in Høyre, the Norwegian Conservative Party. She's advocating for economic liberalisation, free-market policies, and privatisation across the board, thinly veiled as a way to alleviate the stress on the welfare state as Norway continues to move away from oil exports to renewables.'

Simpson raised an eyebrow. 'You've done your homework.'

'Skip the platitudes, okay? This handsome farm-boy act isn't going to get you anywhere.'

'I don't know what you mean?' he asked innocently, raising his eyebrows. Jeez, either he was that far up his own ass, or he genuinely didn't know he was doing it.

Jamie's silence was enough of a hint that he should just continue.

He cleared his throat. 'Hagen is being paid off by Imperium to push an agenda that will benefit them in the long term.'

Jamie nodded. 'I hope the FBI have come up with more than that.'

'Do you know who her predecessor was?'

'Stieg Lange. He went missing twelve months ago, just before Hagen stepped up.'

'Right. And you also know the circumstances surrounding his disappearance?'

Jamie bit her lip. 'Yeah, he pulled in at his home one evening. His wife heard the car arrive, and went out to check after a few minutes when he didn't come inside, found his door open and Stieg gone. His wallet was left on the floor, emptied. It was chalked up to a mugging and the investigation petered out without any leads a week later.'

'Right,' Simpson said, coming a little closer. 'Which tells you what?'

'That Imperium wanted Lange out of the way, that they already had Hagen lined up to replace him.'

'And?'

'That the Norwegian police are on the take, too.'

Simpson opened his mouth, raising his index finger.

'You say *bingo* again and I'm going to kick you.'

He closed his mouth and lowered his finger. 'Noted.'

'So, what's your plan? You want to grab Hagen, interrogate her, find out if she knows anything about Lange's disappearance? Use that to do what, exactly?' Jamie shook her head. 'If I know one thing about Imperium, it's that the people they use don't know anything about *anything.*'

'That's why we're not looking at Hagen.'

'Then who are you looking at?' Jamie tried to sound as nonplussed as she could.

'Lange. And more importantly,' Simpson said, stepping closer again and pulling a folded-up piece of paper from his pocket, offering it to Jamie. 'The man who we believe killed him.'

Jamie took the piece of paper and unfolded it. A grainy long-lens photo of a bald man stared back.

Simpson sighed. 'His name is—'

'Sandbech,' Jamie finished for him, looking up and meeting his eye. 'Yeah, we've already crossed paths.' She remembered the bald man at the chalet. Who'd executed the original Sandbech. Who'd turned and fired and nearly taken her head off from two hundred metres with a fucking pistol.

Simpson raised his eyebrows and cocked his head to the side. 'Then you're lucky,' he said. 'Most people who meet him don't stick around for long.' He sighed then. 'Sandbech's just a moniker... A call sign.'

'I know what a moniker is.' Jamie tried to keep the bite out of her voice, but the legacy of being the smartest, handsomest, most charming, naturally talented and destined-for-greatness guy in his high school obviously hadn't worn off completely, and it was rubbing her up the wrong way. Jamie wondered if that natural cockiness was what got him sent to the farthest reaches of the FBI's global network.

'We don't know his real name,' Simpson said then, trailing off slightly, looking at Jamie.

'You think I do?'

'Do you?'

She smirked. 'And what if I do?'

'Then it'd be in your best interest to tell me, and not intentionally obstruct an official federal investigation.' He tried on a menacing sort of look.

Jamie restrained a laugh. 'Gee, you *Feds* never get tired of throwing that shit around, do you?'

'Perk of the job.'

'I can tell.' Jamie tsked. 'And no, I don't know his name. But I know who trained him. Lars Sandbech. Imperium's original attack dog. Came up through Swedish special forces in the sixties and seventies, was discharged for doing some heinous shit, and Imperium snapped him up, put him to work doing what he did best.' Jamie shivered, remembering how unnerving it had been to be in the presence of a guy like that. A walking, thinking guillotine. 'Grade-A psychopath.'

'Lars Sandbech?' Simpson parroted it back, ingraining it in his mind.

Jamie nodded. 'Yeah, and Imperium had him train the guys who came after. He coined a specific way of murdering and making it look like suicide that seems to have never gone out of fashion. I guess this fucker,' Jamie said, gesturing to the photo Simpson was still holding, 'is paying homage to his teacher. Or maybe it's just a fear thing. Hell, I bet there are a dozen Sandbechs out there. It's like a ghost story – every person who gets sucked into Imperium's orbit fears Sandbech. He's everywhere. In every country. You kill one, and another Sandbech springs right up in his place.'

'Their very own bogeyman,' Simpson said, putting his hands on his hips. 'Well, this specific iteration of Sandbech seems to be one mean son of a gun.'

Son of a gun? Was this guy right out of a mail-order catalogue for good ol' boys? She could picture him on the front of a glossy magazine with cowboy boots, a plaid shirt, leaning on a fence somewhere, staring off into the distance. She figured he was from Arkansas, Oklahoma, maybe East Texas by the accent. But she didn't feel like asking that question and hearing what he thought was a 'charming' answer to it. Jamie had no doubt that there was a well-practised, woman-wooing speech memorised just for that occasion.

'He is,' Jamie said. 'But he's also smart, ruthless, very well connected, funded, and practised, too. At killing, and at not getting caught.'

'Bingo.'

Jamie fired him an icy look.

'Sorry.' Simpson cleared his throat.

'So, if you've got all this figured out,' Jamie said, 'then what do you need me for? Seems like the FBI had everything well in hand. Or are you here just to collect the information I've amassed, and then tell me to go get lost somewhere very far away?'

'Somehow I feel like you've had that mandate before and it's not one that's stuck.'

'People say I have a problem letting things go,' Jamie remarked coolly.

Simpson chuckled a little. 'No, we'd actually very much like you to stick around. You're one of the few people we trust to not be in league with Imperium somehow. And we know exactly how you feel about them. What they've done to you. Your home. Your job. Your father...'

'I'm getting really fucking sick of people throwing his

death in my face,' Jamie said, not keeping the bite from her voice this time.

Simpson squirmed a little, then regained his rugged confidence. 'What I mean is, you've already had a few brushes with Imperium. You know about their operation, you can attest to their involvement, both historical and current, in the Swedish Police Authority, and you can name names.'

It clicked. 'Ah,' Jamie said, 'now I get it.'

Simpson remained quiet.

'It's a sting. Across Norway, Sweden... I'm guessing Denmark, too? Considering that's where the nearest FBI field office is.'

The corner of Simpson's eye twitched almost impercepti-bly. But it was a tell.

She nodded to herself. 'Who's in on it, Europol? They must be heading this up – and for the FBI to have their fingers in it, it must be an American op, too. Though I'm not surprised that Imperium are tangled up in the land of opportu-nity and institutionalised capitalist corruption.'

Simpson's eye twitched again. Oh, he really was a true red-white-and-blue-blooded American. Jamie never under-stood patriotism – she was an orphan of the world.

'And I guess the Norwegian National Police Directorate are in on it. Swedish Chancellor of Justice? And the Danish Ministry of Justice, of course.'

Simpson pursed his lips. 'All I can say is that there's a multi-agency operation in place that's looking to undermine Imperium Holdings on an international scale, and remove those involved from their positions of power in governmental, civil, judicial, and civilian organisations.'

'So basically what I said.' Jamie sighed and nodded. 'And you want me to name the names that I know, go on record, offer a testimony, lay out everything I've learned so far, everything I've seen.'

'It'll be instrumental in building a case against the SPA in Stockholm especially.'

Jamie thought about it.

'We can offer you protection, if that's what you're worried about. Keep you safe,' Simpson said, convincingly, too.

Jamie scoffed a little. 'No, you can't, but that's not the problem.'

'So what's the problem?'

'I'm worried it won't be enough. To get them all. To really finish Imperium off.'

'It will,' Simpson said, again, convincingly.

'Your optimism is admirable, but Imperium have got their hooks in deep.'

'That's why we need your help.' Simpson risked another step closer, so Jamie could now make out the fine lines of his face, the flecks in his eyes. 'Testify, put names in the crosshairs. We're amassing evidence by the day. And once we get them in an interview room, start throwing around the words *witness protection*, well, they're all just gonna start singing.'

Jamie was struggling to believe him. Her cynicism far outweighed his enthusiasm. But her eyes weren't blinkered. She'd been in Bergen for three months, observing from afar, trying to put pieces together. She had information, theories, but no contacts, no support, and nothing to suggest she was about to make any strides in her own investigation. She'd been chased out of Sweden, and was hiding for all it was worth. She was on the back foot, and this was a way to get back in the game. In a serious way, too.

'Okay,' Jamie said then, nodding. 'I'll do it, but don't expect me to just sit on the sidelines.'

'What did you have in mind?' Simpson asked, playing it cool.

Jamie smirked, reading him like a book. 'Oh, I have a few ideas.'

He broke into a grin then, looked down, and shook his head. 'You know, I thought you might.'

29

SIMPSON WASN'T WORKING ALONE. Though that wasn't much of a shock.

There were other groups of agents from different agencies working in cities across Scandinavia. They were given free reign to organise their own investigations, with no oversight, and just one directive: root out Imperium's involvement in the city and provide evidence of it.

Simpson waited in the car while Jamie showered and changed, and then they drove towards Bergen's business district. A cluster of upmarket, low-rise office blocks that occupied several streets.

By all accounts, the city was relatively quiet. And certainly not one that had a major metropolitan vibe. Still, there was plenty for Imperium to be interested in. Despite its relatively small size, Bergen's position on the coast made it the central hub for international shipping, the offshore petroleum industry, and finance, too. Billions of tonnes of cargo moved through the city every year, and Imperium's interest in the place revolved around its power as an import-export behemoth.

They pulled up outside one of the office buildings, a small series of brass signs adorning the stone entryway. On the eight floors, Jamie counted two accountancy firms, two law firms, and a selection of other companies comprising people's names and ampersands. Except there were only seven nameplates.

'Come on,' Simpson said, killing the engine of the smart saloon and getting out.

He crossed the street and Jamie followed.

Simpson made no effort to check if anyone was following them, but Jamie did. And as far as she could see, they were flying under the radar. Which either meant that Simpson was very fucking good at what he did, or they'd made little headway with their operation so far. She guessed it was the latter, which is why they'd spent their time and resources tracking her down instead of trying to get a handle on Imperium's activities.

They walked into the clean and minimal lobby and headed for the bank of four lifts at the back.

The guy behind the security desk glanced up briefly, but didn't seem to even see or acknowledge Simpson. In on it? Or just genuinely disinterested in the job?

Before Jamie could make a firm assessment, they were in the lift and heading up.

They got off on the fifth floor and walked into an empty space. There was probably room for thirty, maybe forty desks, but the room was stark and bare. Grey chequerboard carpet tiles stretched from the entrance hallway to the windows at the far end, and off to both sides, where a line of doors and glass-windowed offices waited, blinds drawn.

They stood at the opening to the floor and Jamie glanced around. She spotted three, no four, concealed cameras covering the lift, and the hallway, as well as the main space from different angles. There'd be no getting in without whoever was behind them watching.

'This way,' Simpson said, walking towards the left-hand offices.

Jamie followed, pricking her ears for any hint of movement. There was nothing. The office was as good as dead.

Simpson stopped at a plain-looking wooden door and then swiped a key card through a reader tucked in the jamb. A magnetic lock released and he pushed inside. The door was sprung and heavy, and Jamie had to shoulder it open as she went through.

It closed behind her and locked instantly.

The air inside was abuzz with clacking keys, a whirring server tower, and a buzzing air conditioner.

Jamie glanced over her shoulder at the internal windows, seeing they were boarded over on the inside with metal plating. She reached out and rapped on it with her knuckles. It was solid, but lightweight.

From the outside, this looked like a normal office. In here, it was pretty much a bunker.

'Gamma titanium,' Simpson muttered, clearly proud of the cladding. 'Bulletproof, blast resistant. You never know, right?'

Jamie said nothing, just gave a polite smile and a quick nod, looking around the room.

The floor-to-ceiling windows were all tinted, making it impossible to see in from outside, and the aspect overlooked shorter buildings, so there was no way anyone could gain a vantage point to spy from.

There were four rows of desks set up in the space. The internal walls between what Jamie thought had been three neighbouring offices had been removed. It was now one large room that could have comfortably fit ten people. Though there were only two present.

Simpson walked forward, pausing at the nearest desk, which she guessed was his, and picked up a file. He opened the lid, looking at the photographs inside, and then spoke to the backs of the two other people – neither of whom seemed bothered by Jamie's presence.

'These the latest from the port authority?' Simpson asked.

A woman in her forties turned on her chair to look at him. She had a fine face, with a pointed chin and a thin nose. 'Yes, they are,' she said, her accent betraying her as Danish. Scandinavians were attuned to the difference in accents across Norway, Sweden, and Denmark, and Jamie's ability had never left her.

'No sign?' Simpson asked, watching the woman for her reaction.

She shook her head, her pinned up, chocolate-coloured hair shaking in its bun. 'Nothing,' she said, 'and we've been watching constantly.'

'Shit,' Simpson said, dropping the file. 'Ottosen,' he called then.

A guy at the far desk turned now. He had close-set eyes, round glasses, and a bald head with greying hair over his ears.

'Any chatter? Hearing anything?'

Ottosen shook his head, not saying a word. He looked sad for a moment, then turned back to his desk.

Simpson put his hands behind his head and looked at Jamie. 'Five days ago, an agent from the Norwegian NCIS went missing in the port authority. He was meeting a contact there – someone who we hoped could connect some dots for us. But he never came back.'

'The National Crime Investigation Service?' Jamie raised an eyebrow.

Simpson nodded. 'Yeah. His name was Klein.' He turned back to the room now. 'That's Caroline Vestergaard,' he pointed to the woman with the tied-up hair. 'Europol, finance expert. She's been tracking the money trails moving through Bergen. And at the back, Ottosen, from the Norwegian Intelligence Service. He's our eyes and ears.'

'And Klein?' Jamie looked at Simpson.

'He was one of our field operatives. Knew the city like the back of his hand. He was good.'

Jamie resisted the urge to say, *not that good.* She cleared her throat instead. 'And now you're at a wall?'

Simpson nodded. 'We've been pursuing the port authority lead for months now, looking for the right way in. But it looks like Imperium have caught up to us. And whatever trail was there will be buried by now.'

Vestergaard turned on her seat and nodded as if to confirm that. 'Two logistics companies that used Bergen to bring in goods from Europe have already been liquidated and broken up, assets shuffled around. Imperium will move their dealings elsewhere now that they know we're looking at Bergen.'

'Thanks, Ves,' Simpson said, nodding solemnly.

She nodded back, then returned to her screen.

'So,' Jamie said, assembling the information in her head. 'The port was your lead, and now that's gone up in smoke, you're missing a man, and trying to keep your heads above water.' She drew a breath. 'Which is why I'm here – and why you're shifting your focus to Emma Hagen and Stieg Lange.'

'They've been on our radar for a while, but the port was looking like our best bet. But now…'

'Hagen will be difficult to remove in a short timeframe. And they need her to keep their long-term goals on course,'

Jamie said, musing as much as anything. 'But they'll be tightening up across the board, now. Especially if they know you're looking at them.' She paused then. She had to ask the hard question. 'If your man, Klein, was found by Imperium – captured, even – you think this operation is still safe?'

Simpson glanced at Ves and Ottosen, who were both looking at him. 'I don't know,' he said. 'This is one of our backup sites. We moved here after Klein missed his check-in,' Simpson said. 'He didn't know about this place.' He glanced at the room again. 'None of us did. We were directed here when I reported his disappearance. Then they sent in a clean-up team, swept the old place. If Imperium do have him, all they'll find is an empty office.'

That was something, at least. 'But Klein could still name names,' Jamie said. 'He knows you guys, your faces?'

'There's that,' Simpson said, looking right at Jamie. 'He's trained not to do that sort of thing. But once you're tied to a chair and someone breaks out a pair of pliers, that training sometimes goes out the window.'

'Which is why I'm here,' she said. 'I'm guessing that before Klein disappeared, you weren't looking for me?'

'We weren't looking for you after he disappeared, either. Ves assembled a list of companies and assets that Imperium had acquired across Norway, Sweden, Finland... Bolstad Oil came up, Heikkinen Investments came up, your name came up. Then we found the incident in the farmers' market, backtracked to Ingrid Falk's death, Rasmus Allinder... And eventually, your father's. It had Imperium's stink all over it. And the way they were splashing your face across the most-wanted lists, we knew you had to be on Imperium's bad side. We figured that if you'd stayed in Sweden, something would have happened in the last few months. And we doubted you'd let it go. You already had one run-in with the Finnish police, so we figured Finland would be off the table for you. And crossing into Denmark wouldn't be easy. Which left Norway as the easiest place to go. You could probably pass for Norwegian, too, so it made sense. We dug a little deeper, found out your father spent a little time in Bergen as a child himself, so we guessed you'd probably visited as a kid, too. You knew the city a little, maybe, so we started asking around.'

Jamie was annoyed with herself that she'd made it that easy. He was right. Her father had spent time here as a child. And he'd brought her here a few times, too. Damn, she didn't even think about that, really. But it must have been in the back of her mind, the reason she chose Bergen. She'd disregarded Oslo almost immediately, too. Landed here without a second thought.

She was pissed at herself, but then again, Simpson was trained for exactly this. The FBI were the elite detectives of the US, so she wasn't wholly surprised. Though it meant if the FBI could find her, so could Imperium. 'You started asking around?'

He grinned again. 'Yeah, Ves could find no electronic trail. Nothing moving through any bank accounts – yours or anyone you were close to.'

'That must have been a long list,' Jamie muttered, still seething.

'Longer than you might think. But you were careful – either using cash or being bankrolled by someone else. We looked at the Bolstad case, and when Ves went through your bank records, saw that you paid for parking near Heikkinen Investments in Helsinki the night you get run off the road and end up in a police station in the middle of nowhere. The same night, you drop off the face of the earth, as does Simon

Heikkinen, and his daughter, Noemi. We tracked down all the assets registered to him, subpoenaed his bank accounts… All but one of his company cars are accounted for. He also moved all the money out of his business accounts into a set of protected Swiss personal accounts – as well as setting up one more and putting twenty-five thousand euros in it.' Simpson took a breath.

Jamie watched him closely, deeply interested in hearing how they'd done it, but kicking herself with every sentence.

He went on. 'We couldn't gain access to them – the point of them, really. But figuring you might be in the city, and that Heikkinen's account was how you were getting by, it was a case of narrowing down the places in the city you can live for cash, no questions, and then looking at banks and ATMs in the area for any regular, sizeable withdrawals. On the first of every month, someone was taking ten thousand Norwegian kroner out of an ATM ten kilometres from your apartment building. So we got hold of the security footage and saw you making the withdrawals at six in the morning. You were in running gear, and a quick check told us that you run. A lot. You did a series of charity half-marathons when you were at the Met. So, we figured that you'd integrated a morning workout with your rent withdrawal. We widened the search area, disregarded anything inside five kilometres, and that gave us a lot to go on. Then, it was boots on the ground,' Simpson said, playing down the sheer scale of that investigation. 'I started asking around with local landlords who rented apartments for cash. Didn't take long to find the right one.' He held his hand up, mimicking his own questioning, '"Hey, have you rented an apartment to a blonde lady, about five-five, long plait or ponytail, a real pissed-off-at-the-world kind of look on her face?"' Simpson glanced at her. 'Yeah, that look.'

Jamie turned away, screwed up her face. 'Okay, okay. What do you want, a pat on the back?'

Simpson shook his head. 'No, I just wanted you to know how serious this is, and what we're capable of. We're up against it here. We could be compromised. As you said, Klein could have rolled on us. Which means they'll be on the lookout.'

'But not for me,' Jamie finished for him.

'They don't know you're in the city. And finding and vetting agents has proved tough so far. With your experience of Imperium, you're a prime candidate to bring on board.'

She looked around at the three of them. Fuck. How could three – or even four – people hope to take on an organisation like Imperium? Even just amassing enough evidence to tackle them on a city-wide scale would prove near impossible. But as unlikely as it was for them to get anywhere as a team of four, it improved Jamie's chances from when she was going it alone. And they had the might of Europol and the Norwegian, Swedish, and Danish governments at their back. They had funding, the authority to plan and act, to get hold of bank records, surveillance tapes. Information. Data. Everything they'd need to stand a fighting chance.

Jamie let out a long breath. 'Okay,' she said. 'I'll help. Emma Hagen is a good target, and there's no doubt she's on Imperium's string. So, what's the plan?'

Simpson, now sat at his desk, rolled back a little, and surveyed Jamie. 'I'm thinking that NIS will be our best bet.'

The Norwegian Intelligence Service. What Klein was a part of.

Ves appeared on the other side of it then, folding her arms. She was taller than Jamie, and lean.

'I'd say so. Or Kripos,' she said.

The Norwegian Criminal Investigation Service.

Jamie caught on then.

'Yeah,' Simpson agreed. 'That's better. She'll be able to move a little more freely then, but still have the sort of pull she needs. Ottosen?' Simpson called.

Ottosen looked over. 'Can you get her backstory together? Get all the documents she needs. I'm thinking… *Overkonstabel?* Should be sufficient.'

Ves nodded in agreement now. 'Yeah,' she said. 'And we just put the focus on Lange. Have a mandate come down from the Ministry of Justice, that Lange's wife made a complaint, and they're looking into the case personally. That should fly.'

Simpson was stone for a few seconds. 'It's going to have to. The fewer people involved in this, the better.'

Jamie stood there like a prized ham, trying not to shift uncomfortably.

Ves bit her lip. 'No, this will work. So long as she keeps her cool, works quietly, doesn't blow her cover. Anyone who checks out her backstory should see what we want them to. Providing they don't look too closely.'

'Or know her face already,' Simpson added.

'Yeah, she's definitely got a *look.'* Ves furrowed her brow.

'A look?' Jamie asked, trying not to scowl.

'She needs a haircut,' Simpson offered.

'What's wrong with my hair?' Her voice definitely sounded strained then. She didn't do much to take care of her appearance generally, but she'd always had long hair. Always.

'It's not hard to pick you out of a crowd,' Simpson said. 'We can't risk you getting spotted. Needs to be cut and dyed.'

'Agreed,' Ves said.

'Don't I get a say?' Jamie asked, finding she was holding

onto her plait now. She hadn't even realised she'd swung it around and taken hold of it.

Simpson and Ves glanced at each other, and then back at Jamie.

And then in unison, they both said, 'No.'

30

JAMIE WAS LEANING against Simpson's desk, turning her head slowly from side to side, inspecting her new 'look' with the camera on her phone.

It was short. Really short. Especially on the back and sides, getting up to maybe five or six inches on top, where it was swept back over her head. And it was black.

'Stop playing with it,' Simpson said, glancing up from the folder he was holding.

'I still don't like it,' Jamie said, sighing, trying to ruffle the mop on top into something she didn't hate.

'You don't have to like it,' Simpson said. 'But it's necessary.'

Jamie was about to offer a witty, cutting retort when Simpson's phone buzzed on his desk and he picked it up.

'They're here,' he said, getting up and straightening his belt. 'Coming up in the elevator. You sure about this?'

Jamie nodded, going for the door. 'One hundred per cent.'

He let out a long breath. 'Okay, well, you're the one who's going out there. This is on you.'

Jamie paused at the threshold of the heavy door and looked back. 'It'll be fine.'

Simpson held his hands up and gestured Jamie out into the empty office.

In the distance, the elevator dinged, and then a voice filled the space.

'—I still don't understand why you can't tell me what it is that the Chancellor of Justice wants with—' Julia Hallberg cut herself off, standing at the corner of the open office, with Ves at her shoulder, looking formal and dignified. The only look she had.

Hallberg's eyes widened, mouth open, eyes fixed on Jamie.

Jamie took a few steps forward, closing the gap. 'Hallberg,' she said, 'I'm sorry we couldn't tell you any—'

Jamie didn't get to finish before Hallberg ran forward and damn near tackled her.

Hallberg's arms locked around Jamie's ribs and she squeezed her tightly enough that it made it hard to breathe.

'Hallberg,' Jamie forced out, reluctantly taking the woman in her arms.

'Jesus, Jamie,' she said, not letting go. 'I thought you were dead.'

Jamie prised her off. 'Not yet,' she said, offering a tentative smile.

'I barely recognised you,' Hallberg said then, shaking her head. 'What happened to your hair?'

Jamie fired a glance at Simpson. 'Don't ask.'

'No, it suits you.' She grinned.

'Thank you!' Simpson chimed in.

'Don't encourage him,' Jamie pleaded.

But Hallberg's attention had already shifted to Simpson, and she girlishly brushed her own hair behind her ear.

'Beau Simpson,' Simpson said, offering a hand. 'Nice to meet you, ma'am.'

Christ, he was really hamming up that East Texas drawl.

Jamie didn't try to hide her eye roll.

Simpson was unphased by it.

'Polisassistent Julia Hallberg,' Hallberg said formally, shaking his hand. 'Stockholm Polis.'

'I know,' Simpson said, offering her a toothy grin. 'I read your file. Very impressive.' He stuck out his bottom lip, nodding. 'Especially for someone so young. The FBI is proud to have an exemplary agent like you working alongside us.'

Hallberg blushed violently.

Jamie nearly gagged.

'I'm, uh,' Hallberg began, looking down, 'glad to be here. How can I help?'

Jamie stepped away, let Simpson explain the situation. All Hallberg was told was that the Swedish Chancellor of Justice was assembling a small team of detectives to assist with an ongoing investigation that needed extra manpower. A simple cover story, but an effective one. It wasn't that rare for detectives to be called up like that. Especially ones with a record like Hallberg's. She was prime material to leapfrog out of the regular SPA and into the security or intelligence services. She was smart as hell, had an eye for detail, numbers, data. And she was shaping up to be decent in the field, too. So, Jamie hoped that it wouldn't raise too many flags or eyebrows.

Ves was coming over as Simpson gave Hallberg a quick debrief on the current situation, and what she'd be doing here.

Jamie grabbed Ves's attention and waved her over towards the window, meeting her there.

'Okay?' Ves asked.

'Any word on our other recruit?' Jamie asked, playing it down.

Ves read her face for a moment, then spoke. 'Detective Wiik is still on leave. He's in Gothenburg, and has been for several months.'

Jamie nodded. 'That's where his son is. Things must have got too hot in Stockholm,' she said, remembering the letter and the mysterious website.

Ves offered no opinion on that. 'Three days after the incident at the farmers' market in Stockholm, he filed a request to be put on administrative leave due to his mental state, citing ongoing depression due to his injuries.'

Jamie listened to that. Wiik may have been depressed, but he would never admit it. He was far too stubborn. And he'd never let it prevent him from doing his job either. Which meant he'd heeded Jamie's advice and got the fuck out of there.

'Do you know if he's alright?' Jamie asked, keeping her voice low.

'His bank statements show that he's actively paying for his hotel stay, as well as other things – dinners, museums, video games.'

'For his son.' Jamie answered her own question before she even asked it. 'At least he's spending time with him,' she said, relieved. 'That's good.'

Ves just sort of stood there.

Wiik's relationship with his ex wasn't really talked about. But in the three months they'd worked together, he'd not ever fielded a call from her, or made any mention of seeing his son. So Jamie had come to the conclusion that their parting probably wasn't amicable, and that custody had gone pretty much solely to his ex-wife.

Whether he'd been forced to flee the city, or just thought it was good sense, Jamie was glad to hear that he was putting his time off to good use.

And while having him here for what came next was what Jamie wanted, she couldn't pull him away from Gothenburg and into this. No, Hallberg would have to do. And at least now she could put that anger she felt at the way Falk's death was handled to good use.

Jamie steeled herself, nodded a quick thanks to Ves, and then went back to Simpson and Hallberg. He was gesturing dynamically, making sure to show off just how tight his polo shirt was, while Hallberg was nodding along, trying to keep her eyes on his and not on his biceps. He was in the process of explaining how they'd been tracking Imperium's money trails, and how they'd ingrained themselves in every level of government, law enforcement, and business.

Hallberg seemed to be taking it all in her stride, but then again, she'd known something was up since Falk, and Wiik must have looped her in to some degree with the whole secret website thing.

Jamie cleared her throat and Simpson glanced at her, arms up, showcased gloriously.

'Hallberg,' she said, 'you want to come with me and actually do some police work, or stay here for the second act?'

Hallberg laughed nervously. It was weirdly loud.

Then she cleared her throat, gave Simpson a quick, polite smile, and nodded to Jamie. 'Of course,' she said diligently. 'I'm ready when you are.'

'Good,' Jamie said. 'Because there's a shitload to do and not a minute to waste.' She was moving then, back into the office.

Ves was already at her desk, and Ottosen was at his.

'Ves, Ottosen,' Jamie announced, gesturing at a free desk for Hallberg.

She went and sat down, spinning on her chair to look at Jamie.

Ves and Ottosen were both doing the same.

'Okay, so now that we're all here, let's get things going. Hallberg, get acquainted with Ottosen. You'll be working closely with him – he can get you any accesses you need. There's a file on your desk that details the disappearance of Stieg Lange, a politician here in Bergen. We have reason to believe his replacement, Emma Hagen, is on Imperium's payroll as they work towards a privatised economic agenda.'

All eyes were on Jamie.

Simpson had slunk back into the room and was hovering behind her. Jamie could feel him wanting to interject, but she carried on regardless.

'Hallberg, I want you to dig into the Lange case. Imperium have an operative going by the name Sandbech. He's been spotted here in Bergen, and is also the prime suspect in the murder of Ingrid Falk.'

Hallberg's nostrils visibly flared, her posture stiffening slightly.

Good. She still gave a damn then. She'd need that drive.

'There's no reason to believe Lange is alive,' Jamie went on, 'but it's likely that before he was removed, that Imperium contacted and tried to coerce him. We'll need to line up interviews with his widow, as well as the two detectives who worked the case.'

Hallberg nodded decisively.

'Ottosen can pull the case file from the Norwegian police's database. I want you to learn it back to front, okay? Then, see what security footage you can pull from that day – traffic cameras from his office to home. I want to know if he was followed and if we can see where the guys who grabbed him came from.'

Another nod from Hallberg.

'After that,' Jamie said, 'work with Ves, comb through

bank records, holdings, everything on the two detectives who swept up Lange's case. I want to know how they were plied, and how much it took. I want to go into this with our eyes wide open. Got all that?'

The corner of Hallberg's mouth curled almost imperceptibly. She gave one final nod, and then turned and opened the file in front of her, hunching over it.

Jamie exhaled, turning to meet Simpson's gaze, which was burning into the side of her head.

'Don't you think that's kind of a lot of legwork?' he asked, keeping his voice hushed.

Jamie smirked. 'You *obviously* don't know Julia Hallberg. For anyone else, sure. For her?' She laughed. 'It's barely a warm-up.'

31

'STIEG LANGE DISAPPEARED at around seven fifteen on the nineteenth of September.'

Jamie drove quickly, with Hallberg in the passenger seat. She had a copy of the case report open in front of her, reading it aloud as they closed in on his address.

They'd both pored over it a hundred times already. Probably more.

Their new badges sat on the dashboard, still fresh from the printer. Both displayed the initials and branding of Kripos, the Norwegian Criminal Investigation Service.

Jamie was going by Overkonstabel Karla Janssen.

And Hallberg's said Konstabel Lillian Heller

It was common practice to keep names fairly close to the original in security services. It made remembering them that much easier. Hallberg's face would be unknown to Imperium, at least that's what they hoped. But still, they couldn't take any chances. She'd had a haircut, too, her tight ponytail now a shoulder-length, wavy side part. Her colour was lightened, too, to a deep chestnut. Jamie didn't hate it at all. Which made her hate her own new cut even more.

Hallberg had called Lange's wife, Nina, the day before, and arranged the meeting. She'd not said anything over the phone other than that they wanted to go over the events of what had happened, and that some new information may have come to light. She had to keep it vague, just in case. There was no way to tell how ingrained Imperium were in Bergen, and whether it was beyond them to be tapping phones and monitoring lines. Kripos, like any other security agency, had airtight background checks, and with their continual monitoring of everyone with any sort of clearance, it was a relatively safe bet that Imperium's reach was halted at the door, or at least limited . But that didn't mean they could be sloppy. And whether Imperium could get any details on an open Kripos case or not was irrelevant, because if they could connect the dots enough to know Kripos was looking at them, they'd button up any loose ends.

If Nina Lange knew anything serious, Jamie suspected she'd already be dead. But they had to start somewhere, and they wanted some background on Stieg before zeroing in on the two detectives responsible for the case.

Jamie pulled in at the kerb outside the smart two-storey home with a sloping roof, wooden cladding, and large windows. There was a new BMW estate on the drive, and a well-manicured lawn told Jamie that there was no shortage of upkeep going on. The house itself was expensive, but Nina Lange didn't work. She'd given up her job four years prior to support Stieg's political career full-time.

Hallberg and her both had their heads on a swivel as they exited the rental car with swapped plates that Ottosen had done some magic with and listed in the official Kripos assets database, and headed for the front door.

Jamie was leading, blowing her errant, overly long fringe out of her mouth as she went. It was supposed to be swept back, and was for the most part, but one strand seemed to have a mind of its own.

She knocked, spitting out the hair and planting it behind her ear, and waited.

She and Hallberg were both wearing trouser suits. Jamie's was grey, with a black turtleneck under it and a pair of low-heeled Chelsea boots below. God, she hated heels. Of any kind.

Hallberg's was navy, with a quarter-collared linen blouse. She seemed more comfortable in heels. But the beads of sweat around the corner of her jaw and the way she kept smacking her lips told Jamie she was nervous.

Jamie looked over, gave her a little nod, then a smile.

Hallberg looked down, exhaled, and then nodded back, clenching and unclenching her hands, and wiping them on the hips of her trousers.

The door opened in front of them and a smartly dressed woman in her sixties stared back. She had a lined mouth and the taut cheeks of someone who was no stranger to Botox, a thick head of dyed, dark hair that framed her face, and a ruffled red blouse. As well as a glass of red wine hanging loosely in her hand.

It was eleven in the morning.

'*Ja?*' she asked, her eyes not focusing on either of them. Yes?

Jamie wondered if it was her first of the day, whether it was because of their impending visit, or simply a daily routine.

'Karla Janssen,' Jamie said, holding her badge up. *'Norsk Sikkerhetsetterretningstjeneste.'* Norwegian Security Intelligence Service. 'Would you mind if we spoke in English?'

The woman's eyes narrowed for a brief second, and then

she seemed to decide she didn't really care why. 'Fine,' she said in curt English. 'I suppose you wish to come in?'

Jamie lowered her badge, and Hallberg kept hers in her hand. Nina Lange didn't seem to care who she was – or at least wasn't especially interested in seeing her credentials.

Jamie had a whole thing planned about their reason to switch to English. It was reasonably close to the truth. She was going to say that she'd transferred to Kripos from the Danish Intelligence Service, as her husband was Norwegian. And that while her Norwegian was more than passable – which it was – her English was better and she wanted to make sure everything was perfectly clear to everyone there.

But again, Nina Lange didn't seem to give a shit.

Before Jamie or Hallberg could even reply, she turned and walked back into the house, her bare feet slapping on the hardwood floors.

Hallberg closed the door behind them and they both followed her inside.

A rack of shoes was sitting in the hallway. The top shelf was all men's, the bottom all women's. And both full.

Jamie wasn't sure if they were supposed to take theirs off, but Nina Lange didn't request it and wasn't around to be asked.

They kept them on, wiping on the bristled welcome mat before entering, and then headed after Lange.

At the end of the hall, the room opened out into a large kitchen and living room with a tall, sloping roof fitted with skylights. The day was cloudy and grey, but the room was still bright.

A clock ticked on the wall and the spotless kitchen gleamed in white marble and gloss black.

Nina Lange had moved behind a wide marble-topped

island and was standing there with her glass of wine, a bottle next to her. 'Well?' she asked tiredly.

Jamie let her eyes drift slowly around the show-home-clean room and fall on Lange. 'Thank you for agreeing to see us,' Jamie said.

'You said you have information about Stieg's disappearance?' She raised an eyebrow, the rest of her face unmoving.

Jamie offered a condolatory smile. 'Not as such. We're simply retreading the ground that the Bergen police have, making sure that nothing was missed.'

Lange scoffed.

'We were hoping to ask a few questions about that night, and the weeks leading up to it, if we could?'

Lange drained her glass, proffered her hand for Jamie to go on, and then refilled it from the bottle.

Jamie kept her smile in place. 'Before Stieg disappeared, did he speak to you about being approached by anyone?'

Nina Lange stopped, her glass halfway to her lips. 'Like who?'

Jamie shook her head and shrugged lightly. 'I don't know. Perhaps someone interested in contributing to his campaign? A new potential donor or backer?'

'My husband wasn't corrupt, if that's what you're asking,' she said haughtily, taking another drink.

Jamie watched her, seeing a perceptive, intelligent woman in front of them. Anything someone said under the influence of alcohol was difficult to use in court. Any solicitor worth their salt would call it a he-said, she-said situation, argue coercion due to inebriation, mistaken testimony, or any other of a number of ways a drunken statement could get thrown out. And Jamie had a feeling that Nina Lange knew that. And that asking skirting questions wasn't going to get them anywhere.

'Let's just cut to the chase then, shall we?' Jamie asked, coming forward to the island.

Hallberg stayed back.

'Please do,' Nina said. 'As you can see, you're keeping me from my busy schedule.' She gestured around to the silent house for emphasis.

'Your husband was abducted. That much we know for certain. What we don't know is why. While the police attested that it was financially motivated, usually in circumstances like this, a ransom is requested. Mr Lange's bank accounts remained untapped, his car was left in the driveway, his phone, too. None of his credit cards have been used, despite being stolen.'

'What are you getting at?'

'That something else was going on,' Jamie said flatly. 'We have no reason to suspect that Mr Lange was involved in any sort of corruption.' In fact, it's likely he refused an advance, and that was why he was killed, she felt like saying. 'But we cannot rule any possibilities out as of yet. Yourself included.'

'What do you mean, "yourself included"?' Nina asked coldly, putting the wine glass down hard enough that the dark liquid sloshed and spat itself onto the counter.

Jamie could tell already that if Nina Lange knew anything about Stieg's disappearance – or at least anything to do with Imperium, whether she knew them by name or not – that she wouldn't say it. Not for fear of her own life, at least.

Which meant if she wanted any truth, she'd need to take off the kid gloves and back Nina into a corner.

She settled herself, then went in hard. 'From where I'm standing,' Jamie said, 'with no seeming motive for the attack, no ransom, no threats made to Stieg, no involvement in corruption, and generally glowing character references, the only person who really stood to benefit from his disappear-ance… was you.'

The woman in front of Jamie stiffened, her jaw clenching in immediate, frozen rage.

'I'm going to ask you a direct question, that I'd like you to answer,' Jamie continued. 'Because it will be just as easy to find out for ourselves after we leave if you don't. And if you make us do that, it won't look good for you.'

The woman glared at Jamie.

'How are you affording to live here considering you're not working?' Jamie already knew the answer but wanted to hear it from her.

'Stieg,' Nina said, 'had a healthy life insurance indemnity that paid out after his disappearance.'

Jamie nodded. 'Interesting. Did they pay out based on his status as "disappeared"?'

'I don't understand what you're asking?'

'Stieg Lange was declared officially dead two months after he disappeared, correct?'

'Why ask,' Nina practically spat, 'if you already know the answer?'

'Honestly, because your reaction tells me more than the truth.'

There was silence in the house then, filled only by the ticking of the clock.

'You fell behind on the mortgage payment on this house the month after Mr Lange disappeared. The following month, he was declared dead, the policy was paid out, and the mort-gage has been taken care of since,' Jamie stated.

'Your point?'

'My point is that of all the people who were affected by Mr Lange's disappearance, you benefited the most.'

'Benefited?' She shook her head in disgust. 'Is that what

you call losing your husband? Having him taken from you? Kidnapped, killed, or—'

'Killed?' Jamie interjected, and Nina fell quiet. 'My question, Mrs Lange, is whether you know for a fact that your husband is dead, whether you took a gamble on it to get the insurance policy to payout, or whether it was pre-planned?'

Nina's pulse had quickened. Jamie could see it in the woman's neck. It was one of the reasons she wanted to get in close.

'Your husband's position in Høyre meant that he had a lot of weight when it came to pushing for policy change. It seems odd to me that during his tenure, those policies remained largely unchanged. And then, without warning or prior threat, he mysteriously disappears, and then his replacement steps up, and immediately pushes for changes to those long-standing policies – most of which stand in opposition to what Stieg stood for.'

'Your point?' Nina Lange said through gritted teeth, her knuckles around the base of her wine glass, ready to snap it.

'My point is that this whole incident is about to come under a very bright spotlight. And currently, I have two burgeoning theories. Either Stieg was forcibly removed from Høyre, as he wasn't willing to change his policies – and that you know more than you're letting on about why that happened. Or, what seems *more* likely, considering his prominence and position in the public eye, is that Stieg Lange – the handsome, charismatic, smart man that he was – was having an affair, or several, and that you found out about it. Then, you had him update his life insurance policy, made a plan, had him kidnapped, waited what seemed like an appropriate and unsuspicious amount of time – let's say, until after the investigation had concluded with zero evidence and no suspects – and then cashed in on his demise. And now here you are, without a care in the world. Sipping wine. At eleven in the morning. On a Tuesday.'

She met Jamie's eye, staying stock-still. And then smirked. And then she laughed. A little at first, then a full-blown, hysterical howl.

Jamie kept her face straight.

'Wow. No wonder they fucked up the original investigation so badly. If you are the best this county has to offer, I shudder to think what they left behind at the *normal* police.' Nina Lange shook her head, her laughter turning to utter disdain. 'I think it's time for you to leave.'

'If we're wrong,' Jamie said, 'then you need to give me something else to go on. Otherwise, we'll tear your life apart, piece by piece. And Stieg's. And every skeleton in the *numerous* closets I'm sure this lovely home has, will all be dragged out and shown to the world.'

'Is that a threat?'

'A statement of fact,' Jamie said.

'Get out.'

'Did you kill your husband?' Jamie asked.

'No. Now get out.'

'Do you know for certain he's dead?'

She couldn't say no, as she'd be admitting to defrauding the insurance company. She also couldn't say yes without admitting to something else.

'Please leave now,' Nina Lange said.

'We're not finished. And we can either do this here, or at Kripos HQ. Your choice.'

She shook her head again, leaning forward, staring down into her glass. 'You honestly have no idea, do you? About anything? How can you stand there and accuse me of… Accuse Stieg of… We loved each other.' Her eyes snapped up to Jamie's, shining with tears. 'Like you'll never understand.

How could you?' She tsked. 'Look at you. You've never known a day of real love in your life!'

Jamie tried to hold her straight face.

'If you had,' Nina went on, her tone growing venomous, 'you'd never ask me these questions, never say these things. Not to me. Not to a wife who gave up her husband!'

'Gave up?' Jamie asked, focusing on the woman's face.

Nina's lip quivered for an instant, and then she regained herself. 'Yes, gave up. Gave up hope! Accepted that if he was alive, if there was any chance of him coming back, that he would have. He would have returned to me. And everyone knows that. They know how much we loved each other. So to give him up – and accept that he was gone… That is what true sacrifice is. That is what true love is.' She stared at Jamie, who stared back. 'I wouldn't expect you to understand,' she said then. 'How could I?'

Jamie swallowed, offered a quick, difficult smile. 'Thank you, Mrs Lange,' Jamie said then. 'We'll see ourselves out.'

She turned, motioned Hallberg towards the door, and then they both left the house.

Jamie swallowed again on the way down the drive, trying to shift the lump in her throat.

When the car door closed, Hallberg finally spoke.

'That wasn't what we agreed,' she said, the respect in her voice meagre.

'Simpson's approach wasn't working,' Jamie said, her words half-choked. 'I had to improvise.'

'Improvise?' Hallberg blew air out of her nose. 'I'd say that was a little more than thinking on your feet. You accused her of killing Lange! You can't think that's remotely a possibility?'

'I don't,' Jamie said, cranking the ignition.

'So then what was the plan? Get her flustered enough to reveal that Lange had been approached by Imperium?'

'No,' Jamie said then, leaning her head back. 'Because Imperium would never have given their name in that situation. They would have been acting as a potential campaign donor – probably through someone who's already donated to other campaigns. Or a previous donor, even. They could move money to Lange that way without raising eyebrows that way. And approach him without it even looking like corruption.'

'So you *do* think she had him killed?' Hallberg didn't seem to be following Jamie's train of thought.

'Yes,' Jamie said plainly.

'So… *she's* in on it with Imperium?'

Jamie cracked a smile and looked at Hallberg then. 'Not quite. I think she planned his disappearance. But didn't do it alone.'

'Someone helped her get rid of Stieg?' Hallberg asked. 'Who?'

Jamie slotted the car into drive and pulled away. 'Stieg.'

'Yeah. But who helped her?' Hallberg was watching Jamie.

'Stieg.'

'I don't understand?'

Jamie slowed for a junction, checked left and right, and then pulled onto the main road and accelerated away. 'Stieg Lange is still alive, Hallberg,' she said, glancing at her partner. 'I think he and his wife staged the whole thing.'

Hallberg was stunned. 'And you're basing that off what?'

'Just a feeling.'

Hallberg drew in a slow breath. 'I was there through that entire interview, and I don't know where you're getting that from, but... you and your damn hunches.' She shook her head. 'Okay, so Stieg Lange is still alive.'

'You believe me?'

'You're usually not wrong about these things,' Hallberg said, laughing a little. 'So where do we start?'

'Well, I guess now we find Stieg Lange,' Jamie said.

'Any ideas how we do that?'

Jamie laughed now. 'Well, now that's your domain. I'm just the one with the hunches, remember?'

32

SIMPSON WAS SITTING BACK in his chair, his hand on his forehead, eyes closed. 'So you're saying you think Stieg Lange is *alive*... based on... his wife saying that she "gave him up"?' He looked at Jamie, who was leaning against his desk.

'Yes,' Jamie said, nodding.

'You realise that isn't proof, right? It's not anything. In fact, it's exactly *nothing*.' Simpson laughed a little.

Jamie drew a slow breath, keeping herself calm. 'You can believe me or not, but I'm telling you, Lange is alive. And his wife knows it.'

'But she didn't tell you?' Simpson said. 'She didn't say anything close. She declared him dead as well, right?'

'You know she did,' Jamie said, keeping her voice even.

'So then I don't understand what we're talking about.' He met Jamie's eye. 'Because we have a plan, don't we? One we agreed on. One which you pretty much formulated *yourself.* Which includes a set of carefully measured steps that take us from where we are now – which is nowhere – to being in Emma Hagen's face and getting her to roll on Imperium.'

'That was before I spoke to Nina Lange,' Jamie said. 'Now the plan has changed.'

'No,' Simpson said, cutting the air with his hand. 'The plan hasn't changed. The plan is solid. All you have is a hunch based on something that a grieving, half-drunk woman said. Hallberg?' he called then.

Hallberg, who was sitting at her desk, stiffened a little behind Jamie.

Simpson went on. 'You were there, what do you think?'

'Don't drag her into this,' Jamie snapped. 'Don't put her in the middle.'

'I have to, Jamie. Because all of our evidence says one thing – as did your calculated decision based on it – that Stieg Lange is dead. And that's what the whole investigation hinges on. And yet, you get in a room with the first person we needed to speak to, and five minutes later, you want to flip this whole thing on its head. So yeah, I am pulling Hallberg into this, because I'm hoping she's going to be the voice of reason here. I didn't think you'd be the gut-feelings-and-hunches kind of detective – I was under the impression you knew how investigative work was *actually* done.'

Hallberg cleared her throat, holding her hand up. 'It may not be solid, but…' She glanced at Jamie, then back at Simpson. '… she's rarely wrong about this kind of thing.'

'But not infallible,' Simpson added.

Jamie kept quiet.

Simpson let the tension ease slightly before he spoke again. 'Whether Lange is alive or not, we don't have the resources to pursue that right now. So we stay on course, and on topic. Because whether his wife and he concocted it, or Imperium snatched him up and dumped him in a ditch, the intel suggests that he was approached, refused their offer, and then disappeared as a result. From where I'm sitting, the facts remain unchanged, and Emma Hagen remains the prime target here.'

'But if we can find Lange,' Jamie said, 'he's far more likely to cooperate. He already has a reason to.'

'Which is what?' Simpson seemed bored with the conversation.

'That he wants to return to his wife. They miss each other – she said it herself that they were inseparable. In love. And if we can promise him total protection for his cooperation, they can both disappear together this time.'

'Is this how they do police work in Stockholm? On *ifs* and vague assumptions?' He shook his head. 'The plan doesn't change. Now don't make me be the bad guy and tell you to do your fucking job, okay, Johansson? We're all working towards a common goal here.' He met her cold gaze. 'Go for a walk or something, cool off, think about which team you're on, and then come back when you're ready to get back to work.'

Simpson, for a sweeter-than-apple-pie farm boy from Texas, had a well-practised assertiveness.

Jamie took his advice. Things here were at a tipping point and she didn't feel like banging her head against the wall anymore. She rose from the desk and headed for the door. As she got through it, she found Hallberg right on her shoulder.

Neither of them spoke until they were on the street and away from the door; the cameras watching the elevator and front door recorded audio, too.

Hallberg spoke first. 'You actually going to drop it this time?'

Jamie rounded on her. 'What's that supposed to mean?'

'Well, you sort of have a habit of ignoring orders when you think you're right.'

Jamie opened her mouth, but didn't really have a retort to

that.

'I'm not saying you're wrong,' Hallberg went on, 'or that Simpson's right. I think there's a chance that Lange could be alive, and I trust your instincts, probably more than anyone's. But he has a point. Our evidence supports our current plan, and if Stieg is alive, then he doesn't want to be found. Which means that doing it isn't going to be easy. And we are just five people. And Imperium is a lot bigger than that. So forget Simpson, it's me asking – just let this sit, okay? Not let it go, not forget about it – just... don't lose sight of what we're doing, as a *team*. Okay, Jamie?'

Jamie had her teeth fastened together, but she managed a little nod. 'Sure, Hallberg,' she said. 'I'll be a team player.'

Hallberg tried to catch her eye and failed. Then she sighed. 'Somehow, I don't quite believe you.'

Jamie looked at her. 'I'm not really selling it, huh?'

Hallberg cracked a little smile. 'No, not really.' She looked out at the road then. The people moving along with their suits and briefcases on the opposite pavement, the cars sliding past, the seagulls cawing and wheeling in circles overhead. 'Come on, we should get back,' she said.

'You going to tell Simpson?' Jamie asked, walking with her.

'That you're going to disobey a direct order and risk the entire operation? No, I think I'll just play dumb when it blows up in your face.'

'That's probably the safest move,' Jamie said. Then she paused and touched Hallberg on the arm.

She looked back.

'You know I'd never do anything to put you in danger, right?' Jamie said, inspecting her reaction.

'I know,' Hallberg replied, offering her a lukewarm smile. 'At least, not intentionally.'

33

JAMIE AND HALLBERG pulled up outside a low-rise apartment block in a reasonable part of the city, and got out. The air was cooler here, and the smell of the coast was thick in the air.

They hadn't called ahead or contacted her, but they knew that Maria Bohle, Stieg Lange's former secretary, was home. They'd been watching her routine, and knew that she worked an early-morning shift at a telecoms company, six until three. And she got home by half-past.

It was a step down from secretary to someone like Stieg Lange, but her apartment was still decent, so the pay couldn't be all bad. Either that or she'd had some sort of money come to her from Imperium.

As they approached the door, Jamie sighed. She didn't like being this cynical, but it felt like Imperium had their hooks into everything. Had poisoned everyone. And it was making her paranoid.

She did what detectives often did when they wanted to surprise someone in an apartment building, and rang every bell but the one they were there for.

A voice rang out of the intercom – a woman. '*Ja, hallo?*' She sounded hurried.

Jamie cleared her throat. 'My name is Karla Janssen. I'm with the Norwegian Security Intelligence Service. We're here to see one of your neighbours. Can you open the door?'

There was silence for a second, then she spoke again. 'Can you hold your badges up to the camera?'

Jamie and Hallberg obliged and held them up.

The door buzzed, and they pushed through, heading for Bohle's apartment.

Jamie let Hallberg catch her breath – she'd not hung around on the stairs – and then knocked.

There was shuffling inside, then the door opened to the chain, a woman's face appearing in the gap. Maria Bohle was in her late twenties, with shoulder-length, wavy blonde hair and a narrow, petite nose. '*Ja?*' she asked, looking from Jamie to Hallberg.

They produced their badges again.

'Karla Janssen, Kripos,' Jamie said.

'Lillian Heller,' Hallberg added.

'Can we come inside?' Jamie said, sliding her foot forwards slightly to catch the door if she tried to close it.

'What is this about?'

The woman already had that look about her that set Jamie's teeth on edge, that slightly wide-eyed, surprised, and frightened look that people had when you caught them doing something they shouldn't be.

Jamie smiled warmly. 'We've been instructed to look into the disappearance of Stieg Lange. We'd just like to go over the witness statement you gave to the detectives during the initial investigation. Would that be alright?'

She looked over her shoulder, two hands on the door. 'I'm

a little busy at the moment,' she said. 'It's not really a good time.'

'What are you busy with?' Jamie asked.

She swallowed. 'I, uh,' she floundered, then regained herself. 'I'm on a video call.'

'With who?'

'My... my...' she began, knowing she was going further down the rabbit hole with every word. She seemed to change then, and smiled back. 'You know what? It's fine, I can call them back.' She closed the door before Jamie could speak and slid the chain off.

Jamie glanced at Hallberg, who offered a little eyebrow raise, and then the door was opening and they were walking in.

Maria Bohle was retreating quickly across the room towards the dining table that sat in front of the sizeable window. She pushed the lid of her laptop closed quickly with a little slap – likely to hide the fact that there was no video call. Though it did little to convince Jamie of anything other than the fact there wasn't one to begin with.

The apartment was a bright, well-appointed one-bed with hardwood floors and white paint. It wasn't audacious by any stretch – and it looked to suit the earnings of someone in Bohle's position.

She was looking at Jamie and Hallberg then. 'Tea? Coffee?' she asked.

They both shook their heads and Jamie gestured to the table. 'Let's just sit,' she said. 'This shouldn't take long.'

Bohle hovered for a moment, then obliged. 'Of course,' she said. 'Sorry, you just caught me a little off guard.'

Off guard? What did she need to be *on* guard over?

Jamie studied her as they sat.

Bohle made a point of pulling her laptop over to her side of the table, as well as her phone, which was next to it.

They were now out of easy reach of both Jamie and Hallberg, both of whom were making sure not to draw more attention to them than necessary. They needed Bohle to feel comfortable, to be truthful. They had no reason to get her all bent out of shape until they knew what she was hiding.

'As we said,' Jamie started casually, 'we're just looking to go over the original investigation into Stieg Lange's disappearance. After so much time and with no new leads developing, we'd just like to make sure nothing has been missed.' She gave Bohle a smile. 'You submitted a witness statement during the investigation, but if we can, we'd like to just go over it. Would that be okay with you?'

Maria Bohle swallowed, breaking eye contact. 'It's such a long time ago,' she said, brushing hair out of her eyes. 'I don't think – I mean, I don't know if I'll be able to remember everything.'

'That's fine,' Jamie said. 'Just tell us what you remember.' She glanced at Hallberg, who produced a notepad and a pen. 'Ready?' she asked Bohle.

Bohle nodded.

'You left your post at the office when Emma Hagen was appointed as Mr Lange's replacement, is that correct?' Jamie asked, just going over some facts to get Bohle comfortable.

She nodded. 'Yes, I continued to work through the investigation, just taking calls and that kind of thing,' she said. 'But then when Ms Hagen arrived for her first day, she gave me a letter saying that I was no longer needed. She gave me six months of full pay and said she'd write a recommendation for me if I needed one.'

'That's generous of her,' Jamie said. 'Did you have any other contact with her?'

A shake of the head. No, of course not. Emma Hagen would have wanted to clean house, start fresh with her own people.

'How did you react when you first found out that Mr Lange was missing?'

'I was…' Bohle began, taking time over her words, 'saddened. I was worried for him.'

'So, you and Mr Lange were close?'

'Close?' Bohle seemed disconcerted by the question.

'Professionally. You worked for him for two years?'

'Oh,' she said. 'Yes, I did.'

'What did you think I meant?' Jamie asked, keeping her smile.

'Nothing, I don't know,' Bohle said, shaking her head.

'You and Mr Lange were never romantically involved?'

'No!' she said it quickly this time, almost forcefully.

Too quickly? Jamie let it slide. She'd get it out of her soon enough. 'Did you miss many days? To sickness, or holiday?'

She shook her head again. 'No, I was there all the time. I don't think I took a single sick day while I was working. And I was only off when Mr Lange was.'

Jamie took a mental note. 'Great. And in the weeks and months leading up to his disappearance, did anything seem amiss or off?'

Hallberg hovered with her pen.

Bohle looked at her, then back at Jamie. 'No,' she said, shaking her head.

'Just no?'

She shrugged then, shook her head again. 'No, everything seemed normal.'

'Any unscheduled meetings or drop-ins? Any meetings with anyone out of the ordinary?'

'Mr Lange met with hundreds of different people, and all of them were scheduled.'

'Did you handle all of his scheduling?'

'Yes, all of his meetings were arranged by me.'

Jamie drew a breath, choosing her next move. 'And how did you schedule them?'

'Using the online diary software at the office.'

'Would his schedule still be on there?' Jamie asked lightly.

'I would think so – but after his disappearance, the Bergen police took the hard drive from my computer, and his laptop, too.'

Jamie nodded, knowing that it would have been corrupted, wiped, damaged, or any other number of things during the investigation that would make accessing that data impossible now. Fucking Imperium. 'What about paper copies? Did Mr Lange ever keep a personal diary or note-book, or—'

'He had his own diary, yes,' Bohle said. 'Every morning, he would give it to me, to transcribe his schedule for the day. And if he needed to take any notes, he'd make them in there. He never went anywhere without it.'

'And I suspect that the police took that, too?' Jamie asked.

'I don't know,' Bohle said, glancing down at her phone, despite it not ringing. 'They cleared out his office, took everything, the diary, too, I think.'

Jamie hadn't seen it on the list of evidence they'd logged. But it wasn't going to be difficult to misplace something like that.

'What about threats?' she asked then. 'Anyone threaten Mr Lange before he disappeared? Any hate mail arrive at the office? Anything like that?'

'No more than usual.'

'He got a lot?'

'As many as any good politician, I think,' Bohle said.

Jamie and Hallberg laughed politely to ease the tension. But Bohle looked on edge.

'Did you keep them? The threats?'

'They were reviewed by the security team at the office,' Bohle said. 'Anything of note was passed along to the police. Any that we had lying around the office would have been—'

'Collected by the police during the investigation.' Jamie nodded. 'Got it. What about Nina Lange?'

'Nina Lange?' Bohle asked, stiffening a little.

'Yes, Mr Lange's wife. Did you meet her?'

'Uh, once or twice, if she came to the office when they had lunch booked or were going out for dinner,' Bohle said.

'And how would you describe their relationship? Did Mr Lange talk about her much?'

'No, he didn't, but they seemed happy – he was always happier on the days they were going for lunch and would come back smiling,' Bohle said, offering a weak one herself.

'And how were campaign donations made to Mr Lange? Did you handle any donations or investments? Was there a campaign fund, or an account that Mr Lange used to handle transactions?'

Maria Bohle's eyes widened slightly, and she looked at her phone again. 'No,' she said, looking back up at Jamie and smiling. 'I never dealt with any money or anything like that. There was a specific campaign fund but someone else was in charge of that. I mostly just handled his appointments and calls.'

'Were they recorded?'

'I'm sorry?'

'The calls. Were they recorded?'

'Uh, I don't know. I don't think so.' She seemed tense now.

'Okay, no problem.' Jamie sat in silence, thinking, watching Maria Bohle. Something was off with her. Jamie didn't know what it was. But she had to take a swing. 'Look, I can see that we're going around in circles a little here, and that if we just ask you the same questions the detectives in charge of the case did, we'll get the same answers.'

Bohle looked back wordlessly.

'So we're going to get right to the heart of things, if that's okay with you? We believe that the person or persons who abducted Stieg Lange would have been in contact with him in the months leading up to his disappearance. He might have been approached in a professional calibre, by a new donor or business who wanted to involve themselves in his campaign. We have access to all of his accounts and will be combing back through them looking for any anomalous money appearing in either his campaign or personal accounts, but if you could give us a place to start, that would be great.' Jamie gave her a smile with just her mouth, her eyes still hard, her gaze cold.

Bohle squirmed.

'I don't believe you had anything to do with his disappearance,' Jamie said. 'You're safe, don't worry. But any information you could provide, anything at all, would be really, really helpful. Everyone's involvement in the initial investigation will come under a microscope, including yours – both inside and outside the office. Do you understand? If anything is being kept from us, we'll find it. Maria? Look at me,' Jamie said, focusing her attention. 'You handled all of his calls, scheduled all of his meetings. Nothing happened without you knowing. So if we find something, we need to know how you missed it, or why you chose not to tell us. So, think hard, okay? If there's anything that comes to mind. Anything at all.'

'I don't…' Maria began, then she bit her lip. 'I have to…' she said, glancing at a door behind Jamie and Hallberg. 'Do you mind if I use the bathroom quickly?' She was beginning to redden, break out in a sweat.

'Of course,' Jamie said, sitting back. 'Take your time.'

Bohle nodded, then got up quickly, grabbing her phone off the table before heading into the bathroom.

She closed it and the lock clicked loudly.

'What do you—?' Hallberg began before Jamie raised her hand to silence her.

Jamie was getting up then, quietly, slowly, and walking towards the door. She paused a little short, holding her ear towards it, straining to hear.

Hallberg watched from the chair.

And then Jamie lunged, suddenly, without warning. She lashed out with the heel of her shoe, right above the handle of the door, and drove straight through it.

The wood splintered, the door flinging open and smashing against the tiled wall with a loud crack.

Jamie burst in, closing ground on the terrified Maria Bohle, who was sitting on the toilet, fully clothed, her phone to her ear.

Her eyes widened in shock, but she didn't get any words out before Jamie snatched the phone from her hand and turned it towards her, ending the dialling call before it could be answered.

'What are you—?' Maria began before Jamie was on her.

She grabbed her flailing hand from the air and dragged her to her feet and back out into the living room, slinging her around and down onto the leather sofa. It hopped backwards a few inches, the metal legs groaning on the hardwood.

Hallberg was on her feet, hands rising to catch the phone Jamie just threw to her. 'She was making a call,' Jamie said, looking at Hallberg. 'We need to find out who to.'

'It was my mother!' Bohle yelled.

'Quiet,' Jamie commanded.

She fell silent.

Jamie drew a slow breath, looking down at her.

Hallberg held onto the phone, watching Jamie. 'What now?'

Jamie swallowed, looked down, and put her hands on her hips. 'Now, I guess we take her in.' She met the eye of the terrified woman on the sofa. 'And find out what she *really* knows.'

34

THE HANDOVER WAS FAST.

Jamie and Hallberg pulled in at the side of the road as Simpson and Ves approached from the opposite direction. They stopped alongside and Simpson got out, opened the back door and pulled Maria Bohle out, then shoved her into the back seat of their waiting SUV. Hallberg handed over the phone and the removed SIM card to Simpson then.

He got back in his car wordlessly and Ves sped away.

Jamie hit the gas, too, and within five seconds, Simpson's car was gone from the rear-view and they were alone again.

Jamie and Hallberg hadn't said a word to each other as they'd driven. And Maria Bohle had sat quietly in the back, staring at her knees. There'd never once been a plea for a solicitor, or to call anyone. She'd just accepted what was happening silently.

Jamie didn't know how to take that. But Bohle had gone into that bathroom, spooked, ready to call someone. And she hadn't done it of her own free will. No, she'd been under instructions that if anyone came sniffing around, she was to call that number.

Jamie managed to get the phone off her before it connected, but whoever was being called would know something was up. Which meant that now, a clock had been set ticking, and they had to move.

While on the phone to Simpson, giving him the rundown and setting up the handover, Ottosen had located the two detectives that had handled the Lange case. Naas and Torgrimson had been partners for fifteen years. Both had topped out at *politiførsteinspectør,* the equivalent to detective inspector, and had been at that rank since their pairing. Neither had a particularly exemplary record, neither was management material, and both looked more than happy to ride that rank until retirement. They were both on the high side of fifty, married with grown children, both holding down mortgages. Naas had a mountain of credit-card debt, and Torgrimson was paying a sizeable maintenance allowance to his ex-wife as part of their divorce settlement. By all accounts, on their pay scales, both men should have been slowly drowning in their finances. And yet both men somehow found the cash to go on two holidays each last year – and not cheap ones. As well as, in Naas's case, do an extension on his house two years ago, and in Torgrimson's, go to Berlin for a long weekend and blow ten thousand euros at a seedy casino.

And while, in court, all this would be circumstantial at best, it was enough to tell Simpson, Jamie, Hallberg, and the others that these two were as dirty as detectives came.

Ottosen said that they'd both scanned into the police HQ, but hadn't scanned out, so they were still there, and would be until their shifts ended at five. Which was thirty minutes from now.

Jamie and Hallberg had no intention of waltzing into police headquarters with fake credentials, no matter how convincing they were. So they planned to ambush the detectives at their favourite post-shift watering hole instead – which they went to every night after work. And if they skipped for some reason, then that'd be a good indicator they knew something was up and they'd grab them wherever they could.

The thirty minutes till shift-end was going to feel long, but it at least gave Simpson a little time to get some information out of Bohle, and Ottosen space to work his magic on the phone and see what he could dig up from the number Bohle was calling. See whether it was a direct line to Imperium, or if it led to some other corrupt police officer or government official. Either way, Bohle was in trouble, and Simpson had the kind of pull to offer her protection in exchange for information. Maybe that would finally get the truth from her.

Jamie sighed, tightening her grip on the wheel, and sped towards the station, checking her watch every minute or so.

Traffic was mercifully light, and at five minutes before five, they parked up a hundred metres down from the main entrance, within view of the bar Torgrimson and Naas headed to before going home.

Hallberg spoke and Jamie jumped a little, her focus completely on the doors in front of her.

'You think Simpson will get anything out of Bohle?' Hallberg asked.

Jamie glanced over. 'Yes.'

'You seem confident.'

'Bohle was crumbling when we were speaking to her. She was easy to goad into running to Imperium or whoever she was calling. Once Simpson gets her in a chair in a dark room and lays out her options – talk and live your life, safe and protected, or don't and go down with the ship that murdered your boss… Well, it's no choice at all, really.'

Hallberg thought on that. 'So you've changed your mind? You think Imperium killed Lange?'

Jamie bit her lip. 'No. I don't know. We'll have to take another run at Nina Lange after we've spoken to Naas and Torgrimson and found out about Lange's diary. I think they'll have misplaced it as evidence. But the big question,' Jamie said, looking at Hallberg, 'is whether they've destroyed it, or think they're clever enough to take on Imperium if they need to.'

'You think they'll have kept it as leverage?' Hallberg asked, raising an eyebrow, following Jamie's train of thought.

'If there's anything useful in there. If it tells us who Imperium used to try and leverage Lange, then they could have hidden it to try and use as a buffer. If they think Imperium are going to get rid of them, or they want out...'

'That's a risk on their part?'

Jamie huffed. 'And taking money under the table to intentionally fuck up investigations isn't?'

'Good point.'

They sat in silence then, watching the clock on the dashboard tick closer to five.

At three minutes past, two men exited, wearing straight-legged jeans and buttoned-up shirts with the sleeves rolled to the elbows. One was taller, the other stouter. The stouter guy had a receding hairline and black-and-grey hair, while the taller guy's was mousy brown, mid-length, and wavy. Naas was the short one, and Torgrimson was the tall one.

Jamie and Hallberg watched them stride up the pavement, laughing and joking, as thick as thieves, heading for the bar.

Neither hesitated before they pushed the door open and went inside without missing a word of conversation.

Jamie was out of the car and moving before the door had even closed. She and Hallberg only had a short window to act in, and confronting the detectives while they were together, off shift, and before news of the phone call from Bohle landed with them was their best option. They were off guard currently and Jamie didn't want to give them a second of forewarning.

The bar was an old, dingy dive-style pub with wooden cladding and was mostly empty. A female bartender in her forties was polishing a beer mug, staring absently into space, and apart from a couple right at the back hunched over a table, talking to each other. The only others inside were Naas and Torgrimson. They were at a booth, a bottle of beer in front of each of them, and Jamie and Hallberg headed straight over.

The two men only noticed when they were six feet away, and both fell silent, staring up at the two approaching women. Jamie figured the suits gave them away, so when they pulled up a pair of chairs and perched on the end of the table, both producing their badges and flashing them at the detectives, there wasn't a whole lot of surprise in their faces. They looked at each other, then both sat a little more upright.

'Karla Janssen,' Jamie said. 'Kripos.'

'Lillian Heller,' Hallberg added.

The guys both rolled their lips into thin lines. Walls up.

Jamie put her badge away. 'I was hoping we could ask you about an investigation you conducted last year into the disappearance of Stieg Lange.'

'What about it?' Naas asked, running his hand over his balding head.

Torgrimson had wedged himself back into the corner of the booth and was watching Jamie.

She kept it light. 'We've just been asked to go over some of the facts to make sure that nothing was missed.' She sighed for emphasis. 'Look, we don't want to be here, and we understand that an abduction like that leaves little room for any investigation to take place. We can see from the reports that no evidence was recovered at the scene and that there was no clear and present threat to Lange leading up to the incident.'

'So, then what's the problem?' Naas snorted, taking a swig of his beer.

Jamie smiled. 'We just wanted to loop you in on the investigation as a matter of courtesy, before we dug into the evidence and reviewed it. We've already spoken to several witnesses, and we wanted to speak to you to hear your side of things before we requisitioned all the evidence – everything recovered from the scene,' Jamie said, eyeing Naas for any sign of a tell. 'As well as everything taken from Lange's office.'

He kept his face straight.

'All of his personal effects, his hard drives, his paper diary.'

An eye twitch.

'I didn't see that it was logged in evidence,' Jamie said, doubling down.

Naas grunted and sneered. 'What paper diary?'

So that was how he was going to play it. 'The paper diary that the other witnesses have sworn never left Stieg Lange's side.'

'So if it never left his side – don't you think it was probably grabbed when he was abducted?' Naas raised an eyebrow, the tone unmistakably condescending.

Jamie smiled back at him. 'It's possible. But the question of why it would be taken remains unanswered then. They took the cash from his wallet, but left his cards, his car keys in the ignition, his phone on the driver's seat. But they take the time to rummage through his bag and take his diary? Doesn't that seem odd to you?'

'I don't know, I wasn't there,' Naas replied, taking another drink of beer.

'That's the thing, though, Naas,' Jamie said. 'You *were* there. You were on the scene less than an hour after the call came in that he was missing. You did the initial assessment, and there was no mention of any of Lange's possessions being taken. In fact, your report said that Lange's belongings were all left at the scene, which suggested that there would be a call for ransom. Then everything was logged – phone, wallet, his coat, and satchel from the back seat. Everything. But no diary. So either the person who took Lange knew to take the diary and put everything back as it was, or it was never logged in evidence.'

'Or it was never there to begin with,' Naas replied, looking at the ceiling. 'We never knew about any paper diary, or heard about it. Until now.' He looked down at Jamie. 'And it very much feels like we're being accused of something.'

Jamie measured the man – the rough stubble, the sunken eyes, the blotchy cheeks, the unclean fingernails wrapped around the neck of his sweating beer.

'Just trying to cover all our bases,' Jamie said, deflecting the accusation of an accusation.

'Thing is,' Naas went on, 'we're good at our jobs. But no witnesses ever mentioned a paper diary. And we took the electronic diary that Lange's secretary kept, and we went through it, and followed up on everything out of place and came up with nothing.' He licked his lips. 'Everyone of interest had an alibi. And none of the people we spoke to had a motive to go after Lange. So we did what we were supposed to, and we waited for a ransom call.'

'Except one never came,' Torgrimson chimed in from his position at the back of the booth. He had his arms stretched out, one along the spine of the bench, and the other on a shelf above the table, running the length of the wall.

Jamie turned her eyes back to Naas after a few seconds. 'Okay, great. Well, we'll need to go over that electronic diary again, just to make sure. We're not here to step on anyone's toes. But with such a high-profile case and no continuing investigation, questions have been asked that we've been instructed to answer. For now, let's go over what happened at the scene, shall we?'

'This isn't exactly a good time,' Naas said, taking another drink. 'But I'd be happy to schedule a meeting for some time this week?'

'No,' Jamie sighed. 'Now is the perfect time, I think. So you and Torgrimson here don't have time to compare stories before you tell them.'

Naas smirked back at her. 'Whatever you want, Overkonstabel,' he said. 'Ask away.'

'Great, we appreciate the cooperation. Now, my partner, Heller, here,' Jamie said, gesturing to Hallberg, 'is going to ask you some questions. And I'm going to take Torgrimson somewhere quiet, and ask him the same ones.'

Torgrimson sat up a little more, his all-too-casual posture stiffening.

Naas ran his rough tongue over his bottom lip.

'Detective Torgrimson?' Jamie said, standing up. 'If you will?'

He glanced at Naas, who just looked back at him, tongue still moving over his bottom lip.

Torgrimson looked up at Jamie then and nodded a little. 'Okay,' he said, and slid out of the booth.

Naas watched them all the way to a table on the other side of the room.

Jamie didn't need to look back to tell.

35

Though Torgrimson brought his beer with him, he didn't touch it throughout the entire conversation, just picked at the label on the neck with his thumb.

Jamie sat him down with his back to the other table, so she could keep an eye on them over his shoulder.

She let the silence hang for a minute or two, let Torgrimson think about the situation, let the gravity of it set in.

When he looked up at her, she started.

'Tell me,' Jamie said, 'what happened on the night Stieg Lange disappeared? Recount it from the top for me.'

He let out a long breath. 'It was… sevenish, I think a little after, when the call came in. Officers had attended the scene, responding to a call that Mr Lange had seemingly vanished. They reported a suspicious scene, signs of a possible abduction – his keys, phone, wallet, all left at the scene, his car door was open, but there was no signs of a struggle. His wife, Nina Lange, had seen him pull into the driveway, and when she went to check on him a few minutes later, she found the car abandoned, and then called the police.'

'The officers then called you to the scene?' Jamie asked, watching his facial expressions, the way he looked almost conflicted over it.

He nodded, taking a chunk of paper under his thumbnail. 'The officers called back to dispatch and instructed Naas and I to investigate and take over the scene.'

'Were you on duty at the time?'

He shook his head. 'No, but we were on call.'

'And what time did you arrive at the scene?'

'Some time around eight.'

Jamie was comparing his story to the report she'd all but memorised. 'Then what happened?'

'We had the attending officers set up a cordon, then canvas the neighbours to see if anyone heard or saw anything or had any security cameras or footage that may have covered the incident.'

'Did they?' Jamie asked, knowing what the report said.

'No,' Torgrimson replied, 'nothing. The closest camera was three houses down, and while it caught Mr Lange arriving home, there was no one following him, and it didn't catch any other vehicles leaving. Which indicates that if a vehicle was used in the abduction, it arrived and departed in the opposite direction.'

Jamie nodded. 'And no one saw anything?'

'No. No shouts or screams were heard, no engines, nothing to suggest that anyone else was on that street at the time.' Torgrimson relayed the information stiffly, but with confidence. 'Whoever took Mr Lange planned it meticulously and executed it perfectly.'

Jamie drew a slow breath, watching Naas sneer and grin at Hallberg in the corner. 'Let me ask you, then – what do you *think* happened?'

Torgrimson narrowed his eyes a little. 'What do you mean?'

'No DNA or evidence was recovered at the scene to suggest who might have taken him or how. No vehicles spotted or heard, no CCTV, no witnesses, nothing. It's as if he just vanished into thin air. So I'm going to ask you again – beyond protocol, beyond the investigation – what do you *think* happened?'

Jamie kept her eyes fixed on his; she could almost see the cogs turning behind them.

He didn't seem to want to answer.

She drew a breath, changed tactic. 'We've been asked to find Stieg Lange, and our investigation has two paths to go down – either we decide that your investigation thus far has been airtight and build on what you have, or we decide that your investigation was botched, and then you and your partner are dragged into the spotlight.'

'The investigation is solid,' Torgrimson said then, almost forcefully. It was the first time Jamie saw something other than reluctance in his eyes. 'We did everything by the book,' he went on, leaving his beer bottle to instead cut the air with his hand. 'We looked for Stieg Lange. Believe me, we *looked*. We did everything we could. We still are.'

Jamie sat back a little, digesting the sternness of that argument. Who was he trying to convince? If he was telling the truth, then it didn't gel with the theory that they tanked the investigation intentionally. And Jamie was all but certain that they were both on the take. So why would they try so hard to find him? Unless it played into her theory that Lange had organised his own disappearance to get away from Imperium, and they were doing their best to find him too. That made sense. If they'd approached him, and he had details of the meeting, however it had gone, whoever it was with, in his diary, then him being on the loose, with that… It wasn't a lot on its own. But put him and Maria Bohle in a room together, with that diary, and the lost or destroyed hard drives from evidence, along with what they had on Torgrimson and Naas already… Sprinkle a little of Emma Hagen's one-eighty on all of Lange's policies. Hell, if they could get that far and get her in a room, she'd crumble. They'd have them. But there were still a few loose ends here.

It all began to come together in Jamie's mind. But so long as they were tip-toeing around the elephant in the room, this wasn't going to go anywhere fast.

Sorry, Simpson, she'd waited too long to put a stake through Imperium's heart. And they'd figure out they were coming for them sooner or later. Jamie was going to strike first, and that was all there was to it.

She pulled out her phone then and opened her files, looking for a photograph. 'Do you recognise this man?' Jamie asked, putting the phone down, rotating it, and sliding it across to Torgrimson.

She kept her eyes on him.

He did his best to hide his surprise – and fear – but Jamie caught it. There for an instant, then gone.

'No,' he said, clearing his throat. 'Who is that?'

'You know who it is,' Jamie said, leaning in, lowering her voice. 'And we know who he works for. We know what they do. And we know who's involved with them. Hey,' she said, grabbing his attention, 'we *know*. Okay? We know.'

She let that sink in.

He watched her carefully.

'The thing is,' Jamie said then, 'we don't want you. Or your partner, Naas. No. We want him. And we want the people he works for. The Lange investigation is at the heart of all this, and if you make the wrong move after walking out of here, then you're going to be caught in the crossfire. Because there will be one. Both sides are gearing up for it, and if you don't make a choice *now,* then this goes one of two ways. You either go down *with* them. Or they put you down themselves.'

His eyes twitched.

'I'm not going to sit here and try and convince you of anything, but what I am going to give you is three names. Ingrid Falk. Rasmus Allinder. Jörgen Johansson.'

'Who are they?' Torgrimson said, trying to feign disinterest.

'They're what happens if you put your faith in these people.' Jamie produced a card then and slid it across the table next to her phone, pulling the device back towards her as she did. 'All suicides. From the outside, at least. So unless you want your wife and kids to find you hanging in your garage one of these days, you'll rethink your position here.' Jamie lifted her eyes towards Naas. 'Your partner is greedy enough and cocky enough to think that he's going to come out of this in one piece. You don't strike me as the stupid type, though. So what I'm going to do is lay out a scenario for you, and you don't have to say anything. I just want you to think about it, and then decide what to do afterwards.' Jamie met his eye again. 'I think that these people you work for approached Stieg Lange to try and get him to represent their interests in Høyre. I think he saw what was coming if he didn't cooperate, and then disappeared before they could get to him. You and Naas were instructed, by your bosses – *both* sets – to find him. Because he's dangerous. But you haven't. Which looks bad. From where I'm sitting, and from where *they* are. Which now means you not only have them breathing down your neck, but Kripos, too. And when they get wind that Kripos are sniffing around, you think they're going to have any interest in you and Naas walking around, knowing what you do? No, the only reason we're talking right now and you're not choking on the barrel of a gun already is because we're ahead of them on this. Not by much, though. So, you can be sure that clock is ticking already. And when it hits zero…' She exhaled, looked down. 'Look – I don't know what they've told you, or what you've got from them in the past, but if you think there's any kind of loyalty to you or your partner, you're wrong. You're tools to them, and you can be thrown away like tools. Remember those names – Ingrid Falk. Rasmus Allinder. Jörgen Johansson. There's your proof of what I'm saying. So make your choice. We can help you. But not if you're dead. You cooperate, and we'll do all we can to protect you. And your family. Get you out of the country, even. If you help us.'

Torgrimson opened his mouth to speak.

'Don't,' Jamie said, cutting him off. She reached over, touched her card. 'That's my number. Call me if you come to your senses. If you don't – let me tell you, from *personal* experience – running doesn't work. Not on your own. You don't have the resources or the contacts. They do. They'll find you. And they'll fucking kill you. Your whole family, too. You have two choices here – side with them and die, or give us something and give yourself a fighting chance.' Jamie pushed back from the table and got up. 'Your window is closing, Torgrimson. I hope your affairs are in order.'

She walked from the table, not looking back, and tapped Hallberg on the shoulder on the way past. 'Come on,' she called. 'We're done here.'

'I'm not finished,' Hallberg replied, twisting on the chair.

'Yeah, you are,' Jamie said. 'You're not getting anything out of him,' she said. 'They've made their choice.'

Hallberg's chair ground on the dirty wooden floor and then she was walking after Jamie.

Naas laughter rang out behind them. 'Bye, bye,' he cooed. 'Nice chatting to you.'

Then Jamie was out in the afternoon light, sucking hard on fresh air and heading for the car.

Hallberg caught up with her halfway across the road. 'What the hell was that?' she asked coldly. 'I was in the middle of an interview.'

'Don't take this the wrong way, Hallberg,' Jamie said, 'but I gave you Naas because I knew he wasn't going to give up anything.'

'So, I was what, just a distraction?'

'Call it what you want,' Jamie said, circling the car and opening the driver's door, 'but what you did might have just given us the biggest break in this investigation yet.'

She stared at Jamie, her eyes cold. 'You know, I'd appreciate being looped in on these kinds of things before you decide them.'

'If I didn't think I could trust you to do your job, I would,' Jamie said, getting in.

Hallberg sat next to her and pulled the door close. 'I don't know whether to take that as a compliment or an insult.'

'When you get your own Hallberg, you'll understand,' Jamie said, giving her a quick grin as she started the engine. 'Now *that* is a compliment.'

Hallberg huffed a little and shook her head. 'I'd still like a heads up next time. Did you get anything out of Torgrimson, at least?'

'Maybe. But Simpson's not going to like it.' Jamie pulled away from the kerb.

Hallberg laughed. 'And why not?'

'Because it supports the theory he already shot down.'

'Of course it does,' Hallberg said. 'See, this is why you keep making decisions without running them by anyone first.' Hallberg put her elbow on the sill and rested her cheek on her hand, watching the city streak by.

'And why is that?'

'Because you're always fucking right.'

36

THE SAFE HOUSE was on the outskirts of Bergen, in a quiet, old neighbourhood full of overgrown trees.

Jamie watched on the monitor from the other room as Maria Bohle sat, drenched in lights, in front of a camera set up on a tripod.

She could see Simpson's shoulder in the left foreground, and Maria Bohle's scared face above it.

'I'm going to ask you again,' he said, slowly, emphatically, 'were you approached prior to Stieg Lange's disappearance by the person who supplied you with the number you were instructed to call?'

'No!' Maria Bohle pleaded, holding back tears.

Simpson sighed. 'If you don't help me, Maria, I can't help you. And if you walk out of here without our protection, then the people who gave you that number to call are going to kill you. Do you understand me?'

'You can't let them do that!' Bohle yelled. 'If you know that's going to happen, you can't do that!'

'I don't even know who you were trying to call,' Simpson said. 'Tell me, and I can help you. If it's who I think it is, then yeah, they'll scoop you up and slit your throat. But I can't offer you anything unless you help me.' His voice was even and calm.

Jamie and Hallberg had got back twenty minutes ago, and Ves had given them a brief of what had gone down. Bohle was pleading total ignorance. It looked convincing.

'I don't know anything,' Bohle sobbed then, hunching forward and burying her face in her hands. 'I don't know anything!'

Simpson let out a long breath. 'Let's go from the top. Once more. How did you receive the instructions to call that number?'

'I already told you,' Bohle said, her words muffled through her fingers.

'And I'm asking you to tell me again. And this time, don't lie to me.'

Her head shot up, throwing her hair everywhere. 'I'm not lying!' she shrieked with the kind of pitch and force of someone fearing for their life.

Simpson just stared at her in silence.

Bohle eventually regained herself, swallowed, and then recounted it. 'I received a letter,' she said, 'about two weeks after Mr Lange went missing. I opened it, and inside was a note that said I needed to save the phone number on the page in my phone – and that if I heard from Mr Lange, or anyone came asking about him, I was to call them immediately.'

'And why would you do that?'

'Because…' She shook her head. 'Because they included pictures of my family, taken recently… My sister in university in Berlin, my mother, my father, my grandparents…'

'How do you know they were taken recently?'

'Because… I was in them,' she said, stifling another sob.

'They were photographs of me with them, taken within the last month.'

Jamie watched her closely, arms folded. Hallberg and Ves were sitting. Jamie was standing behind.

'Okay,' Simpson said. 'What else did the note say?'

'That they could get to them any time – and that if I didn't call, that… that…' There was more sobbing then.

Jamie watched as Simpson shifted in his seat.

Something was niggling at her. She stared at the girl, willing the thought to take form in her head.

'Okay, so where's the note now?' Simpson asked. 'The photographs.'

'I burned them. It said to burn them after I'd saved the number!'

'And you didn't think to go to the police? To call anyone?'

'It said that if I did, they'd kill them, anyway!'

Fuck, Jamie couldn't think with her screaming.

She turned from the screen and walked away, trying to tune out the cries. What was bugging her? What couldn't she put her finger on? Bohle had visited her family, what was the big deal? Her parents and grandparents lived in the city. Her sister lived in Berlin, studying economics at the university there. So what if she'd visited her? Why was that…

Jamie came back to the screen suddenly and shouldered down in between Ves and Hallberg to get at the microphone linked to the bud in Simpson's ear. 'Ask her about Berlin,' she said quickly.

Simpson tensed slightly, then reached up to his ear, touching it, but not saying anything. The silent signal to say again.

'She said she'd visited her sister in Berlin – but she told

me she only took holiday days when Lange was off. Ask her when she visited her and how long for.'

Simpson cleared his throat then. 'You said you visited your sister in the month leading up to receiving the letter, and that it was two weeks after Lange's death. When did you visit her?'

'What?' Bohle asked, looking up, confused.

'When did you travel to Berlin?'

'Uh,' she said, shaking her head. 'It was over a year ago, I don't… Uh… I think about a week before Mr Lange disappeared.'

'Midweek?'

'No,' she said, shaking her head, 'Friday to Sunday, I think.'

'What time did you leave on Friday?'

'In the morning, I think,' she said.

'So, Mr Lange was off that day?'

'I don't know,' she said.

'You told my colleague that you only took holiday days when Mr Lange was off. So was he off, or did you lie to her?'

Maria Bohle's eyes widened a little. 'No, I swear, I didn't lie, I didn't, I, uh…' She screwed her face up, thinking. 'Yes, Mr Lange was off – I remember now. He asked me to rearrange his appointments as he was surprising his wife, taking her away for the weekend. For their anniversary, I think he said.'

Hallberg spun her chair around to another desk to the right and was already hammering on keys. Jamie let her work. Hallberg's mind was sharp, and she'd obviously had her sixth sense twigged, too.

'So, you left on Friday, and came back on the Sunday evening?' Simpson asked. He sat back, touched his ear again, signalling for Jamie to give him something clse, to guide him.

'She didn't mention that to me,' Jamie said over the microphone. 'She said nothing out of the ordinary happened leading up to his disappearance.'

Simpson spoke again. 'Did that strike you as odd? That he asked you to rearrange his appointments for him?'

'No, not really,' Bohle said. 'It was for their anniversary. I thought it was sweet, romantic, you know? He'd been working so hard. Surprising her like that – it was a nice thing. He was a nice guy.'

Hallberg was swinging back to the main desk then, talking for everyone, including Simpson, to hear. 'Our research shows Stieg and Nina Lange were married in April 1998. He disappeared on Tuesday, the nineteenth of September. She's lying.'

Simpson tapped his thumb on his knee, processing that. 'You're lying to me, Maria,' he said, his usually dulcet droll taking on a sharp, cutting tone.

'What?' She stiffened. 'I'm not! I promise!'

'Lange's anniversary was in April. Not September. You're telling me he took his wife away on the weekend of the eighth to the tenth of September. Is that when you visited your sister?'

'Yes! I remember because she didn't come home that summer – she stayed in the city, so... so it was the perfect time to see her, before her term started!' Bohle was growing shrill again.

'So why did Lange tell you he was taking his wife on an impromptu anniversary getaway then? Huh? Tell me that?'

'I don't know!'

'The truth, Maria, the truth! Tell me the fucking truth!' He was out of the chair, standing over her, yelling at her. Loud enough to strain the makeshift soundproofing tacked to the walls in there.

Jamie had a cold sense of dread creep up her spine then. 'His wife,' she said, mostly to herself. Her stomach knotted. She leaned into the mic again. 'The wife, Simpson. Lange's wife. If I'm right and Lange organised his own disappearance, then that was one last weekend for them together before he went. I know you don't like the theory, but we have to act. And we have to do it now. Before it's too late.'

Simpson was still standing, hands balled into fists. But he wasn't saying anything.

'They know, Simpson – Imperium know we're coming for them now. If it wasn't Bohle's phone call, it was speaking to Naas and Torgrimson. And now they're going to be scrambling. If Kripos is already looking at them, they've got nothing to lose. I'm going to get Nina Lange – I'm bringing her in. Okay?'

Simpson was a statue, and Maria Bohle was a bawling mess in front of him.

'Simpson?'

'Go,' he said, under his breath, but loud enough for Jamie to hear.

That was all the encouragement she needed, and was out the door in seconds, with Hallberg hot on her heels.

But as Jamie ran down the front path towards the car, she knew that, just like always, she was already going to be too late.

37

JAMIE DROVE QUICKLY.

She wove through traffic, keeping her speed high and even, aiming for gaps, ignoring the car horns that blared and faded behind her. Watching as headlights strobed in the rear-view.

Hallberg sat with her eyes forward, holding onto the handle above the door, jostling side to side as Jamie closed ground on the Lange residence.

It was dark by the time she wheeled into the street and pushed the car as hard as she could before standing on the brake and sending it to a juddering halt outside Nina Lange's home.

Jamie leapt from the car and bolted straight up the driveway towards the wide-open front door.

Her heart was hammering in her throat. She already knew what she was going to find.

Then her pistol was in her hand and she was holding it outside her hip, both hands on the grip, muzzle to the ground, her pace slowing to a walk. She steadied her breathing, listened for any sign of movement, and found none.

Jamie swallowed, hearing Hallberg come into the hall behind her.

She touched Jamie on the shoulder to let her know to proceed, and they pressed inwards, measuring their steps into the empty house.

Everything was lit brightly, but there was no sound.

Jamie crept towards the corner of the hallway, where it opened out into the spacious living room and kitchen, and paused briefly. One last check for any sound. Nothing.

Jamie peeked around the corner, bringing her weapon up slightly, her eyes going to the counter, a half-eaten plate of food on it. A knife was on the side of the plate, a bottle of red wine lying on its side next to it, the contents spread out across the white marble surface.

She went deeper into the kitchen, seeing a fork on the tiles, the food from its prongs splattered around it and up the polished cabinets.

Wine had crept along the grouting, drifting outwards from the shattered remains of a wine glass. The same kind Jamie had seen Nina Lange sipping on earlier that day.

Shards crunched underfoot as Jamie rounded the island, just to check that Nina Lange's corpse wasn't slumped against the counter.

She lowered the gun and swore. 'Shit.'

Hallberg drew a breath, facing the room, keeping her pistol raised. 'What now?' she asked.

Jamie took stock of things, reached out, stuck her index finger into what looked like a plate of chicken and red pepper pasta. It was still warm.

'We couldn't have missed them by much,' Jamie said then, wiping her finger off on her jeans. 'Head outside, knock on the neighbours' doors, see if anyone saw or heard anything. That's our best bet.'

Hallberg nodded. 'Yeah, okay. What are you going to do?'

Jamie bit her lip, knowing they'd cover ground much quicker with them both working it. But this was a crime scene, and soon enough it would be crawling with police – maybe police who were going to cover up that this was an Imperium abduction. Which meant that if anything valuable or incriminating – like the missing diary – was lying around, then they'd risk it slipping through the fingers.

She needed to take this chance to be alone here while she had it.

Even if that meant gambling with Nina Lange's life.

'Go,' Jamie said, 'quickly.'

Hallberg nodded and then disappeared back out the front door.

Jamie made a beeline for the stairs. The bedroom was the most personal space, and it was where people felt most protected. It was also, statistically, where they were likely to keep something of value or importance. If people hid money, jewellery, if they had a safe – if they kept a weapon in the house – it would be in the bedroom. People feared home invasions, and it's where they slept. Anything that was important, people wanted close at hand in the event of something like that happening. And Bohle had said that Lange never went anywhere without his diary. So if it wasn't with him – which Jamie wasn't discounting – then she'd bet it would be in the house.

It was a long shot, but maybe he'd left it with his wife, or hidden it in somewhere. All they had was the story that he'd never gone inside. And that could be total fabrication. It probably was.

She headed up, not wasting any time.

First door on the left. Bathroom. Nice, but not what Jamie was after.

Second door. Grey bedroom. Upmarket, bland furniture. Pictures of flowers on the wall. No, lacked personality. Guest room.

First floor on the right. No, this was a guest room, too, but in lilac.

Last door.

Jamie burst in, immediately smelling the scent of women's perfume, of night creams. She could see moisturiser on the nightstand, a vanity table with lotions and jewellery boxes on it against the wall.

A full-length mirrored wardrobe spanned the left-hand wall. A regal canopy bed dominated the centre of the room.

Jamie took it all in, her eyes scanning for any potential hiding spots.

Nothing looked out of place, but somehow, the room didn't feel quite right. Though she didn't know why.

She needed to make sure that she wasn't missing anything.

Jamie doubled back into the corridor quickly, and went for the last door at the end of the hall. She pulled it open to find an airing closet. She leaned in and knocked on the walls. Solid, solid, solid. This was against the outer wall.

No hidden compartments, no secret safes.

Okay, back to the bedroom.

The hardwood floors were beautifully grained, a sheep-skin rug covering the open space between the foot of the bed and the bookshelf facing it.

Jamie went to that first, running her hands over the spines. It seemed like they both liked to read. Novels, memoirs, history, everything. There were no cabinets or anywhere else to hide a safe, and the wall the shelf backed onto was solid concrete.

Jamie discounted it and moved on to the vanity table. A plethora of make-up and perfume, but nothing else. Nothing Jamie wanted.

She did her best to keep the fate of the woman who owned these things separate from the task at hand, but she was distinctly aware that every second that passed was one where Nina Lange was in the hands of Imperium, who were doing who knows what to her.

Jamie was on her hands and knees then, looking under the bed. Shoe boxes. She pulled them out, opened them, knowing each would likely contain shoes. Some had old photographs in. Some had little knick-knacks, painting supplies. No diary. Shit.

She stood without bothering to put them back, lifted the paintings on the walls – abstract oils in pastel greens and aquamarines and turquoises. Fuck, nothing!

She circled the bed then, going for the wardrobe, and pulled the mirrored door across, ignoring the terse and anxious look on her own face.

The left-hand side was all Nina Lange's stuff. Two stacked rails – one with beautiful dresses and gowns and other fancy clothes on the top, and below blouses and suits and other everyday wear. She ran her hands through them, found nothing.

Shelves on the left were filled with handbags and belts, more shoes, folded-up cardigans and hats and gloves and scarves and scarves and fucking scarves! Who had so many scarves? They hit the ground behind Jamie as she tore them out of the box-shaped shelf units, searching frantically, feeling sweat beading on her brow as she did.

Fuck, fuck, fuck! There was nothing here!

Jamie closed the door and moved right, to the other half of the wardrobe, her dread that she'd made the wrong call growing, her fear for Nina Lange's life reaching tipping point.

She pulled the wardrobe door aside and was met with a strong wash of men's aftershave. Woody and rich and earthy. Stieg Lange's side.

She ran her hands along a colour-arranged array of suits, then over the more casual clothing below. Nothing. Nothing. Nothing! There was nothing fucking here!

She moved shoes around, lifted hats and T-shirts. A unit of two drawers at the bottom was stuffed with socks and thermal underwear, but nothing of any use.

Jamie leaned in then, pushing the rack of clothes left, seeing a recess that ran behind the corner of the door.

Boxes were stacked up – clear crates, with more... shoes! Jesus, how many shoes could one couple use? Jamie spotted ski goggles, too. Winter-sports clothing. Ski-boot boxes. And... she froze, her eyes searching the stack, that same feeling of something being off niggling her. Maybe a change in the air or just a feeling that something was off... But what was...

Her skin erupted in gooseflesh before she could home in on it and a metallic click ringing out behind her told her she was no longer alone in the room.

Jamie peeled herself out of the bottom of the wardrobe, Stieg Lange's suits brushing her hair as she stood upright, lifting her hands instinctively.

She'd re-holstered her weapon on the way up, but now wished she hadn't.

Jamie's eyes tracked the floor and then climbed the man in front of her. He was tall, with mousy brown hair brushed into a rough, wavy side part. His face was long and angular, but familiar.

'Torgrimson,' Jamie said, hands next to her ears, throat tight as she stared down the barrel of his service-issue SIG Sauer P320 handgun.

It quivered slightly in his grip, but from this range – no more than six feet – there was no way he wasn't putting a bullet through her head if he pulled that trigger.

And that's exactly where he was aiming.

The man in front of her didn't say a word, just retightened his grip on his weapon.

His eyes flitted to the open wardrobe and then back to Jamie.

'There's nothing in there,' Jamie said, 'I swear.'

Torgrimson's jaw flexed as he decided what to do.

'Look – we just…' – Jamie put her hand on her chest – 'I just came… I was worried about Nina Lange – and now she's gone. Okay? She's gone, they took her and—'

Jamie cut herself off, hearing footsteps in the hallway.

Naas stepped into the room, weapon drawn as well, and filed up next to Torgrimson. When he saw Jamie, his look of quiet apprehension turned into a smug grin.

He stood there next to his partner, his lowered pistol slowly rising until it hovered next to Torgrimson's, levelled at Jamie's head too.

'Well, well,' he said. 'Janssen, was it? What a coincidence to find you here.'

'Let's just talk about this for a second—'

'Shut the fuck up,' Naas spat. 'You're inside an active crime scene before the officers who were dispatched to attend the call. You're armed, trespassing. I think we're well within our rights to put a bullet in you. Especially because you tried to draw your weapon on us. What do you think, Torgrimson? Does it look like she's reaching for her gun?'

He didn't say a word.

Jamie swallowed, keeping her eyes on Naas. 'Think about what you're doing,' she said quickly. 'I'm with Kripos. *Kripos*, Naas. And they know I'm here – you shoot me, and they're going to come after you with everything they have. If you thought you were fucked before, you shoot me and you'll never see daylight again. They'll hunt you like a dog.'

He sucked in a breath, then sighed. 'You might be right, but I think I'm still going to shoot you. Because let's face it, if I kill you now, at least I'm giving myself a head start.'

Jamie tensed. 'Don't do this – Nina Lange is missing. Kidnapped,' Jamie added. 'And we're wasting time here – we need to find her. We can still save her.'

'Maybe you kidnapped her,' Naas said. 'Maybe that's what you're doing here – because you kidnapped Maria Bohle, right?'

Jamie said nothing.

'You and your partner, Heller – Maria was seen being manhandled out of her apartment building by two women fitting your descriptions earlier today. So don't tell me this is just a happy fucking coincidence. In fact, I don't even think you're Kripos. I think you're full of shit,' Naas spat, narrowing his eyes at her. 'I don't know who you are, but you're sniffing around, sticking your nose in our case, threatening us, and I think if I put a bullet in you right now, no one's going to give two shits. I think Kripos are going to say they don't even know who you fucking are, and I think I'll probably get a nice fat bonus, too.' He grinned at her again now, his hand steady as he pointed the gun right at Jamie's head.

She turned her attention to Torgrimson then, her only hope.

If he didn't say something, Jamie was going to be dead inside the next five seconds.

But he wouldn't meet her eye.

So she closed hers.

She'd rather not see this coming.

Though frankly, she didn't think it would come like this.

'Jamie?'

Jamie's eyes shot open, Hallberg's voice ringing up the stairs.

Naas and Torgrimson both glanced at the door and then back at the woman they'd been introduced to as Karla Janssen.

'Jamie?' Naas muttered, glaring at her, retraining his gun on her forehead.

'Heller!' Jamie called back, hands still raised. 'I'm in here, Heller.'

Hallberg was coming up the stairs then, and a second later she was in the doorway. Her eyes widened. 'J— Janssen,' she said, correcting herself.

Jamie kept her face straight.

Hallberg's hand hovered at her hip, at the grip of her pistol. She eyed Jamie for confirmation she should draw it.

Jamie gave her no indication, she just stared at Naas, who looked equal parts angry and smug.

'We done here?' Jamie asked coldly.

They stood still for a few more seconds, and then Torgrimson raised his hand and laid it on Naas's wrists, pushing his weapon down slowly, and lowering his own.

Naas let his fall then, and laughed that same laugh from the bar. 'Sure, *Jamie.*'

Jamie wanted nothing more than to dance forward and kick his ugly face right off his shoulders. But there were more pressing matters at hand, and she needed to get out of there.

She moved past Torgrimson, pausing only briefly to say a few words. 'Take a look around,' she muttered, 'this is what you'll come home to find one day if you don't think about what you're doing.'

He looked down at her, met her honest stare, but said nothing.

'Janssen,' Hallberg urged her from the doorway.

Jamie broke their eye contact and left the room, chasing Hallberg down the stairs, into the hallway, and back into the street.

She made for the car, already dialling for Simpson on her phone.

Jamie ran around the bonnet and climbed into the driver's seat, catching a glimpse of Torgrimson in an upstairs window, watching them go.

And then she was in the car and he was gone, and Hallberg's face filled her vision. 'That was close?'

Jamie nodded. 'Yeah, not fun. Tell me you got something?'

'Yeah, hopefully,' Hallberg said as the line connected and Simpson answered.

'Hello? Hallberg? What's wrong?'

Hallberg motioned for Jamie to drive. She didn't need to be asked twice, and spun the tyres, hurling the car forward and away from Nina Lange's house, the growing sounds of sirens echoing behind them.

38

'SIMPSON,' Hallberg said quickly, the car streaking down the quiet residential street. 'Nina Lange is missing – kidnapped by Imperium, has to be.'

'Goddamn it,' he said, sighing. 'What can we do?'

'A neighbour heard a scream, came to the window, saw two guys dragging her down the front lawn and throwing her into the back of an SUV – Range Rover, new model, black, private number plate.'

Simpson was quiet, taking this down, or maybe finding Ottosen and putting them on speaker. Jamie and Hallberg trusted him to make the right choices.

'The neighbour said they went north out of the area, driving fast. That was about eight-ten,' Hallberg.

'Shit, okay – uh, okay – they've got a twenty-minute head start. Let me see what I can do. Ottosen?' he asked into the ether. 'Okay, he's on it – we're pulling traffic cameras now, seeing what we can do. Ves, get Europol on the line, scramble us some more resources – see if we have any access to satellites in the area – we need to find this car. Hallberg? Where are you now?'

'We're moving, heading north…'

'About to join the E-39,' Jamie said. It was the main road out of the city, and there wasn't much north of where they were already. So, she figured if they'd come into the street from the south, they'd be heading north, somewhere quiet, somewhere they could do what they needed to without being disturbed.

She was taking a gamble, but sitting still somewhere only widened the lead they already had, and it could have been time that Nina Lange didn't have.

'Okay, we have you,' Simpson said. 'Ottosen has your position – we'll stay with you. Nothing on the SUV yet, but he's got NPR running across every available camera in the area.'

A voice rang in the background. 'Got something, maybe,' Ottosen called.

'Hang on,' Simpson said, panting and moving towards Ottosen. 'What is it?'

'A matching model just tripped a speed camera at Knarvik – private plate, clocked doing… shit.'

'Shit?' Simpson repeated. 'Where'd it go?'

'It's gone,' Ottosen said. 'The entry has been wiped – someone else is in this system. It's been deleted.'

'Shit,' Simpson said again. 'It has to be them – Imperium. Covering their tracks as they go.' He snapped his fingers. 'Find that SUV. Ves, where are we on support from Europol? Sat coverage? Tell them we need it now, and we know where – Hallberg?'

'I'm here,' Hallberg said.

'Okay, let me call you back. Head for Knarvik. I need to get on the other line. Call me if something comes up.'

'Will do,' Hallberg said, the line going dead as she said it. She looked across at Jamie.

Jamie tightened her grip on the wheel, watched the speedometer climb to one hundred and thirty kilometres per hour as they joined the E-39, and weaved into the road, heading north, and going fast.

They were thirty kilometres behind already, and they needed to catch up.

Jamie drove at full tilt for more than half an hour, nearing double the speed limit most of the time.

Ves's support at Europol had managed to pick up the SUV on satellite and were feeding it back to Ottosen, who was guiding them from the office.

They'd stuck on the E-39 until they'd reached Ostereidet and then pulled off, heading north up one of the finger-like peninsulas that jutted out into the Fensfjorden.

The area was rural, remote, and littered with narrow, barely paved roads that led to even remoter properties.

The streetlights disappeared behind as Jamie wrestled the car down into third and sent it screaming around a corner and onto the street heading to Askeland. They were no more than a few kilometres behind now, but the SUV wasn't hanging around.

Jamie blinked herself clear, her eyes aching from the intense concentration, and listened as Simpson's voice filled the cabin. 'Okay, keep going – they're not far ahead. Stay on this road. You're closing ground.'

The car Jamie and Hallberg were in wasn't built for speed, but it was being pushed to its limits. A nondescript mid-model saloon designed to blend in. Not give high-speed chase.

'Okay, they've just pulled off,' Simpson said, 'heading east now on an old road that leads…' he trailed off. Ves's voice echoing in the background, muffled. 'An old sawmill, it looks like – the turn is a kilometre ahead, and then it's about two kilometres to the mill. You're catching them, guys. Keep going.'

If Jamie could have put her foot harder into the carpet, she would have.

'Europol are on with Kripos – they're scrambling a team – but they're twenty minutes out by helicopter at the earliest,' Simpson carried on, reiterating the situation. 'It's just you guys…' He seemed to drift off for a moment. 'If you want to hold back, no one would blame you,' he said. 'We don't know what you're heading into here.'

Jamie and Hallberg exchanged glances, but neither of them had any doubt in their eyes.

'No,' Hallberg said. 'We're doing this.'

'Okay,' Simpson said then. 'Be careful.' He sighed. 'The turn is coming up on your right any second.'

Jamie searched the blurring tree-line for any hint of an opening. A flash of white caught her eye – an old rusted sign, grown over with weeds, that read *Larsen Tømmer Sagbruk.* Larsen Timber Sawmill.

Jamie stamped on the brake, felt the wheel judder under her hands, and then wheeled it right, down off the tarmac and into the verge, sliding and snaking down onto the gravel-covered track.

The headlights flooded the pine forest and splintered into the darkness, the tyres fighting for grip as they picked up speed again.

Her heart began beating harder, her eyes fixed now on the two fresh tracks in the dirt ahead of them.

'They're closing ground on the mill,' Simpson said. 'Less than a kilometre ahead now.'

Jamie watched the speedometer climb, the steering light

in her grip, the traction-control light blink wildly as the car's back end swung around, the off-camber road sending them pinballing through the forest, churning through one loamy verge, then the other as Jamie tried desperately to keep the thing straight.

A curve loomed and Jamie turned the car in hard. Hallberg sucked air in through her teeth as the nose leapt up over the bulge in the middle of the road, the back wheel dipping into the loose layer of needles and stones, spraying them all over the tree trunks.

The engine roared, wheels spinning, revs hitting the limiter as the safety features on the car tried to decide whether they were crashing or not. And then they were back on the road and accelerating again, the track straightening out. Another sign flashed by, telling them to slow down.

Jamie did no such thing.

'Five hundred metres,' Simpson said.

Jamie could see the faint red spots of brake lights ahead.

She kept her foot planted.

'Two hundred metres.'

The entrance flew out at them, the yard beyond opening into a wide lot before an old, rusted tin-sheet-clad building.

A gate had been pushed open, the sign for the mill riding across the chain-link fence beside it.

The car punched into the lot, the Range Rover suddenly drowned in her headlights.

The doors were open. She could see figures on the gravel next to it.

Two guys on the left. One on the right. Tall, stocky, in dark clothing.

Then another figure was being pulled out – this one smaller, more slender – in a coloured blouse, a white sack over her head.

Nina Lange. It had to be.

They all froze, deer in the headlights, as the saloon ripped across the car park towards them.

'Jamie,' Hallberg said. 'Jamie? Jamie!'

But there was no slowing down. Jamie knew what she had to do, and there was no cover here. These guys were armed, they were trained, and they'd kill them the second they had the chance. No. If they stopped, they were dead.

And Jamie hadn't come this far for nothing.

The men drew their pistols, started forward.

'Hold on!' Jamie yelled, putting one hand on the hand-brake, twisting the wheel with the other.

The tyres bit into the stones and the front left corner of the car sank towards the ground. Jamie jerked the handbrake up, locking the back wheels, and threw the tail out, sending the car into a full sideways slide.

Jamie braced, Hallberg swore, her phone coming out of her grip and flying into the air.

The back wheel of the saloon hit the SUV square in the bumper with an almighty screech of rending metal.

Something clicked horribly in Jamie's neck, and both cars leapt, twisting together.

The guy on the right-hand side of the SUV rolled up over Jamie's bonnet and was flung into the air, his head cracking the windscreen as he went.

The guys on the other side dived for cover, but Jamie lost sight of them before their car came to rest, facing the side of the half-crushed SUV.

Jamie blinked herself clear, coughed violently, then tried to fill her lungs, the belt cutting into her chest and shoulders.

Steam erupted from the bonnet and Jamie fumbled for the belt release, her ears ringing.

Hallberg's head lolled next to her, blood trickling down

her cheek from a cut on her eyebrow. But otherwise, she looked unscathed.

Jamie would come back and check.

Her belt came free on the second try and she pushed the door open, catching sight of the mangled rear quarter of the car.

She flopped down onto the stones, then scrambled to her feet – her knees aching from where they'd slammed against the door, her back throbbing from the impact – and pulled her pistol free of the holster inside her jacket.

She brought it up, breathing hard, wheezing, focusing her vision, and chambered a round, pressing herself towards the gnarled back of the Range Rover.

Nina Lange had been clear of the four-by-four, she just hoped she was okay.

Jamie peeked out, saw one of Imperium's mercenaries first. He was lying face down, his pistol loose, about four feet from his hand.

She couldn't tell if he was breathing, if he was dead or unconscious. She guessed that the impact from her car had sent the SUV sideways straight into him.

Jamie's eyes traced the ground to Nina Lange, lying on her side, hands bound in front of her.

She was groaning softly, whimpering, but she didn't look hurt – she was far enough from the crash to be okay.

But where was the other guy? Jamie had counted one on the right, who'd gone up over the bonnet, and two on the left with Nina Lange. One was down already, where was the other?

She heard a grunt then, a scrabble of stones, and she looked around the car, seeing the front door open, the wide back of one of the mercenaries facing her.

'Stop!' she yelled, stepping into the open. 'Police!'

It happened quickly.

The guy began to turn.

She saw the flash of a weapon.

Jamie fired. Once, twice, three times. Centre mass, close grouping.

Her vision was filled with white light.

More stones being kicked out from under dragged heels as the mercenary twisted awkwardly into the open doorway, the bullets hitting his ribs and chest.

His white shirt exploded with red between the lapels of his blazer.

But he wasn't the only one there.

Muzzle fire leapt from the doorway and Jamie felt the rush of bullets passing her head.

Sparks danced off the metal of the SUV next to her hip.

She went to a knee reflexively, returning fire.

Jamie sank behind the body of the already downed Imperium goon, felt it absorb at least two bullets.

She didn't know if she'd hit whoever was being helped from the car, but she could hear footsteps now. Receding.

She peeked over the guy's shoulder, saw a figure disappearing into the open mouth of the sawmill. She just made out a bald head and the flash of the silver pistol in his grip from the headlights of the SUV before he was swallowed up by the darkness.

Jamie rose, blinking the dust from her eyes, remembered the same flash off that pistol before it was put to the head of an old man back in Sweden.

Sandbech.

39

JAMIE COULD HEAR Hallberg staggering from the car somewhere behind her. Hear her coughs and sliding heels in the gravel. 'Jamie?' she called out.

She turned, already moving, spotting Hallberg coming around the back of the totalled SUV.

'Help Nina Lange!' Jamie yelled, gesturing to the bound woman on the ground.

'What are you—?' Hallberg started, but Jamie was already moving, Hallberg's weak voice swallowed up by her footsteps echoing in the cavernous mill.

Sandbech could only be ten seconds ahead, but in here, in the dark – damn, the place was already a labyrinth.

Jamie paused to catch her breath and looked around. On the main floor, there were two tall stacks of logs stretching away from her into the darkness. A huge machine dominated the space between them, with a conveyor belt running into a set of rolling blades designed to strip and shape the raw pine trunks. The air was heavy with old sap and rust. Long, sinister saw blades hung from the ceiling, waiting to taste fresh wood, lines of blood-red rust stretching their lengths.

A pair of stairs ran up either wall, connecting the ground to a series of catwalks that crisscrossed the mill and would give a bird's-eye view of the processing happening below.

Jamie expected that maybe forty, fifty guys would have worked here in its heyday. Now, the place was a graveyard for rotting trees, an environmental butcher's shop.

As Jamie traced forward, searching the dark paths for any hint of movement, she felt the soft, gritty texture of old sawdust beneath her feet. She looked down and could see that she had carved a rough path through the ancient layer, and then immediately began searching it for any hint of Sandbech.

She spotted the track ahead. It seemed to slow, spread out into a mess as he paused to choose his direction, and then it went left, between the left-hand stack and the great machine.

Jamie followed it quickly, keeping her eyes fixed on the room ahead, glancing down every few seconds to make sure she was still on course.

She could see one of Sandbech's steps was deliberate, one a little dragging. He was limping. Injured from the crash. That's why he was being helped from the car by the third Imperium goon.

Her heart began to beat harder, a strange, cruel excitement riling in her. No, she had to keep herself even, focused. She didn't have him on the ropes yet. And he was still dangerous. A trained, ruthless killer.

Jamie exhaled, slowed her pace, raised her pistol. She was in an alleyway now, pinned between the bulk of the machine and a stack of timber heavy enough to crush her a hundred times over. She reached out and touched the rough, rusty chains that held the stack in place, and wondered whether there was a release clasp on the other side, whether she'd just been lured into a position where she was about to get squashed like a bug.

Jamie quickened her pace then, seeing that it opened out ahead, but also that any leftover light from the headlamps of the cars outside was well and truly gone. She was forging ahead into darkness, and into what she was afraid was going to be a trap.

She had to stop, rethink this. She was going to be outsmarted otherwise.

Jamie glanced back over her shoulder. Was he going to circle around and come from behind? Was the stack going to fall? Was he going to put a bullet in her the second she stepped around the corner? That's what she would do.

Fuck.

As the seconds ticked by, Jamie grew more uneasy.

Her eyes moved to the machine on her right then – the thing designed to slice up great trunks of wood.

The conveyor belt sat at chest height, guard rails on either side stretching over her head.

In front, blades angled down towards it, and corkscrew-shaped rollers designed to strip the trunks hung ominously.

But she could already feel the weight of the stack to her left.

She made the call and reached up, swinging her leg onto the conveyor, and then levering herself upwards and onto the machine.

There'd be no power here, right? The thing wasn't going to spontaneously start up... was it?

Jamie crouched, keeping herself low, minimising herself as a target, and scanned the room, listening for any sound. Listening for any hint of Sandbech.

God, she just hoped Hallberg wouldn't follow her in here.

Jamie edged forward, towards the blades, staring down at

the footprints in the alley below, watching as they went around the edge of the stack and left, towards a steep ladder leading up to the catwalk above.

At least from here she had a vantage point. And she hoped Sandbech wouldn't think she'd be stupid enough to walk herself into a buzz saw. Literally.

Jamie reached up, resting her hand on the cold, rippled metal of the blade above her. It was designed to swing down and slice timber into boards.

She pushed herself past it carefully, keeping her eyes on the catwalk above. She could just see the faint lines of the rails, catching whatever was left of the light coming in through the main doorway.

And then she saw it, the faint glimmer of a polished silver barrel, hovering just above it.

Jamie froze.

Sandbech was there, on the catwalk, right above where she would have been, waiting for her to move underneath him, to put a bullet in the top of her head.

That son of a bitch.

Jamie set her jaw, not daring to move quickly, and parted her heels as much as she could, shuffling them wider. She was half-hidden by the saw blade, shrouded in darkness.

She could barely see him, and she didn't think he could see her at all.

Could she get a clear shot?

Jamie pulled her right hand up slowly, her left coming to hold the heel of her hand and cradle the butt of her pistol.

It hovered close to her chest as she forced her eyes to focus.

The muzzle raised, her breath ragged and fast.

She'd only get one chance at this – and cold-blooded or not, it was time for Sandbech to die. He had too much blood on his hands, and she wasn't about to let him walk out of here.

Not this time.

Jamie raised her pistol, pushing her hands out into the darkness.

The cool, sharp lick of the saw blade touched her forearm, quivering as her hands shook.

You can do this. Deep breath, grip not too tight, slow exhale, wait for the heart to slow, squeeze, don't pull.

Jamie set the man up in her sights and filled her lungs.

This was it.

One muscle twitch. One bullet, centre mass. One less motherfucking killer to worry about.

Jamie let her breath dispel from her chest, let her diaphragm tighten, and her heart slow.

She could feel the tension of the trigger beneath her sweating finger.

And then she heard it.

Her name ringing through the stillness.

'Jamie?'

She pulled the trigger instinctively.

Two muzzle flashes filled her vision, two concurrent shots filling the room.

She heard a grunt, then Hallberg's voice, swearing, yelling out in shock.

Jamie turned her head, watching as Hallberg scrambled for cover.

Sandbech had seen her enter, readjusted his aim, taken a shot at her while she was clear in the doorway.

Fuck!

Jamie searched the catwalk. Nothing! He was fucking gone.

But she'd heard a grunt, and her aim was true. Had she hit him? Was he dead?

Jamie strained her ears, heard footsteps clanging on steel, laboured breath, fading, moving away. The clang of metal on metal, his pistol clipping the rail?

She needed to go after him. Now he was running, and she couldn't let him get away.

The catwalk was ahead, Sandbech's position practically level with hers, but it arced up in a set of stairs to a raised platform over the machine, too high to reach. Shit, she was going to lose him.

Jamie turned, planted her foot on the guardrail of the conveyor belt, felt the sting of the saw blade as she shouldered past it and up.

The rail took her weight, the tread of her boot finding purchase on the rust, and she leapt forwards, right across the gap, and onto the chained stack of timber.

It jostled under her, chains groaning, and she clambered forward, toward the catwalk above it.

The timber shifted and moved, the chains cutting into the wood with the sudden strain.

And then one of them gave way. The ratchet on top twisted and pulled itself apart, flinging the sheared bolt into the darkness.

It hit one of the saw blades like a gong, and a deep, reverberating twang rumbled in the mill.

The wood began to shift.

Jamie gasped, feeling it twisting under her.

She climbed.

One, two, three, gaining momentum, and threw herself at the catwalk just as the other ratchet followed its partner.

Her chest hit the rail and knocked the air from her lungs, her hands hooking over.

There was nothing under her then as the pile avalanched down into the space next to the machine.

Her legs dangled in the air for a moment, then scrambled for the steel girder supporting the catwalk.

The toe of her boot found it, and she was climbing.

Yes, push up. Knee over, turn.

Her heels hit the rough grating and she was running, hard.

Dust plumed into the air around her from the old wood, the impact enough to make the whole building tremble.

Her left hand went out for support, touched the rail on her left. It came away wet.

She held it up in front of her face, saw something black and glistening on it. Tar? No, the smell of iron. She knew it too well.

Blood.

But not hers. Sandbech's. She must have hit him.

He couldn't be far ahead.

Jamie picked up her pace, following the catwalk to the end of the room, then down the only stair set there.

She was in darkness now, her eyes stinging from the dust. She looked around, saw the end of the machine on her right, the fallen timber an impenetrable barrier, and all against the back wall, stacked wood, pallets, and a mountain of discarded, broken boards, wood chips, and shavings. Jamie felt it then; fresh air on her face. The sweat on her brow tingled in the draught and she wiped it off with the back of her sleeve, pressing forward towards an opening ahead.

As she neared, the weak light of the rising moon picked out the newspapered windows in the darkness.

An old steel fire door swung lazily back towards the frame and Jamie approached cautiously.

She could see blood leading through it, from the concrete floor out over the threshold and down the stone step.

Jamie reached the frame and nosed the door back open with her pistol, staring into the wilderness beyond.

Long, pale grass, burnt by the sun, almost glowed in the moonlight. It was parted, broken by churning knees as someone forged through it.

She could just make out shining black flecks on the closest tendrils.

But beyond, it faded to shadow, a line of thick trees standing ten, maybe fifteen yards away.

Jamie could see nothing, and with Sandbech ahead of her, and armed... She swallowed. Going after him would be impossible. At best, she'd run around aimlessly in the dark, trying in vain to track him. At worst, he'd kill her.

And every other option she could come up with wasn't much better.

'Fuck,' she muttered, sighing and lowering her gun.

He was gone.

Jamie swallowed and turned back to the room, climbing the stairs again back onto the catwalk.

Nina Lange was still outside, possibly injured, and Hallberg could have a bullet in her for all Jamie knew.

She picked up her pace, pulling her phone from her pocket. She'd call Simpson, get Kripos to set up a perimeter, roadblocks, comb the area from the air for Sandbech. Scramble a dog team to chase him down.

Depending on how injured he was, she hoped he wouldn't get far. And hell, maybe he'd even bleed out and save them all the trouble.

Though she didn't feel like they'd get that lucky.

For now, she had to consider this a victory, even if a hollow one.

They'd got Nina Lange back, had taken out three of Imperium's goons in Bergen, and injured one of their heavy hitters. And with some luck, Ottosen would be able to track down who messed with the traffic camera records, too.

Jamie descended the catwalk stairs back into the space in front of the cutting machine. 'Hallberg?' she asked into the darkness.

'Jamie?' Hallberg stuck her head out from behind the far stack of logs.

'You okay?' Jamie watched her step out. She wasn't limping, wasn't holding her hand to a bullet wound. Sandbech must have missed. Which was surprising in itself, considering how close he'd been to hitting her from a hundred-odd metres in Sweden.

'Yeah,' she sighed. 'Bullet nicked my shoulder,' she said. 'Few centimetres over and it would have been a different story.' She reached up now, pulled at her collar. Jamie could see the fabric was ripped.

She went closer, pulled on the torn sides. 'Didn't break skin. You're lucky.'

'Yeah,' Hallberg said, rubbing her neck and wincing. 'I feel lucky. I also feel like I have whiplash.'

Jamie smirked a little. 'All part of the fun,' she said, holstering her pistol and motioning Hallberg back towards the crash site. 'Now, come on. Let's see whether Nina Lange was worth saving after all.'

Hallberg eyed her.

'That was a joke, Hallberg,' Jamie said.

'You know, with you, sometimes I just can't tell.'

40

BLUE LIGHTS FLASHED SILENTLY, a sea of them cutting through the darkness and playing against the corrugated metal exterior of the mill.

Black Kripos SUVs with windscreen-set sirens littered the area. Officers in windbreakers and suits stood around talking. Guys in white forensics get-ups pored over the ground, picking up shell casings, snapping photos of the bodies littered around, going over the Imperium Range Rover with tweezers and clear ziplock bags.

Jamie stood, watching Simpson survey the scene, hands on hips.

Nina Lange was about fifteen metres away, sitting on the tailgate of an ambulance, getting her blood pressure taken by a tall paramedic.

Other than shaken up and a little knocked around, she seemed to be okay.

Simpson hung his head, the distant barks of the dog teams combing the forest behind the mill echoing eerily in the still air.

He turned to face Jamie, lips rolled into a wide line.

'You going to say something?' Jamie asked after a few seconds of awkward silence.

Simpson had sent Hallberg away after hearing what had happened. She was hovering next to a Kripos car, watching discreetly.

'I don't know what to say,' Simpson said then. 'This is a bit of a mess. Not exactly how I envisioned this thing going.'

Jamie drew a slow breath, looked over at the totalled cars, the one she was driving still smoking softly, the side a mangled mess. 'Me neither.' She let her breath out. 'But we saved someone's life.' Jamie lifted her chin towards Nina Lange. 'If we hadn't got here when we did, she'd be strapped to a chair in there having her fingernails ripped off with a pair of rusty pliers right now.'

'I don't think they'd have got that far,' Simpson said. 'She doesn't seem the type to hold up under interrogation.'

'That's not really the point, is it?' Jamie said, stepping closer. 'We stopped it from happening, and we put a nail in the Imperium coffin tonight. They wanted something, and we proved they can't just take whatever they please. And we took out three of their men.'

'And let Sandbech escape.'

Jamie set her jaw. 'I got him, though. He's wounded. And bleeding. The dog team will pick him up before dawn. If he doesn't die before then.'

'He's been operating across a dozen countries for years, undetected. He's killed twenty, thirty, forty people. Maybe more. We didn't know he existed until a few months ago. So excuse me if I'm not more optimistic about how all this is going to play out.'

Jamie read the cutting tone in his voice, the unmistakable condescension. 'Simpson, this may not be a win, but it's sure as hell not a loss.'

'No?' Simpson said, shaking his head, his grip tightening on his hips. 'Because it sure as hell feels like one.' He pointed a finger at her then and Jamie resisted the urge to snap it in two. 'You know, before I brought you in, I was trying to decide if something like this was going to happen. If you'd pull the same shit you have before.'

'And what shit is that?' Jamie folded her arms now.

'This gung-ho, do-or-die *shit*. Jesus Christ, Jamie, you rear-ended their car at fifty miles per hour with the person you were trying to save still inside it!'

'She wasn't inside it.'

'Next to it then, the point is the same!'

'She's alive, Simpson. And if I hadn't done that, she might not be.'

'And what if she had died, huh?'

'But she didn't.'

'But what if she did?' He stepped closer now, voice lower, colder. 'You made a judgement call, but with every one you make, I trust yours less and less.' He humphed now. 'Hell, I should have pulled you back the minute you went off book with Nina Lange the first time. Hallberg told me what you did, insisted that I let it go, let it play out, that I should trust you.'

'And you should have. Nina Lange knew something, that's why Imperium wanted her. And what we did, it drew them out. And we almost got them, Simpson. We almost got Sandbech.'

Simpson lifted his eyes. 'But you didn't. He slipped through your fingers. And now they're going to be pissed. And they know we're coming for them. They're going to tighten up, withdraw, plug any leaks they have.'

'They were already doing that, remember?' Jamie said,

unable to control the harshness of her tone. 'After *you* lost Klein.'

Simpson's eyes hardened, his nostrils flaring. 'Go home, Johansson. I'll handle this mess and update you if anything changes. You're done here.'

Jamie didn't move. 'Let me question Nina Lange,' she said then, ignoring the order. She was far from done.

'We can't,' Simpson said. 'The paramedics think she has a concussion, maybe even a brain injury. She's being taken to hospital to have a CAT scan. We're not going to be able to question her until at least tomorrow – if by some miracle she's unharmed. And by then, she'll have lawyered up and we'll get nothing from her.' He turned his back on Jamie now. 'Hallberg said that you thought Lange knew more than she was letting on. But you left her out there instead of bringing her in.'

'No,' Jamie said then, walking around Simpson to look him in the eye while he tried to throw her under the bus. 'You're not putting what happened here on me. This is not my fault. You didn't have *shit* until I came along. In fact, you'd lost your best agent, and knowing that, I still stepped into his shoes and put my own neck on the line.'

Simpson refused to look at her.

'You know, just because you're fucking up your investigation, doesn't mean you can blame that on me.'

He looked at her now, his eyes fire.

Jamie took a breath. 'All I'm saying, is that things may not have gone exactly to plan here, but if we look at this as a loss, then that's what it'll be. We got Nina Lange back, and whether she talks to us or not, she's not in Imperium's hands and talking to them, and that's something. And with Sandbech wounded, this operation of theirs in Bergen coming apart at the seams. They know we're on to them. Which means that, like you said, Simpson' – she leaned forward to catch his eye again – 'that they're going to be cleaning house. And that means we know what their next moves are, right? We know Emma Hagen is on their payroll. We know that Torgrimson and Naas are, too. So we hang back, keep quiet, and we put a watch on them. It's as easy as that.'

He looked at her, but said nothing.

'Look – I know this hasn't worked out the way we thought, and that Maria Bohle was probably a bust too, and the number she called… we'll find out it probably connects to a laundrette in Uzbekistan. But that's how these things go.' She nodded to reassure him. 'We're doing okay. And we're not out of the fight yet.'

He broke eye contact again. 'Get one of these officers to take you home.' His voice was softer now. 'I'll handle things here. Take the day off tomorrow, too. I'll let you know what happens with Nina Lange.'

Jamie nodded slowly. 'Okay.' At least she wasn't being booted off the scene anymore. Even if she did deeply dislike Simpson's knee-jerk to bury her for this just to keep his pristine record clean, she would have bet.

She turned away slowly then, trying not to show her limp. Her left knee was killing her, her hips in agony from where the belt had dug in. And coupled with her aching back and the twenty-kilo bag of cement that was apparently crushing her chest, she could really have done with a day off.

But just like always, things never seem to work out that way.

41

It was five in the morning when Jamie's phone started buzzing.

She groaned and rolled over in bed. Everything hurt, but her neck had now superseded all the other pain, a deep and painful throb erupting at the base of her and shooting up into her skull every second. She was bathed in a cold sweat, her breathing laboured. She felt like she'd been hit by a car.

The reality wasn't far away.

Jamie swung her legs over the edge of the bed in her apartment, and lifted her phone, squinting at the screen. It was an unknown number.

She swallowed, throat like razors, and answered. 'Yeah?' she asked groggily.

A voice on the other end, a man panting. No words yet.

'Who is this?' Jamie asked then, suddenly alert.

'Is that Janssen? Agent Janssen?' His voice was hurried, anxious.

'Yes. Who is this?' Her heart was beating harder now.

'It's Torgrimson. Detective Torgrimson,' he said, grunting. A car door thudded in the background. 'I… I need help. It's my family.'

'Wait, what's wrong, what are you doing?' Jamie asked, on her feet suddenly. The room was dark, and she scanned it for her jeans, not knowing where the hell they were.

'Naas is gone,' he said quickly. 'I can't get hold of him. And… there's a car, outside. It keeps driving past, parking up the street.'

'What car?' Jamie said. 'Are you okay? Tell me what happened.'

He was moving around now, breathing hard. 'Last night, at the Lange house, Naas got a call, left without saying anything, took the car and drove away. And I haven't heard from him since.'

'Hold on,' Jamie said, wishing he'd just take a second. 'Why do you think he's gone? What do you think is happening?'

'I… I don't know,' he said. 'But he's never left like that before – if there's ever been a call, you know, them asking us to do something, we'd always tell the other—'

'You're admitting your involvement with Imperium?' Jamie asked then, unable to stop herself, one leg in her jeans.

He was silent for a second.

'Torgrimson,' Jamie went on. 'You have to be straight with me here if you want me to help you.'

'Yes,' he said then. 'I'm admitting it.'

Jamie bit her lip, stemming the relief rising in her. 'Okay, go on.'

'We'd always tell the other – and most of time we'd both go. But last night, he took a call, and then a second later, he was driving away. And his phone's been off all night. I had a trace run on it, and it was last pinged on the E-39 heading north. Then it went dead.'

The E-39? That was the road they'd taken when following Sandbech. Shit. Had Naas been called to go pick him up? To run interference maybe? She couldn't say anything about that.

'And you haven't heard from him since?' Jamie asked.

'No, I haven't.'

'And who are the people outside your house?'

'I don't know,' Torgrimson said. 'I was up – something didn't feel right. I had a feeling, you know?'

Jamie knew.

'And I checked outside and saw a car parked there I didn't recognise. I know the cars on this street,' he said decisively. 'Then it moved off and parked further up. And every half an hour or so, it does another lap. Pulls off, and then cruises by again.'

Jamie bit her lip. Jesus, was he loading his car up to run? 'Where are you now?' she asked.

'I'm in the house.'

'You're getting ready to run?' she asked.

'Yeah, my family, I have to—'

'Have you been outside?'

'What? No, the car is in the garage.'

'Thank God,' Jamie said, taking a breath. 'What about lights – any on in the house? Can they tell you're loading up?'

'I don't... no. No, they can't,' he said then, more sure. 'The hallway light is on, but the kitchen, living room, they're off.'

'Anyone else up – your wife, kids?'

'No, no one yet. I didn't want to panic them—'

'Good,' Jamie said. 'Don't. And don't run.'

'What?'

'Unpack the car, carry on as normal. But keep an eye out and let me know what happens.'

'You can't just expect me to—'

'Look, Torgrimson,' she said, cutting him off again. 'Trust me, if these people wanted you dead, you'd be dead already. And if you run, they'll see it, and they aren't above running you off the road. Take my word for that.' Jamie's mind flashed back to Finland, and the series of events that had led from there to here.

'So you just expect me to sit here?'

'Yes, that's exactly what I expect you to do. Because if you run now, they'll kill you. If they think you're going to run, they'll kill you. Right now, you're safe – but…' Jamie bit her lip. 'Some things happened last night—'

'What things?' Torgrimson cut in.

'I can't say – but a car showing up outside, Imperium tightening things up… It's not really surprising.' Jamie buttoned up her jeans now, looking for her pistol and jacket. Where the hell had she flung things last night? She didn't even really remember getting home. Hell, maybe *she* was concussed. She shook it off, steeling herself. 'But you running now, that's not going to help anyone. And if you do…' Damn, it pained her to say it. 'There's nothing we'll be able to do to help you. Or your family.'

Torgrimson was silent, but he'd stopped moving at least.

'Look – what you're doing, calling me like this? It's the smartest thing you've done in a long time, okay, but you being involved with Imperium? That's not enough for us. It does nothing for our investigation, understand? But that doesn't mean you're powerless here. We need to nail Imperium, and to do that, we need to know how high up this goes. We need more evidence, and we need to remove the people at the top. You understand what I'm saying?' Jamie finally found her holster and threw it around her shoulders. Boots now.

'I do,' he said quietly. 'But my family?'

'There's no reason you can't run – but how far are you going to get? A car drives by three times and you're already packing. Staying on the run, under the radar, it needs planning, focus, experience, contacts… and lots of money. And doing it with a wife and kids? You won't make it a week. But help us, find us something solid, help us nail whoever's pulling the strings, and I can get your family out. We can disappear you – new names, new country, total immunity.'

'You can guarantee that?'

Jamie pushed her feet into her boots and headed for the door, pausing just as reached it. 'There are no guarantees – especially not when it comes to Imperium – but you're staring down the barrel of a gun here.'

He scoffed a little, then made a weak little noise. 'So what am I supposed to do?'

Jamie opened the door and stepped into the corridor. 'Stay by your phone. Don't move. I'll call you back in few hours.'

'What are you going to do?'

Jamie opened her mouth, already heading down the stairs, but she didn't have an answer for him. 'Just… just pick up when I call you, okay?'

'Okay,' he said, and then hung up.

Jamie paused for breath on the second-floor landing and leaned heavily against the rail, a deep, aggressive pounding building behind her eyes.

She tried to focus them, but everything was swimming in circles.

A wave of nausea rushed through her and her mouth began to salivate like she was going to vomit.

She waited a full minute before it passed and then checked her phone again.

5.17 a.m.

She swiped up with her thumb, found Simpson's number, and dialled without hesitation, on the move again.

There was no time to lose now, and her concussion would have to wait.

42

SIMPSON WAS ALREADY THERE by the time she arrived, coffee in hand. He met her in the lobby and gave it to her. 'Took your time,' he said, eyeing her.

She knew she looked like shit. And the reason she'd taken so long was because she'd pulled over to throw up on the side of the road. Twice.

Her hair was tied back, her eyes heavily bagged, and no doubt her breath smelt like vomit.

'Traffic,' she grunted, then slugged some of the coffee.

Simpson cast his eye over the six-a.m. deserted road outside, said nothing, and then followed her into the elevator. 'So, Torgrimson,' he said.

Jamie nodded. More coffee.

'We need to tread carefully,' Simpson added. 'But I have some ideas.'

'Hmm,' Jamie said. 'Any word on Nina Lange?'

'Still under observation. Her blood work is due back' – he checked his watch – 'any time, really. We should know then where we stand. But her sister is with her, and she called Lange's lawyer, who gave her a script to follow. That Nina

Lange won't be spoken to by anyone until she's cleared by the doctor for any and all brain trauma, and then, and only then, she'll be spoken to in the presence of her legal counsel.'

'So she's untouchable?'

Simpson sighed. 'Yeah, we even tried Norway's equivalent of the Patriot Act, but with no proof of anything and an under-wraps investigation that doesn't officially exist our only foundation to base that on, he pretty much just pissed all over it.'

Jamie sighed as well now. 'So this is basically all we have, then.'

'I'm not saying all our eggs are in one basket, but… If Torgrimson can keep his head, and we can turn this into something real…'

'You're saying it's a pretty important fucking basket. Got it.' Jamie nodded, and they rode up in silence.

'Are you sure you're okay?' he asked after a few more seconds.

The lift levelled out and the doors opened. Jamie stepped forward, finishing the coffee, and glanced back. 'No,' she said. 'But this doesn't feel like a day I can really take off.'

Torgrimson picked up on the first ring.

'Hello?' he said quickly, the nerves in his voice apparent.

It was nearly half-past-six now, but Jamie and Simpson seemed to have worked out a plan that they felt was beneficial and wouldn't get Torgrimson killed. Though they were literally betting his life on that.

'Torgrimson, are you okay?'

He huffed a little.

She took that as a yes. 'I'm here with a colleague of mine

who can get you what you need. He can help you and your family when the time comes.'

'What's his name?' Torgrimson asked.

'My name isn't important,' Simpson said, trying his best to obscure his American accent.

It didn't really work.

'How do you expect me to trust you if you won't even tell me who you are? Like you – Janssen – that's not your real name.'

Simpson narrowed his eyes.

'That other Kripos agent, Heller – she called you Jamie.'

Simpson closed his eyes and exhaled, his nostrils flaring.

Jamie cleared her throat. 'It doesn't matter what our names are,' Jamie said. 'And you can trust us or not – that's your prerogative – but you don't really have another option here, do you?'

Torgrimson grumbled. 'So what do I have to do?'

Simpson stepped back in now, the same chewed-up half-British, half-Jamie-didn't-know-what accent coming out again. 'Right now, we're closing in on Imperium, and we need to find evidence on someone higher up in order to get them to turn, too.'

'I haven't *turned,'* Torgrimson spat, indignant at the accusation.

Jamie waved Simpson to back off a little.

'No, no,' Jamie said, 'of course not. What we mean, is that if you're scared of Imperium, others will be too. And we need your help finding them, and getting them to cooperate.'

They already had someone in mind, of course.

'And what's to stop me from going back to Imperium right now and telling them I've been speaking to you, telling them your plan?' Torgrimson said boldly.

'That's up to you. But if you do that, here's what happens.

We never speak again. You blow the only chance you have. And how do you think they'll react when they find out you've been calling Kripos for help, huh? Forgiving? Somehow, I don't think so.'

He was silent.

'Go if you want, try it. But if you hang up this phone, that's it. In five minutes, the number will be inactive, and you'll never find us again.'

He swallowed audibly, but didn't say anything else.

'Imperium already know we're after them—'

'Is that why Naas disappeared?'

Jamie avoided the question. 'So even if you did tell them our plan was to find out who they'd corrupted and try to gather evidence, how would that be news to them?'

Torgrimson fell quiet again.

'No, Torgrimson, you have no leverage here, and nothing to bargain with. Not yet, at least. Which is why we're in no position to help. Not until you prove we can trust *you.*'

'So what the hell do you expect me to do?' he hissed. It was still early, and Jamie figured his family was still asleep.

She took a second, head still swimming, and gathered herself. They needed to be careful here. 'Looking at the Lange case, we believe that Emma Hagen, Stieg Lange's replacement, may have been installed by Imperium in order to further their business interests.'

Torgrimson was silent.

'We've been looking into her, but so far, she seems clean. Though the suddenness of her appointment, over other more suitable, more experienced candidates, leads us to believe that this isn't the case.'

'And you expect me to, what, break into her office, steal her computer?' he asked, practically incredulous.

Simpson stuck out his bottom lip as if he thought that wasn't such a bad idea.

'No,' Jamie said. 'That's too risky. Imperium will be watching things more closely than ever, so we just need you to be our eyes and ears, okay? It's important that you stay safe, and that you don't take any risks. Keep us informed of any developments.'

He exhaled slowly. She could hear a rustling on the other end of the line, like he was rubbing his face. 'And how will I get in touch with you?'

'We don't want to put you or your family in any extra danger, so pick up a prepaid phone that you can use to call us.'

He exhaled again, shakily. 'Okay, okay,' he said. 'I can do that. But I don't know how I'm going to find out anything about Emma Hagen. I don't have anything to do with politics,' he said, then, the defeat clear in his voice.

Simpson drew a breath. 'Well, Torgrimson,' he said, 'if you want your family to survive, you'll have to figure it out, won't you?'

He reached out and killed the call. The line went dead.

Jamie stood up and laced her hands behind her throbbing skull. 'That was a little harsh, don't you think?'

Simpson had his hands on his hips again, staring down at the phone. 'Yeah,' he said after a while, 'but this isn't a game, Jamie, and I'm not prepared to lose anyone else. I'm already down one agent, Hallberg's still at the hospital, Nina Lange's sedated awaiting her CAT scan, and you...' he looked up at her, his face breaking into a concerned half-smile, 'I appreciate you coming down here, but look at you – you're a fucking mess. And you're in no fit state to be doing this. You need rest.'

Jamie swallowed, holding it together. 'What I *need* is for

this to work. And for Torgrimson's family to survive. They don't have a clue what's going on, and if he screws up... they'll get their throats slit in their beds.'

Simpson was steel then. 'If they do, they do. He knew what he was getting himself into when he started taking bribes.' The contempt was clear. Simpson would no doubt bleed for his badge, and the flag, and anything else vaguely American. Hell, Jamie betted he had the ol' Stars and Stripes hung above his bed. Which meant sympathy wasn't something Torgrimson would get from him.

Which meant Jamie had to be the conscientious one. Which she didn't like. At all.

'There's a difference between trying to save someone and failing, and condemning them to death.'

'He should have thought about that, then, shouldn't he?'

Jamie could see they weren't going to get anywhere with this. 'So what now?'

'Now?' Simpson said, turning to the window and looking out into the dawn-streaked sky. 'Now we wait, hope that Torgrimson comes up with something, and cross our fucking fingers that Imperium doesn't come for him, or us, in the meantime.'

43

Nearly a month went by before they heard anything.

Ottosen was keeping them plugged in to the Bergen Politiet HQ's security system, and Torgrimson was checking himself in and out of the building as normal. There'd still been no sign of Naas. From the system, he was being shown as on annual leave. But without speaking to someone, they couldn't get more information than that.

Was he dead? Was he alive? They didn't know. But Torgrimson still was, and they were growing more uneasy by the day.

Jamie was back at full strength, and despite their apparent lack of progress on the case, Simpson seemed to be in better spirits. He'd insisted that Jamie leave her old apartment, saying that if he could find it, Imperium could, too. She found that difficult to argue with, though she thought that it was probably just a line to get her to move closer to the others.

They'd been set up with a number of apartments in a new block about two kilometres from the office. It was a modern place with underground parking, a view of the coast, and clean Scandinavian design. Though apart from the spartan interiors, Jamie's favourite thing was the communal gym and pool on the ground floor.

She'd been reluctant to move there until she'd seen it. And then she'd gladly accepted.

Simpson had insisted that she not go running as normal – in case someone spotted her around the city. So being able to do lengths in a pool and then hammer out her daily run on a treadmill was something that she found calming. It was the only solace she had from the daily grind. They'd all appear at the office within ten minutes of each other – all travelling from the same place – and then they'd spend the day combing through acquired data from suspected targets of Imperium. As much as they were trying to nail Emma Hagen, the more people they could prove were involved in this thing, the stronger their case. And if they left even one stone unturned, one corrupt official or judge or cop go free, then Imperium would still have a foothold. No, this needed to be total eradication.

And it was that thought that was keeping Jamie going.

That and getting to kick Simpson in the face every morning.

The underground gym and pool at the apartment complex wasn't sprawling by any stretch – the pool was ten metres long – but a hundred lengths was a kilometre, so that suited Jamie well enough – and the gym was about the same size. But another room was attached to that, which was used to store weights and extra gym equipment, but was also lined with mirrors, and intended for use as a yoga studio. Or at least that's what Jamie suspected.

When Simpson came hauling sparring mats through the door, Jamie backed off the treadmill and looked at him.

He didn't meet her eye, but carried on, going back and forth until there was a solid square of them set up in the studio room.

After he'd done that, he left again, and Jamie, piqued, went to investigate. When he came back for the last time, he had a box in his hands. A big one.

She watched cautiously as he put it down and opened the top, pulling out sparring helmets and gloves, ankle and shin pads.

He laid them on the ground – two sets, and then sat back on his knees and looked down at them.

Jamie restrained a smile and went over.

Two minutes after that, they were laying into each other with abandon.

And it had been like that for nearly two weeks now.

'Come on,' Jamie said, feeling the sweat run down under her head guard and over her brow, 'you can do better than that.'

Simpson was dancing around her. He'd kept his cards close to his chest for the most part, but he'd let slip that he wrestled in college, boxed while he was at Houston PD, and the FBI weren't afraid to teach their agents to fight. He was good. Strong. At least fourteen stone, Jamie figured, but surprisingly fast. He liked to grapple and led with his hands, though. Every time they got on the ground, he had her, but she was learning to keep her distance now. And Simpson was beginning to struggle.

He nursed his ribs a little, circling. 'Cheap shot,' he said, catching his breath.

'Maybe you're just getting slow,' Jamie replied, motioning for him to grow a backbone.

'Maybe I let you hit me.'

Jamie dropped her hands a little. 'If you do again, it'll be the biggest mistake you make.'

He grinned, feinted, and then came in at her. He wasn't going full tilt. He never did. But he wasn't pulling punches either, and wasn't afraid to put her on her back.

His right hand came over the top lazily, his left shooting up underneath in a hard jab to the body.

Jamie stepped back out of the way of the overhead and parried the jab with her right forearm, rolling behind it and throwing her left knee up towards his gut.

Simpson dropped his left hand, his elbow connecting with her rising leg, and it sent a bolt of pain down into her ankle.

Jamie grunted, planted it, and then kicked out at his calf.

Her shin struck it squarely, but Simpson was already swinging another heavy right.

Jamie threw her hand up to block and felt his fist smack it into the side of her own head, dulling the blow but not stopping it.

Her eyes lolled a little, but she didn't quit, her sessions with Sung-Sook all coming back.

She hopped, kicking upwards now as she gave him space, and put her foot into his ribs again. Same spot as she had a few minutes before.

Despite Simpson's capabilities, she knew that hurt. His eyes narrowed, teeth baring as he squirmed, his intercostals spasming.

His hands widened for a half a second and Jamie transferred to her other foot, slotting her hand between his wrists, and struck him square in the solar plexus.

He doubled forward now, fighting to keep his balance, but Jamie had hit this combo a thousand times, and there was only one way it ended.

Onto her right foot, left foot, stepping backwards, knee out up, counterbalance, and then over the top. The pad on the front of her shin – what would be the laces on her boot in any other instance – swung up, tracing the line of his back, and then slinging down over the nape of his neck, connecting with the back of his head.

The dull slap of plastic-coated foam hitting plastic-coated foam filled the room, and Simpson sprawled forward, fighting for air.

He landed hard and keeled onto his back, raising his hands and waving for Jamie to stop. Though he didn't seem to be able to find words between the stifled gasps.

'Told you,' Jamie said, pulling off her gloves and tearing off her head guard.

Simpson raked in a breath and threw his own head guard off. 'Damn, I've gotta stop going easy on you.'

Jamie offered her hand and pulled him up. 'Oh, is that what you've been doing?'

He rubbed his ribs. 'Damn, you just gotta keep hitting that same spot, don't you?'

She smirked. 'That's what I practise to do.'

He held up his hand in a fist and Jamie looked down, and then bumped it awkwardly. He'd never done that before.

She looked up and saw that he was looking right at her.

'What?' she said, just as awkwardly.

He shrugged. In the way that he did when he was 'on'. Jamie couldn't explain it, but every so often, he'd just change slightly, break out his pearly smile, close his eyes just a touch, hold his chin a little higher, stand a little straighter.

'In a weird way,' he said, 'I'm gonna miss this.'

'Getting your ass kicked by a woman half your bodyweight?'

He laughed, a little too heartily. A little too toothily. 'No, *this.* Here. This place. Since you came on board, things have been easier.'

Jamie tsked. 'You lost an agent, and you yourself said I've caused you nothing but trouble.' She breezed past him now, towards her kit bag. It was getting on for eight o'clock, and she wanted to be in the office by half-past. She didn't think she'd make it.

'Yeah, well… I think you're putting words in my mouth a little there, Jamie,' he said.

She didn't meet his eye, even though he was trying to catch it.

'You saved Nina Lange's life. That's important.'

'She still won't talk to us,' Jamie said. She refused to, in fact.

'Frankly, I'm surprised she hasn't fled the city.' Simpson rolled his lips into a line. 'I expected her to be out of here the second she was out of the hospital.'

Jamie pursed her lips, pausing her packing for a moment. 'I'm sure she has her reasons.'

Simpson chuckled. 'Don't suppose you know what they are, do you?'

She risked a glance at him. 'Now come on, you hate my conjecture.'

He held his hands up playfully.

She looked away again. This was the last thing she needed. 'I'll see you at the office.'

'Wait,' he said.

Jamie paused, bag in hand, and hung her head, sighing a little. She really didn't want to have to turn him down. 'Look, Simpson,' she started, turning to face him.

But he wasn't looking at her, charm cranked to ten. He was looking down at his phone, face pensive.

'What is it?' Jamie asked.

He finished reading the message from Ottosen. 'It's Torgrimson,' he said, meeting her eye. 'He's reached out, saying he wants to talk.' His expression grew hard. 'In person.'

44

THEY FIGURED that Torgrimson had lost his nerve. That operating as normal, doing Imperium's bidding, was the safest thing possible for him. That he had no intention of crossing them, and that he was quietly looking for a way out. A way to escape.

They'd been keeping a close eye on him, and honestly, had all expected that to be the case and that they were going to need to pick him up the second he tried.

So, the fact that he was reaching out to them, after a month of radio silence, asking to meet…

'Do you think it's a trap?' Simpson asked, driving quickly.

Jamie sat in the passenger seat of the BMW saloon, watching the road ahead as Simpson confidently navigated the early-morning traffic, sliding through gaps, much to the dismay of people behind.

She bit her lip. 'I don't know. What did the message say?'

Ottosen had Jamie's SIM plugged into a device that allowed them to track incoming calls and messages, triangulate the caller, and detect whether anyone was trying to reverse the trace or find out where they were using it.

'Just that he needed to meet with us, and didn't want to tell us what he had over the phone,' Simpson said.

'It could be,' Jamie said. 'I guess we just have to make sure that we do it on our terms. Somewhere we can see him coming, make sure he's not followed.'

'That's a big ask,' Simpson said.

'We'll figure it out.'

'And if he's wired? Or Imperium are tracking him?' Simpson asked.

Jamie drew a slow breath. 'Then I guess we just have to be prepared to grab him, and get his family out, too.'

'His family?' Simpson questioned.

'Yeah,' Jamie said. 'If Imperium see us grab him, they'll go after them. No doubt. Trust me, I know how these guys work.'

'You better than anyone,' he muttered.

She didn't know if that was some sort of snipe, or something else. She ignored it either way. 'So we set the meet, we have him come to us – in a taxi. We have him ditch his phone, his wallet.'

'Drop them at a train or bus station locker?' Simpson added.

Fuck, how many American spy movies had this guy watched? Or was that really how they did things in the FBI?

'Whatever,' Jamie said. 'Then we take him somewhere quiet, and we make sure he's not wired or anything.'

'And that he's not there to kill you.'

Jamie raised her eyebrows. 'What?'

'Well, if Torgrimson's gone back to Imperium, told them everything, maybe he's been instructed to take you out. Been told that'll buy his family's safety. He and Naas have both seen you, have your contact information. Maybe he's been smart, managed to keep his phone call with you quiet.'

Jamie brushed it off. 'No, no, if they had any idea that he'd been talking to us, he'd already been dead.'

'Willing to bet your life on that?'

'Sounds like I am already,' Jamie said, watching with growing dread as a red light turned green and they accelerated towards the office.

'I mean, you're a big fish.'

'A big fish?'

'Yeah, you've been on Imperium's ass for a while now, and wounding Sandbech like you did.' He sucked air between his teeth. 'Maybe they're taking the chance to get rid of you. While they can.'

'So, then you go instead.'

He looked at her. 'They don't know me.'

'Exactly.'

'No, I mean, they don't know me. And I'd rather keep it that way. It benefits no one for any of us to be identified. If you've been made – if Sandbech or anyone else puts two and two together, and realises who you really are…'

Jamie was quiet then. She didn't like the line of thinking, but she couldn't really disagree with it.

They didn't say another word the whole way to the office.

45

Torgrimson came by taxi, as instructed.

Simpson had been outvoted on the train station locker drop.

Instead, the taxi took Torgrimson towards the south end of the city, and dropped him at the public car park for Ulriken, a mountain that overlooked the water and the city itself. There was a public cable car there that took people to the park at the top.

He stepped out of the taxi, his phone ringing the second he did. Simpson and Jamie were already at the top, nonchalantly pressing binoculars to their eyes – like the other visitors and tourists there.

'Torgrimson,' Jamie said. 'Look to your right.'

The big man with the mousy brown hair hung his head and sighed in the distance below. 'Is this really necessary?' he asked tiredly, his voice in both Jamie and Simpson's heads, being fed through their earpieces.

She ignored the question. 'You can see a white Volvo saloon? About twenty metres away.'

He looked up and searched the line of cars parked up. 'I see it.'

'Good,' Jamie said. 'Walk towards it, open the back door. Then take off your jacket, remove your service weapon, your wallet, keys, everything. Empty all your pockets, and put everything on the back seat.'

'You can't be serious?'

'Do it, or this all goes away,' Jamie said flatly.

'For God's sake,' he muttered, sidling over.

When he got there, he reached out tentatively and opened the back door.

Simpson stepped away for a second, touched his ear, hailing Hallberg.

Torgrimson put the phone down on top of the car, pulled off his coat, dropped his wallet and keys on top of it, then seemed to deliberate over his pistol.

Jamie's grip tightened on the binoculars.

Then he gave it up, put it inside, and picked the phone up again. 'Okay,' he said. 'But I can't lose the phone while we're talking. Where are you?' he asked, turning around to search the car park.

He jolted a little, seeing Hallberg standing behind him.

'Torgrimson,' Jamie said, grabbing his attention. 'Hands on the car. Do it.'

He sighed again, turned, and put his hands on the roof of the car as Hallberg patted him down. He knew the procedure well enough, but he still didn't seem to like being on the receiving end for once.

Hallberg moved away from him then, nodding into the distance, signalling that he was clean.

'Happy now?' Torgrimson asked, still looking around.

Not yet, Jamie thought. 'In the back of the driver's seat,'

she said, 'there's a ticket for the tram. Take it, get in, and head to the top.'

'Now?'

'Now, Torgrimson. And you can ditch the phone.' She hung up and watched as he pulled it from his ear, turned his head to squint up into the now mid-morning sun, and then dropped it on top of his coat. He bent down into the car and emerged a second later, closing the door and inspecting the ticket in his hand.

He headed for the station, walking slowly, cautiously, eyes roving the car park. He walked like a man who was afraid he was about to be killed. Not one there to kill someone.

But Jamie wasn't about to let her guard down.

Torgrimson stepped off the cable car a few minutes later and looked around.

Ottosen had been watching surrounding traffic cameras and the camera in the car park for anyone tailing him, and Ves was stationed above the cable car, sitting with a laptop, monitoring with an RFID scanner for any signals that were incoming or outgoing. So far, nothing was telling them that Torgrimson was being watched, tracked, monitored, or tailed.

Nevertheless, Simpson was sitting about ten metres away on a bench with a book, a silenced Glock 19M pistol on his lap under a folded-up coat.

Jamie lifted a hand to wave to Torgrimson. She was standing on a rocky outcropping that had clear line of sight to the cable car, but not to the city below. The last thing she wanted was to catch a bullet from a long rifle looking up from below.

He checked over his shoulders automatically, seemed to fail to pick either Ves or Simpson out of the walkers and tourists moving around, and then headed over.

'Janssen, is it?' he said, raising an eyebrow. 'We still using that name?'

'Let's just dispense with the pleasantries, shall we? You wanted to meet. I hope what you have to say is worth it,' Jamie said curtly, feeling Simpson's eyes on her.

She made sure to give Torgrimson space. There was no need to stand close – the wind was moving quickly up here and their voices wouldn't carry.

He sighed, shivering a little in the cool breeze without his jacket, and met her eye. 'I have something,' he said. 'And I wanted to look you in the eye before I told you.'

'Why?' Jamie kept her voice calm, but felt her heart pick up a little.

'Because if they find out I'm telling you, there's not a doubt in my mind that they'll kill me, my family, and probably my cousins, nieces, nephews, and my barber, too. So if I do, I want your word that you'll make sure my family is safe – I don't care about me. Not anymore. I just need to—' He let out a shaky breath and then settled himself. Jeez, the guy was terrified. 'I need to know they'll be safe. I want your word. And I want to look you in the eye when you say it.'

She had to keep her nerve. 'Tell me what you know first, and then I'll decide if it's enough.'

'Fucking hell,' he muttered, shaking his head. 'Is there any point, then?'

'Torgrimson,' Jamie said, risking a step closer. 'If you know what you have is valuable, then it'll be enough to ensure your family's safety.'

'You promise?' he said suddenly, looking up at her.

She could hear Simpson's sharp tone, even in the dead silence in her ear.

'There are no promises in this game.'

He sagged.

'But I'll do all I can to make sure they don't come to harm, whatever happens. You have my word on that.'

'And how much is your word worth?' he spat. 'I don't even know your name.'

She stood, staring into the distance, collecting herself. 'It's worth a lot. You're just going to have to decide whether you believe me or not.'

He watched her closely, trying to weigh his options.

Jamie awaited the result.

He sighed, mustering the courage to do it. 'I heard from Naas.'

'Go on.'

'He reached out to me yesterday – but he wouldn't tell me where he was or what was going on.'

Jamie hoped he had more than that.

'But he told me that there's an event happening.'

'An event?' Jamie raised an eyebrow. 'What kind of event?'

'The kind where they need security.' He sighed again, grappling with telling her. 'I don't know why Naas was the one to tell me – or where he is, even – but a week from now, I'm to travel to Alesund and await further instructions.'

'Await further instructions?'

'Yes, Naas said that he needed me to come and work security for an event. But he wouldn't say where or what it was.'

Jamie nodded, processing that. 'And what day is that?'

'Next Saturday.'

She drew a breath. 'You're not giving me much to go on, here.'

'I know, I know,' he said. 'But I have more.'

Jamie eyed him. 'You know I can't guarantee anything without knowing the whole story first. You're going to have to tell me, then we can help. Right now, you're not giving me anything.'

'He told me to bring a suit – black tie. And I think… Emma Hagen is going.'

Jamie masked her piqued interest. 'How do you know that?'

'When we were investigating the Lange case, we needed access to the scheduling software they were using. I went back there, told her secretary that I needed to take another look at Lange's history. And then I copied and dumped Emma Hagen's own schedule history, saved it on a flash drive.'

'And you did this after you got the call from Naas?'

'Before – to try and get something on her. Something useful. But after the call from Naas, I remembered that she had that weekend blocked off for a holiday.'

'It's not exactly concrete.'

'No, but every second of every day for the last year has been meticulously planned and annotated. Where, when, travel details, links to voice notes. Everything. Her whole life. Except for next weekend.'

'Where is that flash drive now?' Jamie asked.

'It's somewhere safe.'

'Don't fuck with us here,' Jamie said, her voice dropping a few tones.

'I'm not, but I have to try to protect myself somehow.'

Jamie bit her lip. 'I understand. But we're going to need that flash drive to confirm what you're saying. Otherwise, we have no way of knowing whether what you're telling us is true, or whether you're walking us into a trap.'

He looked angry then, his brow crumpling, nostrils flaring. 'I'm sticking my neck out here for you – risking everything. *Everything.*'

'So are we. And we're only going to get one shot at this.

You're going to have to wear a tracker, some sort of recording device, and—'

'Woah, woah,' he said, stepping back and putting his hands up. 'There's not a chance in hell I'm going to be wearing *anything* walking in there.'

'Torgrimson, you're going to have to. How else do you expect us to get anything worthwhile out of this?' Jamie searched his face for any hint of an inroad here.

He licked his lips, lowering his hands. 'There is another way. I've worked security at these kinds of things before. Events where people get together like this… *privately.* There are no names, no guest lists, but people are invited. Big people. Politicians, judges, business people…'

Jamie kept her expression even, waiting for whatever was coming next.

'It's a way that they can get everyone together, seeing each other's faces. You don't know who's going to be there until you are… But it's' – he snapped his fingers – 'What do you call it? The thing with nuclear weapons?'

It struck her. 'Mutually assured destruction,' Jamie said.

He nodded.

'Fuck. They get everyone on their payroll in a room together, ply them with decadence, make sure everyone knows exactly who brought them there. And that makes sure no one talks. Because if one does, it all comes crashing down.' Jamie shook her head. 'Throw in the threat of having your throat slit and your entire family butchered' – she caught Torgrimson's eye – 'sorry. But it's… elegant. If not a little bit terrifying.'

'And I don't suspect many people pass up that invitation.'

'For fear of their lives,' Jamie finished for him. 'So what are you suggesting? We follow you to Alesund, tail you to wherever the party is being held, and then snap photos of the guests as they come in?'

'Will that be enough?' Torgrimson asked.

'Probably not,' Jamie said. 'Attending a party isn't illegal last time I checked.'

'Then we probably need to go with the other option.'

'Which is what?' Jamie narrowed her eyes slightly.

'Like I said,' he mumbled, turning to look out over the hazy vista, rolling mountains drowned in yellow sunlight. 'These events don't have a guest list. And no one knows exactly who's going to be there.' He glanced at her, met her eye. 'Which means with some luck, a little help, and good timing, pretty much anyone can slip inside unnoticed.'

46

SIMPSON HAD BEEN silent for nearly thirty minutes.

Jamie, Hallberg, and Ves were all watching him closely. Ottosen was still trawling through all the schedules they had access to in order to try and match what Torgrimson had said to people they suspected as being involved with Imperium. So far, everyone was booked to be away that weekend.

Which meant it was looking more and more like they might have to take a chance.

Photographing them arriving would be one thing, but that many people in one room? Under Imperium's wing? If they could get in there… The things they could overhear, the things they could testify about. And if they could get access to a security system or anything like that, well… it could take them from having nothing but hearsay to taking down the whole set-up.

But it involved doing the unthinkable – and heading right into the belly of the beast.

Jamie was scared. Terrified, even. She didn't know whether Sandbech had got a good look at her at the sawmill. She didn't think so. And if they had a picture of Jamie

Johansson on file, they'd see her with long blonde hair, blue eyes. Now, she had short black hair, and coloured contacts wouldn't be a big ask. But was that enough to keep her safe? She didn't know. But they'd made no headway on the case in nearly a month, and everyone they suspected of involvement with Imperium had been going about their normal lives. There was no mysterious money moving, no shady deals being struck. Nothing.

This was maybe the only shot they had.

And the longer they waited, the smarter Imperium would get. The harder it would be to catch them.

Jamie couldn't stick the waiting anymore.

'Well?' she asked, unfolding, and then refolding her arms impatiently.

Simpson massaged his mouth with his fingers. 'I'm thinking.'

'You've been thinking for thirty minutes,' Jamie said.

'Yeah, and I'll be thinking for a while longer,' he said curtly. 'This isn't a quick decision.' He looked up. 'We have to be smart about this. Have to make sure Torgrimson isn't playing us.'

'I don't know if he is,' Jamie said honestly, 'but if he's not, this is the break we've been waiting for.'

Simpson didn't reply.

'Come on, the Lange lead is dead in the water. No one's going near her. Because as many people as they've got on the take, Imperium know that Kripos is watching Nina Lange now, and exposing themselves again is going to be too risky.'

Simpson was still, and then nodded slightly in agreement.

'We went after Torgrimson and Naas specifically to get one of them to flip – and now that one of them has, and we have a chance at doing something real, you don't want to take it?'

'Desire has nothing to do with it, Johansson.'

Jamie watched him. He called her Jamie when they were sparring outside the office. Now it was Johansson again.

'You can't say you don't want to nail them – after everything? After Klein?'

'It's not that I don't want to,' he said slowly, standing up, 'I just think you want to more than anyone else in the room.'

'And what's wrong with that?' Jamie asked defensively.

'It means you don't think about decisions before making them.'

'You're saying my judgement is clouded?'

'Isn't it?' Simpson said.

Damn, he could be a real prick when he wanted to be.

'No,' Jamie said flatly. 'It's not. My vision and my focus are clear. I'm not saying we rush headlong into this – we do our homework, our due diligence, and if everything checks out, we go through with it. If it doesn't, we back out. Even if it's at the last second. And on your word, too. No questions,' she said, holding her hands up.

He measured her, as if deciding whether to believe her. Then he raised his hand slowly, his index finger extended. It bobbed softly in the air. 'I'm not saying okay – but I'm saying we need to look into it. And if – and *only* if everything is watertight, and I mean *watertight* – we do it. But I want there to be no doubt, and I want every second of it mapped out, prepped, and triple-checked. I want to know when this thing is going down, where, who's going to be there, what kind of security we're looking at, what our ingress and egress plan is, how Torgrimson is going to fit in – and how we make sure he doesn't fuck us – and then…' He trailed off and sighed. 'And then, we'll see.'

Jamie had his eyes fully. She held his gaze, her expression hard. Except on the inside, she was a little disappointed.

Disappointed he didn't just shoot the whole thing down then and there. Because now they may actually have to go through with it – and if they did, whether Simpson insisted, Hallberg pleaded, or Ves demanded, she knew that there was no way in hell she'd let any of them walk into whatever was waiting ahead.

No, it was her. It had always been her.

It had always been her fight.

She'd told Hallberg that months ago in Stockholm. She looked at her now, and Hallberg nodded and smiled back reassuringly.

Jamie rattled out a quiet breath and flexed her sweating hands at her sides.

Simpson clapped loudly, and she jolted a little.

'Okay, then,' he said. 'Let's get to work.'

47

THE TIME SEEMED to whirl by.

Jamie's eyes had been permanently embedded with the strobe of passing streetlights, she thought. The amount of time they'd spent on the road was ridiculous. And she didn't think she'd slept for more than a four-hour stretch since they'd begun.

They'd put their heads together to try and figure out where an event like that could be held, and then worked off what they knew.

Alesund was north of Bergen. Seven hours by car. And a drive they'd made half a dozen times in as many days. After checking with all public venues, and eliminating them, they began moving on to suitable private residences. Of which there were a lot. It seemed that every kilometre of the expansive coast surrounding Alesund was home to sprawling estates owned by ultra-wealthy business people, magnates, lords, dukes, and all manner of other high society. It was like finding a gilded needle in a very expensive haystack.

Any attempt to try to narrow it down based on where some of the likely guest list were supposed to be staying wasn't proving easy, either. They'd now resorted to looking for catering companies, party planners, or anything else that might indicate where the thing was going down, to try to trace it through them.

It was now Friday, just twenty-four hours until the event was happening, and they'd whittled it down to a likely suspect. But they couldn't be completely sure, because getting into the grounds was going to be difficult. And if they were caught, if Imperium had any inkling of what was to come, they'd be finished before they even got started.

The former palace was built in 1780, as a 'holiday' home during the reign of Christian VII. The royal family had kept it until the late 1800s, and since, it had changed hands three times. Currently, it was owned by the majority stakeholder in Nordic Oil, the second-largest oil company in Norway.

No one really needed much convincing that this was probably the place.

The palace was huge – probably twenty, maybe thirty bedrooms, a large tower in one corner, a render and wood-cladded exterior complete with red-tiled roof and tall, narrow windows. It nestled in a fjord about thirty miles north of Alesund, and owned the entire thing, pretty much. It even had its own jetty, which faced out onto the private expanse of water. The whole estate stretched across two kilometres of coastline, and took up some twelve-hundred acres of dense, sloped woodland. A single road wound through the forest, beginning at a set of huge iron gates, which themselves were tucked half a mile down a road that led nowhere else. A twelve-foot stone wall ran around the perimeter of the property, and though the construction of that behemoth was done when the palace was built, the motion and pressure sensors now littering every inch of its coping were distinctly modern, and prevented any kind of approach from the ground.

An approach from the water seemed like the best idea, but what kind of security there'd be out there on the night of the party, they didn't know.

Torgrimson was due to arrive in Alesund in less than sixteen hours, at which point they were supposed to give him careful instructions of how this was going to play out, and so far, they had little in the way of a plan, and Simpson was getting nervous.

They all were.

Jamie jolted a little – it seemed to be becoming a habit, much to her dismay – as the door opened and Ves entered the hotel room.

Jamie sat upright, hauling herself out of the deep trance she'd seemingly fallen into, and checked her watch. Shit, it was after six – she'd been sitting there for more than an hour contemplating this.

'Ves,' she said, pushing out of the chair.

Ves swung the garment bag she was carrying over her shoulder and held it up. 'Got it,' she said, smiling briefly. Jamie and she hadn't built what anyone would call a 'bond'. There was a level of professional courtesy at work, but Ves's strait-laced, by-the-book attitude didn't seem to gel well with Jamie's approach. If only she could have met Jamie two years ago, then it would have been a whole different story. Like looking in a mirror.

Shit, how things change.

Ves dropped the hanger on Jamie's bed. 'I hope it fits,' she said.

They had a twin room in a decent four-star hotel. Hallberg was staying in a double room down the street, and Simpson and Ottosen were checked into another hotel on the next street over. They couldn't be too careful.

All of them were spread thin and operating at the ragged edge.

Jamie approached the garment bag cautiously. 'Thanks,' she said. 'I'm sure it will.'

Ves rolled her lips into a line and shrugged. 'Well, Alesund isn't exactly Milan,' she replied, sitting in one of the chairs next to the vanity table opposite the beds. 'And I didn't really know what occasion I was buying for. I did what I could.'

'I'm sure it'll be perf…' Jamie trailed off.

'What's wrong?' Ves asked, looking up from her phone.

Jamie lifted the ruby-red dress out of the bag and held it up. 'Where's the rest of it?' she asked, turning to face Ves, the horror on her face apparent.

'What do you mean?' Ves asked, sticking her bottom lip out.

'What's this?' Jamie said, running her hand up and down the large space between the two straps. She turned it around in the air. 'And where's the back?'

'It's backless,' Ves said, as though that much was obvious. 'And it's plunging.'

'Plunging?' Jamie raised an eyebrow. 'It's fucking non-existent.'

Ves made no effort to hide her eye roll. 'You don't wear a lot of dresses, do you.' It wasn't even a question.

Ves was a smart woman, attractive, naturally feminine, and even in the trousers, heeled boots, and loose blouses she wore to work every day, Jamie could tell she took fastidious care of her appearance. Took pride in it.

That was just one more thing they butted heads over, she supposed.

Ves's eyes went from Jamie's mud-splattered boots – still dirty from trudging around outside the walls of the palace –

up her stretchy function-over-fashion jeans, her loose unisex long-sleeve, right up to the hair that she hadn't brushed for two days and was pinned and ponytailed roughly.

'I can't wear this,' Jamie said, throwing it down on the bed. 'The idea is to *blend in,* not… do whatever this thing is.'

Ves laughed through closed lips, like when a child says something mildly amusing but totally ignorant. 'Trust me, Johansson,' she said, voice dripping with condescension, 'you'll stick out more going into a party like this one wearing anything else. There'll be a hundred women there, and they'll fall into two categories – they'll be dignified wives wearing long gowns, complete with sequins, pearls, diamonds, and all manner of other clanging, bangled jewellery.'

'And the other?' Jamie asked.

'Will be paid more to be there for the night than the jewellery on the wives' necks is worth.' Ves got up and walked towards her. 'And trust me, you're not going to pass for a judge's wife.'

Jamie understood then. 'So you want me to dress like an escort?'

'It'll certainly be the safest option.'

Jamie gritted her teeth.

'If it's any consolation,' Ves said lightly, squeezing her on the shoulders, 'of all the women there, I doubt many of the men will be looking at you.'

Jamie stared up at her, unsure if that was a compliment or the most offensive thing anyone had ever said to her.

'You'll just fall right through the cracks,' she said, patting Jamie's upper arms, and then walking towards the door. 'That's what you want, right? To go unnoticed?' She glanced back.

Jamie didn't have the words.

'I'm going to get some coffee. I'll grab you one, too. You

look like you could use it.' That same closed-mouth chuckle. 'Go on, try it on. We need to know as soon as possible if we need a bigger size. I'll be back in a few.'

And then she was gone, the door closed behind her.

Jamie stood in silence, reeling.

She didn't know what was worse. Looking like a prostitute, or looking like a prostitute no one would want to pay for.

Either way, what little confidence she had before was now totally gone.

And the worst thing of all – even worse than the gut-punch she'd just been given – was that – Jamie held up the dress again, scowling profoundly – in this fucking thing, there'd be nowhere to hide her gun.

48

TORGRIMSON WAS WORKING security along with what seemed like half of the rest of the Bergen police department, and plenty of other trained professionals. All ex-military, with square shoulders, square heads, and tight tuxedos that showed off the telltale lumps of their 'concealed' firearms.

Torgrimson was stationed outside, on the veranda that led down to the lake, which was more heavily patrolled than the grounds themselves.

Which left Jamie and Simpson with only one option – and that was going straight through the front gate.

Ottosen was driving a Mercedes S-Class that they'd managed to secure from a luxury rental company, and Simpson was sitting in the back, with Jamie, queuing up to the gate in a long procession. He was in a three-piece tuxedo with a green-and-black paisley waistcoat. His thick hair was coiffed perfectly and styled back, and his strong jaw was shaven clean. He drummed nervously on his knee with his fingers, looking out of the window at the creeping trees.

'This is stupid,' he muttered for the thousandth time.

Jamie had to agree, and was doing her best to breathe through it.

It was just after eight, and contacting Torgrimson now was too risky. He'd told them there was no strict 'guest list' but Jamie and Simpson figured there had to be some sort of way that they were monitoring who was going in or out. Whether that was collecting IDs, or they had some sort of facial recognition system in place, Jamie didn't know. But whatever it was, she had a feeling that they'd need help getting through the gate.

Torgrimson was to be there for eight. And if he wasn't… Well, Jamie guessed that Simpson and she would be ripping free the pistols taped under the front seats and shoving them in the faces of whoever came to turn them away.

Ottosen was under strict orders to turn around and get them the hell out of there at the first sign of trouble. But as they edged closer to the hulking iron gates, bumper to bumper with black, blacked-out town cars, hemmed in by slippery, mossy banks on each side, turning around here was going to be pretty impossible. Which brought Jamie back to Simpson's point of this being a stupid fucking idea.

She pulled at the hem of her dress, not liking the seemingly endless stretch of bare thigh staring back up at her through the slit in her hem.

In fact, she felt practically naked. Her exposed back was sticking to the leather of the seat, and the fact that she could feel the air conditioning on her sternum told her that 'plunging' was not a neckline she was likely to explore again. Hell, she wasn't even allowed to wear a bra. And she didn't even want to think about the underwear that Ves had made her wear – and just how little of it there was.

The car ahead crawled through the gate and then accelerated away into the woods, heading for the palace to join the other guests.

Ottosen trundled on and then slowed as a man stepped into the road and held his hand up.

Another came to the window and knocked on it.

Neither of them were Torgrimson. But both of them were large, formidable, and armed.

'Fuck,' Simpson said, knees bouncing quickly now.

Jamie could see his fingers flexing, his eyes going to the bottom of the seat in front.

Ottosen glanced at them in the rear-view as the guy knocked for a second time. Simpson swallowed, then nodded.

Ottosen wound it down, and the guy looked inside, then glanced into the back, at Jamie and Simpson, who'd taken to looking out the window as regally as he could.

Jamie smiled easily at him, though she could feel her pulse racing.

'Invitations?' the guy asked, looking at Ottosen.

He looked in the rear-view again, then smiled at the guy, patting his jacket innocently. 'I, uh… I don't…' Ottosen said, shrugging and chuckling nervously.

'Wait here,' the guy said, pulling his head out of the window and heading for the other big guy.

'We're so fucked,' Simpson said under his breath, leaning forward and looking out at the two conversing guards. 'Invitations?' He looked at Jamie then. 'Why the fuck didn't Torgrimson tell us? And where the fuck is he?'

Jamie couldn't answer either of those questions. But unless a miracle happened, she guessed they were about to get murdered… or turned away. She suspected the former.

Yeuch, this was not what she wanted to be wearing when she died.

The guy came back to the window now and bent down.

Out of the corner of her eye, Jamie could see Simpson practically vibrating in the seat.

She kept her eyes fixed on the mercenary with his head in the car.

He opened his mouth to speak, but just as he did, another voice echoed outside.

The guy in the window withdrew and stood up. And past him, Jamie could see Torgrimson jogging down the road, lit up by their headlights.

He was calling out to them, and the two mercenaries turned and walked to greet him.

Torgrimson wasn't small by any stretch, but he was dwarfed by the two guys on either side of him.

He tried to catch his breath, but it was clear he'd run the best part a mile to get there and was red in the face. The mercenaries both focused on him, their backs towards the car, and Simpson took the opportunity and leaned forward, unstrapping his pistol and pulling it onto his lap.

He looked at Jamie, motioning her to do the same, but she had faith in Torgrimson. And even if she didn't, she didn't think a pistol was going to do much good here. They might take out the one guy in front of them, but if they started a fire-fight, with the amount of security waiting ahead, Jamie didn't think they'd be the ones to finish it.

No, the much safer option would be to get out, ditch the car, and run as fast as they could for the main road. And hope that Ves and Hallberg, who were waiting for a distress call, could pick them up before Imperium caught up.

Torgrimson was speaking quickly, gesturing, looking from one guy to the other, and then, he fished in his pocket and pulled out a piece of paper. He handed it to one of the guys and he read it, and then looked at the other, then they both turned to look at the car.

The one with the paper beckoned Ottosen forward, and Simpson reached between his knees and pulled back the slide on the pistol, chambering a round. He held it down between his knees, obscured from view, and assumed an air of nonchalance.

Jamie tried to keep her breathing from sounding like panting. This shit never got easier.

Ottosen began moving and Jamie leaned her head back, filling her lungs.

The guard leaned in again, and she heard Simpson's fingers readjust on the grip of the pistol.

She tensed, hoping to hell he wasn't about to put one in the guy's face. She could already see him lining up a shot through the windscreen at the other in front of them.

The guard held up the piece of paper then, and pushed it through the window. 'You'll need this,' he said gruffly.

Ottosen reached out and took it nervously, and they all watched as the guard stood up and waved them through.

As the car began to pull forward, she locked eyes with Torgrimson through the passenger window, registering the frightened look on his face, and then he was gone, dwindling in the rear window, bathed in the dim glow of their retreating lights.

Simpson reached forward and took the paper from Ottosen's hand, reading what was written on it.

'It's just coordinates,' he said, looking up at Jamie, brow furrowed. 'From a hashed email. Dated this morning.'

She took it from him and looked it over. He was right – it was just a printed email with a pair of coordinates on it that she assumed led to the palace. Which meant the guests had no idea where they were going until that morning.

It was untraceable, seemingly innocent. But she guessed that everyone invited had this email, and if they didn't bring it or weren't able to produce it at the gate, they wouldn't be able to enter. She assumed that there'd been another one some weeks earlier with just a date written on it, too. They really weren't taking any chances here.

As the car wound forward through the undulating forest, she held on to the paper tightly.

Simpson had come to his senses and had put the pistol back under the seat in front.

Neither of them knew what lay ahead, but with Torgrimson now a mile behind them, they didn't have any more help.

They were officially behind enemy lines, and there was no quick way out.

The trees broke suddenly, and then they were climbing up a road hemmed in by manicured, rolling lawns.

The palace rose up in front of them, two rows of tall windows spread across a huge, regal frontage. The corners were rounded like turrets, and a huge, spouting fountain in front of the wide stone front steps made for a roundabout.

Their tyres crunched into it as they rejoined the procession of cars that were circling, dropping their passengers at the foot of the stairs between two more armed guards.

The pairs – guys in tuxes and women in, as Ves had guessed, either dresses that made Jamie's look reserved, or draped in diamonds and sequins and long, modest gowns – moved up a red carpet towards the top, where a barrier had been set out. Two more guards were stationed either side, and were offering trays to the guests to put their phones, wallets, keys, everything in. Then they were wanded, then patted down, before being ushered through the final gate and into the party.

'Glad you put the gun away,' Jamie said, keeping her voice low. 'Looks like heavy security.'

'Wouldn't expect any less,' Simpson said, hunching forward to watch through the windscreen. 'We'll be okay, though.'

Jamie didn't know if he was reassuring himself or her.

Once the cars had passed the steps, they were being directed down a side entrance that moved around the palace. She'd looked at the aerial plans, and there was no other way in or out. They must just be parked up, waiting to ferry their passengers home. Looked like Ottosen had a long night ahead.

Jamie, however, was more concerned with the trays being taken at security. She couldn't see them being handed back. No, shit, the security guard was writing on labels, sticking them to the trays, and then putting them aside. Fuck, they'd have their phones taken from them. Which meant they'd have no way of contacting anyone if anything went wrong.

But so long as they didn't confiscate her bag, they still had a fighting chance.

Jamie leaned forward. 'Ottosen,' she said quickly. 'We won't be able to contact you. So if you see anything going wrong – *anything* – you get out of here, okay? Don't wait for us.'

He looked back at her.

Simpson leaned in. 'She's right. Keep your eyes peeled, and if you suspect anything, go. Full speed, run them down on the way out if you have to.'

Ottosen met Simpson's eye for a second, and then nodded. 'Okay,' he said quietly.

He wasn't a field agent – he was a cyber securities officer, an analyst, a computer expert. He'd not been trained for this kind of thing. Hell, even driving the car was above his pay grade, and Jamie could tell Simpson was thinking the same thing as her. That if something went wrong – which they both had a feeling it would – they didn't want his blood on their hands. They'd both rather be abandoned with no escape plan than to have Ottosen hang on and die with them.

Though neither had any more time to think about it. Because the moment they both leaned back into their seats, Ottosen was stopping again, and the door was being pulled open for Jamie.

She filled her lungs, fastened her smile in place, the red lipstick alien on her mouth, the make-up heavy on her cheeks and eyes, and swung her smooth, well-muscled legs out of the car.

The waiting mercenary held out a hulking hand, and Jamie took it, with painted red nails, and levered herself upwards, clutch bag in her other hand.

She wobbled on the loose gravel, regained her balance, and then took the first stone step, shaking her head a little so her fringe obscured her face from any security cameras that might be trained on them.

The air was chilly, though she wasn't sure if that could be counted on as the reason she was shaking. Simpson was at her side then, offering his arm, and behind, the door had already been closed.

She was led upwards as Ottosen moved away, and then they were alone, moving towards the gate where they knew they'd have their phones taken. Jamie just wondered how long it would be before someone recognised them. And whether, when that happened they'd have any warning at all, any chance of escaping. Or if, before they even knew it, they'd be manhandled into some secluded room and executed.

They got to the top of the staircase, then paused, both looking at each other. Both with big, false, terrified smiles.

'Shall we?' Simpson asked.

Jamie swallowed. 'Don't really think we can back out now.'

'Probably not,' Simpson said. 'I just hope they've got a free bar, because I need a drink.'

It was times like that Jamie wished she did drink.

But that's not why they were here, and she needed to stay sharp.

Her life depended on it.

49

JAMIE AND SIMPSON were told to face each other, and then they were both patted down. Simpson's was rough and thorough. Jamie's was slightly less rough, but even more thorough. You only needed to take one look at the painted-on dress – that perfectly outlined the shape of Jamie's breasts, stomach, hips – to know that there was no way anything could be hidden. And yet the security guard seemed to think that she was concealing something on her upper thighs.

She glanced down at the stilettos Ves had made her wear and wondered if the heel was sharp enough to skewer the security guard's eyeball like a big olive or if it would simply burst if she kicked him in the face.

He finally left her legs alone and got up, nodding them on.

The guy who'd taken their phones, leaving them with just their damaged chastity, had also taken their invitation, and was promptly tearing it up.

Jamie's eyes lingered on the stacked trays containing everyone's phones – everyone's lives. Personal emails, text messages, phone logs, GPS tracking... enough evidence to bring everyone involved with Imperium down. Those trays were all the evidence they ever wanted and more.

And yet Simpson's hand was firmly on Jamie's lower back, steering her towards the party with just a clutch bag containing various little tubes of make-up she had no intention of attempting to badly re-apply – no matter how vital Ves told her it was – in hand. She wasn't interested when her mother told her that she'd never land a husband without wearing make-up, and she wasn't interested now when Ves told her she'd never make a convincing escort without it.

But they sold the illusion, and that was all that mattered.

The security guard had opened it, looked inside, and then handed it back, not even thinking to check the lining for what was hidden there.

Inside, the entrance hall was cavernous. A double-width staircase led up the middle and split off, wrapping around to an open balcony mezzanine, complete with stonework arches, fine art, and a chandelier that sparkled impossibly.

The mercenaries in suits stuck out like sore thumbs, half a head taller than everyone else, and lurking like overly lifelike waxworks.

People stood around – dozens, hundreds, Jamie guessed. High society of every echelon. She didn't recognise anyone, but that was good. Because the fewer people she recognised, the less chance she had of being recognised herself.

Simpson's hand was on her back again then, guiding her left, towards the next room.

It had the feeling of a regal dining room, but it had been cleared of any furniture, and now played host to a sprawling glass-and-gold bar attended by a dozen bartenders.

Laughter echoed from the people in the room, and the cacophony of clinking champagne flutes, backed by the distant, cavernous hum of a string quartet, made the whole place vibrate.

Jamie and Simpson headed for the bar. They needed to get their bearings and decide on a plan of attack. They'd poured over the floor plans of the palace, but of the fifty rooms, they had no way to know which were set up as what.

Simpson stood at the bar and waited for some attention while Jamie turned her back to it and casually surveyed the room through her dark hair. She spotted three security cameras and six guards. She had no idea what kind of technology they'd be employing, but her haircut, combined with Ves's styling, would hopefully disrupt any facial recognition that might be going on and prevent anyone from picking her out easily.

Every inch of the place was being watched, and, she guessed, recorded and chronicled for future blackmailing, so they couldn't be too careful. But, security cameras meant that there was a security *room* somewhere. Which meant that they had something to aim for. Though how the hell they were going to get in there, she didn't know.

How they'd get anywhere was a mystery.

'Come on,' Simpson whispered, turning around and handing Jamie a tumbler filled with a fizzing clear liquid. Her nose told her it was lemonade and a clear spirit – gin, she guessed. But she wouldn't be sipping to find out.

Simpson had a double measure of an amber liquid swirling in his. Whisky. Predictable. But she didn't say anything.

He took a mouthful, then headed towards the middle of the floor, aiming for the door on the far end. This was always the plan – to do a lap of the place, get the lay of the land, scope out which exits were available to them, where things were, and let the plan develop, or die, from there.

They'd made a pact that if the whole thing seemed impossible, that they'd get out cleanly, without making a fuss.

Jamie had settled into a weird sort of calm – more like a fatigue. Her adrenal glands were spent and now she just felt tired, relaxed in an exhausted sort of way.

Simpson was working through his whisky fairly quickly.

Guess they both had their own way of dealing with things.

If nothing else, maybe they could just eat some expensive amuse-bouches, laugh and pretend like they were normal people, maybe dance a little, and then head home. Would that really be so bad?

As Jamie squeezed past what she guessed were judges, politicians, police officers, and business people, she couldn't hold on to the fantasy. Every person here had taken a bribe, betrayed themselves, and what they stood for. Imperium was a cancer, and it had been allowed to run rampant.

So, no, as much as she just wanted to slide under the radar and suck down some crab cakes and caviar, she had no intention of doing that. And as she watched Simpson down the rest of his whisky and place it on the tray of a passing waitress, she figured he was in the same frame of mind.

The decadence was sickening, and arrogance disgusting.

They just needed an opportunity.

They were in the room that opened out through a set of glass doors onto a paved veranda overlooking the fjord and the grass lawn below, lights strung above it in long lines, when Simpson stopped and turned, looking at Jamie.

She paused, full drink still in hand, and met his eyes.

'Behind me,' he said. 'Don't look. It's Emma Hagen.'

Jamie lifted the glass to her lips slowly and tipped the

liquid against them, not letting any pass. She lowered the glass then, resisting the urge to lick them. She knew she wouldn't like the taste, anyway.

'Want me to just tackle her?' Jamie asked.

'Sure, then I'll throw her over my shoulder and we'll just walk on out, shall we?' He smiled easily, though his angst was hard to hide.

Jamie raised her eyebrows. 'May cause a little bit of upset,' she replied.

'We'll call that Plan B then.' He laughed a little. It felt forced.

The small exchange of humour did little to lighten the mood.

Emma Hagen's presence wasn't surprising. But all it did was confirm their suspicions. And that wasn't proof.

It came to them at the same time then. 'We should split up,' they both said in unison.

Each nodded in confirmation.

'I'll meet you on the veranda in twenty minutes?' Simpson asked.

Jamie nodded again. 'Sounds good,' she replied.

Simpson leaned in then, kissing her on the cheek. 'Be safe,' he whispered in her ear, resting his hand on her hip. He let his lips linger for a moment, and the nape of Jamie's neck tingled, his breath hot on her skin.

He pulled away, letting his fingers slide from her side and drop slowly to his own.

Simpson's broad back disappeared into the crowd, and Jamie was on her own once more.

They could cover twice as much ground on their own, and it was easier to play dumb and lost that way too. 'Where's the bathroom?' tended to fly a lot better if you were alone and could feign drunkenness.

Jamie filled her lungs, acutely aware of the expanding patch of bare flesh at her sternum, readjusted and pulled down her dress, and then got moving.

Simpson was going to do a lap, and so was she. The ground floor looked to be where everyone was congregating, but anything worth seeing was going to be hidden away upstairs or off the beaten track. Jamie just wondered how close she could get before she started alarm bells ringing.

Well, she thought, putting down her drink, only one way to find out.

50

Beyond the corner room leading out to the veranda, there was another large, nondescript hall with a vaulted and moulded ceiling. In here, the mood was a little more sultry and subdued. The lights were dimmer, the waitresses and waiters circling with tumblers filled with various cocktails instead of champagne flutes.

A lounge singer stood in the corner in a sequinned dress, her hips bobbing slowly from side to side in time with the band behind her. She was glamorous, with tightly curled black hair. On her right, a double-bassist in sunglasses plucked and nodded his head, and on her left, a saxophonist droned away. A drummer sat at the back, playing with brushes.

Jamie had to admit, it was more relaxing than being drowned in bright light and surrounded by hundreds of people like she had been in the main room.

She held her hand up to fend off a waiter with a tray of citrusy drinks, and then stopped, finding her path barred by a large man. She looked up, smiling automatically, hands tightening on her clutch bag.

Her red dress swung around her bronzed legs and she turned her head to the side to remove the hair from her face, getting a good look at the living roadblock.

The guy in front of her must have been in his sixties, and his stomach draped over the top of his belt. He had a wide face that hung loosely, his jowls tugging on the corners of his eyes. His tuxedo was expensive, the trousers black, his jacket that pale shade of smoking cream, and adorned with a red sash covered in badges and medals. He didn't strike her as the military type, so she assumed the nature of his work was more mayoral.

He licked his thin lips unabashedly, and then exhaled through his open mouth, his breathing husky, eyes roving up and down Jamie's barely covered body.

'Hello,' he panted, drawing in a sharp breath.

'Hi,' Jamie replied, trying not to meet his eyes.

He lifted a wrinkled hand and coughed into it, then grinned at her with crooked teeth. 'Shall we?' he asked.

'Shall we what?' Jamie replied, seeing how coy felt. More like intentional ignorance.

'Go upstairs,' the old man said.

Jamie held onto her smile, but the realisation had suddenly dawned that dressed like this – trying to look like *this* – and without the protection of Simpson on her arm, she was probably going to attract some attention.

'I'm sorry,' Jamie said, looking down bashfully. 'I'm spoken for.'

'By who?' the man asked quickly, looking around. 'You're already paid for.'

Jamie gritted her teeth. *Already paid for?* Had Imperium footed the bill for all of these women? Jamie glanced around, seeing that this room was devoid of the well-dressed wives. It was filled with escorts. Beautiful women in short dresses throwing their heads back and laughing, showing off beautiful teeth and bare, glittered, and perfumed chests. They were rubbing the arms of the men in here, firing them sultry glances over the tops of their glasses. They were kissing, and fondling. Petting in some cases. And in others, being led away through a door at the back of the room…

Fuck. Of all the rooms in this place, Jamie had to walk into this one. The one where the guys looking for a good time came.

She drew a slow breath, wondering if she could flee, and what kind of message that would draw.

The mayor of halitosis was staring at her.

'Don't you want to talk first?' Jamie asked then. 'You may not like me.' She had to try and buy some time.

He stepped forward without warning and reached around, taking a handful of her backside and squeezing hard. 'I've heard all I need to,' he growled.

Jamie couldn't repress a shudder, but she managed not to throw her knee into his crotch.

She laughed strangely and pushed his hand off. 'Hold your horses… tiger?' she said. Fuck. That was about as far from natural as she could get.

He narrowed his eyes at her questioningly.

She cleared her throat then. She needed to tread carefully. If she was the only escort here that was prepaid and not doing her job, then that was going to raise eyebrows.

'I'm sorry,' Jamie said. 'I'm just a little nervous. First time,' she added truthfully.

'Oh, ho, ho,' the mayor said, 'then I'll be honoured to introduce you to a few… *things.'* He grinned at her again and Jamie swallowed the rising bile in her throat. 'So,' he went on, 'what do you say? Shall we head upstairs? The night is wasting.'

Jamie stole another glance around. How normalised this all was here. And this guy – here in his mayor's dress. He wasn't obscuring his identity. He was proud of it. They all were. She could see men draped in clergy stoles, men with military medals on their lapels, men handing women their business cards… There was pride here. They were wearing Imperium's brand as a mark of honour. They were operating freely, under Imperium's protection. Sanctioned, protected debauchery.

It struck her then.

How this snuffling pig in front of her could be useful after all.

'Yes,' Jamie said, giving him a big smile. 'Take me upstairs.'

'That's the spirit,' he chortled, offering her a route to the door.

She expected it to come, but it didn't stop it being any more sickening when his hand hit her backside again, his fingers digging into the crease between her butt and her thigh, lingering there, inches from the place that Jamie had made sure very few people had ever had any access too.

She stepped forward quickly, out of his grasp, and headed for the door, hearing him puffing away behind her as he sidled to keep up.

She pushed through the heavy oak door and into a corridor that ran behind the main staircase.

Jamie glanced out at the dignified party, the bright lights, the champagne flutes on silver trays. She could slip away now, rejoin high society, rethink her approach. But she might just be wasting the best chance she'd get all night.

She felt his bulk behind her, sensed another hand coming, and turned, taking it out of the air.

His fingers danced at her hip, trying to spider their way to her.

'Save some for the room,' Jamie said, as seductively as she could. She never had much practice with it.

'You're here for my pleasure,' the mayor spat, snatching his hand back. 'Remember that.' He glared at her for a second. 'One word from me and you'll be out of here before you can even swallow.'

Jamie held fast. Oh, she couldn't wait to get him behind a locked door.

'You're right,' she said then. 'I am here for your pleasure. Anything you want. So let's not waste any more time, shall we?'

She turned on her heel then and headed past the main staircase, following the red carpet down a long hallway. At the end, she could just see another girl in a dress being guided up what looked like another set of stairs.

Jamie kept walking, kept the mayor following, did what she could to swing her hips without turning over on her ankle, and reached it without further incident. Though she thought if he'd got within arm's reach, he probably would have taken another fistful of whatever he could have.

Jamie made sure he was still in tow, and that he wasn't about to keel over, and started upwards. At the top, Jamie was standing at a fork. To her left, a hallway ran back to the mezzanine and the main staircase that led down to the front door.

Ahead, there was a long corridor. It went straight to the back of the palace, with doors all down both sides, and then hooked left at the end. She knew where she was then, the image of the blueprint in her mind aligning with what she was seeing. This was the west upper hallway – these were bedrooms and bathrooms. What would have once been the guest wing of the palace. And the stairs they'd just come up was the staff stairwell, the corridor they'd come through the staff quarters.

At the end of this corridor, there was a left turn, and a hallway that ran down the length of the back of the building. There was another internal staircase there that led down to the kitchen, pantry, and laundry rooms. And if there was going to be some sort of security centre, Jamie guessed it was going to be somewhere around there.

Beyond that stairs, the corridor hooked left again to run up the east wing, back towards the front – more bedrooms, as well as offices.

While the palace was a private residence, it wasn't lived in permanently. Though it did have a full-time staff to take care of it. The owner, one of the top brass in Nordic Oil, used it to host visitors, parties, and that sort of thing. If she could find his office and get in there…

She heard breathing behind her then and scooted forwards again.

He made a grab for her and missed.

Luckily, he didn't have the breath to say anything else.

Jamie stuck to the right-hand doors, pausing at each to hear the sounds of sex coming through the wood. Some were filled with laughter, others were gratuitous moaning, some just had grunting. Jamie grimaced and pushed on, relieved to find the fifth one down was silent.

She pressed on the handle and the door swung open.

A woman in a dark knee-length dress and apron was in the process of stripping the bed. She was wearing rubber gloves to do it. Jamie didn't blame her.

'Sorry,' she said tiredly. 'Won't be long. Try the one opposite – I just finished up in there.'

Jamie nodded apologetically and backed out, closing the door.

She crossed the corridor and opened that one, the mayor just about catching up, his face red and blotchy, eyes blood-shot from the cardio.

'In here,' she said, not even able to look at him.

He collapsed against the doorframe, puffing hard, and then pushed himself in, swinging the door closed.

Without invitation or delay, he started wrestling with his dickie bow and top button.

Jamie looked around the room for any hint of cameras – thankfully seeing none – and then checked out the rest. A big, fourposter bed sat in the centre. A doorway led to an en-suite bathroom. A dark wooden dresser was sitting against the left-hand wall, an incense stick burning on top of it.

Jamie approached, seeing that the dresser top also played home to two oil-stick air fresheners, a bowl of potpourri, and a ceramic dish with a lid on it. She lifted it, seeing a pile of condoms sitting there.

She grimaced.

The lights went down around her then, and she turned.

The Mayor was unbuttoned fully now, his liver-spotted stomach hanging between the loose, crumpled sides of his shirt. His belt was also open, the ends lolling against his thighs, what hung between hidden by his sagging stomach.

'Take it off,' he commanded, flicking a hand at her dress as he advanced.

Jamie swallowed. Fuck. Okay. No, you can do this. You have your plan.

'How about,' Jamie said, approaching and putting a hand on his hairy chest, 'you learn some manners first? Didn't your mother ever teach you how to treat a woman?'

His lip quivered with sudden rage and his fat hand came up quickly. Though predictably.

Jamie caught it with relative ease, dug her nails into the flesh behind his thumb, and bent it back.

His eyes widened and he squealed a little.

'On your knees,' Jamie commanded.

He sank down.

'You're going to do as I say,' she spat.

He whimpered, looking up at her like a puppy dog. But she could see he was getting off on this. It would make this next part easier, at least.

She threw his hand back to him and walked past, sitting on the bed, sliding back a little.

He followed her with his eyes and Jamie watched them light up as she parted her knees.

She beckoned him over with a finger, pushing her legs wider.

He got the picture and scuttled across the floor like a little fat pig, eagerly diving between them, knees still on the floor, elbows on the duvet.

She kept reminding herself. This was the only way.

Jamie swallowed hard, exhaled, steeled herself, and then lifted her right heel over his shoulder, feeling his hot breath on her inner thighs.

And then she squeezed.

Her right thigh against his throat.

Her left hooked under his armpit. She could feel the moistness of his sweat against the back of her knee as she interlocked her ankles and applied steady pressure.

At first, he seemed to think it was part of the game.

And then realisation dawned on him.

His right arm was pinned up against his right ear, above his head, and his left flailed angrily.

The mayor tried to stand, but Jamie held tight, in what was known as a triangle choke. A powerful ground hold used in mixed martial arts. It was a submission move, and once locked in, was nearly impossible to break. The harder they struggled, the faster their oxygen ran out, and the faster they passed out.

In a sanctioned fight, the person stupid enough to get stuck in a triangle choke would tap out before they lost consciousness.

That wasn't an option for this animal.

Jamie needed to take this all the way.

She could see the top three-quarters of his face, staring up at her over her stomach, eyes wide and wild, face like a beetroot.

He tried to stand, his feet scrabbling on the ground.

Jamie felt her back began to lift, and she arched backwards, batting away his clawing left hand.

He raked it over her ribs, pulled at her dress, exposing her breast.

Then the pain came, sharp and violent, erupting from her thigh.

She looked down, saw his bared yellow teeth sinking into her skin.

Anger surged in her and she squeezed harder. As hard as she could. Fuck it, if she broke his neck, she broke his fucking neck!

He kept biting. She kept squeezing, the muscular legs that carried her twenty kilometres every morning on her runs, the muscular legs that could put Simpson into a crumpled heap, the muscular legs shown off by her slitted dress that had no doubt attracted the mayor in the first place, now siphoning the life out of him.

His clawing grew weaker then, his eyes beginning to roll, a sad, mewling, choked noise escaping his lips.

His teeth withdrew from her thigh, and he collapsed against her, heavy and limp.

Jamie counted to ten for good measure, and then began releasing pressure.

She unclenched her own jaw, feeling it ache, realising only then that she'd had it clamped shut the entire time.

When she was sure he was out, she let go fully, and watched with a certain satisfaction as he slithered off the bed and slumped backwards onto the floor.

Jamie sat up, checking her thigh, seeing deep, purple teeth marks there, a few inches from her groin, and swore under her breath.

Her eyes drifted to the mayor then, his exposed belly flattening upwards, a sharp point erupting between the open halves of his fly. He'd seemingly found that whole process rather exciting.

Would it snap if she stamped on it?

She didn't want to risk waking him, otherwise she likely would have tried.

But as much as she would have loved to have stayed there and neuter him, there was still work to be done. And anyone who would have seen her leave downstairs wouldn't be expecting her back anytime soon.

She had time, and she was upstairs now.

All she had to do was find something that made it all worthwhile, and get out before the mayor came to.

Though, as she traced her way towards the door, listening for any movement in the corridor, she thought that sounded a lot easier in her head than it actually would be.

51

JAMIE SLIPPED from the room and pulled the door shut behind her.

The mayor was still asleep, but Jamie had made sure to strip his trousers from him, along with his shoes, so he'd be less inclined to go scampering back down to the party if he did come to earlier than expected.

And maybe just to humiliate him even more.

She walked along the corridor until she got to the back dog-leg, then peeked out of the window there. There was a flat roof below and she wasted no time in opening it and dumping the trousers and shoes out on top.

Jamie turned her attention back to the corridor and headed forward.

On her right, windows ran the entire length of the hallway, overlooking the expansive back garden. There was a series of patios connected by walkways, shaded and secluded by trees and hedges. Below was a manicured lawn shrouded in darkness, that gave way to a reed-filled pond lit by decorative floodlights. Behind was forest.

To the right, Jamie could see a wide gravel car park filled

with town cars. Somewhere amongst them, Ottosen was waiting. She could make out the drivers congregating, smoking,
talking in the semi-darkness. But it was too dim to make out
anyone in particular.

Below on the patios, people milled around, talking, taking
a breather from the party itself. But no one seemed to be
interested in the upper windows.

She'd not seen a guard up here, either. Though she
figured the people who paid to be here had paid handsomely,
and with more than money. She guessed they deserved to
fuck in peace.

There didn't seem to be a 'host', as such. Not one person,
anyway. And she hadn't spotted the owner of the property,
either. She didn't know if he was here or not. But so long as
he wasn't in his office, it didn't really matter.

Jamie walked the length of the corridor purposefully, like
she was meant to be there, and passed the stairs that led down
to the kitchen on her left. The clattering of pans and the calls
of a fleet of chefs echoed up to her.

She didn't stop. Too many eyes. She'd be too out of place.

No, she'd go for the offices, then circle back if that was a
bust.

Jamie rounded the next corner and was staring down the
east-wing upper hallway. It led back to the front of the palace
and to the mezzanine above the stairs.

She just needed to try every door now, find a computer or
laptop.

Though Ottosen had installed a program on her phone that
would have allowed her to hack into the Wi-Fi network and
search for entry points to connected devices, it wasn't much
good in a tray at the front gate.

Luckily, he'd also sewn a USB key into the lining of her
bag that, when plugged into a terminal, could bypass the

security system and implant a worm that would quietly clone and transmit data back to them. All she'd need was a few minutes alone.

The first door was locked.

As was the second.

She worried that they all would be, but then the third gave.

Jamie pushed into the gloom and looked around. A huge window behind the desk at the back of the room told her that if she hit the lights, everyone on the veranda below would know she was there.

She could see the lamp lights that lined the patios and sloping lawn leading down to the fjord playing off the ripples in the water.

But she wasn't here for pretty lights.

Jamie took in the room and saw the left-hand wall lined with bookcases. On the right, there was a sofa, a coffee table. Nothing of interest. But the desk…

Jamie approached cautiously, making sure she wasn't going to be seen, and searched the top. Empty. She skulked around to the far side, tried the drawers. Empty, too. Fuck.

Okay, okay, this is fine. Just move on.

Jamie went back to the door, hovered, listening for any sound of movement. Nothing. She cracked it and repeated.

Okay, safe.

Jamie slipped out and tried the next door.

Inside, it was much the same. This one was more like a themed sitting room. Everything in florals and pinks. But no electronic devices.

Back in the corridor.

Next room.

Dud.

Fuck. She was running out of doors.

The next one gave, and she slipped into the darkness once more, this time hit with the scent of cigar smoke.

It stung her nostrils, thick and acrid.

She looked around. Bookcases, a pair of sofas facing each other over a coffee table with a stuffed buzzard on it.

Jamie went forward, seeing a sprawling desk stacked with papers and files. Pens. Stationery. An ashtray with a still-smoking cigar. And amongst it, a half-closed laptop.

It's screen gave off a dim glow, and she approached slowly, heart racing all of a sudden. Someone had been in here recently, and with the laptop left open. Did that mean they were liable to come back?

She didn't know, but she wasn't wasting any time and she wasn't wasting this opportunity, either. She opened her clutch and with a quick, deliberate tug, separated the lining from the bag. She emptied the USB key into her waiting hand and went around the desk, opening the laptop a little. She crouched behind it, staring up at the semi-shut screen, and pushed the USB into the port. A little window popped up on the display as the program began to load and a series of green bars filled quickly and then disappeared. A second later, another one flashed up saying *Uploading*. It trundled slowly upwards; the timer telling her it would take a little under two minutes to complete. And then they'd have full access to the computer and everything it was connected to.

Jamie stared at the green progress bar, willing it to go faster, bouncing on her toes, teeth planted in her bottom lip.

Something vibrated on the desktop and Jamie jumped.

She reached over, lifting the lid of a closed folder, to see a phone there.

It was buzzing, the screen illuminated. An email. Jamie craned her neck a little to look at it, not daring to touch it.

The address just read as *no-reply@nordicoil.com* and no preview of the message was displayed.

Her eyes went then to the still-smoking cigar.

Fuck.

Jamie closed the lid of the laptop, hoping the program would continue to run, and then pulled a loose piece of paper six inches to the right to cover the USB key.

She couldn't just stay there and wait. If someone had left their phone, left their cigar, they wouldn't be gone for—

She heard noise in the hallway, footsteps, voices.

Jamie scuttled, staying low, moving on her hands, heading for the sofa, and slid behind it just as the door opened.

Two men walked in, and though she didn't dare look over the top, she could see their shoes underneath.

The one at the front stormed forward, then stopped, turning to the second, who seemed to be limping. 'I want him gone, and I want him gone now.' He exhaled hard. 'I want it done quickly, and quietly,' the guy went on. 'And how the fuck did an FBI agent get in here, anyway?'

Jamie's fingernails dug into the carpet under her hands. Simpson. Fuck.

'You've got a leak,' the first speaker went on, 'and you need to plug it. Now, where the fuck is my…' He moved towards the desk and Jamie watched, holding her breath. He rummaged through some papers, then she heard him pick something up. There was a sudden crackle of burning tobacco, the smell thick in the air again, and then a column of smoke rose above the desk. The feet turned back towards the door. 'What are you still doing here? Go, fix this,' it snapped. 'And find whoever else is here that shouldn't be. I doubt he came alone.'

The man with the limp turned and sidled out, and then the speaker followed him, the door snapping shut.

Their footsteps receded and Jamie pulled herself to her feet, breathing hard. She moved towards the window quickly. Now wasn't the time for stealth.

She pressed her face to the glass and looked up the east side of the palace, towards the veranda where she'd agreed to meet Simpson. She could see him. Shit. He was just standing there, staring out at the fjord, drink in hand.

And they were coming for him.

Whether the guy with the cigar was the owner of the place or just some middleman in charge of the party, she didn't know. But she had a sickening feeling that she knew who the other one was.

Someone used to leading a team of mercenaries. Someone used to enforcing Imperium's will. Someone not afraid to disappear an FBI agent. Someone recently injured and still carrying the effects of that wound.

Sandbech.

Jamie swallowed hard.

Simpson was out of time.

And her shoes were not made for running.

52

Jamie snatched the USB key from the laptop, not bothering to check whether the program had finished, and headed for the door.

She flung it open and stumbled into the corridor, her ankles threatening to roll over. She was already on her tiptoes, so running was tough. She shuffled awkwardly for about ten metres, then reached down and pulled her heels off one at a time, swapping her clutch to her left and the shoes to her right.

She was up to sprint in seconds, the slash in the side of her dress allowing for reasonable freedom of movement, even if the seam was complaining as she went.

Jamie measured her pace – she needed to be careful here, get to Simpson before they did, but at the same time, she didn't want to round the corner and go crashing into Sandbech.

She slowed to a jog, and then as she got to the corner, a walk, getting her breath back.

There were no voices ahead, so she guessed that Sandbech must have headed down the security stairs through the kitchen.

Shit, she must be just ahead of him.

Maybe she could still reach Simpson in time.

Jamie rounded the corner and, heels in hand, moved across the gallery, heading for the main staircase.

She got above it, glancing down at the main foyer, and stopped. There must have been six, no, eight guards down there, heads moving like lighthouses, searching for anything out of place. Like an unaccompanied escort pushing forty with her heels in her hand and her fringe slicked to her forehead with sweat?

Jamie swallowed and made the call, turning and heading across the landing instead, going for the corridor that led back towards the west wing and the staff stairs she'd used to come up.

She'd done an entire lap of the palace now – barely five hundred metres, she guessed – and her feet were aching like she'd just run fifty miles. Christ, why did *anyone* wear heels? The most uncomfortable thing she'd ever had to put on. And that included the thong Ves had made her wear.

Jamie could feel the sweat beading on her back, between her shoulders. She could feel the material of her dress rustling and pulling in all the wrong areas, what little there was of her underwear trying to lodge itself in all the places it shouldn't be.

She reached the staff staircase and swung around the railing, slingshotting herself down.

She counted the steps subconsciously, pounding downwards, then hit the bottom, turned, and ran straight into someone.

Jamie rebounded off in surprise, blinking herself clear. 'I'm sorry,' she said, looking up at the man in front of her. 'I was just—' She cut herself off, recognising the guy in front of her.

'Janssen?' Detective Naas asked, doing a double-take.

Jamie stared at the shocked face of Torgrimson's partner and they stood like that for a moment, neither knowing what the hell to do.

Then Naas moved. One hand towards his earpiece, the other towards the pistol hanging from his ribs.

Jamie didn't have time for this.

She launched herself forward without warning, driving her knee square into Naas's crotch, then swung her heels up and over his shoulder as hard as she could.

They smashed into the side of his head with a dull clatter and he crumpled to the ground, wheezing. There was no honour in fighting like that, but damn, was it effective.

Before he'd even hit the ground, clutching his testicles, Jamie tore the earpiece from his ear and slung it into the wall behind her as hard as she could. It whipped the two-way transmitter from his breast pocket and shattered it against the wooden dado rail, taking a chunk of paint with it.

She was in his jacket then, fishing for his pistol.

He gasped and choked, trying to make a grab for her, so she dropped onto his ribs with her knee, heard one crack.

His eyes widened in pain, and he would have called out if he'd not been so winded from the previous blow.

Jamie unhooked the weapon and pulled it free, stepping over Naas and heading down the corridor.

He rolled over behind her, clawing his way along the floor, but in a second she was out of earshot and picking up speed again. She was breathing hard now, heart hammering in her chest.

The game was up, their covers blown, and all they needed to do now was get out.

Jamie retraced the route from earlier, aiming for the dark room where the mayor had first intercepted her.

She pushed through the heavy door and into semi-darkness again, slowing to an immediate walk. She didn't want to alert anyone here unless she had to. She could just slide between the bodies, slink out onto the veranda, then head left towards the front corner where she knew Simpson was waiting. Okay. She could do this. It was going to be okay. Everything was going to be… fuck.

She halted, turned her back to the room suddenly as Simpson appeared in the doorway, a guy on either arm. He was frogmarched in, but didn't seem to be fighting it.

Jamie guessed he had a pistol jammed against his ribs. Or two.

They cut through the room, pushing people from their paths with their pointed elbows and collective bulk.

Jamie stepped backwards cautiously, lining them up out of the corner of her eye, reaching down, using the cover of the chatter and laughter around her to pull back the slide on Naas's SIG Sauer P320 pistol.

They were shaking, slick with sweat.

She exhaled, trying to decide how to handle this.

From behind would be best. Yes. Let them pass. Put one in the back of the guy on the right, one in the guy on the left, grab Simpson, make a beeline for the veranda and the fjord, dive in, swim for the far shore if they had to. She could swim a mile in open water. Couldn't she?

Fuck, was that really her plan?

Jamie clutched the pistol, turned a little towards the approaching guards, sheltering it against her hip, waiting for her moment.

Simpson looked at her, recognised her. He didn't make a sound, but he shook his head. Just barely. But enough.

Don't. He was telling her *don't*. Don't do whatever you're planning.

Why not?

But then they were passing and their backs were to her.

Jamie kept the pistol low, figuring out her next move. Naas would be rising any minute now, if he wasn't already on his feet.

She should run.

No.

No, she couldn't do that. She couldn't abandon him.

But she should – it was what they agreed. She should run for the door, head out to the car park, find Ottosen, and make a run for the exit. That's what she should do. They had the worm in place now – hopefully – so she needed to get back to base and start figuring out what their next move was going to be.

And yet… she was already following Simpson.

How did they spot him, anyway? How did they know it was him? Had Klein given him up? She'd have to find out the answer to that another time. Right now, there were more pressing things to deal with.

She pushed the pistol into her clutch, keeping her hand on the grip as she traced through the crowd after Simpson.

Her eyes roved the faces of the people as she squeezed past. Fuck, she must look like a mess.

She just hoped that by the time anyone realised that, she'd be past them and gone.

The two mercenaries guided Simpson through the dark room and into a quieter library area. The walls were lined with books, and old-timey sliding ladders clung to the shelves.

Leather seats and sofas were dotted around and people lolled on them, leaning and sitting and lounging, talking to each other, laughing, drinking. A man looked to be eating the face of a young escort in the far corner, his hand up her dress in plain view of the room.

No one seemed to care. About that, or about the two guys frogmarching a guest through the middle of it.

Jamie figured that they were all on Imperium's payroll; they knew what the organisation was about – what it was capable of. Hell, he probably wasn't even the first guest to be escorted out that night.

Everyone just turned their heads away.

Which suited Jamie just fine as she trailed them from the darkened room and into the library.

The trio ahead turned and went towards a door between two bookcases.

The guard on the right reached out and opened it, and Jamie could see then that there was indeed a pistol jammed against Simpson's ribs.

They disappeared through and it closed behind them.

Jamie, who'd hung back a little, crossed the floor quickly and opened it. She let the handle down carefully and pulled it towards her a few inches, looking through the gap.

They were already receding into the distance, down a narrow internal corridor. It was lacking the ostentatiousness of the rest of the house, but was still nicer than any apartment she'd ever lived in.

The trio were maybe twenty metres ahead now, and Jamie needed to make up some ground. No, what she needed to do was figure out how the fuck she was going to get Simpson free.

They were tightly packed in here. She doubted they'd have a lot of space to turn around, to move.

This was as good a place as any.

Beyond them, she could see a door. It had glass panels and led outside.

Okay, right. This was it.

She just needed to get them apart, get that gun out of Simpson's ribs.

Jamie's bare feet thankfully didn't make any noise on the plush carpet as she closed ground on them.

When they were fifteen metres ahead, she crouched for a step and ditched her heels, then the clutch. She kept the USB key in her hand – she needed to make sure they didn't find the worm quickly.

There was a light fixture on the wall and she reached up, dropping the key into the tulip-shaped glass shade.

Jamie exhaled, picking up the pace. They were twenty metres from the far door now.

She would only get one shot at this, and she needed to make it count.

The plan was there.

She'd call out, one would turn, there'd be a moment where their attention was split.

The one on the left had the pistol in Simpson's ribs. She'd take him out first. Get close enough that she could guarantee a headshot. The only way to ensure that trigger wasn't getting pulled. A body shot wouldn't cut it.

She didn't want to kill anyone else – she'd had her fill. But this was Simpson. She couldn't let him die.

Ten metres ahead now. Just a little closer. She had to be sure.

Five metres.

Jamie steadied her breathing, chose her footing, drew a deep breath, raised her pistol, opened her mouth to speak, then froze.

A shape stepped from a side corridor into the space between her and the mercenaries.

A man, alone. He was wearing a black suit, had broad shoulders, was holding the left a little lower, cradling his arm slightly. She knew instantly from the gait and the bald head, despite his back being turned, who this was.

Sandbech.

'Hey,' he called before Jamie could react.

The mercenaries stopped dead, turned in place, Simpson still between them.

Jamie had her pistol up, two metres from Sandbech's back. A few metres in front of him, the mercenaries had turned fully, Simpson still suspended between them.

Fuck.

Their eyes widened, the one with the gun on Simpson reacting first.

'Get down!' he yelled, his weapon flying from Simpson's ribs.

Sandbech reacted instinctively, diving back into the mouth of the adjoining hallway.

Jamie fired twice as he did, not aiming for him. As much as he was due a bullet, Simpson's life still hung in the balance.

The first bullet struck the mercenary with the pistol mid-chest, and he convulsed fired, the bullet ripping into the ceiling, sending plaster pluming down over Jamie's head.

She put her second shot between his cheek and nose.

Blood splattered up the pristine wall.

He tipped backwards, the second mercenary already going for his weapon.

Jamie charged forward, her pistol coming up again, but before she could zero in on the second guard, Simpson threw his elbow into the guy's gut, stepped outside him, and fired a hard punch into his chin.

The guy stumbled, his pistol in his hand, fighting for balance.

Simpson didn't let up though, and led with a sharp hook to the body before he ripped the gun from the guy's grip, twisted it around, and then put three into his chest.

The guy shuddered and then landed flat on his back. But Jamie saw no blood. Ballistic vests.

But now that there'd been shots fired, the whole place was about to erupt into madness.

Simpson's hand was out, waiting for Jamie, and she took it, and then they were sprinting for the exit.

Gunfire rang out behind them and they both ducked, scrambling forward down the narrow corridor.

Sandbech.

Jamie knew before she even turned, firing blindly over her shoulder as she stumbled, fell, landed on her side. She rolled, twisting, levelled the pistol back at the corner.

Sandbech was there, hanging around it, chasing them with bullets.

'Go!' Jamie yelled, putting rounds into the plaster inches from Sandbech's head.

He took cover and Jamie took the chance, getting to her feet and going after Simpson.

More shots behind her.

She ducked again, pinballing from wall to wall as Simpson shoved the door open ahead and burst into the open. Then he was facing her, the pistol he'd taken from the guard raised, and spitting fire over her head.

Jamie crawled under the stream of bullets and into the open air, and a second later Simpson shunted the door closed and grabbed her by the arm, dragging her down the stone steps that cut through the lawn surrounding the palace.

They wound down to a lower driveway, a tarmac road that stretched back towards the front of the building.

They landed, looking right and left, and then decided, taking off. Left. Towards the fjord, if nothing else.

Though Jamie was sure neither of them thought they'd get that far.

As they came up on the corner of the building, the back of a string of black SUVs came into view. They sat there silently, no doubt waiting to ferry the mercenaries back to whatever army surplus hole they huddled in when the sun went down.

Simpson slowed, looking around.

Jamie did the same.

No sign of anyone yet.

But it wouldn't be long.

Ahead, Jamie could see the veranda that Simpson had been collared on. It led down a set of stairs onto a flat patch of gravel and then down more steps towards the water.

The road the SUVs were on led through the middle, back to the turning circle at the front of the palace, a mile of driveway, and then back onto the open road.

Simpson and Jamie got low and moved around to the far side of the four-by-fours. Simpson was leading, running his hands up the side of the first one, going towards the passenger door. He reached for the handle and pulled it. The thing opened, and he leaned inside looking for keys.

Jamie felt a twinge of pain next to her belly button and looked down. Had she scraped it on something? Bumped it?

Her hand came away red.

Soaked red.

A wave of nausea rolled through her then, her mind

replaying the last few minutes over. All the gunfire. How, miraculously, Sandbech hadn't hit her.

Except, he had.

She'd never been shot before. But they were right – you didn't feel it right away.

Jamie exhaled, her whole world rocking back and forth, and then she collapsed against the side of the truck.

Simpson pulled his head out, glanced back at her. 'No keys,' he said, near frantic. Then his expression changed. 'Jamie?' He knelt next to her. 'What's—? Shit, are you? Fuck,' he said, breathless all of a sudden. His hands were on her stomach then, tracing across her ribs. 'You're hit.'

Jamie laughed, then grimaced, the pain setting in now. 'Could you be any more American?'

He met her eyes, not a hint of humour there. 'We need to get you out of here. Now.'

There were voices all around.

Simpson stood, looking through the windows of the SUVs.

'They're looking for us,' he said.

Jamie nodded, her mouth dry. She looked down at her side, lifting her hand to get a better look. The wound was about four inches to the left of her naval. What was there? Anything important? It was her gut. Everything that was in there was important.

There really wasn't a good place to get shot, after all.

Simpson was on her again, then, pressing her hand into her stomach. 'Keep the pressure on,' he ordered her. 'I'll be back.'

He got up and ran to the next truck, checking for keys again.

Jamie could hear voices now, footsteps as Imperium's

guards spread out to look for them. Sandbech's voice echoing, telling the mercenaries' to find them.

She just tried to breathe, keep her heart rate down. Though she could feel it racing in her neck and behind her eyes.

If they discovered her here, she'd be dead before she could even lift her gun.

She looked down at that now. It was still in her hand. But it felt heavy and wet. There was blood on it. Her blood, she thought. It was all up her arms, running down her legs. Fuck. That was a lot of blood.

'Jamie,' Simpson said, appearing again. 'Come on, we have to move. Can you walk?'

She nodded. 'Yeah, I can walk,' she said, letting Simpson pull her to her feet. She suppressed a groan of pain, bared her teeth, and then put weight on her feet. She wobbled, but then held, and started forward, still clutching her stomach as Simpson hauled her along awkwardly.

'This one,' he announced, turning towards an open door and swinging Jamie up onto the passenger seat.

She sprawled in, swearing as she went, still holding the gun. Simpson lifted her legs and swung them in, her dress riding up.

He paused briefly, glancing down at her exposed thighs.

Jamie caught him. 'Not really the time,' she growled through gritted teeth.

'Are those… teeth marks?' he asked, meeting her eye.

'It's a long story,' she said with a pained sigh. 'Now can you please get in the fucking car?'

Simpson looked down again, narrowed his eyes a little, then nodded.

He opened the back passenger door then, to save himself

from being exposed to the palace, and climbed in, and then over the centre console and into the driver's seat.

He reached up and pulled down the sun visor, and a key fell into his lap.

Simpson raised it to the ignition and held it there for a second, looking over at Jamie, eyes wide, breathing ragged. 'You ready?' he asked. 'This could get rough.'

Jamie swallowed, exhaled hard, and then leaned forward, grabbing hold of the door handle and slamming it shut. 'Let's go.'

53

Simpson shoved the key into the slot and turned it, slamming the automatic shifter into drive.

The dashboard lit up, the headlights bursting to life, engine roaring.

The whole car shuddered and then crabbed to the left as Simpson ripped the wheel over, the wheels spinning and spraying the SUV behind with loose gravel and stones.

Jamie could see figures rushing over the lawns now, could hear the dull shouts of guards ordering the guests inside, could see white rosettes punching holes in the night.

The first bullets landed, pinging off the bonnet and windscreen. She ducked instinctively, but they seemed to just bounce off.

'Bulletproof glass,' Simpson practically laughed with relief. He looked over at Jamie quickly as the four-by-four began to snake forward. 'Bet they're regretting that now!'

The SUV slithered through the gravel, searching desperately for traction, and then churned down to the bare earth below and sent them hurtling forwards.

Jamie was forced back into the seat, pain surging through

her gut. She dug her fingers into the raw, turbulent flesh, and screwed her face up.

The SUV jostled forward, the Imperium mercenaries sprinting down the grass towards them, throwing themselves at the vehicle madly, snatching for the door handles.

One grabbed the driver's and managed to get it open a few inches.

Simpson swerved left, then right, swinging it wide and flinging the mercenary off, sending him tumbling into a stone pillar with a sickening crunch.

The rear door was opening suddenly then, the slight shrug-off of speed letting another mercenary get hold.

Jamie twisted awkwardly, the gun in her hand rising up wildly over her shoulder, muzzle swaying violently.

She saw nothing but wide eyes staring back at her, then white spots as she fired three times into the gap.

The door flapped limply, the mercenary tomahawking behind. She didn't know if she hit him or if he let go, but either way, they were moving now and outrunning the others.

The SUV jostled as they passed the path down to the fjord, bodies converging from all sides, and then Simpson was swinging the truck around a loose corner with the sort of confidence that told Jamie he'd probably spent a lot of his high-school career thrashing pickups around the dirt roads of rural East Texas. The water-feature turning circle came into view, now free of arriving cars, and Simpson straight-lined it back onto the entrance road.

The soft layers of deep gravel gave way to tarmac, and she watched as the speedometer climbed, her breathing growing difficult. She closed one eye, her vision doubling, and squinted at the readouts, trying to focus on something to keep her mind straight as Simpson willed the car on.

There were lights in the wing mirror then and Jamie

turned her head to watch a pair of town cars coming up behind them. Big, powerful saloons that carried less weight and had no trouble making up the distance.

The road was only wide enough for two, but the lead car wasted no time trying to fill the space.

It came up fast on the right and Simpson reacted, turning the wheel, sending the SUV lurching across the smooth surface with a sudden shriek of hot rubber.

The car behind braked hard, the nose diving, and the second car pulled out and gunned it, slotting into the space on Simpson's side instead.

His window was peppered with spiders' webs then as bullets buried themselves in the glass, the impacts making the whole car shudder.

'Fuck!' he yelled, wincing away from them.

They traded paint, fighting for road as the town car tried to send them into the verge and the waiting tree trunks.

Jamie was going to throw up.

She tried to breathe through it, the pain making her vision split and reform ten times a second.

'Hold on!' Simpson yelled, grappling with the wheel. The weight shifted, and the nose plunged as he took the car wide, rumbling through the loose leaf litter at its edge, and then sent them hurtling right across the two lanes and square into the side of the saloon.

It jumped, skidded, wobbled, then dug its tyres into the dirt on the far edge of the road, before jackknifing and spinning into a birch tree.

It wrapped itself around it with a deafening, metal-tearing crash, and smoke and steam exploded from under the buckled bonnet.

Jamie looked past Simpson now, their car practically sideways in the road, and saw the second car catching up. Sandbech's determined, furious face was stark in the passenger seat, his arm out the window, pistol homed in on them.

And then their driver's door was open, and Simpson was brandishing his own pistol. They fired simultaneously, emptying their chambers.

Bullets hit the door, the interior door pillars, the dashboard, spraying sparks all over them as one ripped through the GPS screen.

Jamie shielded her head, smearing blood all over her hair and face.

Simpson seemed to hit nothing, and a second later, they were moving again, his door slamming shut, the engine screaming, wheels spinning.

They set off, Simpson's heel grinding the accelerator into the floor.

Just breathe, you have to breathe. You have to stay awake.

Her vision was pulsing black now, her legs soaked. The seat soaked.

She felt woozy, mouth dry, lips shaking, cold spreading from her fingertips and into her arms.

Sandbech's car rammed them from behind.

Jamie lurched forwards, then slumped back, groaning. Pain. So much pain.

They snaked, tyres squealing.

Simpson kept it straight.

Then again, from the side now as Sandbech wrestled up their flank, drawing level, each turning into the other and vying for space, trying to run the other off the road.

She looked over, saw Sandbech leaning down over the driver, the fierce mouth of his silver pistol snarling at her. And then it spat through open window of their car, blotting out her view of him as impact welts filled the glass of her own window

She stared at them, studying the intricate cracks with fascination. They multiplied. Like raindrops, she thought. Like rain starting.

How pretty.

She could hear it. Roaring. Roaring in her ears.

A calmness settled over everything.

Then there was a distant bang, an eruption of white smoke or steam in her peripheral and the car next to theirs weaved, spewing the gas from its front end.

The radiator, she thought, her mind vague. Simpson must have shot the radiator.

She smiled.

Clever.

He was so clever.

She looked over at him.

He looked back at her, face shining with sweat, eyes full of fear, mouth moving. Talking. Simpson was talking? She couldn't hear him. Was he miming? How funny.

God, she was so tired. Why was she so tired?

She needed to sleep.

She should sleep.

Weakly, she reached out, squeezed Simpson's arm, and then closed her eyes.

And then, Jamie slept.

54

THE FIRST THING Jamie became aware of was the soft beeping of the heart monitor.

And then the pain. She moved slightly, winced, then tried to swear, her throat stinging and dry. The smell of a hospital room filled her nostrils and her eyes opened, aching in the glow of the halogens overhead.

The world swam into focus and Jamie lifted a hand to her neck, massaging the pain away. She'd been intubated, she thought.

'Hey,' a voice said out of the ether, 'don't move, you're okay.'

'Simpson?' Jamie croaked, squinting at the shape taking form at her right elbow.

'Not quite,' came the reply, a square, sharp jawline coming into view. She saw his keen eyes, his slicked-back hair. A compassionate expression on his face. The most she'd ever seen.

'Wiik,' Jamie said, still not quite believing he was here. Wherever 'here' was. Where was she? Jamie blinked a few times, coming back to the moment. 'What are you doing here?' she asked.

He smiled, amused slightly. 'Turns out I'm listed as your emergency contact.'

Jamie laughed a little, then groaned. 'Where am I?' Was she safe? How long had she been out? Why hadn't Imperium come for her? Would they? They needed to get out of there.

'Oslo,' Wiik answered.

'Oslo?' Jamie shook her head. 'No, I can't be... We were...' She screwed up her face, trying to figure out what the last thing she remembered was.

'You were rushed to a local hospital, treated there, stabilised, then air-lifted to Oslo for surgery,' he said plainly. 'They said it was touch-and-go.'

'You don't seem too broken up about that.'

He shrugged and ran his hand over his head, pressing his hair to his scalp. 'They don't know you like I do.'

She laughed again. Then cried a little. Fuck. Wiik looked better, though – time away had been good for him, it seemed. He looked like his old self again.

'Are we... is it safe here?' Jamie asked, keeping her voice low.

His smile broadened. 'Yeah,' he said. 'You're safe.' He hooked a thumb over his shoulder towards the door. 'There's been two Kripos agents out there since you got here. And that Simpson guy is back and forth ten times a day. Hallberg, too.'

'Everyone's okay?'

He nodded. 'Not a scratch on them.' He sat back and picked up the remote from the side table. 'It was about time you got a taste of it for yourself.'

'Gotta say,' Jamie said, pushing herself up with great difficulty. 'I'm not a fan.'

She saw Wiik swap the remote from his broken hand to

his good one and press the power button. She could see now that her entire midriff was bandaged.

The TV flickered to life on the wall, the news playing on it. Wiik turned the volume up, and Jamie read the banners scrolling along the bottom.

A newscaster was trapped in a little box at the corner of the screen as footage of people exiting their homes, shielding their faces, getting into cars, running into restaurants and offices, played. Reporters, cameras, microphones chased them around as the caster spoke.

'—evidence of widespread corruption through every echelon of government, public office, and private business continues to surface. With resignations and disappearances pouring in, this is set to be the largest unseating of political party members and public officials in Norway's history. Several high-profile arrests have already been made, and the public have decided, with calls for re-elections already sounding. The army have been brought in to assist with peace-keeping as protests begin to erupt in major cities, and with hundreds of police officers and administrators stepping back from active duty, Norway is calling on neighbouring nations to help maintain order as we—'

Wiik muted the TV and looked back at Jamie. 'You get the picture.'

'Jesus,' she said. 'We did that?'

He nodded. 'Looks like. Simpson will explain the finer details, I'm sure. But whatever you traded that for' – he pointed to her wound – 'it was worth it.' He kept looking at her then, as if wanting to say something.

'What is it?'

'Was it… him? Did you catch him? The man who killed your father?' He asked it plainly, as was his way.

'I met him,' Jamie said.

'And?' Wiik asked, measuring her, stopping short of asking if she pulled the trigger.

'Probably the most frightening person I ever met.'

Wiik kept her eyes. 'Did you get what you wanted?'

She swallowed, winced again. Fuck, what had they put down her throat? A drainpipe? 'He's dead, if that's what you mean.' She looked away, out of the window, at the gloomy Oslo skyline drowned in cloud and drizzle. 'But I didn't kill him.'

'Did he…'

'Do this to me?' Jamie shook her head. 'No, but he trained the man who did. Real charmer. Bet you two would get on.'

'And what about him?'

'Alive,' she said. 'I don't doubt that. He's slippery. Smart. Skilled. Ruthless.'

There was a rap at the door and Simpson's face appeared there in the gap. 'Knock, knock,' he said.

Wiik raised his eyebrows and rolled his eyes. Jamie didn't need to ask what his take was on Americans.

Simpson let himself into the room wearing a pair of jeans and a loose chequered blue shirt. 'How you feeling?' he asked.

'Ready for action,' Jamie replied. 'I just finished up my morning 10km, can't you tell?'

'That good, huh?' He grinned with perfect white teeth. 'Glad to hear it – my ribs still need a few more days to heal.' He came over and clapped Wiik on the shoulder, much to his dismay. 'She kicks like a horse, you know that?' Simpson asked him.

'I'm aware,' Wiik growled.

He stood then, shrugging off Simpson's hand. 'I'll leave you two to talk,' he said quickly, turning away.

'Wiik,' Jamie called after him.

He paused and looked back.

'Thanks,' she said. 'For being here. For coming.'

He lingered for a moment, then just nodded, rolling his lips into a line. And then he was gone, the door closed behind him.

Simpson took his seat then and picked up Jamie's hand without invitation. 'Well, we did it,' he said, still grinning. '*You* did it.'

'I'm overflowing with glee.'

He laughed, looking up at the TV. 'When we finally got time to breathe and knew you were safe and were going to make it, Ottosen checked out what the worm had found. Turns out that laptop belonged to Martin Iverson, an executive at Nordic Oil. He was staying at the palace during the party, and once we got into his email account and onto the Wi-Fi network...' Simpson clapped, and then made a rocketing motion with his hands. 'The guests' phones were mostly out of reach, but a select few staff, guards, high-ranking Imperium employees' weren't.'

'Won't this damage the case? Everything being out there like this?'

He closed his lips a little and sighed. 'Kripos and Europol were... dubious about our methods – and weren't sure the gathered evidence could be relied upon. They thought Imperium would claim it was fabricated. And with no photo or video evidence from the party – of the people inside...'

'What about our witnesses? Torgrimson? Maria Bohle?'

'There's no sign of Torgrimson,' Simpson said. 'He's gone. His family, too. In the night after the party. Looks like he drove straight there, collected them, then...'

Jamie drew a slow breath, regretting filling her lungs all

the way. 'He'll show up. Once he realises how hard running is. And he'll talk.'

'Maybe. But we weren't prepared to wait around,' Simpson said.

'So you leaked it?'

He broke into a gentle smile. 'No, no,' he said, lifting his hands. 'That would be wholly irresponsible. Kripos and Europol are denying all knowledge of an investigation into any alleged corruption.' He shrugged. 'But now that it's out there and plastered across every news outlet, they're pretty much obligated to launch one and review the evidence presented.'

Jamie leaned her head back. 'That's good.' She coughed, whimpered a little. 'Fuck Imperium.'

'Yeah,' Simpson added. 'Fuck Imperium. They get every-thing they deserve.' He sighed. 'Just a shame we never managed to find Stieg Lange. His testimony would go a long way here.'

Jamie let out a low, close-lipped chuckle.

'What's so funny?' Simpson asked, raising an eyebrow.

'Oh, just another one of my hunches,' Jamie replied.

'This really the time to be coy?'

She looked at him. 'You tell me?'

'Okay, okay, I'll bite. You get a lead on Stieg Lange while you were unconscious that you're not telling me about?'

'Something like that. But I'll keep you in suspense for now.'

'You know withholding information during an active investigation is a crime, right?'

Jamie smirked at him. 'Yeah, I do. Except there is no investigation. Not really, because Stieg Lange isn't missing. He never disappeared.'

'I'm not following? What do you mean he's not missing? If he never disappeared, then where is he?' Simpson asked, leaning in.

'He's still in his house,' Jamie said, looking at him. 'He never left.'

55

IT WAS NEARLY two weeks later that Jamie and Simpson pulled up outside the Lange house in Bergen.

It felt strange to be back, especially outside the guise of her assumed identity. Outside of the investigation. She was back in her trusty jeans and boots – the dress long gone, thankfully – her hair back to its natural blonde and pinned back. Though still a lot shorter than she would have liked. She was walking unassisted now, but it was painful and awkward. She was limping badly. But she was on her feet. And that was something.

The doctor told her it would be three months before she could run again. She'd be there within one. She promised herself that.

They moved slowly up the drive, Simpson hovering at her shoulder, ready to catch her if she stumbled.

'Any more thoughts about what comes after this?' he asked.

It'd been a whirlwind twelve days since she woke up. The bullet had done damage, but missed everything vital. It had ended up puncturing her small intestine, and they'd taken two inches out. The surgery had taken seven hours and she'd been unconscious for nearly three days before they brought her out of sedation. Everything leading up to those final moments in the car was blurry and grey. She remembered being in the palace, chasing down Simpson and the guards, Sandbech, gunfire, realising she'd been shot... but not much else. No details. Just snatches. Flashes. Simpson's face, his frightened expression.

'No,' Jamie said. 'Some time to recover, get myself back,' she said. 'I'll go somewhere quiet, drop off the map for a while. I'm pretty good at that.' She needed it. Though Imperium were on the back foot, on their knees by public standards, Jamie didn't think this was quite over. They might have lost their pull in the political and business world, but they still had men at their disposal, and they'd be looking to make someone pay for what happened.

And it wasn't like they didn't know her name already.

'Sounds good to me,' Simpson said. 'Think we could all do with a break after the last few months.'

He was talking like it was over. And she hoped for him it was. That he could go back to Texas, or Virginia, or wherever it was they had him stationed before this, and go on with his life. Imperium had recognised him at the party, but so long as he was very far from here, maybe they'd just let him go, the risk of going after him greater than the reward.

But for Jamie... she had no intention of running. When they came for her, she'd know it, and she'd be ready.

She reached out and knocked, the reverberation from the door making her stomach ache with each rap.

After a while, it opened and Nina Lange stood there. She eyed Jamie and Simpson in turn, saying nothing, and then wrapped the draping hems of her cream cardigan around her waist, raising her eyebrows in waiting.

'Mrs Lange,' Jamie said, 'We're sorry to bother you.'

'All communications with the police regarding the investigations into my husband's disappearance, or the incident that took place, must be directed to my legal counsel,' she said formally. 'I'll thank you to respect that.'

She tried to close the door, but Jamie put her hand out to stop it, regretting the action as soon as she did. She suppressed the pain as well as she could, breathing through it. 'Mrs Lange,' she went on, voice strained. 'Let me introduce myself properly – my name is Jamie Johansson, and like your husband, I was a victim of Imperium Holdings.'

She drew a breath and straightened, but said nothing. There wasn't a person in Europe who didn't now know that name or hadn't heard about what had been going.

'My partner and I were working undercover, trying to expose their actions – and we've succeeded in doing so.'

Nina Lange said nothing.

'We're not saying that it's over – far from it. But what we are saying is that it's time for Mr Lange to come forward.'

Nina Lange measured her, then let her face settle into a scowl. 'Is that supposed to be some kind of joke? My husband is still missing—'

'Mrs Lange,' Jamie cut in. 'I know it's frightening, and that you have no guarantees of anything, but with his testimony, we can keep building the case, keep putting people away for this. He's going to be needed at work, too. Emma Hagen has stepped down from her position at the head of Høyre. If he stands up now, he can make a difference.'

She swallowed, then hardened. 'You're sick. Coming here, to my *home,* saying these things. When you should be… out there' – she flung her hand into the air – 'finding him! God, he's probably… he's probably dead already, and you're here accusing me of what?' She laughed incredulously.

Simpson stepped forward a little, laid his hand on Jamie's shoulder. 'How sure are you?' he asked her.

Jamie looked at Nina Lange, smirked a little. 'I'm sure.'

'Good enough for me.' Simpson pulled out his badge and held it up. 'Special Agent Beau Simpson, FBI, acting under the authority of the National Criminal Investigation Service and Europol. We need to come inside.'

'Absolutely not.' Nina Lange snorted.

'Mrs Lange, wilfully lying during a federal investigation is a felony that carries serious jail time. Falsifying evidence is also a felony. As is falsely reporting a crime. And quite frankly, we can go on and on. Now, my partner here,' he said, gesturing to Jamie, 'has been polite, but in the spirit of helping things along, I'll say it again. We need to come inside. And if you decline, then I'll put you on the ground and in handcuffs, and then when my partner finds Mr Lange, you'll be remanded into custody and charged with as many crimes as I feel like slapping you with.' He grinned at her. 'And thanks to that friendly look you're giving me, I might just feel like booking off the whole day just for you. So, what do you say?'

She shifted from side to side, grinding her teeth as she decided whether to continue lying or to just give up.

Eventually, she made the right choice and stepped aside. 'Though I don't know what you expect to find,' she muttered as Jamie limped past, heading for the stairs.

Simpson went up behind her, giving her space, but holding his hands out to catch her if she fell backwards. Which she refused to do, but almost did.

Nina Lange watched carefully from the bottom of the stairs.

Jamie was breathing hard, sweating by the time she got to

the top and ambled towards the master bedroom. 'In here,' she said to Simpson, and he followed her in.

The room still had that slightly off quality that it had when she'd been confronted by Torgrimson and Naas. And now she knew why.

Jamie approached the mirrored wardrobes and slid the furthest one back. 'Would you mind?' she asked Simpson, gesturing to the boxes stacked up against the inside wall.

'Uh... sure?' he said, walking over and taking them out.

They were all fairly light, and he stacked them neatly on the floor.

While he did, Jamie watched Nina Lange, who was now hovering silently in the doorway, trying to keep herself calm.

'There,' Simpson said, standing up and proffering the empty closet to Jamie.

She moved passed him, reaching up and brushing the clothes on the rail aside. She took one last look at Nina Lange, and then reached out, running her hand over the inside panel that would have been the outside wall of the house.

She let her fingers trace the smooth surface, her eyes inspect it. And then she paused, looking back at Simpson, who was standing at her shoulder, peering into the gloomy wardrobe.

Jamie pressed. Not hard, but enough to activate the mechanism.

The latch gave, and then the wall sprang back towards her.

She pulled the hidden doorway out, revealing a space about two feet in width.

The compartment turned right, and led down a steep and narrow staircase that ran behind the headboard of the bed, into darkness.

'Damn,' Simpson said, surprised.

Nina Lange was in the room now, kneading her hands, tears in her eyes. But she was saying nothing.

Jamie drew a breath, eased herself down onto the little plinth inside the wardrobe, and stared into the darkness. 'Stieg Lange,' she called.

There was no response.

'My name is Jamie Johansson, formerly of Stockholm Polis and the London Metropolitan Police. As I'm sure you've seen, Imperium Holdings' operations have been exposed, and Europol and Kripos would very much like to hear your experiences. We're here to formally offer you protection in exchange for your cooperation. There's a car waiting outside, and we can take you straight to Kripos HQ for you to give a statement.'

Still no response from the darkness.

'Please don't make me come down there, Mr Lange,' Jamie said tiredly. 'I got shot to make all this happen, and stairs are my least favourite thing right now.' She looked back at Simpson, who offered a little shrug, then gestured to the hole, asking if Jamie wanted him to go down.

She shook her head, gathered her thoughts again.

'Mr Lange,' she went on. 'I know you're scared. And I know it seems impossible to trust anyone right now, but I promise you can trust me. I've given everything to bring Imperium down, and now, we need your help to do it. The city is in chaos. Høyre is imploding. Bergen needs you, Stieg. Your country needs you.'

That little patriotic push made Simpson offer Jamie a nod of approval and a thumbs up. Americans.

There was a creak from the darkness then and Jamie turned her attention back to the stairs, squinting down into the hole.

Slowly, a man's face began to take shape. He looked pale, drawn, tired. But there was no denying it.

The man crawling up the steps, out of the basement panic room that he'd been hiding in for more than a year, was Stieg Lange.

56

Jamie and Simpson stood on the front lawn of the Lange house, staring out at the grey sky. Winter was fast approaching now, and there was an undeniable chill in the air.

'How did you know?' Simpson asked, still flabbergasted by the whole thing. 'Droves of officers, detectives, investigators were in and out of that house. Crime scene techs, too, who went over everything. *Everything.*'

Jamie cracked a smile, trying not to feel too smug. 'We had all the information,' she said. 'I guess it just never occurred to anyone.'

He looked over at her and folded his arms. 'Come on, you've gotta give me more than that.'

'Nina Lange's bank records – before Stieg disappeared, their food bill was about fourteen hundred kroner a week.'

'Okay?'

'And after he disappeared…'

Simpson scoffed, shook his head. 'It was still fourteen hundred kroner a week. Fuck.'

'If she was alone, it should have halved. Half the food. Half the price.'

He laughed to himself. 'Okay, so how did you know about the secret panic room?'

Jamie looked up and down the expensive street, seeing expensive cars and security systems blinking on the front of everyone's house. 'You know how many millionaires live on this street?'

Simpson took a quick survey. 'Lots, I'm guessing.'

'Yep. And people who are well off are afraid of getting burgled.' She turned and looked back up at the house. 'Stieg Lange built this house himself. And being a prominent figure in Høyre, having such a deep, known love for his wife... I don't know, I had a feeling. And when Hallberg and I came back here to find her, I went upstairs to see what I could see. The landing had a cupboard at the end, but the bedroom felt... off. Small, somehow. The walls didn't seem to line up. So I pulled the blueprints when I had time, looked over them.'

'And they showed the panic room?'

Jamie shook her head. 'No, they didn't. That's the point. The back wall in that bedroom was supposed to be solid block, in line with the back of the house. It wasn't. There was space behind it that shouldn't have been there.'

Simpson put his hands on his hips now. 'Goddamn. So while everyone was scouring the city – every ditch and shallow grave – for Stieg Lange, he was hiding in his own damn bedroom, sleeping in his own bed.'

Jamie raised her shoulders slowly. 'I thought he'd run away in order to protect his wife, but then I realised that he wouldn't leave her. There'd be nowhere he could go they wouldn't find him, and it'd be tough for them both to disappear. So, the simplest option...'

'If it walks like a duck...'

'Quack, quack,' Jamie said.

57

JAMIE FIRST KNEW they were coming for her when her phone lit up.

The camera she'd set up facing the front door, had been tripped, and by the time she'd opened the video stream, six guys were already inside her apartment, wearing black special-ops gear, masks, and carrying what looked like compact sub-machine guns. Suppressed MP5s, she guessed by the grainy night-vision feed.

It wasn't unexpected. In fact, she'd been waiting for it. And had she been in the apartment at the time, she'd already be dead.

It took them three minutes to do a full sweep, and then they were gone.

The last one through the door was the leader. He lingered for a second, then drove his fist through the plasterboard next to the door, and then walked out. She'd not have known him except for the silver pistol strapped to his thigh.

Jamie sat up in bed and smiled to herself. Sandbech.

It had been more than a month since Stieg Lange had publicly announced his return to Høyre, and then denounced

Imperium on national television. And two weeks since Jamie had rented a small apartment in southern Stockholm using her own bank account.

She wasn't there, of course. She was hundreds of miles away. Doing what she promised Simpson she was going to do. Drop off the map for a while, recover, ready herself.

She knew that Imperium would want to come for her. That Sandbech would have an axe to grind. Maybe they'd never stop coming for her. Or maybe, once she extracted this particular thorn from her side, they'd finally back off. There were thousands of people responsible for Imperium's sudden demise. And as their first line of defence seemed to be claiming they didn't exist in any meaningful capacity, she thought waging a continuing war against those who'd crossed them seemed counter-intuitive. But she also thought that she might be an exception. At this point, she figured it was a matter of principle more than anything else.

But she wasn't strong yet.

Not strong enough.

And she wasn't ready.

When she was, they'd know.

58

It was January and twenty-two below zero.

The wind rode up over the top of the ridge and whipped down into the bowl, dragging slews of icy powder into the air and sending it swirling across the surface of the frozen lake.

Jamie sat in the doorway of the hunting cabin, a fire in front of her. It crackled, spluttering in the frigid air. She reached behind her, into the protection of the interior, and pulled out another split log, pushing it on the flames.

Jamie watched it catch, then turned her attention to the swaying pines ahead, and the track that cut through the snow down to the shore and out onto the lake.

The road in had been covered over with nearly five feet of snow for over a week now. Though that wasn't a problem for her – she had everything she needed to spend the entire winter here. She just wondered whether they'd wait for it to clear before they came.

It had been four days since Jamie had sent word to Wiik – a simple text saying that it was good to be back there, at the lake. That it made her feel close to her father again.

So either they were losing their touch and hadn't worked it out yet, or they were just biding their time.

Would it be today? She squinted into the colourless, flat sky, struggling to pick the line of the ridge from the clouds. Visibility was low, a thin, frozen mist moving across the frozen water. The wind was up, too, which would mask any sounds of an approach. Though she wouldn't need to hear them coming.

Jamie stared out at the point of the horizon line where she knew the track came over the top, her hand moving an oiled rag up and down the stock of the Remington hunting rifle on her lap. She cleaned it every day so it was always ready.

Whether it was a change in the air, some sort of sixth sense, or just pure coincidence, she didn't know. But as Jamie reached out for the satphone at her side, it lit up.

She turned it over and looked at the dim green screen, then answered. 'Hello?' she said, her voice as cold and hard as the frozen ground under her heels.

'Hello, I was instructed to call this number to report anything unusual.'

'Talk,' Jamie said, feeling her heart beating low and fast.

'We have three vehicles approaching the designated location. Black SUVs. What's your order?'

Jamie took a breath, rolling the last year over in her head. Wondering how close to the day it was that she'd come rolling over that ridge towards someone else with a rifle in their hands.

'Go,' she said, hanging up before there was a response.

She stood then, slinging the rifle over her shoulder, picking up her pack, and reached for her snowshoes.

If they'd been picked up by the camera that was being monitored, it meant they were just ten kilometres away. She checked her watch before leaning down and picking up the enamel mug of coffee warming on the stones around her fire. She drained it.

Jamie took one last clean, calm breath of crisp air, arched out her back, feeling her abdomen ache and stretch, and then set off down the track, leaving a trail of breath mist behind her.

The SUVs must have pulled up at the foot of the rise on the far side. Jamie wasn't surprised to see them coming over the brow by foot. They had even dressed for the occasion.

They were wearing snow-camouflaged gear, white over-alls, and body armour, their weapons wrapped with white tape to make them less visible.

Except Jamie wasn't looking with her eyes.

She was on her belly in a hide two hundred metres away, in the middle of the lake. She'd been steadily compacting a patch of snow over the last few weeks, and was perched on top of it, a white fly-sheet overhead protecting her from the elements.

She had the rifle laid on a bedroll next to her, the chamber full.

Her eye was pressed to the eyepiece of an infrared spotter's scope, and she watched the twelve men come over the hill cautiously, skulking low through the snow. Their bodies were blue against the blue backdrop, but their hands, their faces, glowed yellow and red.

Picking them off from here was not her intention.

First, one against twelve wasn't great odds when it came to a firefight, even if they were only armed with – Jamie switched views on the electronic scope and dialled up the zoom – AK5 assault rifles. Standard issue Swedish military weaponry. Though the only gun she cared about was the shining silver pistol stuck to the thigh of one of them. She didn't know which, yet.

Second, killing them wasn't prudent either.

They were just doing a job, and while that job was coming to mount her head on a pike, she couldn't blame them for it. And she'd much rather see them all rot in a cell than die out here with a bullet in their gut. She reached down instinctively and rubbed her stomach. That wasn't a pretty way to go for anyone.

Still, if they fired, she'd fire back.

Though she hoped that she'd not need to.

Jamie repositioned and looked down the spotter's scope again, watching them trace down the hill towards the cabin, her fire still smoking in front of the open door.

They'd head right for it – they had no reason not to.

They were at the bottom of the slope now, on flat ground, pushing through the snow. It was up to their waists – four feet of loose powder. Not easy to move through. They'd be tired, their footing unsure, the blanket of snow ahead forming an undulating, unreadable surface.

It's why she'd waited until then to make that text to Wiik.

Jamie held her breath, watching as the first two guys, walking shoulder to shoulder, rifles raised, plunged beneath the surface.

She held her smile, waiting to see what happened next.

The remaining men all backed up, ducked, hid themselves beneath the powder, crouching.

Now she smiled. It was freezing out here. Colder than freezing. A lot colder. And they couldn't wait around all day without going hypothermic. Jamie also knew what that was like. But this time she was wrapped up in half a dozen layers, snow boots, a full neoprene face mask. She wasn't taking any chances.

The two men who went under didn't re-appear. She wondered whether the others had figured it out yet – that before the snow set in, she'd dug a six-foot-deep trench across the road in, and laid a series of thin boughs across it. Ones which would bear the weight of snow, but not of burly mercenaries.

They were in there now covered with snow, no doubt screaming, wondering what the hell had happened.

They wouldn't die – at least they wouldn't if they didn't panic and fill their throats with snow.

But it also would be impossible to get them out without the others being vulnerable. She could still see them trying to decide. It would be so easy now to pick up her rifle, put a bullet into their masses, send them scuttling home.

That would give away her position, though, and she'd barely thinned the herd at all.

No, they'd go exactly where she wanted them to, and that was right towards her.

Off to the other side of the track, up the slope, the ground was uneven, boggy even. Deep, soft, wet earth and gorse that made movement even more difficult.

Sandbech would know the terrain, though. He would come here prepared, having viewed satellite images and topo-graphical maps. And he'd know at twenty-two below, that the lake ice would be solid, and flat, and predictable.

But Jamie knew a lot about lake ice, too. She remembered what her father had taught her. About how to cut a hole in it to fish. About how to move across it. About how to know if it was strong enough. And about how *not* to cause it to break. She'd learned that lesson that hard way.

She remembered him carrying a chainsaw out onto the ice, standing with his legs splayed, cutting out a chunk as big as their old box-television at home. Then using these rusted iron pincers to drag it out.

It was far too cold for that kind of shit now. And Jamie needed something a little more… *concerted* than an old chainsaw.

The group began moving off, spread out to distribute their weight, two guys holding behind to stay with their buried comrades.

That left eight moving down onto the ice.

Jamie watched them, the rangefinder on her scope telling her that they were a hundred and eighty metres away.

A few more should do it.

They kept descending, wading down through the snow, and then levelled out, reaching the shore.

Jamie pulled back from the rangefinder, and lifted the rifle, bringing it to her eye. They were in the open now. And the ridge was a long way behind them.

If she engaged, they'd have to face her and push forward.

There'd be nowhere to hide. But they'd use the snow for cover, get down low to minimise themselves as targets, spread out so they weren't clustered, so they couldn't be fired on easily.

This was it.

They were on the ice now.

She'd only get one shot at this.

Jamie exhaled, pulled the rifle against her shoulder, kept both eyes open, zeroed in loosely on the mercenary on the outer left-hand side, and squeezed the trigger.

The roll of fabric taped to the end of the muzzle hid the flash, dampened the sound – along with the speed of the bullet, but it didn't matter. She wasn't trying to punch a hole through his Kevlar body armour.

Snow plumed into the air a metre to his left and they all dived forward onto their bellies.

Jamie pulled back the bolt, chambered another round, and fired again, at the same place.

This one hit closer, and the mercenary scrambled sideways.

Jamie wheeled right, ejecting another spent casing and chambering another, firing to the other side.

They began to cluster.

She saw an arm flailing, ordering the men to stay in formation. She saw a head rise above the surface of the snow, thinner here on the ice.

There you are, you motherfucker.

Jamie put another one in the chamber, steadied herself, and then fired, right at him.

A near miss.

Another geyser of snow just behind him.

No matter.

She wanted to goad him into coming for her, not take his head off.

Well, maybe a little.

They got to their knees now, began returning fire. Though they didn't know what they were aiming at. Jamie had checked how easy it would be to see her, and the answer was pretty fucking difficult. And in this wind, with this much powder flying around? They were as good as shooting blind.

But they knew the direction the bullets were coming from, and spurred on by Jamie's poor aim, they kept advancing.

She lowered the rifle now, letting it rest on its side. Her father's old Remington Model 700 hunting rifle had a six-round internal magazine. She'd fired four.

Jamie fished in the box next to her, counting four into her

fingerless-gloved hand, and brought them up, pushing them into the body... Two, three, four. She counted in her head, then leaned over, glancing into the rangefinder. One hundred and fifty metres and closing. Yeah, that was close enough.

Jamie reached over and picked up the little black transponder sitting next to the spotter's scope, flicking the switch guard up with her thumb. It had a number '1' written on it. 'Sorry, Dad,' she muttered, narrowing her eyes. 'This is definitely going to scare off the fish.'

She pushed the switch upwards and there was a moment of stillness.

Then snow jetted into the air like a synchronised fountain, running in a line away from her, past the left-hand side of the mercenaries and around behind them.

The remotely detonated explosives, normally used in precision demolitions, had been buried under the snow for the better part of a week, sunk into drill holes in the ice. Each charge was no bigger than a cocktail sausage, but more than large enough to send a series of fractures through it.

Jamie watched as the surface ahead began to move, the snow rippling as the ice broke itself into miniature bergs. The shock waves from the explosives sent waves through the water, causing the snow on them to collect and divide in drifts.

Weight began to stack up, and the first jagged tail of ice poked up, the up-ending piece dumping snow into the freezing lake water.

Screams reached her. Yells of shock and surprise as the men got up and started running, legs pumping through the snow.

Jamie put down the first transponder and picked up the second, labelled number '2'. She tried to pick Sandbech out of the clamouring mercenaries, couldn't, then decided it didn't matter.

They were all going swimming either way.

She flicked up the guard and pushed the switch.

More explosions rippled outwards, this time running right, and then back towards the shore, forming the second half of the oval, trapping them all inside.

The ice creaked and groaned under her. It had to be more than a foot thick, but that much explosive was putting a lot of pressure on the rest of the shelf, too. The shock waves moving through the water were forcing it to bend and crack. Jamie could already feel the telltale popping under her as microfractures began to stack up.

Another berg upended itself ahead and Jamie saw the first body lifted into the air. The guy lost his footing, landed on his back, and slid down the sudden ramp, disappearing into the water.

She checked her watch.

It had been more than twenty-five minutes since she'd had the phone call. They had to be close by now.

The men ahead of her were closing in now, running and jumping from piece to piece, leaping across widening stretches of water as the chunks of ice collided, broke up, churned themselves into smaller fragments, and flipped over.

The smooth layer of snow had disappeared, and in its place a frozen, frothing battleground.

Jamie watched as the numbers dwindled, with body after body slipping through the gaps and into the water.

They'd be fine, she told herself. They'd make it. They'd survive.

She didn't harbour any guilt, but she wasn't keen to add any more lives to her conscience.

She could only make out four now, still hammering

towards her, towards the explosives line, where the ice turned solid. Except, it wasn't.

A crack rumbled beneath her and she felt her stomach sink as the ice rose and fell suddenly.

The fractures were spreading.

Fuck.

Jamie rolled over, snatching up the rifle, and climbed out of her hide, standing up.

She could feel the whole of the lake shuddering under her heels.

A quick glance towards Sandbech's men. Down to three now.

The shore, she needed to head for shore.

Jamie started running. She was too heavy, too bulky.

She unzipped her parka, shed it, and kept moving, her chunky boots scooping snow out of the way with every step.

Her stomach ached, pain bursting through her muscles with every awkward heel-flicked stride.

She heard a shot behind her. Loud and resounding, and then an instant later, heard it unzip the air above her head.

Jamie stumbled and dived into the snow, feeling it soaking her fingers instantly, her woollen gloves gathering powder.

She checked over her shoulder, getting to her feet. She could still see three bodies – one looked to be in the water at the explosives line now, another trying to help him up. Then he went in, too, the edge he was kneeling on giving way, and then they were both thrashing, looking for purchase on the slick ice, trying to haul themselves out.

But neither of them had fired.

The third mercenary was moving across a piece of rocking ice, weapon raised. Silver pistol raised.

This fucking guy!

He moved from one to the next, skidding and staggering before he took a run towards the edge, and jumped the last stretch of water, landing on what appeared to be solid ground.

He got to his feet and started charging, ignoring his men yelling for help, brandishing their hands at him from the water's edge.

Sandbech was coming for her.

Jamie started moving again, running hard.

Another shot.

She sidestepped, turned, pulled her own pistol from the holster at her hip, and fired back.

Sandbech strafed, moving low and fast, his bulk much more efficient at ploughing the snow from his path.

Jamie lined him up, held tight on the grip, and fired again.

The shot flew high, her aim thrown off as the ice beneath her rose a foot and then plunged back down, knocking her off balance.

Another deep, bellowing crack rang out, and she stumbled backwards, then forwards, finding her balance.

Sandbech was doing the same.

They both threw their weapons up, like western duellers, and fired.

She hit him centre mass, and his bullet hit her in the shoulder, no more than three inches from her heart.

Shit, he could shoot.

The impact blew her off her feet, the ballistic vest she was wearing stopping it from tearing her shoulder in two, but doing little to dull the pain.

Jamie gasped, opening her eyes, and got a mouthful of snow. She pulled her head from it and got to her knees.

But before she could stand, she felt a hand on the back of her head.

It ripped the beanie cap from her head, and then came back for more.

His fingers dug into her scalp, scraping roughly against her skin, and took a fistful of her hair.

Jamie was dragged to her feet, and then they came free of the ground.

She was flying, and then she hit, landing square on her back.

Sandbech assumed her vision, standing over her.

Jamie's fingers flexed, looking for her pistol, but it was gone, out of her grip.

She was breathing hard, fighting to catch her breath. She reached up, pulling down her mask, letting the cold air rush between her lips and into her lungs.

The ice groaned and wailed beneath her, shaking and splitting across the entire lake.

Sandbech took hold of his helmet then and pulled it off, peeling his white balaclava off with it.

She looked at him then for the first time, the first time she'd clearly seen his face.

He was bald, his skin pale, face square. He had the pronounced cheekbones of a Balkan, his pale eyes grey in the flat light. They were narrow and sharp and lifeless. Focused and dead.

His mouth was nothing but a carved slit in his joyless face.

'Jamie Johansson,' he spat. 'I've waited a long time for this.'

Jamie swallowed, staring up at Sandbech.

He let his pistol hang loosely at his side, the cries of his drowning men echoing unanswered around them.

She watched as his boot rose, traced a path over her head,

and then lowered, grinding down under her chin, forcing it upwards.

The sharp treads cut into her skin, the pain behind her eyes immediately blinding as she felt her windpipe being forced closed.

She sucked in as deep a breath as she could, listening to the cracking of the ice be replaced by the roaring of blood in her ears.

She'd been here before. She knew how this ended. And this time, there was no fighting it. There was no kicking him off. There was no one to save her.

Jamie conserved her strength, conserved her breath, feeling his boot crushing her throat.

She listened to her heart beat, focused on keeping calm despite it all. And had she not lived through everything she had, had she not survived this long despite the numerous attempts to kill her, had she not persisted, and endured, and fought every step of the way, she might have panicked.

But what Sandbech didn't know, and what Jamie did, was this place.

Was the snow-covered ridge coming in, was the distance from the cabin to the shore, from one shore to the other. Was the ice they were on, was how not to break it when you didn't want to, how to break it when you did, and what happened then.

Another deafening crack rang out. The ice moved, fractured, buckled, bucked.

And by the time Sandbech realised that Jamie's hands, locked around his ankle, weren't trying to push him off, but were, in fact, holding him in place, it was too late.

Jamie felt the coldness of the water on her back first, then suddenly around her ears, spilling over her face, into her nose and stinging her closed eyes.

And then the pressure was gone from her throat and she was underwater, the coldness setting her skin alight.

She opened her eyes, still holding fast on Sandbech's boot, and watched him kick and claw in front of her, the lighting fading above them by the second as the ice closed up overhead and they sank lower.

And then she let go, drifting backwards, the pain in her neck receding, the burn in her lungs low and tolerable.

Her time at the lake had not been misspent.

But for Sandbech, in his heavy tactical gear, writhing above her, clawing his way towards the surface, banging and hammering on the underside of the ice, it was already too late.

Jamie watched him for a few more seconds, his movements growing frantic, more panicked by the moment.

And then she turned away, squinting into the distance.

She could see a patch of light, a long way ahead.

But she was strong.

And she'd done what she said, been running in a month. She was swimming a week after. Knowing each day, each plunge, each swearing, cursing mission into the slushy, freezing waters was all leading up to this moment. And now, kicking off her boots and slipping out of her heavy snow-trousers, moving smoothly, swiftly through the water, this finally felt like the end.

In the darkness around her, she found comfort. She found solace. There was nothing, and no one.

As Jamie Johansson swam beneath the ice, she'd never felt more alone, or more at home.

Her time here as a child, with her father, had been the happiest of her life.

And it was fitting now that this was where it ended. Where she could finally lay him to rest.

His face loomed ahead, calling her towards the light.

With each kick and pull of her numb fingers, it grew dimmer.

And dimmer.

She didn't know how long she'd been down there, how far she'd swum.

But it felt like far enough.

Jamie slowed, letting a quiet smile play across her lips, a faint glow of pale daylight filtering down from above.

She turned her face skywards, feeling a distant warmth against her skin.

And then, after everything, Jamie Johansson closed her eyes and just stopped fighting.

EPILOGUE

THE SPRING WAS WANING, the last of the snow clinging to the tops of the mountains in the north.

Simpson drove with eyes tired, slowing the car into the small village of Arvidsjaur. He sighed, the window open, and rubbed his forehead, keeping his eye out for the sign.

He indicated left and pulled off the empty road into the car park of a dimly lit roadside restaurant.

Finding a space was easy, and he killed the engine, looking out at the deserted town. It was only nine in the evening, but it might as well have been four in the morning.

He stepped into the cool northern air and cracked his back. A longer drive than he expected.

Simpson headed for the restaurant, skirting the backs of the few odd four-by-fours parked up.

A haggard, one-eared dog hurled itself against the back windscreen of one, barking and gnashing its teeth through the glass, filling it with fog.

'Fuck,' Simpson muttered, exhaling and removing his hand from the pistol holstered at his hip. 'Stupid dog,' he said, shaking his head and walking away towards the entrance.

The place looked tired. As tired as he felt. The outside was clad in dark wood and a dirty backlit sign said something he had no hope of reading. Mercifully, the word *restaurant* was in English, though he didn't know whether he'd trust the food there.

Inside, it was dim. A row of tables stretched down the middle, and on either side were booths. One line against the back wall, the other down the front, each with its own window.

It wasn't hard to spot her – there was no one else in there.

He headed down the line of windowed booths and slid in opposite.

The light overhead was making her hair glow practically white.

She turned her head to look at him and smiled warmly.

He returned it. The last time he'd seen her face, he'd pulled her out of a frozen lake and done CPR for nearly two solid minutes before she'd thrown up two lungfuls of water and opened her eyes. She was bundled into a helicopter right after, wrapped in foil blankets, and then she was gone.

And now here she was, sitting in a roadside restaurant in the middle of nowhere, looking wistfully out the window.

'Hey,' he said.

'Hey,' she replied.

'It's good to see you.'

She looked at him for a few seconds. 'It's good to see you, too. Drive okay?'

'Long,' he replied, rubbing the back of his neck and looking around for any of the wait staff.

'I told you,' Jamie said, 'you didn't need to come.'

'I wanted to,' he replied, waving at the woman at the back of the room on her phone. She didn't look up. He returned his attention to Jamie then. 'I wanted to see you. Though,' he said, laughing and hooking a thumb over his shoulder towards the door, 'I did almost get eaten by a dog on my way in here.'

'He hasn't got out, has he?' Jamie asked, her eyes widening a little in alarm.

'No, no,' Simpson said quickly, 'he was in a car – wait, that's *your* dog?'

She sighed. 'Sadly, yeah.'

'When did you get a dog?' he asked, picturing the bedraggled mutt. *'Why* did you get a dog? Why that one?'

She shook her head and closed her eyes. 'Don't ask,' she replied, laughing to herself.

He watched her laugh, felt at ease in her presence. He'd missed her. 'Anyway,' he said, reaching into his inside pocket. 'Here it is.' He withdrew an envelope and put it on the table, sliding it across to her.

She looked at it.

'You don't have to take it,' he said. 'My offer still stands.'

She looked at him then, grinned a little. 'Thanks, but I don't quite think I'm cut out for the Bureau.'

He offered a shrug. 'Don't know if you don't try.'

'It's not really my scene.'

'And this is?' he asked, gesturing around.

'It suits me.'

'For now.'

She took the envelope and pulled it towards her. 'For now.'

Jamie slid her thumb under the flap and opened it, pulling out the appointment letter. She glanced over it.

'Look okay?' Simpson asked.

Jamie nodded slowly, then folded it back up and slipped it into the envelope again. 'Thanks for this,' she said.

'The least I could do. But the Minister for Justice would have given you pretty much anything you asked for after what you did. Though I think your friend Wiik will be sad to lose you from the department.' Simpson sat back, folding his arms.

Jamie smirked at that. 'Wiik's never been sad about anything in his life. He's not good at the whole "showing your emotions" thing.'

'Coming from the expert?' Simpson raised an eyebrow.

She feigned a sneer. 'But it'll make him an excellent Kriminalkommissarie. He'll do well at the SPA.'

'He's got big shoes to fill. I hear his predecessor was smart. Capable,' Simpson added.

Jamie nodded. 'Ingrid Falk was... a good person. She made mistakes.'

'Haven't we all?'

Jamie let that hang for a few seconds. 'If anything, Wiik will be more upset about losing Hallberg than me.'

Simpson chuckled. 'I doubt that. She'll go far – and Europol will be a great fit for her. Better than the SPA, I think.'

'Time will tell.'

'It always does.'

Jamie sighed, lifting the envelope and tapping the corner on the table.

'You really want to go through with this?' Simpson asked then. 'Kurrajakk is a long way from Stockholm.'

Jamie couldn't help but smile at the pronunciation. Or lack thereof. Swedish place names didn't really lend them-selves to the East-Texan drawl.

'I'm sure,' she said. 'Small, quiet municipality, open

spaces, clean air, one of the lowest crime rates in all of Sweden. I need a break, a fresh start, you know? A little normality.' She looked up then, met his eye, hand tightening on the envelope. 'I mean seriously, what's the worst that could happen?'

AUTHOR'S NOTE

Well, that's it. Whether you started with *Angel Maker*, or you've been with Jamie since *Bare Skin*, you know it's been a journey for her. And to get here, she's gone through a lot. More close shaves that we can count. And during that time, she's changed and evolved. It's always been my intention to create an arc for Jamie, one that gives her closure and a sense of peace, no matter how bittersweet.

There were elements about this trilogy that I doubted all the way through, but I knew I was working towards something that was as much one whole as three individual parts, and now that it's finished, I feel like I've done right by Jamie — at least for *that* part of her story. There's more to come, don't worry!

There are themes here which recur, scenes from previous books which come back around, a sense of cyclicality that shows how things have progressed for Jamie, that show how she's changed. The lake and the hunting cabin were crucial parts of *Angel Maker*, and getting to end here, where, for Jamie, everything sort of began, that was something I was so glad I could do for her. I wrote and re-wrote the final lines a bunch of times until I got them as they are now. I never had any intention of killing Jamie off, or of making it seem like she was destined to die. It was the reason I didn't explore the scene where the choppers arrive, Simpson leaps out, pulls Jamie from the icy waters, breathes life into her... I was set on having that as the final scene. But when I was imagining her beneath the ice, swimming for her life, that felt natural. Symbolic. Powerful. It felt like the end was there. That Jamie had reached it. That the story and the fate of Imperium were secondary to what Jamie deserved. It wasn't death, but simply peace.

At this point, I don't really want to unpack everything in the story or in the previous novels. Know that there is much there, lurking below the surface. That the interplays between the characters are layered, that introducing new characters and excluding old, that the time jumps, that the way this whole narrative, from *Angel Maker* through to this point – that it was all done in a way that aimed to produce a coherent series of novels that told a whole story. That delivered something as one solid unit, as well as a story with each instalment.

If you ever read them again, I'd hope there'd be more to extricate the second time around, then the third. That Jamie would continue to grow and solidify in your mind until she feels as real to you as she does to me.

The question of what's next then, may be hanging in the air.

Where do we take Jamie now, and what does the future hold?

Her story isn't 'finished' by any stretch. I consider these six first novels as her introduction, her maturation. The Jamie we know moving forward is wholly different from the one we met in London two years ago. But that's not a bad thing. I want each novel to feel different, and each time Jamie comes to the page, to be different, to seem different, like she's carrying the burdens of her life on her shoulders. And I hope that I can achieve that, and that what I deliver next will be your favourite novel. And that the one after will be your new favourite. And so on forever until Jamie's too old to catch bad guys. And then who knows, maybe we'll just go cosy crime and have her chasing down crooks on a walker at an old folks' home. That's in vogue, right?

But there's a long way to go before that.

Like all of us after trauma, we need to rebuild. Ourselves, our minds. And Jamie is no different. This author's note used to be different. I changed it to this because things changed. The next book wasn't done when I wrote this originally. I needed time to reflect, to think about what I wanted to do with the series next.

Luckily for you, I did, and I have, and now, the stage is set for the next three books at least! The next instalment, *Death Chorus,* comes out on December 31st 2021. If that date has passed, then it's already out, and you can find the link to it next, along with the blurb to see if it's something you might like!

I've taken everything I've learned so far, all the feedback I've received from readers, reviewers, fellow authors, and I've channelled it into the next book. The style is more on the psychological side of things, leaning into what we did with *Angel Maker,* returning Jamie to her role as a detective. It's a new place, a new case. There are new characters, new challenges. A new partner. One Jamie might even hold onto for a few books! We'll see. She does go through them, doesn't she?

Anyway — what I meant to say is that the last two years of writing Jamie have been the most enjoyable of my career.

So if you're not tired of her yet, take a breath, turn the page, and let's keep going. Because I'm a long way off done. And so is she!

All the best,
 Morgan

DEATH CHORUS
DI JAMIE JOHANSSON BOOK 4

The quiet northern Swedish town of Kurrajakk is rocked when a popular teenager is found dead, mounted on a sacrificial altar, body covered in strange cuts, a crow shoved down his throat. Rumours begin to swirl. **A local ghost story, *Krakornås Kung,* The King Of Crows, is back.**

Jamie left the Violent Crimes department in Stockholm to rebuild her life. Her body. Her mind. To get away from cases like this. But Jamie can't let injustice go unpunished – and now, she's all out of compassion. **The King may think Kurrjakk is his for the taking, but he's never met Jamie Johansson.**

As strange occurrences begin to plague the town, the residents are whipped into paranoia. Jamie and her new partner must race to unmask the King, but find themselves at the centre of a deadly game. The rules are simple – survive. **But when your greatest enemy is your own mind, winning isn't so easy...**

Find Death Chorus, book 4 in the DI Jamie Johansson series on Amazon now.

STAY UP TO DATE

Currently, the next Jamie Johansson novel is not available for pre-order, but as soon as I have news, I'd love to let you know.

I don't do spam, don't bombard my subscribers with emails. I think I've sent three in the last twelve months. But when I have news, this is how I tell my readers. So if you'd like to stay in the loop, head to my website, and join my mailing list.

I also run giveaways for book vouchers, audio versions, signed copies, and lots more!

Thank you so much for all your time and energy. I hope you'll join, and that we can go on more adventures together!

morgangreene.co.uk/mailing-list

ALSO BY MORGAN GREENE

The DS Johansson Prequel Trilogy:

Bare Skin (Book 1)

Fresh Meat (Book 2)

Idle Hands (Book 3)

The DS Johansson Prequel Trilogy Boxset

———

The DI Jamie Johansson Series

Angel Maker (Book 1)

Rising Tide (Book 2)

Old Blood (Book 3)

Death Chorus (Book 4)

Printed in Great Britain
by Amazon